I0535636

PHOENIX PROJECT

ROBERT BLANCHARD

Phoenix Project

By Robert Blanchard

Copyright 2013

All Rights Reserved

Copyright © 2013 Robert Blanchard

First Print Edition May 2014

First eBook Edition November 2013

This is a work of fiction. The events and characters described herein are imaginary and not intended to refer to specific places or living persons. The opinions expressed in this manuscript are solely the opinions of the author. The author has represented and warranted full ownership and/or legal right to publish all materials in this book.

This book may not be reproduced or transmitted or stored in whole or in part by any means, including graphic, electronic, or mechanical without the express written consent of the author except in the case of brief quotations embodied in critical articles and reviews.

Cover design by Javier Canto

Architectural drawings by Robert Blanchard

Formatting by First Steps Self-Publishing Services

Please provide feedback

Printed in U.S.A.

ISBN-10: 0991344405

ISBN-13: 9780991344406

Library of Congress Control Number: 2014903080
Phoenix 26, Miami, FL

Website: www.phoenixproject-thenovel.com

For my boys

Acknowledgments

I would like, first and foremost, to thank Eduardo "Wato" Canto. Best screenwriter in Hollywood and the first person to bleed red ink all over my manuscript. Wato showed me that I really had a great story with a heck of a lot of grammatical errors. Next, my editor Theodora O'Brien. Dorrie is a no-holds-barred type of editor. She tells it like it is and sticks to her guns. I tried to battle, but eventually realized that she was right all along. Dorrie took my story and made it flow, and for that I can't thank you enough. Cris Wanzer, my proofreader. I must have proofread my manuscript dozens of times before I sent it out to you. I now realize how important and difficult your work can be. Thank you for your time and knowledge.

Captain Johnny M. Bittick (Ret) with 600 carrier landings and 320 combat missions under his belt. It is because of you that my book has that "real feel" to it. Thank you for your editing and for your service to our country. And H.P. "Viking" Lillebo, F-8 Crusader pilot, Fighter Squadron 13 (VF-13) on *USS Shangri-La,* thank you for your website on the annotated guide to Navy pilots' lingo and bringing together Captain Bittick and I.

Rashid Siahpoosh, who I consider a very good critic and friend. Thanks for being honest and straightforward with your analysis. To my two best friends: Javier Canto, best graphic designer in the business. Thank you for your help in designing the cover for the book. You knew exactly what was needed even though I held you back a bit! And Valerio Vitoria, crazy, over-the-top, best pilot, military, and policeman I know. Now retired (or so he says). Yes, the character of Val is based on this crazy guy.

I would also like to thank my family: My uncle "OC," the smartest, most kind and generous man I know. Thank you for taking me under your wings and giving me the knowledge and education, which I now pass on to my children. My cousin, Vincent Perez. He was the first person to lay eyes on my story, and once done, he came knocking at my door insisting that I share it with the world. His brother, Steve. Whenever I am stuck or have a problem I always ask, "What would Steve do?" And to date he has always been right. My one and only brother, James Blanchard, who by publishing his book before me, made me want to beat him at his own game. Thank you, James, for all your help and walking me through the process that is the publishing and marketing world of books. It is always nice to have another writer in the family to talk about our passion.

Author Matthew Reilly. Thank you for sharing your genius gift of writing. Your work is my inspiration. Your writing style opened my eyes to a new form of storytelling. Keep bringing those wonderful stories to light.

Lastly, to my wife and kids. Honey, I know I can disappear when I am writing, so I wanted to thank you for taking care of the world around us when I am lost in thought. You are the glue that keeps everything together and in order. And our kids, Jean-Luc, Jacques, and Xavier...the inquisitive look in your eyes when I test my stories on you always lets me know if I am onto something or if I need a rewrite. Always know that life is full of wonder. So go out there and explore...then sit down and write about it.

1

Berlin, April 30, 1945

Nicoli opened his eyes wide. It took him a few seconds to realize where he was. He blinked repeatedly, trying to wipe away the recurring nightmare, but the memories of the past four years remained fresh. He regained his composure as he scanned the expanse of burning and destroyed buildings around him, and calculated that in those few precious minutes of sleep, nothing had changed in his kill zone.

Years of combat had made Nicoli into one of the best sharpshooters in Stalin's elite Red Army sniper squad. He remained motionless, even while in sleep. Melding in with the destroyed architecture, his clothing part of the insane scenery.

A worn and discolored cape made him invisible to the untrained eye. It was a perfect accessory for a sniper, and the reason it was on Nicoli's back was because of its previous owner's, a German sniper, inability to remain still. He had won that shootout, and many more after. Now he just waited, like he always did, for a target to come across his line of sight.

Nicoli was in a precarious but well-thought-out sniper position, perched up high on one of the few standing buildings in the Berlin area near the infamous Reichstag Building. The building below him was partially destroyed and Nicoli knew that he ran the risk of it collapsing under him at any moment. Still, he remained.

He was an expert at choosing his targets, which had given him 14 kills from his current position. The secret to his high body count was to make sure that the enemy was alone; if not, whoever was with the victim would figure out from where the shot had originated and call in support to take the sniper out.

*Berlin...*he thought. *Soon the Red Army will triumph and end this war.*

He had to be cautious...he couldn't risk making any mistakes now.

The constant cracking of bullets breaking the sound barrier echoed off the rubble below. Its sound was almost rhythmic at times, only to be interrupted by the occasional mortar round exploding, sending its concussion wave into the surrounding structures and shaking the dust off the wood rafters above his head. Nicoli noted that the sounds of war were quieter 40 meters above the city. His mind began to wander off to how life would be after the war. He missed the solitary sound of a calm wind, or the water from a stream cascading over countless boulders. Serenity, that's what he wanted most, but all he heard was the sound of war...all around him and down below, where personal battles were being won and lost.

A glint in the horizon caught his eye, breaking his focus. He aimed the Mosin-Nagant 1891/30 PU sniper rifle's scope to the object in the sky. He knew what it was, or could be...or was his mind playing a trick on him? Nicoli closed his eyes to remove any fogging and opened them again.

• • •

Otto Von Ludger swore out loud, and forced the aircraft into a deep bank as another bullet flew through one of the many Plexiglas panes in the small cockpit of the Flettner Fl 282 Kolibri "Hummingbird"—an open cockpit, intermeshing rotor helicopter, or synchropter. He knew that he had no choice but to endure this suicidal ride to freedom, or at least into an American prison, because if he were to be caught by the Russian army, he was as good as dead. Worst of all, he knew that if he was going to make it out, pleasing the SS officer sitting in the rear-facing seat behind him would be key.

Otto was lucky in retrospect, because the choice he had made to become an experimental test pilot kept him away from the dangers of war. First, he flew the Folk Wolf FW-190 G9—the first Folk Wolf fighter plane with a 12-cylinder, inline fuel-injected engine—a vast improvement over the original radial engine. Then came the fast Messerschmitt jets, but his true curiosity led him to fly the new concept of controlled hover-flight.

It was a radical change for him to be hovering in midair 100 meters off the ground and with the immediate responsiveness of the machine to move in whatever direction he pleased, even backward. What amazed him most was its ability to land and take off from almost anywhere, including the stern deck of a battleship.

The technological advances were great, but his love for the machine sprang from how it felt—as though it were an extension of his body. He would climb over the flat Plexiglas panels and strap himself into the uncomfortable leather seat, becoming one with the machine. That connection made him the best helicopter pilot in the Luftwaffe, but that caught the eye of a high-ranking SS scientist from one of the most feared units in Germany. The scientist sporting the rank of an SS colonel recruited him just before he'd been about to make his escape.

"*Scheissen!*" Otto yelled as another bullet bounced off the thick steel plate surrounding the fuel tanks. Otto eyed the tanks, and smiled at his foresight in bulletproofing his helicopter. Scanning the remnants of the city below, he made another sharp turn and followed a wide boulevard until he saw red smoke rising from a ruined courtyard. He banked the helicopter once more and flew toward it.

Otto looked down and hoped the pick-up would be fast. He wondered what package was so dammed important to send him into hell and back. What he did know was that his helicopter was to be refueled for the trip back, and that alone would allow him to get far away from the Russian army, but he had to drop off the package first.

• • •

"No wings?" Nicoli asked himself. "Look, Satlana, no wings. What do you think it is?" he asked his dead wife. As always, there was no response.

Nicoli adjusted his prone position on the top floor of the building and checked his rifle by feel. Satisfied, he let out a deep breath and cleared his mind.

"Just follow him and see what he is up to," he whispered.

Nicoli eyed the aircraft through his scope as it flew closer. He noticed its four spinning blades perched atop the fuselage. As the aircraft turned, changing its flight path, he could now see that the blades were counter-rotating. It pitched its nose up and slowed down to a complete midair stop.

Nicoli's mouth opened, amazed at the flying feat the aircraft was performing 400 meters in front and below him.

It's hovering like a hummingbird.

The pilot in the cockpit moved his head from side to side, trying hard to keep the aircraft rotor blades from striking the walls surrounding the courtyard as it descended.

"*Bljat!*" Nicoli swore as he focused on the seven German youth Brown Shirts and two military officers who had gathered in the courtyard of the dilapidated building under the aircraft.

Nicoli tried to line up a shot, but he wasn't feeling lucky enough to shoot through the spinning blades. Shooting the pilot was now out of the equation. He waited and scoped out the targets below him and made up his mind. He made a mental note that he could register two kills before they dispersed, and picked out the most decorated officer as his first target.

Take two shots and leave.

He began to calculate distance-and-wind to target. His four-power magnification scope had a fence post pointer in place of the traditional crosshairs. He aligned the tip of the post on the mass of the SS officer's black tunic uniform, and focused between the rotors and target, trying to judge when he could take his shot, but the spinning blades kept his target safe.

The helicopter's wheels licked the rubble-strewn floor of the destroyed courtyard before the full weight of the aircraft pushed out the sidewalls of the rubber tires. One SS officer bent down and held on to his visor as he walked toward the pilot underneath the spinning blades. Nicoli watched as the air pressure being produced by the blades picked up loose material on the ground, whipping it about, making a shot even more difficult. He paused, taking his eyes off his target, and looked up when he heard the familiar and frightening sound of a bomber's radial engines high above.

18,000 feet above Berlin

"Jerry, 10 o'clock high, coming in fast!" came through the headset.

The .50 caliber machine gun behind Captain McCormick shot multiple short bursts at the German Luftwaffe Me-262 jet diving toward the cockpit of his B-17 Flying Fortress. Thomason, Captain McCormick's flight engineer, ducked as instinct took over when the jet fighter's bullets ripped through the cockpit, killing Stevens, the 22-year-old copilot.

McCormick turned to see his copilot's head was missing. All that remained was a shredded jaw and the leftover remnants of what had been in the cavity just a few seconds before. McCormick's facemask ruptured violently as he vomited into it. He turned his head back, and during convulsions and spraying bile, managed to get an order out to Thomason.

"Thomason! Get him out of the seat and take his place!"

Thomason looked forward and saw McCormick trying to wipe the blood off the instruments and windshield. "Jesus Christ..." he mumbled as he noticed what was left of his friend's head.

A frightened voice crackled over the intercom. "Sir, we have a problem back here."

"What is it now?" McCormick asked.

"We lost a bomb bay door! I can see a fuse on one of the lower bombs spinning!"

McCormick answered after a moment of shocked speechlessness. "Can you reach it?"

"No, sir. It's hanging out of the fuselage."

"How long?"

"We have maybe 30 seconds, sir."

The fuse on the 500-pound bomb had a small propeller that would spin a given amount of time before it would arm. This fuse, when hit, would set off the bomb. McCormick and the others knew that, once armed, the bomb could go off if it hit the sides of the plane during turbulence or evasive maneuvering.

"Crap...." McCormick weighed the importance of the mission, looked at his watch and decided on the spot. "Little! Change of plans. We are dropping our load now! Engaging autopilot!"

"On it, sir," Little said as another Me-262 took a potshot at the Fortress.

McCormick reached down and toggled the autopilot switches, giving control to the bombardier. Once the autopilot was engaged, the bomber would remain on a straight and level course for the bombing run, thus increasing the accuracy of the drop, but it also made the bomber an easy target for the enemy fighters.

"Little, autopilot engaged," McCormick called out to his bombardier.

"I have control!" Little responded as Thomason pulled the body from the copilot's seat.

"Pick a safe target. Remember, there are many friendlies about in Berlin."

"I'll try my best, sir," Little said, who knew that a millimeter mistake at 18,000 feet could cause enormous collateral damage below.

"Okay, boys, phase one is snafu. Phase two still a go—"

"Jerry, 12 o'clock!"

"Jesus!" McCormick screamed as another Me-262 came head on, its 30MM MK-108 cannons blasting at the Fortress. "Crap, how many 262s are out there?"

"Sir, I count five. Maybe six."

"Seven," Sesperela, the tail gunner, said. "The others are taking on the Mustangs."

"Eight o'clock!" yelled the belly gunner from his ball turret, which hung under the plane. The waist, belly, and top turret gunners let out a volley of .50 caliber bullets at the fighter plane. The bullets tracked to the oncoming plane and found their mark, tearing through the plane's left jet engine pod. A puff of smoke came out the rear of the jet engine and a second later the 262 exploded in a ball of fire.

"Yehaw! Take that, you fucking Nazi!" screamed Kilroy, the red-headed, 19-year-old waist gunner.

"Good shot! Little, release the bombs so we can drop these Marine Jarheads and get home in one piece." He heard a small chuckle through the intercom.

"Roger, Captain. Target acquired. Ready to drop in five," Little said, voice pitched high, shaken up by the intense firefight. "Bombs away!"

The B-17 shot up into the air as it released its tonnage of death.

Nicoli could see that the blades were not slowing down, so his shot would have to be after the flying machine took off. He relaxed a bit more, but the sounds of the bomber overhead made him nervous.

Following the SS officer's orders, the Brown Shirts took up positions around the helicopter with their submachine guns at the ready. After a few seconds, two more German officers came through a door carrying what looked like a gray, rolled-up rug between them. Nicoli pulled out his 8x30 binoculars to get a closer look at the action. The binoculars gave him a different perspective on the scene playing out over four football fields away and below his perch. He could see the flying machine, its pilot, and the Hitler youth in their brown shirts; two were pouring gasoline into the side tanks of the machine. He also caught a closer look at his target. The man was SS, and by the look of his tunic, a high-ranking officer of the German Armored Panzer Divisions.

The two officers moved low under the spinning blades and placed the rug into the backward-facing seat next to the SS passenger behind the engine compartment. One of the soldiers saluted the pilot. Nicoli heard the engine rev, saw the flying machine lift off the ground, spin around, and pick up speed, heading away from the courtyard and Nicoli's position.

• • •

Otto swore as he took off from the courtyard. "More weight; that's just what I needed." Otto thought he'd be picking up some kind of paperwork, but the extra weight in the back had changed his plans. Not only would he burn more fuel, but also the helicopter was past its weight limit, and a greater danger to fly. Otto went over the map strapped to his thigh, searching for the new coordinates that he had been given, and ignoring the bullets ricocheting off the steel plating.

Otto adjusted the map on his lap and banked the helicopter right, yet again trying to avoid heavy incoming fire. He thought of his luck as he pondered the reasoning behind flying into Russian-occupied territory.

He calculated the distance.

Eighty miles south-southeast. I am not going to make it back.

He was flying away from the Americans, and the trip back would take longer. That was fine as long as he could get fuel at the next stop. Otto went over his situation. He looked up and around at the many contrails and spotted the jet escort the German SS general on the ground had said would protect him.

One by one the jets dove toward his position. He recalled the general's last words that if he was not able to reach the drop-off site, the jets would make sure that he would not be captured by the Russians.

Otto banked yet again and said out loud, "You mean you'll shoot me out of the sky, you Goddamned Nazi." Damn, he hated the SS.

I knew it, there had to be a catch. He was beginning to doubt he could make his plan work.

Otto looked once more at the small duffel bag tucked behind his feet containing his civilian clothes, some money, and a Spanish passport. He banked the aircraft around some tall pines and headed out of the Berlin outskirts and straight into Russian-occupied territory.

• • •

Nicoli immersed himself in the world he now viewed through the scope of his sniper rifle, ignoring the flying machine as it lifted out of the courtyard. All that mattered now was the target. The wind had died down and the post point drawn on the scope's lens found its mark within the red haze of smoke.

The officer in black shouted a couple of orders at the Brown Shirts, then stood in front of the tallest boy and began to speak to him. Nicoli took a deep breath, calmed his mind, and began to squeeze the trigger.

Inside the rifle, the firing pin flew forward and into the primer on the 7.62x54R round. The primer ignited the powder within the casing, forcing the copper bullet forward under incredible pressure. The bullet began to spin while traveling through the barrel, following the barrel's grooves, and exiting into the clean air after traveling 27.8 inches in less than a hundredth of a second.

At the same time the copper bullet passed the broken window into its free horizontal trajectory toward its target, a mass weighing thousands of times heavier was finishing its own vertical trajectory. Within its mass, a mechanism much more complicated than that of the bullet armed itself. The tip of the fuse depressed as it hit a broken roof rafter, producing a chemical reaction, igniting the 500-pound explosive charge inside it, disintegrating itself and all the material and life within the building it had just entered. Nicoli was evaporated, but his last action remained flying as a couple of similar explosions occurred behind the bullet's flight path.

Nicoli's bullet beat the shock waves; it even beat the human reaction of the bombs from the B-17 Flying Fortress going off. The bullet, after traveling 407 meters, reached its mark.

Nicoli never saw his bullet penetrate the SS general's head, and he never saw one Brown Shirt's reaction as the bullet exploded out through the general's face, covering the boy in bone, brain matter, and burnt flesh. The bullet continued its deadly path, penetrating the outer skin of the Brown Shirt's jaw and running along the outside of his face, leaving a long, open wound as it embedded itself into the wood beam behind the Brown Shirt's head.

The boy stood there in shock for a few seconds until another 500-pound bomb went off where the rest of the group had taken cover. He was thrown back by the concussion wave, past the wood beam, and down a flight of steps, ending up unconscious at the entrance to a collapsed basement.

"11 o'clock high!" a voice screamed over the Fortress's intercom.

The .50 caliber machine gun, which Thomason had just left, fired yet again at another incoming fighter. Thomason looked back to see that one of the Marines had taken his place on the roof turret.

He was amazed at his calm. He, and the other passengers sitting in the radio compartment past the bomb rack, looked as comfortable as if they were on a regular plane ride from D.C. to New York. The funny-looking, shaggy suits, camouflaged uniforms, oxygen masks, and equipment were the signs that they, too, were at war.

Earlier in the day the group of five Marines had marched themselves onto the flight line, called out to Captain McCormick, and given him a letter. He read it, nodded, and received a sharp salute from the Marine major. The captain then called the crew together and told them about the change in mission.

The lone crew of the B-17 was to head east, covered by two P-51 Mustang fighter interceptors over Berlin, all acting as a photographic reconnaissance flight. Once over Berlin they were to head south-southeast, drop to 14,000 feet, and offload the bombs over a predetermined pocket of German resistance. The Marines were then to jump out. After dropping their cargo, the B-17 would turn west and head back to base.

The new flight plan was reviewed and the crew told to keep their mouths shut. The captain ordered them to remove four of the 10, 500-pound bombs, and replace their weight with extra ammunition and fuel for the extended flight.

Thomason was shocked back to reality as the flight controls exploded in front of him and a searing pain shot through his arm. "Shit! I'm hit!" he yelled as McCormick saw his new copilot grabbing his left arm. Blood ran through his fingers as he squeezed.

"Major!" McCormick hollered back to his passenger, who was busy firing at the attacking planes. "Get your medic up here to take care of Thomason's injuries." McCormick looked to his right as the Marine stepped over Stevens's lifeless body and entered the cockpit, wielding a knife.

He cut the sleeve off Thomason's B-3 leather sheepskin jacket, took a quick look and spoke to McCormick. "Shrapnel. You want me to dope him before I take it out?"

McCormick turned, looked at Thomason, then at the Marine. "Yeah, go ahead, I can fly the Fortress alone if I have to."

"Captain, we are coming up on second waypoint in two minutes," the bombardier said over the intercom.

"Roger that." McCormick looked back as the Marine went past the engineer's compartment to the narrow bridge between the empty bomb racks to get the morphine from the first aid kit in the radio compartment. He removed his mask and yelled back to the Marine major, "Major, you have two minutes till dro—"

The major was blown past the bomb racks and landed face first onto the radio compartment floor with a force that came close to knocking him out. A cold rush of wind hit him as he opened his eyes. He was stunned as his team gathered around him and helped him up.

"Major! You okay?" screamed Marine Sergeant Collins over the rush of wind blowing through the aircraft hull.

Major Dean DuMonde blinked his eyes, adjusting his focus. He staggered up and turned around to see that where the cockpit and nose of the plane were supposed to be was now blue sky. Realizing the fate that awaited the remaining crew, Dean yelled to the radioman to tell the remaining crew to jump. The belly gunner quickly climbed out of his spherical pod as one of the waist gunners rushed back to pass the message to the tail gunner. Dean looked forward one last time and admired the B-17 as it kept flying straight and level.

Dean watched on as the tail and waist gunners jumped out, followed by the belly gunner and radioman. The B-17 started to bank and Dean knew they only had a few remaining seconds to jump. He looked down through the open bomb bay doors at the passing landscape and got his bearings. They were close to the target, but would have to watch out on their short hike for any leftover German Panzer tank groups.

He looked up and yelled over the howling wind, "Sarge! Your lead!"

The sergeant and the other Marines dropped down through the bomb bay doors. Dean took one more look, rechecked his equipment, and dove head first into the open air.

2

80 miles south-southwest of Berlin

Three SS soldiers, hidden in a machine gun nest, looked up as they saw a strange craft trailing black smoke fly over them.

Dean, taking advantage of the noise and distraction, took careful aim at the SS soldier smoking a cigarette 20 meters away. He calmed his breath and paid attention to his heart rate. The line of sight through the De Lisle suppressed rifle moved up and down along the torso of the intended target.

He squeezed the trigger, and the muffled puffing sound of the exiting .45 caliber copper bullet was the only noise that emanated from the suppressed rifle barrel. As the target began to fall, Dean heard the distinctive puffing sounds from two other De Lisle rifles on either side of him and the other two SS soldiers collapsed under their own dead weight.

Dean got up, shouldered his rifle, and replaced it with another weapon as he ran to the machine gun nest. He pointed his OSS M3-A1 suppressed submachine gun—also known as the grease gun because of its uncanny resemblance to a real grease gun—at the three bodies. One of the soldiers squirmed in pain. Dean squeezed the trigger, silencing the man.

Seconds later, Dean was surrounded by lumps of leaves and burlap. The Marines, wearing Ghillie suits, pointed their grease guns at all points of the compass. The Ghillie suit each man wore was the result of a suggestion of the man now kneeling next to Dean, Master Sergeant Collins.

Collins was a first-generation American of Scottish descent. It was his father who had instructed him on how to construct a suit out of burlap and surrounding foliage which, when put together, would break up the silhouette of the human form and, in turn, the wearer would blend into the surrounding scenery, essentially making him invisible. It was the old way of keeping the herd safe from poachers and became a very useful tool in a time of war.

Collins first introduced the idea to Dean in Italy during a scouting mission. He told Dean to go into the château the Army was using as a forward command center, count to 10, then come out and try to find him.

Dean gave up after a few minutes of walking around and getting pelted by rocks. He was convinced of the Ghillie's use when he saw Collins waving at him from a squatting position, acting like an ivy-covered tree stump. That day Dean ordered Collins to teach all his men, including himself, the art and use of the Scottish Ghillie suit.

"Sir, what was that thing?" Vic asked.

"Helicopter. Germans have been using them for a few years now. Impressive machines." Dean looked to the right. "Vic, hide the bodies, and stay out here for the next patrol. Once you take them out, follow us in."

Vic jumped his five-foot-two-inch skinny Italian body into the machinegun nest and started moving the bodies from sight.

Dean pulled out an aerial picture of the site and pointed to a dot on the black and white photo. "This is our entry point. An air vent. We are here..." He moved his finger down the photo to the machine gun nest they now occupied. "According to intelligence, the V-2 rocket manufacturing facility is right under our feet. Part of the First Armored Division has been sent our way, and should be here within the hour. As per our briefing, we are here to make it easy for the Army boys, and to keep the Russians out if they get here first...and it looks like it's going to be a close one from what I saw when we jumped. Any questions?"

The men shook their heads.

"Good, let's go then."

Dean and Corporal William "Bill" Sertain, the radioman and electrical wizard, crouched as they hurried to the air vent.

"Yep. The vent is wired. Should take me a minute or so," Bill said. He reached into his pack and retrieved his electrical kit.

By the time Bill had bypassed the alarm system, the rest of the team had formed a perimeter circle around the vent. Dean tied the climbing rope around the concrete shaft and then helped Bill slide the iron grate off the manhole-sized opening.

The shaft's diameter was too small for him to wear his pack, so he left it behind to be sent down after him. Dean removed his Ghillie suit and was the first to repel down the shaft. His feet touched a hard concrete bend in the pipe 75 feet down. The horizontal pipe's diameter was tall enough to allow a man to maneuver within; he figured it was designed for a cleanup crew to inspect.

Dean shook the rope and held it tight for the next team member. Second down was Sergeant Jackson, the unit's explosives expert. Jackson was a Puerto Rican native who'd joined the Marines to see the world. The Marines discovered he had a knack for blowing things up, and a man with such gifts was not to be overlooked when Dean had put his unit together.

Jack, as the rest of the team called him, knew to use sign language in the tunnels. Noises had a tendency to travel long distances in such conditions. He shook the rope and it went flying up the shaft. As they waited, Dean tapped him on the shoulder and motioned that he was going to go deeper into the pipe. Jack nodded that he understood and turned his attention to the backpacks coming down the shaft.

Otto made a high-speed wheel landing on the grass field, and by doing so, kept the temperatures of the cylinders low enough to coax a few more seconds of function out of the burning radial engine before it would seize. After a 200-meter rollout, Otto saw a group of men with a fire hose running toward him from a dark, ominous, concrete cave. The helicopter was showered by pressurized water as it rolled past the overhang and through a bomber-sized hangar door. Otto jumped out of his seat as the helicopter came to a stop, and ran past the hose men. He stood back and watched as a crowd of soldiers and medical teams rushed to the aid of the burnt SS colonel in the rear compartment of the helicopter.

Otto turned from the commotion and took in his new surroundings. The cavern was made of concrete. It's ceiling rose over 10 meters to accommodate the tail height of transport aircraft. To his right were the remains of six Me-262 jets that had clearly been cannibalized for parts. To his left over a dozen Tiger tanks began to spew black smoke from their exhausts. It was orchestrated chaos in the hangar.

The crowd that had gathered around his helicopter moved as one away from it and down toward the back of the concrete hangar. Otto ignored the commotion around him as he tried to figure out his next move. He sat alone on the right landing gear wheel, staring aimlessly over the fire-damaged BMW radial engine until two soldiers approached from his left.

The corporal cleared his throat to get Otto's attention. "Sir, excuse me. Could you give me an estimated number on the troop movements?"

Otto looked up from the engine bay. "There were three platoons that I could see. All had Russian markings. Four kilometers to the east."

Around him, soldiers prepared for an upcoming battle.

"Off to the west was a line of 10 Sherman tanks, moving fast."

Workers moved planes around to make space for four Tiger tanks, which took defensive positions around the entrance to the hangar.

Otto looked around, worried about where he could ride out the battle and stay alive for another day. "Looks like we have less than an hour."

"Thank you for the update, Major. If you would follow me now, the general is asking for you," he said as he handed a note to the private standing behind him, who ran off toward the Tiger tanks.

"Corporal, do I look like I'm presentable to meet a member of the High Command?" He turned as the remaining Tiger tanks accelerated out of the hangar.

"Sir, we do have a change of clothes for you. Please follow me."

"Hold on, Corporal, let me get my flight bag." He stepped up to the cockpit of the helicopter and reached in, grabbing the wet duffel bag containing his falsified papers and civilian clothes. Last thing he needed was for one of the SS guards to go fishing through his bag and arrest him for attempted desertion.

He was led through a side door, which took him inside the Me-262 jet fighter pilots' locker room.

"This is Major Schneider's locker; you can use his uniform. The showers have cold water," the corporal said as he opened the locker.

"Don't you think he will mind?"

"No, sir. The flight squadron had orders not to return." He looked down at a stopwatch in his hand. "You have exactly 10 minutes." The corporal sidestepped and waited by the door for Otto to get ready.

The cold shower felt great considering the amount of sweat that had poured out of his body during the mission. He dried off and put on the major's clothes, transferred his insignia and awards onto the shirt, and threw on his damp, brown leather jacket. He picked up his duffel bag, followed the corporal back into the hangar, and noticed that his helicopter was gone.

"Where is my helicopter?"

"It is being moved to a safe location for repair."

Otto thought that maybe, just maybe, he could still fly out. He walked behind the corporal and looked around, knowing all too well that all of the men around him were in for a losing fight.

Otto noticed that he was heading much deeper underground. An SS platoon three rows deep, guarding a meter-thick steel door, parted and saluted at Otto. Otto found it strange, but returned the salute. He and the corporal walked through the door and watched as it closed behind them.

"Well, the Russians will have a hard time getting through there."

"Yes, they will. Because of you those men have volunteered to guard the door at all costs."

The steel door closed with a resounding thud and locked behind them.

Scheissen...I meant the door, not the soldiers. What the hell am I into now?

A small rail cart sat 10 meters in front of them. Otto stepped onboard along with the corporal. The corporal turned a few dials and the small cart began to move, picking up speed with every meter it traveled.

"Where is everybody?"

"Waiting for you."

Otto stopped asking questions; to him each answer was not what he wanted to hear. He took his mind off the subject, concentrating on the speedometer on the panel. For such a small rail car, he was amazed that they were speeding past 100 kilometers per hour. Then the cart began to slow. They had been traveling for only a few minutes when they reached the stop.

The underground station was deserted. Otto got an eerie feeling when he heard a constant humming coming from in front of them. Once on the platform, they walked over to another steel door. The corporal slid it open and Otto stepped into a pantry-sized room.

The door then shut behind them and Otto felt the pressure change as his ears began to pop. Thirty seconds later a door in front of him slid open. The corporal moved forward, but Otto stood still, amazed at what lay before him.

The crawl through the pipe took some time before Dean came across a sliding steel hatch. He pressed his ear to it and listened.

Nobody's home, but just to be safe...

Dean pulled out his good luck charm—an 1875 single-action Smith & Wesson Schofield Model 3, five-inch revolver. The gun was converted to fire the powerful and abundant .45 ACP bullets loaded in a circular moon clip, making it very quick to load and unload. The Schofield was a family heirloom and was given to him before being sent to war. To date it had kept him safe. Dean adjusted himself and got into a squatting position as he waited for Jack to arrive.

Once together, Jack aimed his grease gun and nodded at the revolver. "Luck, don't fail us now..." he whispered.

Dean cocked the hammer.

Jack winked and pulled hard on the hatch.

The hatch slid open and Dean swept the room from the safety of the pipe. "Clear."

Jack jumped down into the 10-foot by 10-foot room. It was the left wall that caught his attention. Nestled within it was an array of lights, switches, and gauges. Dean approached the wall and holstered the Schofield in its leather cross-draw holster as he watched the needles in the gauges rotating counterclockwise.

"Wow, only seen such a set-up in a sub," Collins said as he jumped down from the hatch.

Dean looked back to see his team had gathered in the small room, minus Vic, who remained up top waiting for the patrol. A small alarm went off and the steel door to the vent tunnel slid shut.

"It's stuck, sir," Jack said as he tried to pry it open.

Dean looked at the other door in the room. Above it a small green light began to strobe.

"Never mind that. We'll blow it if we have to."

"What about Vic?"

"He's a big boy, he'll figure it out," Collins said as he stepped toward the door that Bill was inspecting.

"Is it wired, Bill?" Dean asked.

"Um…yes, but looks like it's wired to this panel, just like the vent door we came through." He pointed at the black electrical cords attached to the bare concrete wall.

"And what do you make of this?" Dean gestured to the gauges on the panels.

"Looks like pressure gauges, sir, and they're moving counterclockwise."

"Jesus, that tunnel is huge," Collins said as he looked through the hubcap-sized window embedded in the steel door opposite the hatch.

"Sir, what do you want to do?" Jack asked.

"Well, it is definitely not like what we found six weeks ago. Bill, take some pictures and let's move on."

"We did not come here to relax, men. Let's open her up," Collins said.

Bill pulled hard on the door and the edges whistled. Dean could feel the suction as the door gave way. A buzzing alarm began to sound as Dean stepped through. "Hurry!" he yelled as Collins jumped through.

Jack just made it as the door closed, separating Bill from the group.

"Don't worry, sir," Bill said, his voice muffled by the thick window. "I'll bypass it. Should take me a couple of minutes."

Dean gave him a thumbs-up and stepped down the concrete ladder, which was molded into the curved wall.

I am now two men short. Bill could get back, but thinking that way could get one killed. As far as I know, I have two men left. Not good.

Dean turned around to find Collins and Jack staring at the immense tunnel around them. It was unlike anything he had ever seen. The tunnel was over 90 feet wide, and it had rails running around its circumference wall, much like the rifling inside a gun barrel. Between the rails and fastened to the circumference of the tunnel were cargo-pallet-sized black rectangular plates.

"Sir, did you feel the pressure change?"

"Yes." Dean looked to both ends of the tunnel. "Let's head toward the brighter side of the tunnel while Bill tries to get the door open."

"Sir," Collins asked, "what is this place?"

"I don't know, but it sure doesn't look like a V-2 rocket facility. Jack, you're taking pictures, right?"

"Yes, sir."

"Well, save your film. I have a feeling things are going to get stranger."

Dean noticed a slight curve to the tunnel as the group began to walk through it. He stopped 10 minutes into his walk when he caught a glimpse of an object in the distance.

"Sir, what is that?" Jack asked.

Dean put his binoculars to his eyes and began to focus.

"What do you see, sir?" Collins asked as Dean handed him the binoculars.

"You tell me," Dean said.

Collins looked at the object. "Um...well, sir, it looks like a floating subway train."

"Good. For a minute I thought I was going crazy."

"Herr General, what is this thing, sir?" Otto asked the general.

The general smiled. He put the Iron Cross around Otto's neck. "It's our past, and our future. Your actions have earned you and your ship..." The general looked to his left. Otto followed his gaze to see that his helicopter was being pushed into the train. "...Germany's highest honor...to be invited to such an event."

"Sir, I still don't understand."

"All your questions will soon be answered." The SS general stepped back and performed a perfect salute. "Heil Hitler!"

All in the small gathering, including Otto, saluted back. "Heil Hitler!"

Otto always felt uncomfortable saying it, but now was not a good time to protest.

A corporal stepped up to the group. "Sir, it is time. The automatic settings are now active. In a few minutes the tunnel will become a vacuum. We need to step in and seal all doors."

"*Danka.*" The general turned back to Otto. "Major, you will be seated with me in the second cabin. Corporal, please escort the major to his seat."

The general and his team walked away toward the front of the train.

"Sir, you have to come with me for processing," the corporal said as he spun on his heels and headed to the train door.

Otto looked around, trying to make sense of what was happening around him. The corporal turned and motioned to him. Otto took a labored breath and followed.

"Sir, I'm feeling short of breath," Jack said.

Collins looked back at Jack. "Yeah, me too."

Dean felt the same but kept silent. He picked up his pace as the lack of air began to take a toll on his lungs, and stopped a few meters from the train, studying it as it floated in midair. He pointed out the thin steel wires to Collins. The train was huge, around three times the width of a typical New York subway car. It was hung in the center of the massive tunnel about 20 feet above their heads. Its mystique was partly discredited by the hundreds of thin wires holding it up. Dean looked around as the sound of hundreds of clicks resonated through the tunnel, followed by a steady electric hum.

"What was that?" Jack asked.

Dean stepped closer to the train and began to notice a strange pull on his weapon, as if some unseen force were trying to pry the machine gun from his grip. The closer he got to the train, the stronger the pull became. He stopped once again as his dog tag chain leaped out off his shirt and magically hovered in the air.

It took a moment to register. *Magnetism.*

Dean's hand shot up in a closed fist. Collins and Jack froze, aiming their weapons at the unseen danger. He turned his head around and whispered, "Gentlemen, stop and check that all your metal equipment is secure."

Jack kneeled down, covering the others as they checked for loose items, when the Bowie Knife that he kept secure to his backpack strap flew out of its sheaf and toward Dean. Dean ducked away from the deadly object, but not before the tip of the blade nicked his right cheek.

All three watched the knife as it picked up speed until it hit a dark, cargo-pallet-sized metallic plate on the wall where it stuck, oblivious to gravity. Dean looked at the tunnel's walls and now noticed that the plates were placed closer together.

"Jack, leave the knife, but get a couple of shots before you put that camera away."

Dean was careful as he took each step toward what he guessed to be the rear of the train. With all the metal he had on him, any misstep could send him flying into one of the hundreds of plates now surrounding them, and the closer he got to the train the more he felt the pull of the magnets.

Dean found a wooden grab-handle at the rear of the train, suspended under it by a thin rope. He dragged his steel-toe boots forward five yards on the magnetic metal plates and reached up, taking hold of the wood handle. He pulled down and a long, thin ladder unfolded from the bottom of the train. The ladder's main pivot point led to steps built into the rear structure. He grabbed the sides, checked that it was secure, and with great effort lifted his boots onto the bottom rung and began to climb. It took a few moments to reach the top, where he found a perch on a thin outcropping. He crouched on the ledge and moved up to the square window in the steel hatch, grabbing the vertical handhold next to it with one hand. He then aimed the Schofield with the other hand, peeked through the window, and saw an empty mechanical compartment. Dean looked down and with a small nod motioned for the rest of his team to head on up.

"Collins, you take point." Dean took a labored breath. "Jack, you're next." He turned the handle. The door slid open, letting out a whistle of air, and like before, a small alarm went off. The door began to shut, but not before they were all in the small cabin.

Dean, feeling lightheaded, struggled for each breath. A small green light on top of the opposite door began to strobe and a shot of cool air was released into the compartment. They took in deep breaths of the fresh air as it filled the small cabin.

"Everybody good?" he whispered as he looked past the porthole window of a secondary door, scanning the long, thin hallway.

"Yeah, almost passed out there. It was like the air was being sucked out of me," Jack said.

"Recheck weapons. I'll take point," Dean said as he holstered his Schofield, swung the grease gun around from his back, and stepped in front of Jack. "Ready?"

His team nodded once, then Jack reached across and pulled on the door handle.

The train car they were walking through contained a multitude of wooden boxes and furniture. Most were marked with personal names. Collins took a few seconds to pry one open and found photo albums, stock notes, civilian and military clothing.

"Looks like the inside of a moving truck," Collins said.

As the team stepped through the car, Dean counted the paces he took before reaching the next compartment.

"One hundred meters," he said as he grabbed the latch in front of him.

Dean nodded to Jack. Jack nodded back, and Dean slid the door open to his right. This time there was no rush of air, just a small hissing sound. As Dean stepped through he took note that the cars were separated by a pressure room large enough to hold four people. They walked through the first door, closed it, and waited for the green strobe before opening the next door. As the door slid open, the strong smell of gasoline filled the space. Dean could see swollen black rubber bags on both sides of the compartment that extended the length of the car.

"No smoking," Jack said comically.

Collins chuckled, then reached over and touched one of the rubber bags. "Feels like they are filled to capacity."

"Jack, lay one charge, but don't set it," Collins said.

Dean kept guard as Jack hid the explosive between the rubber bag and train wall. "All you have to do is activate it and run like hell," Jack told them.

"Let's keep going. I'm a little worried that we haven't run into anyone."

Dean began to turn as a crack, a whistle, and puffing sounds occurred within the span of a second. The nine-millimeter copper bullet passed under Dean's chin and smacked into the sliding door behind him. At the same time, in the opposite direction, two .45 caliber slugs entered the body of an SS soldier, killing him on the spot.

"Guess I spoke too soon!"

Dean sprinted forward, and red lights illuminated the compartment. A German voice announced over an intercom that there were two minutes to launch.

"Good shot, Jack. Collins, did I hear right?" Dean asked as he reached the dead soldier.

"Yes, looks like somebody is going to try to get a V-2 rocket off without our permission."

"Still doesn't make sense."

"What?"

"All this." He pointed with his chin. "This strange train, the gasoline, the personal effects." Dean peeked through the window of the next car. "Well, now this is even stranger," he said as he slid open the door.

Packed all around them were cars, trucks, and motorcycles. The team ran through the train, zigzagging around all the machinery.

"What the hell is this?" Jack whispered.

"It looks like a garage for all things German."

"Is that the helicopter we saw earlier?"

"Looks like it."

"Sir, look at this car," Jack said as he went ahead of Dean.

The car had the dimensions of a light truck but the looks of a convertible limousine. It was a black Mercedes Benz convertible with one front and two rear wheels on each side of the car.

"Oh, I'm taking this one back with me."

"Sure, but first we have a few things to do."

Dean was back at point when he noticed the group of barrels pointed at him.

"Cover!" he yelled as all three threw themselves behind a box marked "headlights/glass" half a second before a barrage of bullets began to disintegrate the items within the boxes.

Whoever led the firing squad in front of them made one critical mistake, which Dean picked out and used to his advantage. Dean waited a few more seconds. Then it came.

Silence.

"Cover fire!" Dean yelled out as he hurdled the box, took four strides, then jumped over another box. Dean turned his body in midair, landing hard on his back, and slid on the metal floor as he emptied a full clip at the four surprised SS soldiers who were all caught reloading at the same time.

"Clear!" Dean reloaded and turned to face the door behind him.

"Well, I guess they know we're here!" Collins said as he took a knee next to Dean, who was now inside the pressure room, looking around as an electrical humming noise filled the compartment. Then the walls of the train and everything within began to vibrate.

Collins looked at Jack as he grabbed the handle on the sliding door. He could feel the door handle vibrating in his hand, nodded, and pulled. Jack went in first, followed by Dean, then Collins. He took stock of the cabin and didn't like what he saw. The cabin was six triple rows wide with seats, but every one was empty.

"Keep a sharp eye, Jack; I don't like our situation," Dean said as he walked behind him.

Jack never had time to reply as a wall of bullets entered his body, sending him back into Dean. Dean, in turn, stumbled backward and was caught by Collins, who had just thrown a grenade. Jack's body became a human shield, blocking the deadly bullets, saving the lives of Dean and Collins.

Dean crawled to the open door behind them, then past it, just as Collins's grenade exploded. He heard a creaking sound and turned his head to see the middle of the car's ceiling explode outward. The suction was so great that their bodies began to lift off the floor. Everything not tied down was lifted up, including Jack's body. A couple of German soldiers standing near the hole were gruesomely folded in half as they were sucked out through it. It took but a few seconds of mayhem for the pressure between the tunnel and the train car to equalize. Dean and Collins fell back down to the floor of the small compartment, unable to breathe.

A red strobe went off, and the compartment door shut. Like before, the strobe turned green and a blast of air was released into the space between the cars. With every passing second the vibration and humming within the cars became deafening as Dean took a much-needed breath, got up, and peeked through the window to see an army of masked SS soldiers running to the door.

"Collins, give me the satchel charge. Hold your breath and slide open that door."

Collins handed the satchel to Dean. Dean placed one foot on either side of the doorframe, bracing himself, and pulled on the satchel arming ring. The timer began to run as he held the explosive on his chest. He aimed his grease gun at the door and winked at Collins.

Collins took a deep breath, held it, and pulled as hard as he could. The door gave in and slid on its tracks. The pressure difference between the compartment and the vacuum created another smaller blowout that sent the satchel flying out over the first 10 soldiers. Dean also fired his grease gun, which took down six of the masked men. Once the pressure between both spaces equalized, he knelt as he emptied the rest of his bullets at the running crowd.

The alarm went off and the door began to slide closed as Dean's eyes grew wide at what appeared before him.

It was at that exact time that one of the SS soldiers shot back. Dean did not react as his last bullet exited his barrel and 30 feet away a German nine-millimeter bullet flew toward his head. The German bullet went traveling over the speed of sound toward its target, and right behind it a bright wall of light was catching up.

Dean stared in awe as the white light rushed toward him.

The light passed through the hot copper nine-millimeter bullet a meter in front of Dean, and a split second later engulfed him.

The space where Dean stood turned to fire as the automatic self-destruct systems activated. The enormous explosion disintegrated everything within its radius. Its concussion wave swallowed up the miles-long subway tunnel and in that instant the ground above bellowed from the enormous pressure below, and then collapsed within itself, burying the complex and sending all its contents into oblivion.

3

Off the coast of Libya, October, 2010

The whining sound of the turboprop engines resonated within the small, four-foot-wide cabin of the surveillance aircraft as Lieutenant Commander Max DuMonde reviewed the instruments depicted on the flat screen in front of him. He checked his altimeter and reduced speed as he approached the intended target, a small island just off the nose of the aircraft. The plane he flew was the Navy's new project surveillance aircraft, code named Condor. Condor was an evolution of the little-known skunkworks project made to create a silent, manned, night-aircraft observation platform during the Vietnam conflict.

The first aircraft used for that early project was a Schweizer 2-32 sailplane converted to run on its own power by using a piston engine and a multi-blade wooden propeller spinning at very low rpms, which minimized the sound signature of the rotating propeller.

Once the project became active, it surpassed all expectations. It was able to fly down to 200 feet at night without detection. The North Vietnamese even had stories circulating around their ranks of a flying ghost ship. The project was such a success that the Schweizer Company began its own stealth aircraft project dedicated to providing silent, night patrol aircraft for surveillance and observation. Eventually, Sikorsky bought out Schweizer Aircraft Company and continued building and improving on the surveillance aircraft program.

The Sikorsky SA-38BN, the "N" being its Navy designation, was the latest in this type of aircraft design, and the most sophisticated surveillance platform aircraft to leave the Schweizer assembly line, thanks to U.S. Navy funding. Operation Condor was the Navy's answer to the growing compromise between the use of manned and unmanned aircraft surveillance vehicles that provided longer aloft times and the ultimate in safety for pilots, since the pilot would be flying the plane via remote control from a comfortable chair thousands of miles away from the danger.

On the other hand, the Navy and Marine higher-ups were old-fashioned and believed that the human element in the battlefields was an important and justifiable method to get the job done. The Marines had already reactivated the OV-10 Bronco, an old and trusted Forward Air Control (FAC) conventional twin turboprop aircraft. The Navy went the opposite way and invested in a new aircraft to fill the FAC role. The Air Force, on the other hand, was known for testing the unknown so they went with the drones, as did the Army. The test reports did show the advantages and also the disadvantages of the unmanned aircraft. So, as always, the land- and ocean-based warriors agreed to disagree and chose different paths.

Even with all the Navy's backing, the Condor project was still in jeopardy. The techs in the Pentagon had to please the politicians who disliked spending more money on putting a human in harm's way, especially in the economic downturn. So it was down to the test phase of the project, which would determine the final decision to add the Condor to the Navy's military arsenal or into the Naval archive of failed projects.

At first glance, the two Condors the Navy had ordered appeared to be like the other surveillance aircraft that rolled out of the Schweizer plant. The original fuselage contained room for a crew of three: pilot, copilot, and dedicated surveillance engineer; or a crew of two, working with the extra surveillance package. Its power came from two Pratt & Whitney PT6A-34A turboprop jet engines put in center thrust configuration. One engine lay in front of the cockpit, the second facing rearward behind the cockpit.

The wing roots extended toward twin booms from the cockpit sides and the wings stretched out from the booms in sailplane fashion, long and thin, allowing the aircraft to soar quietly in a thermal updraft if the occasion called for it.

Within these booms were a mired mix of electronic equipment, including the AN/APG-78 Longbow millimeter-wave Fire Control Radar (FCR) target acquisition system, and the Radar Frequency Interferometer (RFI) all redesigned and connected to a forward-looking infrared surveillance unit (FLIR). Both these booms extended rearward out past the rear engine and were connected by a rudder/elevator wing.

The major difference in the Navy's Condors lay in their extensive prototype electronics equipment that took up all available space, including the right seat, which in the military was reserved for the copilot. It included the replacement of stronger and taller landing gear, along with a tail hook, to accommodate the harsh aircraft carrier landings. Armor plating was also installed. The armor hugged the pilot in his seat, protecting him from bullets on both sides, including the seat base and back, and a single .50 caliber machine gun on a rotating ball turret was under the cockpit.

It was this .50 caliber automatic rifle that gave the Condor's pilot, Lieutenant Commander Max DuMonde, a sense of comfort, knowing that, if needed in a combat situation, he could help instead of flying around helplessly waiting for the gunships to arrive. They also gave the Condor an edge over its competition, allowing the pilot of the aircraft to hit any target with surgical precision. Its competition, the unmanned drones, used the Hellfire missiles to kill.

The Hellfire missiles were considered a waste of good money and firepower by the Navy. They, in turn, figured that the same mission could be done with the precision of the .50 caliber bullet from high above. Max, a former Navy SEAL, also had firsthand experience and knew the importance of friendly .50 caliber bullets covering fighting men on the ground.

"Condor One, Control. Do you copy?" crackled the voice of the radar operator flying in the Navy AWACS air control plane 20,000 feet above the Condor's position.

Max clicked the mike button. "Control, this is Condor One. Copy five-by-five," he responded and began his much-practiced routine inside the Condor. "Control, Condor approaching vector. Turning to target in two, switching frequency. Over."

"Roger, Condor, have you on scope, good hunting. Out."

Max reached out his gloved hand and pressed on the touch screen of the rectangular 8x20-inch LCD in front of him. He found the corresponding radio frequency and touched it with his bare finger that stuck out of the tip of his Nomex fireproof glove. The white numbers switched to red, signifying that that radio frequency was now on and active. The new touch screen was a marvel. It worked much like his iPad, allowing him to touch and set up the screen as he wished. Right now he had the center occupied by a synthetic vision of the outside world, along with the primary flight control systems overlay. The far left of the screen displayed the radio and transponder information, and to the far right, the digital readout of the aircraft's engines, temperature, and fuel status.

"Fish, this is Condor, you read?" Max said into the mike.

A thousand feet below and two miles to the east, two black shadows scaled the rock cliff of a small deserted island off the coast of Libya. The first shadow stopped and spoke into his neck microphone, which picked up and transmitted the vibrations from the wearer's vocal cords.

"Condor, this is Fish. We copy."

"Roger, Fish. How you doing?"

"Fine. How about you?"

"Coming up on your position. Can you detect my sound signature?"

"Yep, I hear you."

"Good, give me a second. Activating silent mode." Max pressed the silent icon on the right of the LCD screen and the rear engine began to wind down. He felt the automatic flight control system move the corresponding throttle quadrant back into its idle position and watched through his rearview mirror as the rear propeller spun down, feathering itself and allowing it to cut into the wind, which minimized the aerodynamic drag. The front propeller still turned, but at a much slower rate, giving just enough thrust to keep the Condor aloft. "Fish. How do I sound now?"

"All went silent from down here. As far as I know, you don't exist."

"Good, activating HMD." He had yet to try out the new generation-five Helmet Mounted Display in a real-mission scenario. Up to now all his experiences using the HMD had been within California airspace or inside the simulator at the Naval Base in San Diego. He touched the HMD icon with his exposed finger. The world around him flickered and suddenly contained 3D floating icons of all types. The new system reflected off the mirrors in his line of sight and onto the visor much like the heads-up display in the jet fighters. The biggest difference was that his heads-up display was the helmet he now wore, giving him a 360-degree, 3D view of the world around him. The icons would remain in place despite his direction of sight, much like the stars at night.

Max looked up as a new icon came into view from the top left-hand corner of the visor. He turned his head once more and the icon got brighter as it centered on the middle of his visor. He knew that all he had to do was press the small button on the control stick next to his ring finger and the computer would set the radio to the AWACS aircraft above. Each button on the control stick and throttle quadrant was connected to the HMD, allowing him to control the Condor's equipment without moving his hands from the controls.

What gave the HMD such power was the new Active Electronically Scanned Array radar, or AESA radar, as it was known. The new radar worked in tandem with all the other electronics in the plane. It had fast processing times, which gave the HMD the possibility of viewing the world around it in real-time, three-dimensional space. The other hidden treat in the Condor's arsenal was the experimental Forward-Looking Infrared Radar and listening device, or FLIR. The new FLIR he worked with now was different in that its lens had more magnifying power than the previous model, and contained a sophisticated gyroscopic and computer system that reduced vibration in the image on the screen.

"FLIR coming online." He controlled the zoom lens with his left thumb, and rotated the FLIR pod by turning his head toward the intended target. The target appeared on both his HMD and on the top left of the LCD screen. The helmet and FLIR slave connection was cut when he clicked on the spot he was looking at, allowing him to turn his head around in the cockpit without changing the line of sight on the FLIR scope, which was now locked on the target, its image projected onto a small area of his HMD. "HMD functioning, FLIR... *Fliring*."

A laugh echoed in his headset. "Don't quit your day job, Max."

"Guess I am not feeling it today, but I'm here all night, so get used to it," Max said as he course-corrected the Condor.

"How do you see us?"

Max zoomed in even closer and was amazed at not only the clarity of the new lens that was installed just days before, but also the stillness of the picture it produced. The camera picked up the figure of Max's best friend and Navy SEAL Commander Val Vittoria, as he stood upright on a boulder five times his size perched on the edge of a cliff. Val was dressed in his black combat outfit and carried his M4 rifle slung across his chest. Max reactivated the FLIR for manual adjustments and focused even closer. "Fish, your shoelace is untied."

"What?" Val looked down and noticed that his shoelace was indeed untied. "That's fuckin' amazing. You can see that?"

"Obviously...but I didn't have to look to know that you're too dumb to know how to tie your own shoes." Max zoomed out and saw Val's teammate below hanging off one of the many cliff outcroppings. "Why don't you ask Sergeant Perez to tie them for you?"

"Ha, ha, asshole."

"All right, back to business. You guys do your thing and I'll start the test run."

"Copy. Doing our thing."

Max went through his checklist for the night's exercise. He was to run a mock-up target identification and acquisition procedure using all the systems at hand. He looked around once more and allowed himself to relax, let go of control of the Condor to the computer and set the autopilot to circle the island at 1,000 feet. He eased his grip on the controls and played with the FLIR, watching his best friend looking down at Perez, encouraging him in Val's usual way.

Let's see what you're saying.

Max pushed one of the buttons on his throttle quadrant and listened as the computers began to adjust for ambient noise.

"Jesus, Perez, my grandmother can climb faster than that. You'd better hurry. Lt. Commander DuMonde will get pissed if they cancel his program because you took so fuckin' long that the technology surpassed us and we all became obsolete."

Max laughed out loud and hit his communications button. "Val, take it easy on the sergeant. You keep that up and he may just jump back in the water and swim home."

"You can hear me? Shit, I didn't think it could work that well in the real world. Anyway, if you're still listening, I don't know where you are, but I am sure you can see this," Val said as he shot his middle finger up into the air.

• • •

Sergeant Steven Perez reached Val's position and stood next to him.

"About time," Val said as he smiled at his new team scout.

Val had specifically picked Perez for the mission. Perez was not new to the SEALs, but he was new to Val's team, so Val took it upon himself to make sure he was a good fit. So far Perez was proving to be a patient and quiet man—just what Val was looking for.

"By the way, do you speak?"

Perez looked back, smirked, and nodded.

"Shit, you're worse than my last girlfriend. She spoke too much, and you have yet to say a word."

Val went over the aerial photos of the island they were standing on and double-checked them with the portable GPS unit. Satisfied, they went on to set up the laser and markers for the night's exercise. They placed the markers at random distances from each other. Once done, they headed over to a football-field-sized flat clearing to set up the laser system.

• • •

A crackle came through Max's headset. "Condor, Fish is set up."

"Roger Fish. Switching frequencies." Max turned his head toward the green icon floating in midair to his right. The HMD adjusted the brightness of the icon and turned it red once Max clicked on it. "Dragonfly One, this is Condor One. Do you copy?"

"Copy, Condor. Dragonfly One is out 10 miles north of target. Standing by for orders," warbled the voice of the Navy Black Hawk helicopter pilot who had dropped Val and Perez a mile off shore.

"Copy, Dragonfly One, evolution is beginning, return for pick-up in three zero."

"Copy, Condor. Dragonfly One will be back in three zero. Out."

Max switched back to Val's radio frequency and told them to be ready for pick-up in 30 minutes. He pressed another one of the dozens of buttons on the flight controls and slaved the FLIR back to the HMD. Thirty new icons appeared superimposed on the ground. A small green halo appeared as Max pressed another button. The halo flew over to one of the icons.

Blip...

The computer identified it with a number designation before scrolling off to the next icon. It did this 30 times in less than two seconds. Next, the computer zoomed onto the icons and waited until Max allowed it to head to the next one. Max read the letter on the marker and recorded a few seconds of the sound frequency emanating from it before moving on to the next target. It took Max less than two minutes to read and record all 28 markers. The last two icons were the infrared signatures of Val and Perez taking cover a few hundred meters from the test area.

Once done, he activated the ground laser aiming system. The computer took over and maneuvered the FLIR over to each spot the laser illuminated. Max was finishing the digital backup of the night's exercise when the emergency channel flashed on the radar screen.

He looked up at the AWACS icon and clicked on it. "Control. Condor One. What is the nature of the emergency?"

"Condor, Control. Dragonfly One has lost an engine due to a bird strike. They are RTB at this time. Base has Dragonfly Two running up, will be there in five zero. Copy."

RTB meant Return to Base.

"Control, Condor copies Dragonfly One is out, new bird running up. ETA five zero. Over and out." Max switched frequencies. "Fish."

"Copy, Condor. What's up?"

"Dragonfly One lost an engine. He's heading back to the carrier. There's another bird running up and should get here in 50. I'll hang out until they pick you up. Looks like we've had our gremlin for tonight."

"Don't jinx it, Condor. How did the exercise go?"

"Everything ran well, and I finished two minutes ahead of time. Give me a minute, then you can start to pick up. I'm going to do a little more limit testing while we wait."

"Roger."

Max made sure all the systems had recorded and saved the night's exercise in a MPG-4 high-definition file. He removed the postage-stamp-sized flash storage card and replaced it with a new one. A green light first flickered, then glowed a steady green hue as the system began to record once more. He aimed the scope, switched to night vision, then back to infrared, taking his time to get accustomed to working the controls. He then began to test the limits of all his sensors as he followed Val and Perez picking up the markers they'd placed around the west coast of the island.

Max watched as Val jumped across a car-sized boulder, followed by Perez. They were practicing maneuvers as they picked up the markers. Max would pan out, analyzing the terrain in front of them, and tried to guess which way Val would take. After a few minutes he guessed he was right 90 percent of the time.

Val picked up the last marker and found a suitable area in which to sit and rest. They sat back to back, sipping water from their camelback water bladders. Max licked his lips and reached down for his water bottle, tilting his head down, which in turn moved the FLIR downward, and out of the corner of his right eye he saw something familiar and out of place.

He was careful not to move his head as his hands fell back onto the flight instruments. Max zoomed out in search of the straight, light gray rifle barrel he thought he had seen.

He switched all the sensors to infrared and patiently waited as the Condor's flight plan took it around the cliff edge. Max clicked on the spot where he had last seen the object, and disconnected the helmet from the movement of the scope. He froze as a white figure began to appear behind a boulder. "Oh, shit..." Max heard a blipping sound as the HMD lit a green halo on the newfound object. "Fish, we might have a problem."

"What is it?" Val asked, recognizing the change of tone in Max's voice.

Blip, blip.

His view began to fill with small green circles. "We have three..."

Blip.

"Correction, four tangos heading in your direction..."

Blip.

"Shit, five. Looks like they're coming out of a small cave." Max shut off the icon activation sound.

"You're sure they're hostiles?"

"All carrying AK-47s. Start heading east. They're 500 meters southwest, coming up on you fast."

"Roger. Your eyes, Condor."

This was the code that told Max it was up to him to tell Val where to go.

Max reconnected the helmet to the main aiming device. When he looked up, he saw many more glowing white figures surrounded by the computer-animated green halos approaching Val and Perez's position from the south and east.

"Val, you're surrounded. Head northeast and fast. Have you taken fire?"

"No. Heading northeast." Val's breathing was fast and hard as he sprinted away.

"Contacting Control." Max switched frequencies and started to run the sound software. "Control, Condor. Fish has encountered unfriendlies, all bearing weapons. Sending sound now."

"Roger. Receiving sound. Do not engage. Wait for orders." The AWACS officer manning the radios connected to Max's home base, the aircraft carrier. Inside were numerous interpreters who started to translate, as the voices Max was recording were sent over the radio. "Condor, relaying your communication direct to ground base. Switch to Alfa. Over."

"Roger, switching Alfa."

"Good luck, Control out."

Max touched the Alfa radio frequency icon for the carrier. "Base, do you copy?"

"Condor, this is base. Copy you loud and clear. Acknowledge orders," a woman said, who was sitting in the center of the operations room deep inside the aircraft carrier.

"Orders are not to engage."

"Condor, standby."

Max saw that it was going to be tight for Val and Perez and began the arming procedure for the .50 caliber machine gun. Below, and to the rear left of the cockpit, a thin hatch opened and a long barrel dropped down from the belly of the plane. It chambered a round and slaved itself to the FLIR, rotating around to point in the same direction Max was looking.

"Condor, translation confirms unfriendly. Do not engage unless engaged upon."

"Copy, relaying message." Max switched to Val's frequency. "Val, usual bullshit. Do not engage unless engaged upon. Here it gets tight, go right of that boulder. I have the .50 cal, slaved, online, and hot. I got you covered, buddy."

"Roger. How many BBs you got?" Val's breathing was heavy as he rounded another boulder. A bullet whizzed by his head. "Shit! We're engaged! How many hostiles?"

"I count 40. I have 30 shots, 10 full metal jacket, 10 tracers, and 10 uranium."

"Start with the FMJ's, make them count," Val yelled, as he and Perez began taking evasive maneuvers.

"Go east, on my mark, toward unfriendlies. I'll clear a path." Max flipped the arming switch and called base. "Base, we are taking fire, engaging."

"Roger, Condor. Fire at will. Fighters on the way. ETA in 10."

Max looked at the situation below. *Ten minutes...crap.*

Max saw more unfriendlies coming out from the ground. "Val." Max took aim. "Wait for it..." He squeezed the trigger. "NOW!"

One .50 caliber copper bullet spit out of the long barrel and headed toward two hostiles. The bullet hit and disintegrated both targets. "Go! Go! Go!" Max could already see Val and Perez running at full speed. "Forward

20 meters, then turn hard left, then head north to the edge of open field. Take cover around the tower-looking boulder. I'll keep them at bay while I think of something." Max switched frequencies. "Base, how are those fighters coming along?"

"Condor, still on the cat," the woman said, referring to the two planes on the steam catapults that would accelerate the fighter jets to take-off speed and off the front of the aircraft carrier.

"Roger that." Max shot two more rounds, killing one hostile, missing the other by millimeters. He swung the barrel around and noticed the hostiles were starting to wonder where the bullets were coming from.

Shit, shit, shit ...this is getting worse by the second. Think, Max!

He looked at the open field and started to run a scenario in his head. He went over it again, rechecking the wind direction, and decided. He took a deep breath and began to mentally prepare himself for what he was about to do.

"Fish, they look to be organizing. I'm going to try to keep them busy. Once I start, I want you to head out into the field and wait."

"Out in the open? You have to be fuckin' kidding me!"

"Val, just do it. There is no way we can hold them off." Max started shooting into the small crowds. They started shooting up out of desperation, trying to kill the invisible hunter. "Go Val, and stay low. I'm coming in."

"You're what?" Val shouted as he shot a burst into a crowd of five hostiles running at him.

Perez took down two of them, Val the rest. They both picked up and began to run into the open field.

Max was busier than he had ever been, shooting the .50 caliber gun and restarting the rear engine as he banked and dove the plane toward the ground. Alarms began to sound within the cockpit, warning Max of a stall, and then another alarm signaling the ground was coming up too fast.

"Pull up! Pull up!" announced the onboard speaker as Max leveled the wings before a final turn onto the small patch of flat land below him. He watched through his infrared heads-up display as Val and Perez shot at the oncoming opposing force. Max helped out and was surprised to see green lines heading toward the ground.

Ah, shit.

Max had given away his position and plan to the enemy. "Fuck it!" he screamed as he emptied the remaining tracer bullets into the enemy, taking a few more lives. Max flicked down the landing gear and at the same time the .50 caliber machine gun rotated and hid in the belly of the fuselage.

The Condor approached sideways as it slipped, making it lose altitude while maintaining its forward air speed. The plane came down hard on the dirt plateau. Its wingtips flexed down, narrowly missing the ground, and bounced up again. Max fought it back down to the ground as the engines roared when he applied full reverse pitch on the propeller blades. The plane stopped and gave Val and Perez a few precious moments of cover from the hostiles now shooting at the plane from the opposite side.

The right canopy swung open and Max yelled at his stunned friend, "Come on, I don't have all day!"

The left side of the canopy shattered. The bullets ricocheted off the interior. Max ducked and heard Val empty his machine gun. At the same time Max released his Medusa model 47 revolver from its holster, aimed at a shadow, and shot. The gun spit out its .357 magnum-caliber bullet and hit the shadow center mass, sending the body back onto itself.

Max heard Perez throw himself in the back on top of all the electrical equipment, and pushed the throttles to full power as Val yelled at him to go. Max, still shooting his gun out the hole in his canopy, controlled the plane with his feet on the rudder pedals in a straight track toward the cliff's edge. He holstered his empty gun as Val emptied another clip into the receding crowd from inside the cockpit.

Max reached up with his right arm and pulled Val down. Val shut the canopy just as the plane came up to the edge of the cliff.

"Hold on!" Max screamed.

The Condor rolled out into thin air...and dropped.

Max could hear bullets smack into the belly of the plane as the dark ocean filled his windshield.

"SHIIIIIT!" he yelled as he forced himself to keep from pulling back on the control stick, because if he did he'd force the plane into a stall, ending their efforts there and then.

"Pull up. Pull up," the computerized voice warned once more, as three little green lights came on, informing Max that the landing gear was up.

"Jesus, Max, do what the plane tells you!" Val yelled.

"A few more seconds!" Max yelled back, then pulled back on the stick as his airspeed indicator rolled up 20 knots past rotation speed.

His body became heavy. He began to take quick and shallow breaths as the G-forces increased. The plane got closer and closer to the sea as the stall alarms began to wail once more.

"Pull up. Pull up."

The stall-warning horn boomed throughout the cabin and the plane began to buffet as its wings lost lift. The buffeting decreased, and the stall-warning horn lowered in decibels as the Condor leveled off. It was only then that Max knew they were going to make it. He let out the breath he had been holding and was shocked to breathe in the salty ocean mist coming through the grapefruit-sized hole in the canopy. He took a quick glance out to his right, and became fixated on the top of the wave he was skimming just a few feet below.

Max's senses told him there was something wrong with the plane. He looked at the engine temperatures and saw that the rear engine was running hot, eased off on the rear engine power level and began a slow climb, then turned his attention to his passengers.

"Val, you all right?"

"Yeah, I'm fine, you crazy fuck!"

"How about you, Perez?"

"Steven?" Val said as he reached back in the small space where Perez lay on top of electronic boxes.

"Shit! Perez is hit!"

"How bad?"

"Not good." Val searched for injury. "He's losing blood. Looks like a through-and-through upper chest wound. Bullet just missed his vest. Call it in. I can stop the bleeding...but we have to get him help."

"Base, this is Condor."

"Condor, Base. Update?"

Max was about to answer when, below and to his right on the HMD, he saw three new icons. The small round halos assigned designations as Max zoomed in on the white wakes of three boats leaving the small island.

"Base, I have three new contacts. Looks like go-fast boats. I have one injured onboard. Requesting vector to base ASAP."

"Negative, take out targets with your gun, Condor."

Max looked at his ammunition counter. "Base, Condor has two shots left. Over."

"Condor. Take the shots. Then paint the targets for incoming Delta flight, out two minutes."

"Roger. Taking shots and painting remaining targets." He turned to Val. "Val...need to do some more work before we go home."

"I got control of the bleeding," Val said as he covered the exit wound. "But we need to get him taken care of. I can only do so much."

"Should be quick. Hold on." Max armed and aimed the .50 cal at the rear of the closest boat. He squeezed the trigger twice. The last shot hit the magic spot and the boat blew up into a ball of fire. "Holy shit!" he shouted.

A new voice came over the radio. "Condor, this is Delta flight. Two Rhinos. Delta One has four AIM 9, four Mavericks, two Harpoons, plus mike-mike, same Delta Two. Over."

The F-18 pilot had told Max that each plane carried four AIM sidewinder air-to-air missiles, four AGM-65 Maverick air-to-ground missiles, two AGM-84 Harpoon anti-ship missiles, and 578 20-millimeter bullets for the nose-mounted M61 Vulcan Gatling gun.

"Delta, this is Condor. Painting targets." Max aimed two separate infrared lasers, one for each of the remaining boats. The F-18 fighters would now be able to read the targets and take them out.

"I take it that that huge fireball is of your making."

"That's one of three. Instead of missiles I want you to use your guns. Let's see if we can get us some prisoners. Let me get clearance first." Base gave Max clearance to take out the targets using the Gatling guns. "Good news, boys, you get to shoot your guns today. Do you have my paint?"

"Roger. Delta One has FAC and target in sight."

Satisfied that the flight of F-18s knew where he was, Max gave his clearance for the attack. The two new small halos designated the two F-18s on his visor. "Delta. I have you in my sights. Delta One, take out the north target. Two, you have the south target. Pull out to the east and remain at 3,000. Delta One, call out FAC and north target. You are cleared in hot."

"Delta One has FAC and north target in sight. Engaging."

Max watched as Delta One dove, spitting fire from its nose cannon as it made its pass, destroying the lead boat's stern.

"Delta One is off." The pilot grunted under the G-forces as he pulled up vertically to 3,000 feet.

"Roger, Delta One. Good run. Remain at 3,000. East orbit. Delta Two call FAC and south target. You are cleared in hot."

"Roger, Delta Two engaging south target. FAC and target in sight."

Max watched as Delta Two's aim cut the second boat in half.

"Two's off."

"Good run, Two. Delta flight targets are down. Can you remain until Dragonfly Two gets here? I have one injury onboard, and my rear engine is running hot."

"Roger, Condor, we have your back. Good luck."

"Thanks, Delta. You both scored 100 percent. I will pass it on to your squadron leader. Condor out." Max switched frequency. "Base, Condor One, need to vector home. One injured, number two engine's running hot. Delta flight is in a circuit, waiting for Dragonfly Two. Over."

"Condor, vector to base. Good work. What is status of injury?"

"He is stable but has lost blood."

"Medic team is on deck. Call two miles out. Foxtrot Corpen is 270."

Foxtrot Corpen was the ship's heading.

"Calling two miles out."

Max banked the plane toward the small icon floating on the visor on the 270-degree compass heading, located in the vast darkness of the ocean. Val worked to stabilized Perez, who was now lying sideways on the electronic equipment. The Condor traveled at a steady 200 knots toward the aircraft carrier. The plane could fly faster, but the big hole in the side canopy forced Max to keep the speed down as he finished checking all the equipment.

• • •

Twenty minutes had passed when Max turned his body around to see how Perez was doing. He winced as a sharp pain shot through his chest, and shook as a cold shiver ran through his body.

"You okay?" Val asked.

"Just a little jumpy from the adrenaline. How's Perez?"

"He's a strong kid; he'll be fine. I'm just dreading all the bullshit stories that will come out of his mouth when he wakes up."

"We all did that our first time in combat. Can't blame him." Max shook again, then coughed.

"What's wrong?"

"Hold on. Base. Condor two miles out." Max had maneuvered the plane to the correct altitude, in landing configuration, and angled for final bearing. The landing area of the flight deck was built at a 10-degree angle offset to the ship's center line, so Max had to calculate that into his final approach.

"Roger, Condor, call the ball," said the Air Boss in the tower. The Air Boss was the officer who, from his perch in the Primary Flight Control, the Tower, controlled what was happening in the airspace around the ship, including the flight deck.

"Condor ball. Point three," Max said, telling him he had 300 pounds of fuel left. He told the Air Boss how much fuel he had left in his tanks so the arresting wires could be set to the proper weight setting. These wires were stretched across the small flight deck and were grabbed by the tail hook of the landing plane, allowing it to slow down to a complete stop before the flight deck ended. "The ball" referred to lights on the left side of the flight deck that told Max if he was on the correct glide path to land and hit the arresting wires. There were four wires in total that Max could grab with his tail hook. The number three wire was considered a perfect approach landing and gave one bragging rights when they hooked it.

"Roger ball," the LSO replied, letting Max know he was lined up on the flight deck's landing area, and was on speed and glide slope. The LSO, or Landing Signal Officer, now had a direct connection with Max, telling him if he was too high, low, fast, or slow. He also had the right to abort the landing and send the pilot to go around if he thought the landing to be off and/or dangerous. All the Navy pilots on the aircraft carrier treated the LSO with respect because he kept the landings safe—and he also graded them.

"Roger." Max squirmed in his seat as he slapped the landing gear, and watched as he received green lights in return, telling him that the landing gear was locked for landing. He then reached down and released the tail hook.

Max blinked hard as he started losing focus, then coughed and a spray of blood splattered on the windshield.

"Shit!" Val said as he reached over to Max. "You're hit, Max."

"You think?" Max said as he coughed some more.

"A little high, ease it down," said the LSO from the flight deck.

Max clicked the mike button twice and reduced power, trying hard not to cough again as blood began to fill one of his lungs. He reached up and snapped off his chin strap, while Val desperately searched for the entry wound. Max clumsily removed his helmet and gave it to Val, pointed at the mike, then at Val. Val knew that Max couldn't talk anymore, and took the helmet.

The Condor was diving down to regain the glide path; Max had less than a minute before he was over the stern of the ship. He reached up and pressed the speaker icon, which allowed Max to hear the LSO screaming over the speaker to wave off. "Wave off" meant the pilot was to abort the landing and circle around once more for a second approach.

Max looked at Val, nodded, then Val spoke into the mike. "Paddles, pilot is wounded, fading fast. No wave off. Repeat, no wave off!"

"Roger, Condor, keep it coming," the LSO replied.

The radio went silent when the ship's emergency alarm went off. Everyone within eyesight of the ship's closed-circuit TV stopped what they were doing and watched the live broadcast of Max's landing. "Keep it right there, Max, steady, steady, a little more power..." the LSO said, trying to guide Max down onto the flight deck.

Max was hurting bad. He had been holding his breath for over a minute and was drowning in his own blood. The ball was centered as the plane was about to cross the aft of the ship's deck, known as "the ramp." He had to keep it together for a few more seconds.

Max's vision began to fade; his lungs screamed at him to breathe. The plane crossed the ramp. He waited what seemed like an eternity for the landing gear to hit the deck.

"Power! Power! Power!" the LSO screamed, but it was too late.

Max had slumped unconscious and dove the plane down onto the deck, breaking the left strut as the tail hook grabbed the third wire, sending Max's body forward against the shoulder harness, pushing all the blood that had pooled in his lung out and over the whole windshield.

The emergency flight deck fire crew, all wearing red jackets, rushed over to the crippled plane. Both its propellers bit dangerously into the humid ocean air. All they could see from the outside was red on the glass canopy.

Inside the cockpit, Val unzipped Max's flight suit, exposing his chest. He reached into his thigh pocket, ripped the plastic off a bag with his teeth and produced a thick needle with a valve at the end. He felt around Max's chest and shoved the needle in. A quick hiss emanated from the valve, depressurizing his chest cavity and allowing Max to breathe again.

At the same time one of the younger fire rescue team members ran over to the side of the Condor, staying clear of the rotating front propeller as he reached out to a handle embedded into the fuselage. He prodded it out and turned it, releasing the canopy lock. The canopy popped open. Perez was still stuck to the front right side of the instrument panel as Val worked to stabilize the valve that now protruded out of Max's chest. "Kill the engines!" he screamed at Val.

Val grabbed the throttles and idled the two engines as the fire rescue team member reached in and began the shutdown sequence. The medical team in white jackets with red crosses on them rushed in once the fire rescue team waved them in. It took the ship's medical team less than a minute to pull both

Max and Perez out of the aircraft and onto stretchers. Val watched as they were rushed off across the deck, through a dark hatch in the superstructure and down to the hospital below.

• • •

Val stood leaning against the Condor, its engines making the clicking sound they make when the superheated metal starts to cool. Max's squadron commanding officer jogged up to him. Captain Van Strong took note of the countless bullet holes on the whole of the fuselage, then peered in to see the bloody mess that had been left behind. He looked at Val holding his M-4 rifle across his chest.

"Val. What happened out there?"

Val took a deep breath and adjusted the M-4. "The Navy Cross is what happened."

Val was referring to the highest medal commendation for bravery in the Navy. Val took a step forward and patted the captain on the shoulder. They both walked away from the plane toward one of the few hatches that led into the superstructure. Both turned to look at the Condor as the Air Boss gave orders over the loudspeaker to get the Condor off the flight deck. A small army of men dressed in red and brown swarmed around the Condor, manipulating the plane onto a crane. The crane lifted the Condor up off the deck, where it swung with the movement of the ship as the crew worked at a slow but steady pace, walking the Condor from the landing deck and toward a plane elevator that led down into the massive hangar below the steel deck.

Val was always impressed by the orchestrated flight deck ballet on the aircraft carriers and took a few minutes to lose himself as he smoked a not-allowed cigarette. He remained within the dark hatch under the "No Smoking" sign until one of the F-18s from the night's firefight snatched one of the four wires minutes after the deck was cleared. Val took one last drag of the cigarette and smashed the lit end against the gray, steel bulkhead, making sure all the embers were out, and disappeared into the massive structure.

"You have a visitor," the cheerful nurse said as she let Val enter the room. "I will be on the call button if you need me."

Val stepped aside and watched the brunette exit the room with a purposeful swing to her hips. "You getting some of that?" he whispered to Max from the doorway.

"Dude...just look at me. Do I look like I am?"

Val looked his friend over. Max was pale and much skinnier. His eyes had dark rings and the two-day-old stubble didn't help, either. His friend looked terrible.

"Well, you look much better than when I saw you last, but as always, you came through with flying colors." Val took a seat next to Max in the small hospital room, put his feet up on Max's bed, and made himself at home. "Well, how are you feeling? A few weeks in the hospital being served hand-and-foot sure has done its thing."

"Val, can you do me a favor?"

"Sure, anything."

"Get me the fuck off this floating hospital. Man, its been 20 days... I can't take it anymore. I have a serious case of cabin fever."

"Funny you should ask, my friend, I have here a letter..." Val put the bundle of mail he had carried in on the small desk next to Max and summarized the opened letter. "Navy Department of Cabin Fever Victims has handed this letter to me, allowing you to get off this boat as soon as the doctor gives you your release papers...which should take place in the next couple of minutes. The Navy has also asked for your debriefing report of our mission. So from here, you're to go back to the carrier for debrief. Good news is that you have been given three weeks' leave after you file the report." Val put the letter down. "I guess you'll be off to Hawaii to see the family. Oh, and don't forget to tell your mom my mom says hi."

"Does she know what happened?"

"Nope, but I think you should at least call her. Not only that, but I think your stepbrothers and sister want to hear from you, too."

"Yeah, I guess you're right. How is Steven?"

"Perez? He's fine. The boys are all ragging on him for passing out. You know how harsh the teams can be. He's a good kid and handled himself well in the situation. Not bad. Not bad at all. He is fitting in with the rest of the team."

"So, what's his call sign now?"

"Monk. 'Cause the son of a bitch never talks. Anyway, I'm off tomorrow with the teams to Germany for some training, so I thought it would be nice to stop by and thank you for what you did."

Max nodded. Boasting for being a hero was not in his genes, so he changed the subject. "Is that my mail?"

Val reached over and handed him a package and some letters. "Who's the package from?"

"I don't know." Max turned the package around to read the address. "That's strange. It's from Paris."

Max took his time as he ripped the brown packaging and opened the cardboard box. Inside were three old journals, a photo album, a taped-up green box, and two letters. He opened the first envelope and a set of keys fell out. He held them up, studied them for a second, then turned his attention to the letter. After a few seconds of silence he read it once more.

"Well, what does it say?" Val asked when he saw the blank expression on Max's face.

"Its about my father's death."

Val straightened up from his casual position. "Your real father? Is it about how he died in Vietnam?"

"No...it's about how he died last week."

4

Outskirts of Paris, November 15, 2010

Max stared out the window at the passing French landscape. The scattered rain clouds darkened the sky and fought the sun for space in the morning air. His eyes focused on the water droplets streaking past on the long, panoramic window to his left. The never-ending gentle gray hills occasionally broke his focus by allowing a deep-green pasture to taint the winter seasons' landscape.

The train rocked his body side to side as the cold rain beat down on the dining car where he sat alone at his table, sipping his latte. His eyes scanned the long room, coming to rest on its three inhabitants—two lovers in conversation, and the waiter staring out the window clearly lost in thought.

He reread the letter once more. It was his father's handwriting, according to the lawyer who'd sent him the package. Max looked up again, searching for his waiter, who had moved toward the back of the car, and made eye contact. The waiter knew he could not ignore him anymore, and cursed under his breath as he began to walk toward Max.

Funny. Why is he annoyed? He's got nothing else to do. Typical, Max thought.

The waiter approached him, expertly dodging around the tables as the train swayed back and forth.

"*Oui, monsieur?*"

"*Oui, la addition, s'il vous plait,*" Max said in perfect French.

The waiter turned and followed his previous path back to the kitchen. Max scanned the letter yet again and folded it back into his satchel. He reclined back in his chair and stared through the window at a distant, infinite point, wondering about his past.

His mother had told him that from the start of their marriage his father was never around due to his position with the Army. The Vietnam conflict and his job as an intelligence officer kept him away from home; he was off to D.C. once a week, and he traveled overseas once every few months.

A preacher and an Army officer had come to his home during one of his father's overseas trips. Max was a few months old and could have never recalled that day, but his mother never let him forget about it once he became old enough to understand. His father had been shot down while on an incursion mission in Vietnam, and was presumed dead.

A few years later, Max's mother married a fellow named James, a good and supportive man, and gave Max two stepbrothers and a sister. He loved his siblings; there'd never been any animosity or favoritism in the family.

Thomas, Max's father, had been presumed dead but had been alive in a small bamboo cell somewhere near the Cambodian-Vietnamese border. He'd managed to escape from the POW camp and was found close to death by a Long Army Reconnaissance Patrol a few months before the United States pulled out of Vietnam.

He had been devastated by the war, his recuperation, and by losing his wife to another man. Thomas also knew that he wasn't in a balanced mental state. He had nightmares every night. One night he had attacked a nurse, thinking she was the enemy. The doctors told him he would get better in time, but that he could still be a danger to others.

Once back home, he'd naturally wanted to meet his boy. Max's mother had never told him what he now knew—that Thomas had shown up out of the blue one day while Max was at preschool.

Thomas, knowing how the meeting would end up, still went to talk with his ex-wife in person. After a long discussion, he realized that his son might have a better childhood with a stable and good man in his life. He waited that day for his son.

Max was brought home from school by his stepfather James to find a strange man with a gift for him. Max was happy as could be with his new toy, a red car the stranger had given him.

"Do you mind if I take a picture of him?" the man had asked.

James nodded. "Go ahead."

Thomas took his picture, turned, and shook hands with James. "Take care of him as if he were your own."

"Don't worry, Thomas, I will. Please do think about stopping by every now and then as a 'friend of the family.' This way we will not confuse him and you can spend time with him."

"Thank you, James." Thomas turned, leaned forward, and gave his ex-wife a soft kiss. He smiled at her, took one last look at his son, patted him on his head, and walked away.

The story was all there in the letters Max now held.

His thoughts were interrupted as the waiter handed over the check. Max pulled some Euros from his pocket and left him a more than generous tip. The waiter took the cash, smiled at his small fortune, and gave Max a pleasant look. Max stood, turned, and caught his reflection in the window. He was well dressed in his All-Weather Navy overcoat and Service Dress uniform. His hair was closely cropped and receding. His sharp jawline was even more pronounced since the weight loss after the surgery. The nose bent to the side about two degrees off-center—a casualty of his boxing stint. He was six feet tall and held his weight in check with a constant workout regimen. That, in turn, kept him looking much younger than his true age. Max buttoned his coat, put on his white visor, and readjusted it. He picked up his satchel, looked around once more, and headed back to his seat.

To his surprise, he found the train's couché empty. Max plopped down into the firm seat and took the opportunity to open his airline-approved, carry-on rolling suitcase. He pulled out the three journals that had come with the package, put his feet up, and reread his father's second letter.

Dear Max,

Well, I guess I'm dead if you're reading this. I won't go into apologies. The previous letter briefly explained the situation. In any case, you can read more about it in my journals, if that's what you want. You'll also find here a photo album and a box containing your grandfather, Dean DuMonde's, medals and family history. Lastly, these are journals 1 through 3, out of a total of 11. Inside them is my life from when I was a small boy to my last days, excluding the time in my little jungle bamboo hotel room. My host would not let me write during my stay—how inconsiderate. After the war I decided to keep journaling, as it kept me sane and gave me the opportunity to know that one day you could read about not only me, but also our family's history. I hope this can ease your mind. Just always know that, although I was not there beside you in your good times and bad, I always loved you and supported you in my own way.

You'll find a set of keys on a chain—put them around your neck, and don't lose them. One will open a safe deposit box. All its contents are yours. You'll also find some paperwork. Its explanation can be found in the sixth journal. Do what you will with that, too, since I never got around to it. Now you'll ask yourself, "Where are the other journals and this safe deposit box?" Well, for that you have to take a train from Paris to a small town called La Fertée-Milon. There find the old aerodrome and ask for Pierre Bouvier. Show him the other key and he'll tell you what to do.

Your Father

Max reached out and grabbed the photo album next to the journals. He placed it on his lap and turned to the first page, which had two photos of an era long gone. He took out the first picture from the plastic slip. It showed two men, a woman, and five kids all sitting in a Model T. On the back it read "1917, Uncle Jake, dad and mom with family. Maximus 5, George 11, Carolina 7, Thomas 9, and Dean 2." He pulled out a much older picture that read "1878 London, Uncle Jake and Constable Philip McGovern" written in cursive below the picture. Jake wore a bowler hat, cape coat, black vest, and peeking out of the left side of his waist was a revolver in a cross-draw holster. "Looks like a bad ass," he whispered. He placed the picture back in its sleeve and flipped through the album. The following pages were of Jake at the Giza pyramids in Egypt, then somewhere in China. There were some other pictures of carvings on walls and hieroglyphs. It looked like Jake was some sort of explorer. He wore his distinctive bowler hat and cross-draw holster in every picture he was in. He carried what looked like a shotgun held loosely across his chest in one of them. A few pages in, the scenery changed to that of more modern times and pictures of another man. Judging by the uniform he wore and his surroundings, Max guessed it to be his grandfather, Dean. Some of the pictures looked to have been taken in the United States, the rest showed Europe during the war. Toward the end of the album were pictures of Thomas, Max's father. The family resemblance was uncanny. Max had his grandfather's square jawline, long face, and nose, but he had his father's height and eyes. Unfortunately, he had both their receding hairlines. Max removed a Western Union message from under the clear plastic and read it.

His grandfather had died on April 30, 1945.

Man, so close to the end of the war.

Max pulled out a green box and opened it. Inside he found a faded-dark blue velvet case on top of military medals and ribbons. He opened it, and a metal badge much like the ones you would see the marshals wearing in the Old West stared back at him. It had a five-pointed star at its center and a ring molded from copper made up the circumference. Stamped into this ring, along the top, it read "United States," and on the bottom, "Secret Service." Inscribed on the back of the badge was the name Jake DuMonde. *Very cool,* he thought as he held the badge in between his fingers. He put it back in its case and picked up a Navy Cross. Inscribed on the back was the name Dean DuMonde. Alongside it was a Purple Heart, silver star, bronze star, and many others he could not recognize. In the other compartment, separated by a thin wooden strip, were his father's awards. Thomas had earned many of the same as his father before him, including the Purple Heart, still in its velvet box. He assumed his father had received it after escaping from the POW camp.

Max closed the lid and tucked the box, along with the photo album, safely back into his carry-on bag, then leaned back into the plush chair. He reached around his neck, produced the keys his father had left him and examined them as they swayed with the movement of the train. He leaned forward and picked up the journal mark "1," placed it on his lap, and began to read.

• • •

Thomas, Max's father, had had an interesting childhood. He was an only child. His stepfather was an engineer who'd worked well away from the influences of the military life. He'd loved his stepfather, but couldn't forget the bond between a five-year-old and his real father. The death of the father had been difficult for such a young boy.

First came the sadness, then the anger, and then the rebellion. Thomas became a problem in his early teens. He respected his mother and stepfather, but the rest of society became his outlet. He took his anger out on the world, from the fights to the petty theft. Finally, on his 18th birthday, and out of pure frustration, his parents gave him an ultimatum.

Thomas's mother's deal was for him to join the Army or face the world completely on his own. One thing Thomas knew about his mother was that once she made up her mind, it was locked in stone forever. She wanted him to become a man, and she thought best that the Army could control that which she could not. Thomas was also a smart kid and he chose wisely.

He spent the next couple of days with his stepfather in a small motel close to the bus station where he would board the bus to his new life. During those two days he got to know his stepfather better than ever before. Simon, like his father, also fought in World War II with the Army. He, too, saw his share of death and victory and Simon allowed Thomas to enter that side of his life that he had locked away in his mind and never spoke of at home. Thomas was grateful for his stepfather's advice, especially on how to survive boot camp, and for the first time in Thomas's life he saw Simon not as his stepfather, but as a man who cared deeply for him. For the first time he saw Simon as his father.

The train's brakes screeched as it pulled up to La Fertée-Milon station. Max gathered his belongings and stood next to the exit. The train came to a stop and its door swooshed open, letting in the cold, damp air. He took a few moments and helped an older lady with her luggage before exiting himself. The rain had turned to a slight mist collecting on his wool overcoat as he followed along with a small group into the station and through an arched stone doorway, which led to a street. He looked up at the sky as a ray of sunlight peeked through the cloud-covered sky and heated his face.

Max heard the click-clacking of the train's wheels, and turned to watch as it accelerated away from the empty station. He had not planned ahead, figuring he could catch the late train back to Paris, but if the meeting turned interesting he'd have to find a place to stay, thus the overnight bag rolling behind him.

After a short walk Max turned right onto Rue de la Chaussée, and found himself transported back in time. To his left stood an old church. Farther down the street, typical early 1900s two-story French architecture stretched out into the distance. Except for the modern cars and the odd advertisement, he could have imagined himself in 1920s France. After a 10-minute walk, the thin boulevard opened up. What lay in front of him was the quintessential French town painting. A lazy river bisected the town. To his left a cobblestone boat ramp and a beautiful tree-lined peninsula park jutted out into the river. An old wooden paddlewheel turned just opposite the boat ramp and beyond it a ruined castle sat proudly perched at the highest point of the town. Max walked over the bridge and to the end of the street. He then turned left, then right, and walked off the paved road onto a cobblestone street.

Twenty yards ahead loomed a 15-story medieval tower. A plaque on its wall read Eglise Notre Dame et ses Quatre Tourelles. Opposite the tower was the old ruined castle. He found his way to the castle grounds and took in the abandoned stone structure. After some time exploring, Max decided to go back to town and find someplace to sit down and have a hot cup of coffee.

To his delight he found a small café hidden in the far corner of the plaza. Max took a deep breath of fresh, cool air and headed there. Its tables were empty, but the front door was open, so he found a dry table nearest to the doorway, and took a few moments to take in the scenery around him. There was a comfortable feeling about the town, as if all was just right.

Through the window, Max saw an older man stocking a shelf. So, he dragged the wrought iron chair out from the table and sat down. The noise it made would have awakened the dead as its screeching echoed off the medieval walls. A few minutes passed, and Max decided to take out his map. He shook it open and cleared his throat. Satisfied with his attention-getting scheme, Max studied the map and from time to time gazed up with a puzzled look.

"Oui, monsieur?"

"Bonjour. Are you open?"

"Ah, American soldier." The waiter paused.

"Yes, good afternoon, sir. Are you open?"

"If we were not, the chairs would have been gone by now," the waiter said in French.

"Yes, very true," Max agreed in French. "I was wondering if I could bother you for a latte?"

"It's never a bother. You speak my language very well." He paused. "Surprising," the old man said as he walked away.

Max listened as an espresso machine spit out steam into milk. A few minutes passed and the old man came out with two coffee cups. "My name is Jacques."

Max stood and presented his hand, accepting the cup with the other. "Max, *enchanté*."

"What brings you to Fertée-Milon? We are not accustomed to tourists in the winter."

"Well, now that you ask, I was wondering if you could help me out. I'm here trying to find the old aerodrome."

"Ah, not many people come here for that unless it is a time of war," Jacques said as he pulled out a chair and made himself comfortable, preparing to tell Max a story. Max shrugged and settled in, too. Jacques took a sip of his coffee and began. "The aerodromes in the area are very important. During the First World War the Germans found one of them to be a perfect site to keep their planes. The story goes that a French aristocrat owned the land that this particular aerodrome is currently located on. His wife had a love for oak trees. The specific area where the interesting part of this story takes place is in her oak road. Many years before the First World War this aristocrat decided to plant these 100 rows of oak trees on each side of her 'boulevard' that led to her château. Halfway through the war somebody decided to drop a bomb on the château, leveling it." Jacques spread out his arms and made a big boom sound. "Once the Germans got to the area, they decided to use the boulevard as a runway. The planes would start their run under the trees and fly up and out where the old house foundation still lay. Not only that, but the rows of trees on each side provided great cover for parking the planes." He drank some more and continued. "The war went on, the field changed sides, and in the end it just disappeared from the history books. It stayed that way until Hitler came by. Germany, once more, used the field until they were pushed out.

"After the war, the field, once again, went into obscurity. The owner's great-grandson took it over, built a small grass runway within the tree line, along with some hangars, and now it's just a private airport. Once in a while you'll get some old-timers coming to reminisce, but that's about it." He looked at Max's empty cup and asked him if he would like another.

"No, thank you, Jacques. You know a lot about this place."

"Lived here all my life. I was a baby during World War I, and I fought with the resistance in World War II. After all this town and I have been through, I think I will die here, as well." He looked around and then back at the café.

"You were with the resistance?"

Jacques nodded. "I had just turned 17 and helped lead a raid on the airfield, but they dropped the bombs off target and onto a makeshift runway with fake planes. I had told them over the radio of their error, but twice they made the same mistake. It didn't matter because the American Army rolled in a few days after the last bombing raid. Then the Army Air Force took it over. *C'est la vie.*" He took a deep breath and slapped his thighs. "Strange thing is that fake runway is now a working airfield." He took one last sip and looked at Max. "We seem to have forgotten why you're here."

"To make a long story short, my father recently passed away," Max said. "He asked me to come to this town."

"I am sorry for your loss."

"Thank you."

"It's just occurred to me that when I first saw you, you looked familiar. What was your father's name?"

"Thomas. Thomas DuMonde. Did you know him?"

Jacques bowed his head. He shifted in his seat and put his hand on Max's shoulder. "*Mon ami*. He talked a lot about you. He was a good man, and a good friend. Your father helped me out in times of trouble, but he never asked for anything in return. I, of course, paid him back, but he never wanted the money, just the friendship."

"Thank you." Max paused, feeling a little taken aback. "Well, could you possibly help me in finding this man my father wanted me to meet?"

"*Bien sur*. What is his name?" Jacques asked with a slight tilt of his head.

"Pierre Bouvier."

Jacques' French demeanor returned. "*Je le savais!*" His hands went up in surprise. "To think that we have been talking about Pierre all this time!" He saw the puzzled look on Max's face. "Pierre, he's the owner of the aerodrome. Ha! I'll take you there. Wait here while I tell the wife that I'm stepping out." Jacques yelled into the café and a high-pitched voice screamed back. He waved it off and ran around back.

Max was gathering his bags and leaving some change on the table when he heard a popping sound and a high rumble as an old gray BMW motorcycle with a sidecar came out from the alley next to the cafe.

"*Voilà!*" Jacques motioned to the sidecar of the motorcycle.

Max stood there looking at the old man dressed in a long overcoat, aviator helmet, and goggles as he jumped off and opened the rear compartment of the sidecar. He grabbed Max's bags and with little effort threw them inside the trunk of the sidecar. "Well, what are you waiting for?" he asked, pointing to the sidecar.

Just as Max fit himself into the small seat within the sidecar, Jacques took off. Max held on for dear life as Jacques executed some tight maneuvering through the town, ending up on a long, winding road.

Max turned to see the Cheshire Cat smile on his driver's face. The old man began to look younger with each increasing mile per hour.

"Hold on! I know a shortcut!" he yelled over the high-revving engine.

A split second later the BMW flew off the road and into a field of grass. Max bounced around in his seat. As he held on, he could hear Jacques tell him about the motorcycle.

"She's a BMW R-75 survivor, mostly due to my actions. Even after all these years, still purring like a kitten. I liberated her from a German soldier as he pulled over to take a crap." He laughed out loud. "You should have seen his face as I drove off. Look, there is Pierre!" Jacques pointed up.

Max followed Jacques' finger. He saw a sailplane soaring a thermal above a plowed field. Max loved soaring; it was the only way he could get away from the issues of everyday life. Once in a while he would rent out the local soaring club's motor glider. The biggest challenge for him was not the time he spent flying, but the distance he could travel. His record to date was 820 miles without the use of the engine, but his career made him a busy man. He gave it up a few years back and got busy with life. Max knew he would make friends with this man.

"There is the runway." Jacques pointed with his chin as he accelerated over a small hill, which sent the BMW flying over its crest.

Holding on even tighter, Max looked forward and saw what Jacques had described earlier. The runway was wide enough to accommodate a good-sized private plane. What took his breath away were the old oaks that lined the runway. Based on their sheer size alone, they must have been over 200 years old. One could even build a small town under the canopies.

The sailplane came very close to them as it dove on final approach toward the runway, and with its passing came a spray of water from its ballasts that missed them by a few feet.

"You missed! You bastard!" Jacques yelled as he shook his fist at the sailplane.

The sailplane touched on the grass runway, rolling uphill toward an open hangar under the first row of oaks, where it stopped short.

Jacques pulled up next to the hangar and shut off the engine. Max could see Pierre within the sailplane, apparently writing something down. Pierre then unlatched the canopy, swung it open, and with a little difficulty, climbed out.

He was a tall man, about six feet five inches, skinny and tanned. He wore a baggy khaki shirt, matching shorts, and a floppy hat, which was decorated with over a dozen pins. Pierre smiled, and waved the two of them over.

Jacques walked between them and broke the silence. "Pierre Bouvier, this is Max DuMonde."

They looked at each other and nodded, then shook hands.

"*Enchanté,*" Max said.

"The pleasure is mine," Pierre said in a British accent. "Would you mind helping me out?" Pierre motioned to the opposite wing.

"Sure." Max walked over to the tip of the wing, held and led it, as Pierre attached a small electric tow to the tail wheel that helped in pulling the sailplane into the hangar.

Once inside the hangar they worked together rotating the plane to fit among the other aircraft. They led the wing around the hangar, making sure that the tip would not accidentally hit the wall or one of the other planes.

"Seems as if you have done this before," Pierre said.

"I used to fly motor gliders like yours back home." Max looked around at the planes inside the hangar. One in particular caught his attention. "You have a very interesting collection," he said to Pierre.

"My hobby. When I'm not teaching others to fly, I'm restoring aircraft. I started with the old Spad in the back, then the Albatross. I've restored and sold many others over time, but I kept these three," Pierre said as he looked over his work.

"Yes." Max nodded and looked toward the last aircraft. "What is that one? Looks like a..." Max paused as he approached the short left wing of the aircraft, and took in the strange rotor blades that drooped downward. Then it hit him. "Is this a—?"

"Cierva Autogiro!" Pierre finished the sentence. "PA-19 four-to-five place cabin 'Giro. She was created for the elite. Unfortunately, the aircraft was so far ahead of its time that people began to question it. How does it fly?

What happens if the rotors break off? This mentality made it difficult for Cierva to sell the 'Giro. Well, that and the disappearing funds and clientele this specific model was designed for. The Great Depression made sure of that. Not the best time for such a forward-looking and expensive machine. Four 'Giros like this one were made, two stayed in the United States, and the other two ended up in the UK. This is the only survivor. Found it, or what was left of it, in a barn." Pierre looked over the silver machine like a loving parent would his child. "Took us a *very* long time to get it this far," he whispered as he touched the fabric-painted skin fuselage.

"Wow…" Max looked over the polished silver exterior. "I saw an open-cabin 'Giro at the Experimental Aircraft Association Museum at Oshkosh, Wisconsin. That particular one was in static display, but it had been flown there before its retirement. Last one left of its kind, as well," Max said as he walked over to the cabin hatch.

"*Oui.* There is one other flying, but that one is the smaller, open-cockpit version. The PC-18, or what some called the poor man's 'Giro. It is in America, owned by an old friend, Jack Tiffiny." He patted the fuselage. "Soon this old girl will be back up in the sky where she belongs."

"When do you think you will have her in flying condition?"

"When you help me attach the engine."

"Me?" he asked, taking his eyes away from the 'Giro. "What?"

"Well, since you now own half the 'Giro, I figured you might want to see it fly. All we need to do is hook up the electrics, fuel lines, and such, then we can take her on her maiden flight," Pierre said enthusiastically.

"Hold on. What do you mean by half mine?" Max asked, wondering if the man in front of him was a little crazy.

"All in good time. Frankly, I think if you did not come along, I would not have had time to get the 'Giro ready for the air show in Madrid. Now with two brains and four hands we will make a lot of people excited," Pierre replied back in his English accent as he gestured at the radial engine hanging from its cradle in front of the Cierva. "Come," Pierre said, waving Max toward him. "And thank you."

"Thank you for what?" Max asked, still staring at the aviation treasure that this man claimed he now owned.

"For walking in my motor glider," Pierre said, waving his hand at the sailplane.

"No problem."

Pierre stayed quiet for a moment, as if searching for the correct words, and changed the subject. "I'm sorry for your loss, Max. Your father was a good man and a dear friend. I am really glad you came. I was unsure if you would once you had received the paperwork." He paused, lost in thought, nodded his head in approval, and continued. "Here, help me close the hangar doors."

They went to opposite sides of the hangar and slid the doors together. Once shut, all three men walked to an old log house within the oak forest. Once inside, Pierre motioned to Max and Jacques to take a seat.

"Pardon, Pierre," Jacques said, "but I have to go before the wife sends the dogs out for me." He turned to Max. "Maybe you two can come into town tonight and we shall all toast your father."

"Sounds like a plan," Max said. He looked at Pierre.

"*Oui,*" Pierre said. "We'll see you tonight."

Jacques turned and skipped out of the log house as the door closed after him. A few moments passed before both Max and Pierre heard the BMW motorcycle drive away.

Pierre stood in front of the stove lost in thought as he watched the flames heat up a pot of coffee. "You look like him; a little taller but with the same features," he said, looking down at the pot and adjusting its position on the stove.

"I'm at a loss here, Pierre. My father told me to find you and give you one of these keys." Max pulled out the chain from under his shirt.

Pierre turned and looked at the keys, then back at the pot of coffee. "*Oui,* the famous keys. Come with me and I'll explain it to you." He turned off the flame on the gas stove and headed to the front door.

Max followed Pierre out and listened.

"Your father was a good man; he helped me build this small airport with the condition that he be allowed to own a hangar where he could live." Pierre turned past the 'Giro's hangar and headed to a set of hangars at the other end of the runway. "We met during the early years of the Vietnam conflict, before the escalation. I was his interpreter back then. We both went our different ways, but then a few years later he showed up looking to see if I would help him restore a plane. I accepted the challenge on the condition that he would lend a hand restoring my planes, thus our friendship resumed." Pierre paused as he kicked a small rock away from the runway. "You know that I almost became his brother-in-law, your uncle! But it was not to be. My sister passed away a few years ago from cancer. It hit your father as hard as me, but we helped each other through it. Then the disease came for him. The last time that I saw him was a few months ago. We went on a rally across the Asian and European continents. After those 35 days of racing he gave me his papers and instructions, and told me to give it all to you. Your father was a good friend to the end." He pointed to the far left hangar. "That is the restoration shop." He headed to the blue hangar on the right and stopped in front of a box. "Well, here we are!"

Max saw Pierre place one of the keys in a small lock box. He opened it and pressed a button within.

The hangar door shuddered and started to squeak upward. Inside, the fluorescent lights flickered on. Max stood there watching as a strange object began to unfold before his eyes. To the far right was a Cessna 337. The 337 was a fantastic plane that had the same push-pull engine configuration as the Condor. They were even used by the Air Force as Forward Air Control planes during Vietnam. But it was the plane parked right next to the 337 that gathered all his attention. It looked strange, to say the least.

"Beautiful, aren't they?" Pierre said with excitement in his voice.

"They sure are. But what is this one?" he said, pointing at the tail-dragger with the six-foot-diameter propeller standing proud in front of him.

"Well, I am sure you recognize the 337A. It is actually serial number Two. We restored it around 10 years ago. Your father went everywhere in her. She is as original as when she came off the assembly line, but this one..." He walked up to the tail-dragger and placed his hand on the propeller. "...is the Storch. An Fi-156 C Fieseler Storch, the most functional short take-off and landing plane ever built." Pierre walked around the front of the plane. "This Storch is one of the last built by the Germans during World War II. Your father never told me how he came by it, but here it is, after a long restoration."

Max studied the plane with its long wheel struts and its angular shapes jutting out all over the structure. He figured the front view looked like the offspring of a mechanical bird and a dragonfly. It was not a plane built for speed, but for slow and deliberate flight. He walked closer to it and touched its surface. The skin was made of fabric, which meant the structure was tubular steel. It had taken Max a split second to recognize the plane after he heard the name. It was named after a stork due to its long strut landing gears and high wings, which rose far above Max's head. Its stance looked much like a stork coming in for a landing. True to its form, it was an impressive flyer. Max turned and asked Pierre about its flight characteristics.

"Well, why don't we go up and find out?" answered Pierre.

"You sure?"

"Your father left it and the 337 to you, just like he did with the 'Giro. So you can do whatever you like. As a matter of fact, Thomas asked me to check you out on all three."

"They are also mine?"

"And everything else in here, including the hangar and a few other odds and ends."

Max was in a state of disbelief and tried to find the right words. After a moment he gave up and just asked the question at hand. "Is she flight ready?"

"Here, just help me roll her out. We'll go up for a quick spin before the sun sets."

They both pushed the Storch out onto the runway. Max looked at the hangar and back at the plane.

Pierre saw how Max was reacting to the news and offered some advice. "Max, I know this is a bit of a shock to you, but let's just go up in the Storch and I promise that it will set your mind at ease."

Max smiled back at him.

"Why don't you start with the walk-around inspection?"

"Sure." Max stood back and admired the simplicity of the plane. He began at the front and walked around it, checking its surfaces, hinges, and all-around structure. "How about the fuel?"

"Don't worry, I'll do that. Just watch and you can do it tomorrow." Pierre took out a small stepladder and a cup on a stick and pushed it up against the bottom of the wing. A small amount of fuel poured into the cup. He checked it for water droplets, then went to the other wing and finished up under the engine. "No water, so we put it back into the fuel tank." He climbed up the side of the plane and onto the wing, opened one of the fuel caps and poured the fuel back into the wing tank. Pierre made sure the cap was tight and jumped off the wheel strut. "Now for the fun part—let's get strapped in!"

Max climbed into the Storch and fiddled with the old belt harness, managing to lock it after two tries. He looked up and took in the view. It was amazing—by leaning left or right one could even look below the plane.

"Good visibility? Well, that was its purpose in the war," Pierre answered his own question. "Wait until we start her up and fly out, then you will appreciate the plane even more."

Max studied the instruments while Pierre strapped himself in. They were familiar except that the dials were metric and marked up in German.

Pierre took note as Max looked over the instrument panel. "Don't worry too much about the instruments; you'll get the hang of it after a few flights. So, ready, Max?"

"Yes."

"I've gone through the checklist, so just plug in the headset to your left—we rewired the plane's mike and radio system to accept these new headsets. Put the key in and switch the magnetos to both. Good. Now, step on the brakes, move the throttle a few centimeters forward, and mixture full forward when the engine begins to fire. Ready?"

"As I'll ever be."

"Prime the pump a few times, then push the red button, bottom left of the instrument panel."

Max yelled out an open side window. "Clear!" Then flipped up the metal switch cover labeled "Anlasser" and pressed the starter button. The plane shook from side to side as the six-foot propeller rotated in front of them. There was a loud bang followed by a puff of smoke as the spark plugs within the cylinders began to ignite the fuel. Max waited one more cycle, then applied full mixture. The Storch jumped as all cylinders began to fire with the addition of more fuel. The thundering sound of the inverted V-8 engine resonated through the cabin as the plane found its balance. A gust of fresh air and smoke came in through the window as he watched the throttle lever move up by itself.

Pierre adjusted the throttle control forward another eighth of an inch, using the rear throttle control levers.

"She takes some time to get to know what she likes and doesn't," Pierre yelled from the back seat over the engine noise.

The engine popped once more, then smoothed out in a pleasant, rhythmic sound.

"Now, turn the avionics switch on."

Pierre waited a few moments, then spoke into the new Bose microphone, "Can you hear me?"

"Yes, I hear you." Max adjusted his headset.

"Press the button on the headset wire. It's the noise-canceling device."

Max did and was rewarded with a much quieter world.

"These Bose headsets are much improved over the original ones." He laughed. "Just remember to let the plane do what it wants to. This is not a jet where you tell it what you want. By the way, what plane did you learn to fly in?"

"A Cessna Birddog."

"Well, that was an unusual airplane to learn to fly in; very tricky to control on the ground."

"Yes, it was. I came close to ground-lopping the Birddog a few times but the old-timer who owned the plane taught me to use a light touch, keep the stick back, and to feel what the plane wanted to do. He flew them in Korea, and after the war used to run a glider school with one as a tow plane. Anyway, he was the best instructor I ever had."

"Good. Now give it some throttle, but not too much. Ease off the brakes, and just taxi her to the end of the tree line."

Max found the plane to be very responsive as he maneuvered it down the grass runway. He approached the end of the tree line and realized that the distance to the low stone wall in front of them was too close for a safe take-off.

"You can stop here. Now run her up and do a mag check. I'll look over your shoulder at the gauges."

Max applied the brakes and pushed the throttle until the rpm gauge read out at 2,000. He switched each magneto to off and watched the gauge drop around 100 rpms for each magneto.

"Now throttle to idle and let it stay there for a few seconds. Good. Bring her back up a bit and when you are ready to take off, apply 75-percent power and increase it after your tail lifts off. Remember, she'll react quicker than you're used to."

"Um, Pierre, I don't think we have enough space to clear that stone wall." He pointed at the wall a few hundred feet in front of him. Max heard a small chuckle behind him.

"Don't worry, I'm not suicidal."

Max hesitated, and then pushed the throttle forward, watching the prop pick up speed. After a few yards the tail flew up. He was careful not to overcompensate. It had been a long time since he had flown a tail-dragger, but once the tail became horizontal, the flight characteristics were the same as any other regular light plane.

He pulled the stick back gradually and was surprised as the plane almost hopped into the air, clearing the wall by well over 50 feet. He banked the plane away from some tall trees and gained altitude.

"Go ahead and test the limits of flight when you hit 1,400 meters."

Max nodded and continued to climb. He, like Pierre, wanted a safe altitude before they started playing with the plane. Max took the time to look at his surroundings, noticing that the plane had excellent visibility. The Storch was exactly what it looked to be; an observation aircraft. The glass atrium that surrounded them was an odd shape. It was built with flat glass angled so as to try to maximize aerodynamics. The cockpit was about two feet wide up to the waistline of a seated pilot where the glass then jutted out 12 inches at a 45-degree angle away from the sides of the seats. From there it went vertical about three feet, angling inward once again and connecting to the wing above.

Most of the glass panels were rectangular, some triangular, each separated by steel tubing. He looked all around and found that the tubing did not hinder the view outside, and looking down both sides he could see the ground below him.

Some time had passed while he enjoyed the view outside, but he always kept the aerodrome in sight. Last thing he wanted to do was ask for directions back home. He figured they were at least 4,000 feet from the ground. Then he looked at the altimeter and saw a reading near 1,400 meters.

"Close enough," he said and pulled the stick back while decreasing the engine power to 50 percent.

He started to pay attention to the airspeed indicator and watched it drop. He pulled back even more on the stick.

Okay, we should start feeling the onset of the wings shuddering as they lose lift and the plane enters into a stall, he thought.

Max had stalled in many different planes, and each one gave a warning shudder before it would stop flying, but for some reason the average speed at which most general aviation airplanes stalled had come and gone. Max watched as the speedometer dropped to 45 kph, or about 20 mph. He first heard the audible sound of the stall-warning alarm, and then felt the plane starting to react sluggishly to the inputs on the stick and rudder. The plane's stall alarm increased in decibels and the structure began to shudder at around 38 kph. He kept the stick back, forcing the plane to enter the stall. At 32 kph—19 mph—the plane shuddered hard and the right wing began to drop.

Max let the wing drop and followed it by pressing hard with his foot on the left rudder pedal, and moved the control stick forward. The plane dove and cut into the increasing wind, happily righting itself out of the stall.

"That was pretty amazing," he told Pierre.

"Amazing is when you have a 40-kilometer-per-hour headwind and you can even fly this thing in reverse. Now do some steep turns so you can get used to its turning radius."

Max couldn't remember the last time he'd had so much fun in an airplane. He performed more stalls, both with the power on and off, and some steep 45-degree turns, enjoying the cloudy afternoon as he looked out the windows. He felt like a bird and got lost in the moment, until Pierre snapped him back to reality when he told him it was time to head home.

"Let me land her, you just follow me on the controls," Pierre said as he shook the stick to let Max know that he had control of the plane. "The landing will feel as if we are going to smash into the ground, but don't worry. It was built for exactly this kind of flying."

Pierre handled the Storch like the veteran he was. He made a few tight turns and was lined up on final approach to the grass strip runway. Max positioned the flaps and set the throttle as he was told.

The Storch fell straight down from Max's perspective. *Jesus! This guy thinks he is landing on a carrier!* He tensed up, squirming in his seat.

"Relax, Max, this is the fun part," Pierre said.

Max expected the flare out; it didn't happen. He squinted his eyes and lifted his legs, trying to avoid the deadly impact moments away. When the wheels hit the ground, the plane settled down as the long shock absorbers reduced the impact force to a gentle push against the seat. After the shock of such a landing, Max realized the Storch had rolled to a stop within its own length.

"Of course, the landing rollout would be a little longer if we'd landed on a flat surface and not uphill. Just always remember that you'll need three times your landing space to take off," Pierre said.

"Do you recommend I always land like that?"

"No, of course not, but we will practice it over the next couple of days so that you'll know it if you have to use it. Better overdressed than underdressed."

Pierre taxied over to Max's hangar. He pulled the mixture back to the stop, which cut the fuel flowing into the cylinders, and shut down the engine. Pierre, with the Storch still rolling, turned it 180 degrees until it came to a complete stop facing down the runway in front of the open hangar.

Show off.

"Magnetos off."

"Check," Pierre responded.

"Radio off."

"Check. You're a natural flyer; you should be a expert with the Storch in no time."

"Thanks," Max said, giving the instruments a onceover. He shut off the electrics, turned the key to the off position, and removed the headset.

"Don't thank me yet. You still have some studying to do on the flight characteristics, general maintenance, and some odds and ends before I check you off on the Storch. And same goes with the other toys."

"Just as long as it's all in a language I can read," Max said as he unbuckled himself.

They both checked over the exterior of the plane to make sure nothing had changed or broken off, and with an electric tow moved the Storch back into its hangar, tail wheel first. Pierre waited until Max returned with his logbook, filled it out, and handed it back.

"Get acquainted with your hangar, unpack, then we'll head out to dinner." Pierre turned around at the hangar door. "You're driving," he said, grinning.

"Driving? Driving what?"

"In the hangar, Max. Look in the hangar," Pierre said from a distance. "I will see you, say, 5:30?"

Max waved at Pierre, then looked toward the back of the hangar, where he saw four car-sized lumps of canvas behind the Cessna 337's tail. He walked by the 337 and took some time to check it out. Pierre was right. The seats and even the instruments looked to be designed exactly like they had been built in the '60s. It was a time warp to say the least. He closed the hatch and went to the back of the hangar. Along the back wall were two motorcycles. Max walked up to them. One was clearly a dirt bike. It was a Honda CR125 Elsinore. Next to it was what looked like a vintage café racer bike painted black, it had a menacing stance. On the tank it read "Vincent." Max reached out and ran his hands up to the low slung handlebars and gave a mischievous smile as he twisted the throttle. "Cool," he said as he let go and turned his attention to the closest faded-green cover. He reached out and pulled it off the object it was covering.

"Sweet! A Model T!" He stared at the antique black car. It had wooden spoke wheels and a convertible top that covered two rows of bench seats. The seats were in black leather and tufted, looking much like a library couch one would find in a Victorian house. On the driver's side was a brass searchlight alongside a Klaxon horn. Max pressed down on it and smiled at the "Oooga- oooga" sound it made. He gave it a good onceover, then climbed in through the passenger's side door. There was no door on the driver's side.

"How the hell do you drive this thing?" he asked as he saw what looked like a hand brake to his left and three pedals on the floor. From what he could recall, the pedals' functions were very different from a regular car. So he slid back out and made a mental note to check YouTube for an instructional video on how to start and drive the Model T. The car bounced back on its rudimentary springs as Max jumped off and took three steps to the next lump.

Max's eyes grew wide as the jet-black and chrome trim revealed itself as the cover slid off. He dropped the rest of the dusty tarp on the floor next to him and stepped back. In front of him was a restored four-door sedan he did not recognize. On closer inspection, he found a red emblem with the word "Tatra" written in white script on the front. The car was oddly aerodynamic, with four front headlights mashed together within a long oval that took up one-third of the front of the car. There was no radiator grill up front and in the center of where it would be, there were three numbers: 603.

Max opened the driver's door and hopped in. It had a very spacious interior. The front seat looked like a couch, much like the Model T's, but a bit more spacious. The whole interior was black vinyl with red cloth inserts and almond-colored headlining. It had a late '50s, early '60s look to it. Strange, yet practical.

Max looked around the dash; the keys were in the ignition. He turned the key but nothing happened. He tried the knobs and switches. Each one worked, turning on the lights, the fan, even the horn. He noticed a small button and pressed it. The car surged forward.

"Ha!" Max said in victory.

He pushed in the clutch and pressed the starter button once again, and was surprised to hear the engine fire up behind him. It was a strange sound. There was the telltale sound as a V-8 gurgled along with a whining sound of a turbine. He stepped on the accelerator and the car torqued with anger. The sound was brutal and with purpose, telling the driver that it was all business. He found neutral, after a few tries, on the column stick shift, then stepped out of the car and walked to the back. He lifted up the trunk and smiled at the air-cooled V-8 engine nestled inside. There were two spinning turbine fans at the back of the engine that regulated the flow of air, keeping the engine cool. It was a brilliant design, much like the air-cooled Porsche engine, but with four more cylinders for fun.

"Very cool," Max said as he closed the trunk lid. He walked back to the driver's seat, reached in and shut the engine off. He closed the door and turned his attention to the next long, flat green lump of canvas. Under it was a left-hand-drive 1960s sand-colored Land Rover, but not like the ones in the African safaris; in fact, it was a type of Land Rover he'd never seen. The hood was very long with vent louvers running the length of it. Four silver exhaust pipes came out from both sides inside the engine bay and went down to connect into a horizontal exhaust tube that led the exhaust gases back under the Land Rover and out the tailpipe, which exited in front of the rear wheel below the passenger's door.

He opened the driver's door and was surprised at the detail within. The Land Rover had leather burgundy bucket seats stitched in a vintage 1930s quilted pattern. The steering wheel was wrapped in leather and finished off with coiled string, also giving it a vintage feel. The windshield was very short and folded forward. The only thing that could keep the bugs and wind from the driver's face were two small aero-windscreens, much like the ones one would see on a 1920s Bentley. It was a two-seat Land Rover and the rear tailgate area was set up for cargo purposes. But the oddest thing was the stick shift ball. It took Max a while to figure out what it was until the writing on the top gave it away. It was a cricket ball. Very odd, but it did fit the part.

The name of the manufacturer, Bell Aurens, was written on the center of the steering wheel, and below that the model, Longnose. Max had never heard of them, but by the looks of the Land Rover they knew how to engineer and build such a car. Everything was perfectly detailed. Everything had its function.

Max looked at the leather-covered aluminum dash and saw two bread-plate-sized dials; one was the speedometer and the other the fuel, amp, and temperature indicator. He lifted his body up and into the soft, comfortable, but supportive seat. Max ran his hands around the steering wheel. His right hand comfortably fell onto the cricket ball that he pulled out of first gear and into neutral. Max reached down, turned the key, and started her up. A roar came out the side as the V-8 engine growled and barked as he depressed the accelerator a few times. Max was smiling from ear to ear with the feel of the raw horsepower coming from within the engine bay. He accelerated once more, then shut off the engine.

He stepped out of the Bell Aurens Longnose and stood staring at the last lump. It was much shorter and smaller than the other two. Max took a deep breath and pulled off the canvas tarp.

"You've got to be kidding me," Max said with a sigh.

In front of him was a beautiful silver Porsche. The second he saw the car Max recognized it as the Porsche 550 Spyder. He had seen pictures of the famous 1950s actor, James Dean, alongside the same racer. It was the same model that the actor had lost his life in, in a freak, tragic accident. He went up to the Spyder and put his hand on the cold aluminum body, and ran his fingers along the length of it, feeling the imperfections of over 50 years of use. The Spyder was not a restored example like the others. It had the character of a well-traveled playboy and a life force all its own.

Max pulled open the small door and was surprised to find it very light. He dropped into the car and adjusted himself into the contoured seat. The seat hugged his body, giving him the same strange sensation he felt when he strapped himself into a jet fighter. He reached out and caressed the faded ivory-rimmed and aluminum-spoke steering wheel. He moved his hand to the key and turned it. Next he pressed the starter button to the right of the key and the car ignited with a roar. Max depressed the accelerator a few times and smiled yet again at the raw power in the engine behind him. He turned the engine off and looked at his watch.

He still had plenty of time.

Max put his hands in his lap and looked around the hangar from the inside of the Porsche. *So much time,* he thought, *so many years*. He wondered how it would have been, knowing his father, flying with him, even just talking with him. He shook his head at the lost opportunity, opened the car door, and climbed out.

To his left was a built-in room on the side of the hangar. Max walked to it and opened the metal door, reached in, and flipped the switch to the overhead lights. The fluorescent lights flickered for a few seconds, then lit the trailer-sized room. The side closest to the door looked like a small office. There was an engineering table set up against the wall. All around it were old pictures of planes. Above the desk was a long, three-foot panoramic photo of a Zeppelin, and next to it a series of photos showing an open-cockpit 'Giro performing a loop. To the right of the engineer's desk was a five-foot-tall file cabinet. Toward the center of the room was a small kitchen with a refrigerator that hummed in the background. Past the kitchen was a living room with a 50" plasma flat-screen TV.

At the end of the room was the bed. It was low and thin, looking more like a Japanese-style bed than anything else. Max looked back at the drafting table and noticed that there was an envelope on it, along with some books looking much like the journals he already had. He picked up the envelope and saw that it was addressed to him. Pulling out the drafting chair, Max took a seat and opened it.

Max,

If you made it this far you might want to take the next step. No doubt that you have seen the planes. And knowing Pierre you have already flown in the Storch by now. I'll get to the Storch story later, but first, how do you like the cars?

These are my babies and the Storch my mistress. All I ask is that you take good care of the collection. As you have noticed, the Model T, Tatra, and Bell Aurens Longnose are fully restored so you should have no problems with them. If you do, tell Pierre and he will let you know who to take them to.

I use the Tatra the most; it is better for long trips than the other three. In fact, it is a fantastic car to take fast on mountain high-ways. The Tatra was purposely built to take on any road condition short of going on a 4x4 expedition, and its very reliable, I might add. If you're looking for a greater challenge try the Model T. She was made in 1917 and has been in our family since new. I am sure you have seen the picture in the photo album and I am sure you will have no clue how to drive her—just ask Pierre, he will teach you. The Longnose will get you in and out of any trouble you can think of. Very powerful four-wheel-drive and a blast to run on rally events.

Now for the 550 Spyder. Yes, she is original, and has never been restored. I try to put her on the road at least twice a month when the weather is nice, and run her for a few miles. Once a year I take her to the Porsche rally in Germany. People love her and you will get some outrageous offers for her. Try not to fall for the temptation and keep her in the family.

The 337 is my work horse. I flew one of these during my time in the war. You will not find a better plane to get the job done. She's a six-passenger plane, but is usually set up to carry two plus cargo. Once a year I take her down to Africa and help out the missionaries and the national preserves counting herds and keeping an eye out for poachers. Pierre has all the information and I think you might enjoy doing this type of work.

Now for my pride and joy, the Storch. Pierre and I have spent many, many years restoring her, and she is 99 percent original, with a few things added for safety and convenience. Now, how I came into possession of the Storch is an interesting story. You will find it in the journals, sixth book starting on page 83.

Finally, the safe deposit box key. First, you have to get your check ride on the Storch. This way you get to take time to just enjoy flying her. Pierre will tell you what to do with her once you're ready.

Well, welcome to your new dwelling, and tell my old friend that I said hello. Good luck, my son.

Your Father

Max put the letter down, and then grabbed his bags from inside the hangar. After unpacking, he went into the small bathroom, which he found through the door next to the refrigerator, undressed, jumped in the shower, and let the hot water run.

He dried his head with a plush white Egyptian cotton bath towel as he came out of the bathroom. The steam from within escaped through the door and dissipated into the room. Max walked up to the desk wearing one of the towels wrapped around his waist and looked down at the journals. He flipped through the top one, then put it aside. He did this with each journal, checking the dates on the front inside cover, until coming across the journal marked "6." Max separated it from the others and placed it on the bed, looked at his watch, and dressed for the night's activities. Before leaving he took a quick look inside the closet for a jacket. Inside and front and center was a canvas three-quarter cut trench coat. He took it off its hanger and put it on. The coat felt slightly big on his frame, but it was better than wearing his military coat out to dinner. He strapped the belt on the coat and gave himself a quick look in the mirror. "All I need is a pencil-thin mustache, silk scarf, a biplane, and I am good to go." Max shut off the light and walked into the hangar.

He pointed the Longnose down the grass runway toward Pierre's house. Inside, Max felt as if he were in an African safari, grinning from ear to ear like a child waking up on Christmas day.

Pierre watched as Max skidded to a full stop in front of the cabin's porch, sending a fine cloud of dust up into the air, where the wind grabbed hold of it and took it away into the oak forest.

"I told your father that you would take the Tatra. We both knew the T was out of the equation...unless you could figure out how to drive the thing. Tricky at first, but a very fun car to drive once you understand how it works," Pierre said as he got up from the rocking chair, stepped down off the porch, and walked toward the Longnose. "Your father said you would take the Spyder. I guess we were both wrong."

Pierre settled himself in the passenger's seat and closed the door.

"Let's go eat," Max said as he popped the clutch.

The Longnose spun all four wheels in the loose gravel as it accelerated away. After a short ride through the oak forest, Pierre told him to leave the dirt road. The Longnose bounced up on the slick tarmac and onto a winding road. Max drove around the bend, as the cold afternoon air blew around him, and he began to think about his day, the planes, the cars, and his future flights—but for the most part he thought about the journal, and the story he had yet to read.

5

Somewhere deep in the mountains of the Colombian jungle,

1966

———

The bugs were the worst part. They would crawl onto the body, biting and burying into the skin, and even though every instinct in his body told him to squirm, he kept still. To move would bring attention. Attention would mean detection, and detection meant death.

The temperature was cooling off as the sun began to set behind one of the many lush green Amazonian mountain peaks. Soon it would get cold, and with the cold, the flies, ants, mosquitoes, and whatever else had crawled through and around his groin would hopefully quiet down. Thomas looked down at his hand and saw a fat mosquito nestled among the countless bumps of swollen flesh, taking his fill for the night.

Drink up while you can. His thought was drowned out by thousands of insect and animal noises emanating from the jungle around him.

Thomas DuMonde knew this week would be a hard one, if not the hardest since his return from Vietnam. He had a few days left in his leave and he wanted to make each day count. His time in the Green Berets had prepared him well for situations like this, but for the most part, his job in the military had just benefited the generals and politicians. Now was his time. It was his little adventure and it was going to pay off. This time, risking his life was his choice and this choice would make him rich—or dead, if he screwed up.

Pedro's short and stocky body lumbered around the path surrounding the old, overgrown coffee farm. He hated this post time. Usually he would walk the same track over and over again until his relief came five hours later, but tonight Pedro was stuck pulling two shifts guarding the coffee farm that would soon be turned into an emerald mine. He adjusted the old and rusty M1 Garand on his right shoulder and soldiered on.

Ten hours...Ten hours of walking around in circles guarding this plot of land, and for what?

That was the bet that he had lost earlier in the day...Javier's midnight guard shift at the mine. Pedro kicked a baseball-sized rock into the jungle brush as he thought of Javier laughing it up with the local whores at the cantina, spending his money and wasting his time.

"Javier...*ese hijo de puta*," Pedro murmured. He pulled aside from the worn path, and continued cursing his cousin as he unzipped his fly to relieve himself in the bushes.

Thomas's eyes were still, and focused on that infinite point in the dark distance, when the stream of warm urine struck the rotted log a few inches from his face. The strong, musty smell of the urine told Thomas this man was dehydrated and in need of a drink of water. It was all he could do to ignore the mist of urine collecting on his face and lips. A long minute passed before Thomas exhaled as the sound of receding footsteps dissipated into the night.

That was too close.

He sighed again, and waited for the sentry to get far enough away to move. Thomas pulled on the damp green towel around his neck, removed the leaf-covered Skullguard MSA hardhat, and vigorously wiped the towel across his face. The guard was now a safe distance away as Thomas looked up and waited a few more minutes until the daylight was almost gone.

It was time to make his next move. He crawled out of his hiding place and out into the open.

The crawl was very slow and deliberate. Thomas's arms were underneath his body, elbows bent, and hands in front of his face. This position, which all Green Berets were taught, allowed him to slowly and methodically inch forward with minimal detectable movement. A mound of foliage above his back hid him from view. Thomas's pace took him close to five minutes to reach the barbed wire fence 40 feet ahead of him.

He passed through the depression under the fence, covered the opening with loose growth, and took cover inside a small trench cut into the field by the rainy season water runoff. The trench was dry and followed the natural contour of the land. Thomas crawled inside it for 10 more minutes until he came upon the makeshift dig site.

The site was invisible to the naked eye even from a short distance. He had camouflaged it using a canvas tarp covered by mud and shrubbery, which melded itself into the surrounding landscape. Thomas pushed aside the fake mud wall and slid into what would be his work environment for the next 10 hours.

The space was small and cramped, even after two days of digging. Thomas had picked the spot because he found it favorable to do his work, and as an incentive, the fist-sized emerald jutting out from the side of the trench wall had given him the final say as to where he would set up camp. He contorted himself into the space, trying to find a comfortable position, and began to dig at the wall in front of him.

Nine hours passed. Thomas sat with his sweaty back against the trench wall, and lifted the clear Bourke face shield that hung from the front of his full-brim hardhat. The two small shields split from their vertical, angular position in front of Thomas's eyes to a horizontal position, giving him an unobstructed view of his small workspace. The Bourke face shield had been invented a year earlier by a fireman; to Thomas, it was the perfect addition to the hardhat. It protected his eyes from flying debris as he pickaxed the mountain rock and did not fog up in the hot, damp space he was working in. After removing his leather gloves, he opened a brown paper bag at his side. Inside lay the only meal of the night, a peanut butter and strawberry jelly sandwich, which he consumed while watching a scorpion make its way across the opposite wall.

"Not one fucking rock," he snapped at the scorpion. "Another nine hours, and nothing to show but the emerald I found two days ago. I'm going to kill Esteban when I get back. 'Es full ofse Emeraldas. Sey are efrywhere ew dig.'" Thomas imitated Esteban's bad English pronunciation. "That bastard," he grumbled as his heel flew forward and crushed the scorpion against the dirt wall.

Thomas moved his boot and a chunk of rock came loose, falling down between his legs. The light from the flashlight, which was strapped to the side of the hardhat, reflected green as it bounced off the rock. Thomas picked it up and wiped the crushed scorpion off. Turning the rock over, he admired the dirty, golf-ball-sized emerald embedded within the rock.

"I take that back, Esteban," he said as he looked up at the area the emerald had come from. Thomas tilted his head and aimed the light beam into the dark hole. His eyes grew wide as the small opening glowed a greenish hue.

Thomas put the gloves on, grabbed the trowel, and stuck it into the hole. The small opening grew as he pulled the stone surrounding the perimeter off its perch. Within the ever-expanding hole lay a nest of scorpions, surrounded by an enclave of emeralds. One of the angered homeowners jumped at Thomas's face, but he managed to slap it off before the deadly stinger found its mark. He put the Bourke shield back down for protection from another jumper, and spent the next few minutes killing off the scorpion family. Once done with the massacre, he began to pry the emeralds loose from the rocks.

The minute hand on Thomas's watch counted down to the zero hour... sunrise. Forty minutes had passed since the discovery. In that time he had managed to fill his small backpack and all the available pockets in his clothing with the precious stones.

He leaned against the far trench wall and took a long breath. The air was dusty and humid as he looked at the watch once more.

It was time to go. Thomas contemplated staying, but he knew better.

Greed will kill you. Now, go!

He reached up to the hard hat and turned off the flashlight. Thomas crawled toward the exit with the backpack securely closed, and pulled back the canvas covering the opening. He heard the starter of an engine a few hundred yards from the dig site on the far side of the field turn over a few times. The engine shook and let out a loud bang as the fuel ignited, sending out across the field the unmistakable rattling sound that only a diesel engine can make. But what took Thomas by surprise, and worried him the most, were the countless spotlights that began to illuminate the field, looking as bright as a noon-day sun.

Shit.

Thomas crawled outside and peeked above the trench rim. Another engine started in the distance. This time it was the old rusty farm tractor that leaped forward and struggled as it dragged a plow. At first the field had seemed bright as day, but as Thomas's eyes adjusted, relief came over him. The lights were not as bright as he had initially thought, and because they were so close to the ground and so few and far between, they caused a strange casting of shadows in all directions.

Thomas didn't waste any time, and headed away from the emerald cave. By the time he reached the fence, the first rays of sun had begun to pierce through the mountain fog. He pulled the fence up and crawled under it just as the tractor fell into the hidden trench at the center of the field. Hearing this, Thomas worked the rest of his body through, and had just begun to crawl toward the safety of the jungle when a sharp crack of a bullet breaking the sound barrier sounded above his head.

He scrambled to his feet, not waiting for the next shot, and dove the last two yards into the protection of the jungle, rolled once, and reached out for his secondary backpack.

A few more pops sounded above his head as the bullets tore through the foliage. He pushed off the ground and started the rehearsed sprint away from the flat plateau and down the mountain toward the river. Thomas dodged around some massive trees and hopped over the thin metallic trip wires he had set up for such an occasion as he strapped on the secondary backpack.

"*Esta llendo para el rio!*" came a loud voice from behind, notifying Thomas that they were on his path down to the river.

He kept a steady pace and laughed out loud as he heard a couple of soldiers swearing; they had run right into the trip wire.

Thomas arrived at the foot of a massive ficus tree, jumped out into midair, grabbed one of its dangling roots, and shimmied down over 20 feet to the riverbed below. He ran across the sand and rock surface, and began to hop from boulder to boulder, crossing the gentle river where, on a long, shallow sand bank a dirty green airplane rested on bulbous tires each the size of a beach ball.

Thomas jumped over the last boulder, and with his right hand reached down to a small box and turned the handle protruding from the top. Dozens of flashes ignited, and the far side of the river was engulfed in phosphorous smoke. As the pyrotechnics covered the forest in a blanket of white smoke, Thomas threw the backpacks in the rear seat and climbed into his Piper Super Cub, started it, and waited as long as he dared before pushing the throttle forward.

• • •

In the confusion of the smoke some of the guards went off the river's steep bank, falling hard onto the rocky riverbed. A few broke their arms; others, their legs. Pedro, after falling face first from the trip wire, was far enough back to see where the previous men had disappeared. The smoke made it impossible to see what was going on two meters ahead of him, but he managed to climb down the embankment to the rocky shore and follow the sound of an idling engine.

Pedro moved forward through the dissipating smoke, careful not to slip into the river water. He recognized the telltale sound of a propeller chopping through the thick, humid morning air as it echoed off the riverbank walls.

Pedro aimed his M1 Garand rifle and began to shoot through the smoke toward the noise while still navigating over the boulders. He emptied the clip and reloaded just as the smoke gave him a line of sight to the small plane, its engine now revving up as it pulled away and lifted off the sand bank.

• • •

Thomas had just pulled the stick back into his gut and pointed the plane's nose up to the sky when a shower of hot copper peppered the front of the Piper, shattering the side of the Plexiglas canopy, and unbeknownst to Thomas, mortally wounding one of the plane's cylinders.

Thomas looked himself over. He was unhurt, but not so the plane as he noted a change in the engine's tone. He scanned what was left of the instrument panel. The compass and the altimeter had been spared destruction. Thomas would have to make do with what he had. A few more minutes passed as the plane climbed higher into the sky and the unusual noise emanating from the engine kept up a steady rhythm. His situation was stable...for the moment.

Thomas looked once more at the receding riverbed, then reached back for his flight helmet. He unbuckled the hardhat chin strap and flicked it off his head, replacing it with the helmet. He slid the clear Plexiglas shield down, protecting his face from the strong wind coming into the cockpit through the jagged hole in the windshield.

Thomas set the trim tab to gain altitude and pointed the nose east toward the Venezuelan border, hoping the plane would manage to get that far. He knew that if worse came to worst and the engine failed, he could find a nice, suitable landing spot near a road or village and crash land, hopefully surviving, and hike the rest of the way home.

Thomas's mind wandered and began to calculate the fortune nestled in the rear seat. He was jolted from his reverie when the engine began to sputter.

Damn it!

He looked at his watch and judged he was about 10 minutes away from the border.

"Come on, baby, you've given me 30 minutes, be a sweetheart and lend me another 10," he said, caressing the shattered dashboard. At that same moment the engine let out a scream and the plane shook violently. The propeller stopped spinning, now frozen in the vertical position.

Not good.

He adjusted the plane's trim to the best glide ratio, which would allow the plane to travel the longest distance possible in proportion to its altitude. A few seconds passed, and the altimeter kept spinning counterclockwise at a high rate of descent, which told Thomas the plane was not going to make it over the mountain range ahead. He began to scan the area for a suitable landing spot when a bright flash illuminated the cockpit for a second. He turned his head toward its suspected origin and caught a glimpse of a tin roof to his right and 1,000 feet below.

He banked the plane toward a nearby hill. After scanning the area, he found what he had been looking for: A narrow farmer's field cut into the base of the mountain a few hundred feet down and away from the tin roof.

"Well, it doesn't get any better than that," he said sarcastically.

Thomas knew he would get one chance at landing on the field, so he strapped himself in tight and began to prepare for a short-field landing.

"Okay, here we go."

Thomas lined up the plane for its final approach onto the field ahead. He corrected for a slight crosswind as he leveled the wings and lowered the flaps, giving the plane more lift at slower speeds. He was now slightly relaxed, knowing he would make the landing, when suddenly an unseen, strong wind eddy coming off the treetops sucked the plane down and off course as it flew right into its vortex. Thomas slammed the control stick back, overcorrecting, but it was too late as the plane headed directly into one of many trees now in its path.

"Too short!" Thomas screamed through his teeth as he physically lifted himself off the seat.

Ah, crap!

The Piper smashed into the top of the tree, leaving its landing gear and part of the tail behind in the foliage. Thomas was thrown forward in his seat, but managed to coax what was left of the plane down onto the field, where it hit hard, then flipped over twice before skidding over the side, down a steep hill, and into the jungle.

Thomas's eyes opened to an upside-down world. He shook his head, got his bearings, and checked for serious injuries.

No pain...that's always good. Uh-oh, fuel smell. Mags off.

Thomas reached out and turned the ignition key, his body still hanging from the seat harness.

Main battery... He flicked the switch marked battery to the off position. *Off.*

Seatbelt o—

Thomas unbuckled himself and fell hard onto the ceiling of the fuselage. He crawled out and collapsed flat on his face. After brushing the last few terrifying seconds off his mind, he flipped onto his back and took in the thick jungle canopy above. He crawled back into the fuselage, grabbed all his belongings, and then pulled himself up on his feet with the help from a dangling vine. He staggered away from the plane, removed his dented Army flight helmet, and replaced it with the hardhat.

You lucky son of a bitch.

Thomas looked back at his plane, and after getting his bearings, took some time to remove all identification from it—last thing he needed was to be tracked down. He touched his palm on the destroyed fuselage one last time, picked up his belongings, threw on his backpack, and climbed up the wooded hill to the field above.

It took some time to scale the 50-foot hillside, the weight of the pack dragging him down with every misstep. After a struggle he was standing on a flat, low, uncut grass surface. He gulped some water from his canteen and surveyed the field. A tall tree to his right held tight to part of the plane's tail section. Below it was what looked to be a wide hut. Next to the hut was an overgrown path following the contour of the hill.

Thomas took in his new surroundings as he walked to the path. A few parrots flew across the trees at the end of the field. Nature called out in song all around him.

His short walk ended in front of a wide barn door kept closed by a rusty padlock. He tugged on the lock and tried to peek through the small crack in the dried-out wood paneling. His face lit up when he saw the outline of a plane sitting in the darkness. Thomas couldn't see much else, but his hopes were high once more. He turned and headed up the path to try to find the airplane's owner.

The structure before Thomas was well hidden by countless vines. After a few moments his eyes picked out the front of a gate to his left. Beyond the rusty iron gate lay even more tree cover.

"*Se encuentra el dueño de la casa*?" he yelled for the owner of the house.

Thomas gave it some time, shrugged, and pushed the gate open, cringing at the squealing sound the gate's rusty hinges made as they pivoted.

"That will sure get anybody's attention," he said as he stepped onto the property, but still no sign of life.

Ten paces in he found himself in the middle of a lush courtyard. Behind was the gate embedded in the tall, ivy-covered wall. To the left was a gray, three-foot-high flat rock wall with a view of the lush green valley below. Within the courtyard was a very impressive botanical garden, bearing many plants, including some rather exotic-looking orchids and ferns. He walked on the gray, decomposed granite path through the courtyard, and saw the main house in the distance peeking through the dense foliage.

Thomas followed the path through Eden. On his way he picked a pear from its tree and mulled it over, wondering how hard it must have been to grow them in such a temperate climate, took a bite, and marveled at its incredible taste.

"Damn, that's a great pear!" He looked around and reached up to pull down more of the lush fruit, stuffing them alongside the emeralds within his safari jacket's lower pockets.

Thomas's tour of the gardens ended in front of a wide porch built from the same stone as the walls surrounding the property. A few hammocks and a couple of wicker chairs made up the décor. A soft breeze fluttered dead leaves around as an open French glass door at the back banged up against the whitewashed wall with each gust.

"*Algien se enquentra*?" Thomas called out again, asking if anyone was home. He stepped up onto the porch, then moved forward and peeked in through the door. It was a mess inside. Leaves had accumulated in the corners of the room, chairs were tipped over, and all the cabinets were open. He reached under his jacket, pulled out with his gloved hand his "borrowed" CIA suppressed .22, and pulled back on the action, checking to see that it was loaded. Being extra cautious always kept one alive.

He sidestepped around the perimeter of the living room, the .22 by his side at the ready.

The room was square. It had a river rock fireplace flanked by two paintings opposite the front entrance. To the left was the dining room with a picturesque view of the valley; to his right, a den lined with bookshelves.

He did a double take on the paintings. The artist who had painted the colorful, deep-green landscape, which swirled into and out of texture, seemed so familiar to him. He just couldn't pinpoint it. He walked up to the one on the right and read the artist's name.

"Van Gogh. You have to be shitting me," he gasped.

Thomas went on to see the other artist on the wall. Matisse. He then stepped into the dining room. On the wall hung a Renoir and a Pizarro. Four paintings worth a fortune. Astonished by the find, he went looking around the rest of the house, careful not to let his guard down. His luck struck once more with a Picasso in the master bedroom.

The main house was small, with only two bedrooms. The single-story house had been abandoned in a hurry. Luckily for Thomas, whoever had ransacked the place had no clue what they were doing. The house was intact but messy, and the food and silverware were gone. Next to the main house stood the servants quarters; they, too, were empty, but it was a different story. All that was left were the walls, everything else was gone, even the toilets and sinks. It looked to Thomas that the thieves either respected the owner's property or feared what might happen if they took anything of real worth.

Thomas ended his search back in the living room. He went through the pair of doors that led into the den, and looked over the untouched books on the shelf. Some titles he recognized; Hemingway, Edgar Allen Poe, Kafka. Others were in German. He then came across an unusual title.

"*Mein Kampf*," he whispered.

Thomas pulled the book from its shelf and noticed an awful but familiar smell, easily recognized from time spent at war: The smell of death. He moved closer and sniffed, noticing that the smell got stronger.

Is it coming from behind the bookshelf?

He put the book back and began to probe the wood structure.

"There you are," he said as he found the locking mechanism and pulled on it.

Click.

The shelf shifted. Thomas grabbed the side with his empty hand and pulled it open, revealing a hallway into another room.

A fluorescent tube flickered above him as he inched ahead, pointing his weapon forward. The smell was overpowering. He reached up and removed the dirty towel from around his neck and covered his nose and mouth, trying hard to ignore the smell of rotting flesh coming through the towel.

The windowless room was half the size of a typical garage. Two of its walls were lined with bookshelves and the other two covered in pictures. There was a solitary mahogany desk in the center of the room, stacked with papers, and a slumped swollen human body.

Thomas holstered his gun and walked to the body, grabbed it, and pulled it with considerable difficulty up and back onto its chair. The body was stiff with rigor mortis. Thomas calculated the man had been dead at most for about 72 hours. After checking it for wounds, he concluded that the old man had most likely died of natural causes.

There was a partially written letter on the desk, along with the usual artifacts—pens, a paperweight, stationary, and a letter opener. Thomas picked up a half-written letter and tried reading it. He recognized a few German words, but not enough to make any sense of what was written there. He lifted his head and scanned the room once more.

In front of the desk was a reverse-mirror image of the library wall in the den, lined with books of all sizes and colors. In the center of the wall hung a one-by-two-foot painting of a government building. The painting was mediocre and Thomas wondered why it would be hidden in such a room, away from view of the casual stranger. He walked up to it and found out why.

"A. Hitler," Thomas whispered in amazement.

He looked back at the body, then again at the picture. The thought crossed his mind, but the dead man at the table bore no resemblance to the artist of the painting on the wall. Thomas looked over the body once more. The man seemed to be in his early fifties, tall and well built, but the swelling and rigor mortis made it hard to guess any better. With that thought aside, he began to search the room.

The books seemed to be of a scientific nature, most with pages upon pages of calculations. Some were of astronomical charts, the rest German novels. Thomas then came across a photo album. What he found inside left a chill in his bones.

The first few pages were those of what looked like military friends, and the dead man sitting in the back seat of an observation plane at an earlier time in his life. The next pages showed some scenic pictures of a mountain retreat, followed by the dead man alongside Adolph Hitler and his entourage. Thomas looked at the pictures in disbelief. The next pages were of another mountain range and an ominous-looking castle perched on the mountainside. Then came the disturbing pictures, first of some labs, then of malnourished people alive in one picture, and grossly dismembered or disfigured and dead in the next. The progression of pictures depicted continuous experiments that produced horrible deaths until the last pictures that showed a few souls alive in the before-and-after pictures.

Thomas looked back at the dead man, but this time in true disgust.

"You son of a bitch." He walked over to the body and pushed it aside. It tilted over and thumped on the hard concrete floor. "Let's see who you are."

Thomas, now determined, began to open the desk drawers. All he found were more files and papers he couldn't read. He flipped through them, but none had a closing signature or any sort of identification as to who had written them.

Thomas looked up from the desk and focused on the painting, noticing something he had not seen before. It was at an angle from the wall, much like an open door. He went around the desk and stood in front of the painting, reached out, pulled on the edge of the frame, and pivoted it out.

Hello there.

"Sure," he said, looking back at the body, "where else would you keep it?" Thomas studied the safe embedded in the wall. Its door was smaller in size than the painting and had a combination lock with a steel handle. He wrapped his gloved fingers around the handle, closed his eyes, and pulled the lever down.

Click.

Thomas smirked as he pulled open the heavy safe door.

A thimble size light bulb flickered inside the safe, dimly illuminating a thick manila folder, a small dark-blue velvet box, and a few papers. He pulled the contents out of the safe, one at a time, and found what he was looking for.

The small booklet was burgundy-colored with a gold inlaid eagle perched atop the Nazi swastika. He opened the passport and flipped to the picture of a much younger Nazi SS officer, who now lay dead on the floor. The man's name was Hans Kammler, a name Thomas did not recognize.

There were some medals inside the velvet box. The thick manila envelope contained a set of plans, more paperwork with calculations, and pictures of scientists working around a donut shaped, cylindrical machine the size of a truck's tire.

Thomas looked in once more and found a set of keys against one of the corners of the safe. As he took the keys out, the leather on his index finger got caught up on a fine metal ridge embedded into the side of the safe.

There you go...one more surprise.

Thomas pushed against the opposite side of the ridge and a lid swung open. He reached in and found a tin, shoebox-sized box within. The box was heavy and rattled as if something were loose inside. It also had a key lock. Thomas picked up the keys he had found in the safe, but none fit the small lock.

He looked around the room and found an old leather briefcase in which he put the contents of the safe along with the tin box. The thought of taking the Hitler painting crossed his mind, but he decided it was not worth the effort to carry it across the jungle.

Thomas left the stench of the secret room and entered the living room. He put his backpack down and began to empty its unnecessary contents to make space for his emeralds by taking out all the extra clothing, a couple of paperback books, the waterproof poncho, and his digging tools.

He sat on one of the lush couches in the living room and rearranged the pack to maximize the space within. Thomas grabbed the throw pillow on the couch, took out the stuffing inside and emptied the emeralds from his pockets into it. After adjusting both emerald bags at the bottom of the larger backpack, he put the old leather briefcase inside, along with what he deemed essential supplies for the trip ahead. That left the tin box, which he put on top of the backpack and flapped the canvas lid over it, securing everything inside.

Thomas collected all the paintings by removing the priceless works of art from their intricate frames, and wrapped each one in sheets from the bedrooms. He then placed one on top of the other, covered them in the waterproof poncho and secured the bundle to the outside of the backpack above the smaller pack now hooked securely to the main pack. He shook the backpack, making sure everything was strapped on tight, ran his arms through the straps, and adjusted the weight comfortably on his shoulder. Suddenly, Thomas looked up as he heard a distinctive chopping sound echoing through the valley, the telltale sound of a helicopter.

Shit!

He pulled down on the straps, tightening the backpack to his body, checked the living room once more, and jogged out into the courtyard. Thomas didn't know if they were hostile, and even though the sound was far away, he wasn't going to take the chance. He would have to disappear into the jungle. He took off running through the garden past the rusty front gate, and down the path.

The helicopter was getting closer as he reached the old barn at the end of the path. He stopped in mid-stride and looked back at the wood structure.

"Might as well check." He removed his triple barrel rifle from the sheaf that was strapped to the side of the pack, cocked the exposed top hammer, aimed and squeezed the trigger, blowing out the lock along with the surrounding wood with a powerful 45-70 buckshot round. He pulled on the long door, letting in the light that revealed an unusual shape within.

Thomas let go of the door as gravity took it and swung it open. He stood there and stared at the weirdest-looking plane he had ever seen. Time was of the essence, so he jumped onto the left wheel strut, found a perch, then climbed up to the wing to check the fuel tanks. To his good fortune the plane was fueled up. He stepped down, opened the side hatch, and stuck his head into the cockpit and moved the battery switch, checking to see that it had a charge. The battery indicator dial swung its needle to full charge.

So far so good.

Next he moved the control stick, making sure all the control surfaces were in working order. Satisfied that the plane was safe to fly, he took off his pack, put it in the rear seat, and sat himself in the front seat. Thomas took a few moments fiddling with the rest of the gauges, trying to figure out what each one did.

Key? Need the keys!

"Damn, I don't have time to hot-wire you," he grumbled. Thomas determined that he had about a minute left before he would have to abandon the plane and hop into the jungle. He reached back and started emptying his backpack.

"Ha!" he said in triumph as he found the keys in the old leather briefcase. "Now let's see if this is the luckiest day of my life!"

Thomas began to slip each key into the slot on the flight panel. On the third try the key slid in and turned, and a green light lit up above the key. Next to it was a dime-sized button, which Thomas pressed. The long, two-bladed propeller spun twice, shaking the plane from side to side.

Okay, that should be enough to lubricate the cylinders.

Thomas turned the magneto switch to both, set the mixture to full, pumped what he figured out was the primer, and advanced the throttle a half an inch forward. He closed his eyes, and hit the starter switch once more.

The long, two-bladed wood propeller swung, but this time it was accompanied by a popping sound. He kept the starter depressed while he fiddled with the throttle, and with a loud bang the engine caught on. Each of the eight cylinders began to fire. It was music to his ears. He pulled the throttle back and settled the plane into a smooth but loud idle.

Thomas patiently scanned the gauges, making sure everything was in working order. Then from above, the hangar shook as a Bell 47 helicopter sporting the Colombian colors flew right over and down the grass strip, heading to the smoke rising up from the crash site. Thomas had not noticed the smoke as he ran down the hillside, and now figured that the spilled fuel must have ignited when it touched the hot engine exhaust tube.

He stared at the helicopter as it hovered a few feet above the ground. The two passengers shifted inside, trying to get a better view at the burning wreckage below. The helicopter then fired a burst of bullets into the jungle from its twin .50 caliber machine guns, each one mounted on the outside of the helicopter's skids. The copilot threw a round object out and toward the smoke plume. After a few seconds, Thomas felt the concussion of a grenade exploding.

Swell, they've got machine guns and grenades.

He looked at the end of the runway, then at the helicopter hovering in his path. "Fuck it!" He set the flaps to 40 degrees and pushed the throttle lever forward until it stopped.

The plane leaned to the left and Thomas applied right rudder to compensate for the torque the engine produced. Inside the hut it became a blinding whirlwind of dust as the plane accelerated out into the open field. The tail rose up, catching Thomas by surprise. He pulled back on the control stick and the tail came back down, only to rise again. Thomas stabilized the plane and felt as the wings bit into the wind, lifting the plane up and away from the grass runway.

"Hey, assholes! Look left!" he screamed as he got closer and his speed increased. "Look, damn it!" Thomas screamed again as he calculated that the helicopter was not high enough off the ground for his plane to safely pass under it.

The plane closed the distance between the two aircraft. Thomas saw the helicopter pilot turn his head, and the two of them made eye contact. Thomas cut the throttle and flared the plane, forcing it back down onto the runway.

The pilot pulled on the collective, and the helicopter began to lift just as Thomas's propeller reached the point where the landing skids had been. The propeller completed its rotation and the tip of the blade nicked the bottom of the left skid.

The helicopter pilot's first reaction was instinctive. He pulled up in time for the two aircraft to miss each other by millimeters. Unfortunately, the helicopter pilot's second reaction was panic, and the third anger. These three separate reactions became one as the pilot input them into the control systems.

The rising helicopter swung around, machine guns blazing, as the tail rotor rotated the fuselage right, trying to track the plane that had almost collided into it. But the inputs were too much for the helicopter as the extreme vibrations and .50 caliber machine guns' fire and kickback made the pilot overexert, sending the helicopter into a dangerous pitch.

Thomas had the best seat in the house as he pushed the throttles forward once more. He watched through the greenhouse canopy as the helicopter maneuvered into firing position. But what he saw that the pilot of the helicopter did not, was the tree vine dangling innocently in the flight path of the helicopter's tail rotor.

The tail rotor and vine exploded as one, sending the helicopter completely out of control. Thomas ducked as one of the tail rotor blades flew toward him. The blade made contact with one of the many small glass windows that made up the top of the canopy structure of the plane, and sprayed the broken glass all over the cockpit interior. He felt the shards hit his hardhat and shoulders, cutting through his clothes and slashing his skin, but he didn't care. Not because he had cheated death once more, but because he now faced a solid wall of green jungle.

The helicopter pilot and his passenger froze in fear as the blades struck the ground, sending the frame of the helicopter cartwheeling out of control and into the mountainside of the runway. The pilot was thrown out of the cockpit, and cut in half by the remaining rotor blade. The rest of the helicopter smashed into the mountain. Thomas felt the concussion of the explosion as the helicopter disintegrated when the armed grenade that the copilot had accidentally dropped, exploded.

Like the pilot in the helicopter, Thomas needed to go up, so he pulled back on the control stick and tried to push the throttle past its stop. The plane reacted as he put the stick into his gut. His eyes grew wider as the engine revved up, spinning the propeller as it cut its way through the dense foliage. He heard the landing gear snap some branches, and just as quick as the mayhem began, it was replaced by blue sky and the rhythmic hum of the airplane's engine.

Thomas banked the plane, and looked back over his shoulder to see the burning grass runway, and the smoldering black smoke rising out of the pile of jumbled steel. He convulsed once, twice, and burst into nervous laughter. After a few seconds he took a deep breath, let it out, and released his death grip on the stick and throttle.

He took his bearings and headed east to the safety of the Venezuelan border, looking around every so often just to make sure he was the only one in the air. The plane flew at a steady 80 knots and bounced through some unstable air as it crested over a lush green mountain peak. Thomas banked the plane and descended into the valley, looking for signs of civilization. After some time he made out the faint outline of a dirt road peeking through the green Amazonian canopy. The road hugged the mountain's base, winding its way down to a riverbed, then crossed the river at a rickety bridge. He mimicked its every turn, flying slow and low until coming to a small town surrounded by plowed fields. It had been 40 minutes since his escape, and by the looks of the town below, Thomas recognized that he was now in Venezuelan airspace.

The plane hit another mild patch of turbulence, and something rattled below his seat. Thomas reached down between the control stick and seat, pulled out the tin box that he'd found in the safe, and flipped it in his hands, mulling over the faded address: Cullinan, South Africa.

He held the control stick between his legs, pulled out the K-bar knife from its sheath on his belt, and worked the tip of the knife into the small lock attached to the top lid, all the while keeping the plane level with his knees. After a few turns and a twist, the box lid flew open.

Thomas's grin showed his crooked teeth as he stared down into the tin box.

This is the luckiest day of my life!

Inside sparkled hundreds of uncut diamonds.

6

12,000 feet above the French Alps, November 20ᵗʰ, 2010

Max was buffeted around by the mountain air turbulence as he checked the GPS unit for the runway icon one more time before looking over and ahead of the Storch's nose. It took him a few seconds to pick out the runway located on the edge of a mountainous cliff.

There it is. Damn. This is going to be interesting.

Max let out a sigh and spoke to the control tower. "Courchevel Tower, this is Romeo-Bravo-Charlie-Papa. Five miles to the north, full stop." The plane bounced again as another warm thermal pushed up on the 20-foot-long wings. Max took a quick glance at the rear seat, making sure the aluminum urn carrying his father's ashes remained firmly buckled in.

Max was en route to Geneva, but first he had to head south past the city to the small ski resort town of Courchevel, located high up in the French Alps. Once there he was to take the chairlift to the highest peak, and release his father's ashes while skiing down the slopes.

"Charlie Papa. Courchevel Tower, you are cleared to land," said a metallic voice over the headphones. "Winds from the west, one-zero knots, temperature, one two. Charlie Papa is number one in pattern, visibility clear."

"Roger, tower, turning on approach. Charlie Papa has the runway in sight, number one in pattern, cleared to land." Max had called earlier to advise the airport that he would be arriving at this given time, but what Max saw ahead worried him a little.

Earlier in the week, between getting his body back in shape, having some fun with his new toys, and helping Pierre put the finishing touches on the 'Giro, he had spent most of his time practicing short take-offs and landings in the Storch. Max was pretty sure he could fly it into almost any short runway, but what lay in front of him was unusual.

The Courchevel Airport runway was built on the edge of a cliff at an angle following up the contour of the mountain at an 18-degree slope. He would have to land the plane uphill.

Max lowered the flaps and set throttle and mixture. He picked a point on the runway and began to glide the plane toward it. His line of sight was a little threatening. At around 30 feet from touchdown all he could see in front of him was a wall of tarmac. As the plane crossed the threshold of the runway, he was slammed into the seat as an unseen updraft forced the Storch up.

• • •

An older man sat on his wooden, snow-covered balcony, facing out into a valley with a clear view of the landing approach to the airport. He lost his grip and spilled his coffee on his lap as he exploded in laughter after seeing the pilot of the Storch lose control at the edge of the runway.

"*Was ist so lustig*, Grandpapa?" The question came from inside the chateau. The beautiful girl behind the voice stepped out into the cold morning mountain air. She looked down at the mess he had just made and spoke to her grandfather in his preferred language, German. "*Schau, was du getan hast.* The coffee is all over your ski pants."

Solange's grandfather's smiling eyes looked up at her and then back at the plane. "Solange, *sehen*, I made the same mistake when I first landed here." He pointed at the struggling Storch in the distance. "And in all these years,

I have yet to see somebody screw up like I did until now." He laughed again. "Just look at him!"

• • •

"Jesus Christ!" Max screamed as he fought the plane back down onto the runway. He worked all his senses as he managed to overcompensate every move he made, making a spectacle to watch from the ground.

Max managed to calm himself down, and glided the Storch up on top of the air current eddy, where he skillfully caught the wave of air coming up and over the runway's edge, and rode it much like a surfer on an ocean wave. Max had done this before, when he'd gone ridge-soaring in California, flying off the waves of air the wind made as it crested over the top of the mountain ridge. It was an exhilarating ride. One could spend hours soaring with them, back and forth. Ridge-soaring was one of the few never-ending rides that Mother Nature was kind enough to provide, stopped short only by the limitations of the human body.

• • •

"*Phantastisch!* That is a man who can fly. He lost all control, and then regained it back by doing something that most pilots would have ignored." The old man nodded as he heard the plane apply power, easing itself off the current of air, and descend toward the runway.

He and his granddaughter stood in silence on the porch as the pilot made a perfect three-point landing, touching all three wheels on the runway at the same time.

"I must meet that man," he said to Solange.

"Why?"

"Well, because he is a damn good pilot, and flies almost as well as I do." He stared, lost in thought at the Storch taxiing up the runway. "And because he is flying the same type of plane I flew in the war."

• • •

Max's heart was still racing as he was guided to his tie-down spot on the tarmac between two Swissair turboprops. The lineman, leading Max, crossed his fists over his head, signaling to come to a complete stop. Max kept his feet pressed down on the brake pedals as he let the engine idle. He looked over to see the lineman put a pair of wooden chocks around each wheel, then give Max a thumbs-up.

Max pulled back the mixture control, which starved the engine from its fuel. The engine complained until the remaining gasoline was spent, and abruptly shut down. He called the tower once more to thank them, and they responded with laughter.

Max began his shutdown checklist and took his time to fill out his flight and the plane's logbook when a tapping on the canopy distracted him. He held his finger up, telling the lineman outside to hold on as he removed his Bose headset and reached down to the hatch handle. The cold mountain air hit his face as the hatch opened.

"*Belle reprise.*" The young man told Max that he had made a nice recovery.

"*Merci. Bonjour, je suis Max DuMonde,*" he said as he stuck out his hand.

The lineman shook Max's hand. "*Enchanté. Je suis Jean-Luc. Max? Americain?*"

Max nodded.

"Your French is excellent," he continued in French.

"I had to learn your language or I was going to have a hard time going through life as a DuMonde that didn't speak French! Here, help me out with these bags."

"*Certainement.*" He looked around the inside of the plane. "Never seen one of these. What is it?"

"Storch. Fi-156," a man behind Jean-Luc said. "*C modéle, je crois que, mais la vitre de toit arrière a été modifié.*" The man knew it was the C model Storch, and pointed out that the rear roof glass was modified.

"I'll take your bags into the terminal so you can pay your landing fees and close your flight plan," Jean-Luc said as he watched the old man look over the plane.

"*Merci*, I'll be right in." Max turned to talk to the old man now standing under the right wing strut, but was distracted by the beautiful, brown-haired woman engulfed in a plush fur coat next to him.

"*Excusez-moi. Je suis Ditter Von Ludger, et...*" Ditter turned. "*C'est Solange Ludger, ma petite-fille,*" he said to Max, saying that the woman next to him was his granddaughter.

Max nodded at Solange, and leaned out of the cockpit and shook Ditter's hand. "*Je suis Lieutenant Commander Maximus DuMonde, mais mes amis m'appellent Max,*" Max answered in French, giving his rank much like a rookie would, trying to impress a girl. He felt stupid a split second later.

"Well, we have two things in common now," Ditter said in English. "I am a retired major of the Luftwaffe."

"And the second?" Max smiled, already liking the major for switching to English.

"We have both flown the Storch!" Ditter looked in the cockpit.

"Really?" Max asked, still pumping the major's hand.

Ditter nodded. "You speak French fluently?" he asked as he stepped back to allow Max to climb out of the cockpit.

"In my line of work it is good to know more than one language."

"Yes, very smart," nodded Ditter.

Solange walked around her grandfather and tilted her head as she looked Max over.

"*Hallo, Herr DuMonde,*" she said in German as she walked up to shake his hand.

Max was surprised at her strong grip. "*Sie können mich anrufen Max, Frau Ludger,*" Max retorted in the broken but proper German manner, but that was as far as he could go in the language.

She was beautiful. Her piercing green eyes looked straight at him as her wavy brown hair flowed in the wind. She was a tall woman, close to six feet, but Max could not tell much else due to the long fur coat covering the rest of her body.

"*Du siehst aus wie die rote baron,*" she said, looking into his gray eyes. "*Und Sie können mich anrufen Solange.*"

"I must apologize, but I only understand a bit of German," Max said. "Did you say something about the Red Baron?" he asked in English. It was then that Max realized he must have looked ridiculous. His idea to wear his father's reproduction Willis & Geiger WWI trench coat, leather head aviator cap, and knee-high brown leather boots seemed almost fashionable as he stepped out of the WWII plane, but he never thought that he would meet a girl in the getup. Now, slightly uncomfortable, he made the best of the moment. "Ha! I get it, Red Baron. Well, I have been known to be a trendsetter in my realm."

"Well, I don't know you, but it does suit you," she responded in a European accent. They both laughed it off. "And you can call me Solange."

"*Ja, ja.*" Ditter waved them off. "Do you prefer English?"

Max nodded.

"*Gut!* If you two are done, I would like to ask our new friend about his aircraft."

Max let go of Solange's hand, wondering how long he had held it. She gave him a nod, and stood next to her grandfather.

"*Alles zu seiner Zeit, Grandpapa.*" She turned to face Max once more. "Will you be in town long?"

"Unfortunately not. I have to leave for Geneva tomorrow morning if I want to stay ahead of the weather, but I could leave..." Max looked up at the sky as if trying to read the weather. "...a bit later. Let me check the forecast to see if anything has changed. Then I'll know. Can you recommend a place where I could stay for the night?"

"*Mach dir keine Sorgen.* Sorry, English: Don't worry, I'll make a call to the main hotel in town. They should be able to set you up for the night," Ditter said, still looking over the Storch. "I flew one in Africa, then in Germany toward the last years of the war." He touched the cold fabric fuselage.

"Well, I'll let you two be," Solange said. She paused in mid-thought and turned to her grandfather. "Grandpapa, why don't we have the Lieutenant Commander over to the family's formal dinner?" Solange looked back at Max. "Every year we throw a weekend of formal dinners to discuss the family's winter activities. It is a fun night, watching them all discuss if we are to stay here or go to a warmer place."

"I am staying right here! I had enough of the beach last winter," Ditter proclaimed.

"Strange. You seemed to enjoy all the half-naked women in the Mediterranean." She smirked at the jab.

"Oh, no. I would not want to impose." Max smiled back, not sure if he wanted to get involved with some unknown family.

"*Phantastisch*, Solange." Ditter turned to Max. "You will be my honored guest for tonight. As you can see, we need a mediator! I won't take no for an answer," he said in his stern voice.

"In that case, it will be my honor, Major Ludger." Max bowed.

Ditter stood even taller when Max called him by his rank. He turned to Solange. "Oh, I like this one."

"Finally, a dinner with some intrigue," Solange said. "I can't wait to get to know you, Lieutenant Commander. Eight sharp. Grandpapa will tell you where to go." She looked him up and down. "I cannot wait to see how you will dress tonight!" She winked, spun on her heels and walked briskly away.

Max watched her leave as Ditter asked permission to sit in the pilot's seat. He motioned him to enter, held the hatch open and turned to watch Solange disappear around the corner of the control tower building.

"She's a feisty one," Ditter said as he touched the controls. "You two will get along famously."

Max slammed the iron, fist-shaped knocker on the old wooden door, which was twice Max's height. The chateau looked like a miniature castle from the outside. He waited, then reached out to knock again, but stopped when he heard someone behind the door.

The three-inch-thick door creaked as it opened inward. "Hello, Lieutenant Commander," Solange said as she stepped forward and gave Max a soft kiss on his cheek.

"Hello, Solange, you look..." Max paused, looking for the perfect word. "Beautiful."

Simplicity is always best.

"Come in, everyone is here and the spirits are freely flowing! It will be an interesting night to say the least!" Solange grabbed Max's hand and pulled him in. She led him into a grand foyer lined with intricately carved, wood-paneled walls that reached high above his head. The ceiling had a wonderful, painted, fox-hunting scene. Max looked to the corner to find the fox hidden and looking out from a hollowed-out tree stump as the dogs rushed by.

"Here, let me take your coat and visor." Max removed his visor as Solange reached up and helped him take off his black overcoat. She looked Max over. "Another surprise. I've always liked a man in uniform."

"I feel a little overdressed, but it was the only suit I had with me."

"Don't worry, you're dressed right for the occasion. It shows authority, especially since everyone now knows you will be the referee for the night." Solange stepped closer to Max. Max could smell her intoxicating perfume. "Just so you know, many in the next room will try to lie, cheat, and even bribe you to pick their vacation spot." Solange moved even closer, their lips just inches apart. "I am up for a Caribbean trip to the Virgin Islands via catamarans."

"Are you bribing me?" Max smirked as he handed over his visor.

Solange winked, turned around, and disappeared through a door with his coat and white visor in hand. Max took the opportunity to check himself out in the standalone mirror in the corner of the foyer and made sure that all was in place. He was dressed in his Navy class-A uniform. He straightened the ribbons above his left chest pocket and pulled down on the jacket, adjusting it square to his shoulders. The double-breasted suit looked very slick when seen straight on, its gold buttons standing out against the dark wool. Max's sleeves had the three gold stripes and one star above them, the rank of a lieutenant commander. It was also cut tight on the soldier's body, which in turn forced most officers to keep in relatively good shape. The pants were straight-legged, and the shoes patent leather, rising up to mid-ankle for support.

"Stop fussing, you look very distinguished," Solange said as she walked over from the coat closet and wrapped her arm around his, leading him into a hallway.

Max took a last, quick glance at the mirror, adjusted his flat black tie against the white shirt, and gave himself an encouraging nod.

"I have never seen my grandfather so full of life as when he got back from flying in your plane."

Max looked at the beautiful woman at his side. "Well, I'll tell you this much, he certainly is the youngest 85-year-old man I have ever met."

"You should see him ski!" Solange laughed. "Everyone is already here, waiting in the library."

Max quickly checked his watch, making sure that he had not arrived late. He had not. They stepped through another wood frame that led down into a room surrounded by book-filled shelves that reached up two stories. At its mid-point was an iron walkway giving access to the books 20 feet above his head.

Max looked around the room and saw over a dozen people mingling, in separate groups, but all eyes were on them. He noticed that although he stood next to a beautiful woman, it was he they looked over.

Ditter stepped out from the far right of the library and rushed over to them. "*Wunderbar!* Max, it's a pleasure to have you here this evening. I have taken the liberty to inform everyone to speak English, since you will be our mediator for the night."

"That will be of great help, Herr Ludger." Max felt relieved.

"Let me introduce you to my family and friends." Ditter wrapped his arm around Max's shoulders and lowered his voice. "If you would like to get to know Solange a bit more, may I suggest that staying this winter in my Swiss chateau sounds like a perfect family vacation." Ditter squeezed Max's shoulder to get his point across and led him around the room.

"I see your family pulls no punches."

Ditter winked at Max as they approached one of the groups. "Lieutenant Commander Max DuMonde, this is my wife, Helga."

"Pleasure, Frau Ludger," Max said as they shook hands.

"I heard you have been having fun with my old man." Helga smiled.

Max was relieved that she spoke to him in English. "I hope I will have the energy he has when I reach his age."

"As do I," Solange said, to Max's surprise.

"Now, now, Solange. You must show a little restraint," said the lady next to Helga. She raised her right hand. "Eva Ludger."

Max looked at Ditter, but did not see a resemblance.

As if reading his thoughts, Eva said, "I was married to Ditter's brother, Otto. He was killed in the last days of the war. You would have liked him; he was also a pilot."

"It is a pleasure to meet you, Frau Ludger." Max nodded at Eva.

"So, I hear you are to be the referee for tonight's discussions," Eva said as she dragged him away from Ditter. "I will help you out if you help me out," she whispered in his ear.

Max kept his poker face. "So, how do you plan to help me? You have to give me a bit of something before I decide to help you out."

"I will start by giving you the lay of the land."

Eva saw that Ditter was approaching, so she grabbed Max by the arm and moved him toward the bar at the far corner of the room. Once there she began to spill the information. "Ditter is an old *ziege*—goat—and he wants to stay here in this cold mountain skiing all day and drinking at night. All I want is not to be here. Pick wherever you like, just as long as it's not in the cold."

At that moment a tall, older man and what looked like his son approached the couple.

"Eva, who is this you have here?" the older man asked in a raspy voice.

Eva could tell that he, too, was looking for a way to bribe Max. She smiled politely. "Lieutenant Max DuMonde, this is Klaus, Solange's stepfather, and his son, Hermann Wehr."

They both shook hands with Max. Max caught the handoff from father to son.

"So, Max, English is fine?" said Hermann.

"Yes, thank you. But I know French if need be."

"Rare to find an American that speaks more than one language. Glad to see it!" He patted Max on the back. "You know I am a pilot, as well," Hermann said. "Here, let me pour you a drink." He walked up to the bar and turned back to face Max. "What is your drink?"

"Whiskey. Neat."

Hermann was over six foot five, his hands were large, and easily fit two tumblers into one. He poured whiskey into the glasses, handed one to Max, and clinked the glasses together. "Cheers." He took a sip of the smoky liquor. "So, let me cut to the chase, as you Americans like to say. What offers have you received?"

"As the referee in this discussion, I must maintain a neutral position." Max smiled back.

"*Verdammt!* They have already started getting to you. I am late to the game!" He looked to Ditter, who was eyeing the conversation. "That old man," Hermann pointed with his glass to Ditter, "used my idea already, didn't he? Well, I will let you know that as Solange's stepbrother, I know much more about her quirks than her grandfather there. But Austria is a much better place to ski than here. Have you ever been to Austria?"

"Can't say that I have."

"Well, you—"

"Excuse me, brother, but I would like Max to meet the rest of the family," Solange interrupted and dragged Max away. Behind him he heard Hermann whisper to his sister, "Don't you dare use what God gave you to get him to choose the Caribbean. It's only right to go skiing after the Mediterranean last winter," he hissed.

Solange leaned her head back. "Advantage me, brother." She smirked at the fact that she had the upper hand.

Hermann looked at his father and shrugged.

"These are our longtime friends, the Meiseners, and Herr Klien." Max shook hands with each of them.

"I am glad that for once an outsider gets to choose! Usually I end up having someone *hate* me for a year after this dinner. I am in debt to you for taking on this assignment," Michael Meisener said.

"Let me guess—you must be on Solange's side," Max said.

Michael raised his drink and smiled. "Well, I would not want such a pretty lady mad at me for a year..." He let the thought hang there for a few moments. "Solange tells me that you are staying in our hotel?"

"Yes, and I want to thank your staff for finding a room for me. I hear you are booked at this time of the year."

"Usually, but we always have a room or two for the unexpected guest."

Ditter cut in, "Let me finish the presentations. You will all have enough time this evening to interrogate my guest," he said as he escorted Max to the other side of the room.

"Ditter, where are your manners? Max's glass is low," Helga told her fleeing husband.

"I'll get right to it, Your Highness." He whispered to Max, "Even after 61 years of marriage I'm still a private in her army."

"I heard that," Helga said from a distance.

"With ears like a fox." Ditter leaned in and spoke as they walked toward two women. "Max, now pay attention. The lady on the left is Olga, Solange's mother. She was married to my son Christopher, who passed away many years ago."

Max caught the deep sadness in Ditter's eyes when he spoke his son's name.

Ditter paused for a brief moment, then shook off the darkness. "A few years later she married Klaus, himself a widower." He pointed to Klaus. Olga turned and smiled as they approached. Max immediately saw the resemblance between Solange and her mother. "Olga, this is my guest, Lieutenant Commander Max DuMonde."

"Max will be just fine," he said and leaned forward, giving her a cheek-to-cheek kiss. "Pleasure, Frau Wehr."

"Elegant try, Max, but I still need to make up my mind about someone my little girl has brought home." She turned to the lady next to her. "This is Fraulein Klien. You have already met her husband." She gestured to Herr Klien.

Max also gave her a cheek-to-cheek, making sure that Olga noticed that his greeting to her was equal to the woman next to her. Olga looked him up and down. "Well, you are smart, I will give you that, so let me let you in on a little secret. I like skiing, especially in Austria."

"And just so you know, Olga is a difficult woman to please so I hope you make the right choice," Mrs. Klien interjected.

Christ, I was just double-teamed!

Ditter came up from behind and whisked Max away. "Excuse me, Olga, as I continue the introductions."

Max excused himself, as well.

"Here, let me take you to the younger side of the crowd. These are Eva's grandchildren. Eric, Samantha, and Gertrude." Ditter heard a commotion from across the room. "Excuse me while I see to my other guests. It seems that the quarreling has begun."

Max politely shook the hands of the 30ish-year-olds. "Let me guess, Caribbean?"

They looked at each other and laughed at Max's insight.

"So, I take it that the rest of the crowd has begun their attacks? How are you holding up?" Eric asked.

"Well, so far the skiers have the advantage but only because you did the Mediterranean last year, but the night is young," Max said as he looked around the room. It had been quite some time since he'd been around such a family gathering. Max felt a twinge of loss that his career had taken this part of his family life away, and he made a mental note to call them when he had the chance.

Klaus approached and was now on the attack as he entered the conversation. He put his hand on Max's shoulder. "How long have you been in the military?"

"I started right after graduating from high school when I received my acceptance letter to Annapolis. Spent my years there until I graduated and headed to flight training. I have been in ever since."

"Do you ever think about joining the civilian world?" Samantha asked.

"Lately I have, but I just don't know what I would do out in the real world. I've had some offers from the private industry, but nothing concrete."

"So, what brings you here?" Klaus was now back in control.

Max caught on to what was happening. Klaus was coming in the opposite way from everyone else, trying to play the card that he didn't care and just wanted to chat, but Max knew better. "I am here on leave."

"But you flew in what Ditter tells me is a World War II plane. I take it is yours?"

"My father's, actually. It was his wish for me to fly out in his plane and spread his ashes on the top of his favorite mountain ski resort."

"Oh, well, I am sorry for your loss. He did pick a beautiful place to rest."

Ditter stepped in. "Did I hear talk of the Storch?"

A butler stepped out of an adjacent room, rang a bell, and everyone turned. He then called out that dinner was served.

The small crowd slipped into the dining hall, itself as tall and wide as the library. The room was adorned with wall-to-wall medieval armor, and the odd animal head. The dining table, situated in the center, had the ability to seat three times as many people as were gathered this evening. A stone fireplace crackled and spit embers up and into the chimney flue opposite the entrance on the far wall, giving the whole room a warm, eerie orange glow. Above the center of the table were two chandeliers made entirely from antlers.

Max stepped up to the table alongside Solange and pulled out her chair, and remained standing until all the women at the table were seated. He looked at Ditter, who nodded in approval, and then sat down between him and Solange.

"Not all the family is here; in fact, Klaus and Hermann surprised me and graced us with their presence tonight. They must be desperate to get their vacation location, especially since they flew in from Austria."

"We will not make the same mistake we did last year by not attending," Hermann said.

"As I was saying, the rest of the family is too busy to attend this dinner. Most just leave it up to this group to decide where to go for winter vacation," Ditter said.

"So, do you live here all year round?" Max asked.

"No, just during ski season. The rest of my time is spent on the outskirts of Zurich."

Max turned to Solange. "What about you and your family?"

"Geneva is my home."

"What do you do in Geneva?" Out of the corner of his eye, Max could see Ditter smiling at the conversation between him and his granddaughter.

"I'm a jeweler. I design my own jewelry. Here, look." She turned, and lifted her chest to Max, showing him the necklace that followed her features, lying directly in the center of her magnificent cleavage.

Max took a quick look, determined not to look like a pervert. "Do you have your own store?"

"Yes, I'll be there on Monday if you're still in the city."

"I'll be in town for a few days, so I would be more than happy to run into you. Maybe you could show me around?"

Solange smiled and took a drink of her wine.

Hermann changed the subject as she was about to answer. "Max, did you have a chance to ski the slopes today?" he asked from across the table.

"Unfortunately, I only had two hours before the mountain closed so I did not get to enjoy it as much as I would have liked. That said, it is a different kind of skiing over here. You have fewer restrictions than you do in the U.S. and if you go flying off a cliff, it's your fault for not reading the sign." Max took a sip of wine. "It has been a while since I put on skis, but I will have to say that the Alps are beautiful. I really enjoyed it and I can see why my father liked it so much."

"So, how long are you on leave?"

"I have two weeks left. I figured I'd end my trip in Italy. I've always had this thing for archeology and I've never been to Pompeii."

"Don't stay in Naples," Samantha said. "One of my favorite places is Capri, and they have the emperor's ruins up on the top of the mountain. Just take a checkbook, because it is expensive."

"Everything is expensive now. I would recommend renting a car when you are in the Amalfi coast. The taxi service there is plain and simple robbery," Eric said from across the table.

"Yes, prices are through the roof, but if you get the chance, stop by Sorrento. They have the best Limonchelo liquor. Small place where this family has been making it for centuries! I will give you the address after dinner."

Ditter looked at Max and Solange, making sure that his guest was having a good time. Hermann looked at Ditter and asked him about flying the Storch. Ditter straightened up and began to tell everyone, in English, the story of Max's encounter with the ridge air.

"He is beginning to tell the story," Solange whispered into Max's ear. "You had better listen so as to correct his usual exaggerations." She smiled and placed her hand on his.

Max felt a nervous tingle, like a schoolboy trying to get a date for the prom.

What's wrong with me? God, has it been so long?

Max left his hand in place until Solange let go to get her wine glass. Max did as well, and started to listen to the marvelous way Ditter told the account from his perspective. They would all laugh and smile at the same moments, and then Ditter asked Max to tell it from his side.

After a hearty onion soup and a puff pastry, the main course arrived at the table. Ditter looked at Max. "Elk. I shot this one myself."

"Nothing like a good hunt, Herr Ditter," Klaus responded, holding his glass up. The rest of the men at the table did the same. "To the elk that gave his life so that we could enjoy this dinner tonight."

A few glasses clinked. Max took another sip and put his glass down. "So, you like to hunt?" he asked Ditter.

"We all do." He gestured with his glass at the table. "Klaus there is a member of an exclusive hunting club in Austria."

"The Wehrs have been members there going on close to 150 years," Klaus said.

"We go there every year," Ditter said. "This year we hunted elk. Some years we hunt boar. Lots of fun!"

Hermann spoke as he dove into his meal. "If you are ever in these parts during hunting season you are more than welcome to join us. These old—"

"But wise!" said his father.

The table erupted in laughter.

"Yes, but wise men—" He slapped his father's back. "—can be a bore. It would be nice to have new stories around the fire."

"That is very generous of you. Thank you for the invitation." Max was starting to feel a bit tipsy and he knew he did not stand a chance staying sober at these altitudes with the locals, so he began to substitute the wine with water.

"So, tell us about flying off an aircraft carrier," said Eric.

"Most fun you can have with your clothes on."

The small crowd laughed once more.

"But it can be very challenging and downright frightening at times."

"Like when?" Solange asked.

Max took a breath and recalled one of his many nights on the aircraft carrier. "One particular night, a few months wet-behind-the-ears from carrier flight school, I was flying the F-18 Super Hornet from a land base to the carrier. It was a new moon so it was pitch dark and weather was rolling in.

I was a bit nervous to say the least, so I punched it all the way to the carrier, but the weather got there before I did. I was last in line to land. The minutes ticked by with each landing in front of me, and the weather really began to pick up. Finally, I was given clearance to land and bad luck decided to strike when a bird hit my canopy and shattered the glass. I couldn't see forward. So there I am, alone in pitch darkness in the middle of a storm with zero visibility, and I had to land on a moving postage-stamp-sized airport in the middle of the ocean. Worst part was that I was running out of fuel and the air tanker, the plane we use to refuel in the air, was also out of fuel. Poor judgment by me to say the least, to burn up most of my fuel on the way in," he reiterated. "So I had two choices. Land or ditch. Since I was so new to the program and ditching the very expensive plane would most likely ruin my career, I decided to land or die trying." Max took a sip of water.

"I guess it's just the way you think when you are young. Nothing can hurt you, so you're willing to take risks. Anyway, I call in my situation with the zero visibility and luckily for me my commanding officer was the LSO that night." He looked around the table and noticed that they had no clue what LSO was, so he quickly explained. "The LSO, Landing Signal Officer, is the man who helps you land by talking to you over the radio as one comes in for landing, also known as Paddles. So as I came in for my first attempt, the deck came up from a large ocean wave and he waved me off, telling me to go around once more because it was unsafe to land. Now, that did wonders to my confidence because I had maybe two go-rounds left before I'd have to ditch the plane. Now understand that the weather was bad, very bad, so ditching was out 'cause the odds of rescuing me in that weather would have been very low, not to say very dangerous for the rescue helicopter if they could find me to begin with."

The table was now quiet as everyone listened to Max's story.

"So here I come around once more and I tell them I can't see the ball once more. The balls are these lights that tell you if you are lined up with the runway. The LSO clears me, and with the kindest, most calming voice starts telling me to increase or decrease power. He leads me down. Now I am a few seconds from landing when a rogue wave hits the ship, sending the deck flying up. Neither the LSO, who was thrown off his feet, nor I had enough time to abort. So the ship's deck slams up into my plane, which is coming down, and sends the landing gear up through the fuselage. The plane's fuselage comes crashing down onto its belly and crushes the engine, sending dangerous hot shrapnel in all directions. The crew on the deck had the good fortune not to get hit and I was lucky that the plane got caught in one of the arresting wires—they are wires that lie across the deck, which the planes hook onto to stop them. Anyway, the force of the crash was so great that it knocked me out. The last thing I remembered that night was coming in those last seconds and going full throttle. Everything else was, and still is, a blank. The next thing I remember was opening my eyes in the hospital ward on the ship. To everyone's amazement, I was fine. Except the excruciating lower back pain that eventually went away through months of yoga and exercise. To this day I watch that landing—all landings are recorded—and thank my lucky stars."

The table was full of awestruck people who began to ask follow-up questions. Max answered as best as he could, using humor to tone down the event. Eventually Ditter noticed Max was getting flustered and took over the conversation with a few untold stories about flying the Storch in the desert. The conversation continued through the night. The subjects wandered from the steel business, in which each member of the family had a stake in, to the world economy, to selling either the ski trip or the Caribbean trip.

Dinner was delicious and ended with a wonderful apple tart dessert with vanilla ice cream. Max knew it was now his time. He had to make a decision, but his choice would be a difficult one. For one, he had to make the girl happy; on the other hand, he had to help his host.

In just the few hours Max had spent with Solange, he had gathered enough information to know what he might be getting himself into with her. She was a smart girl, and made her own way in the world. She didn't like to be told what to do, but did enjoy sharing what she was going to do. If Solange's grandparents were anything to go by, he knew that she would be honest and kind.

Ditter raised his glass and said, "It is time, my friends. We have a few choices from what I gather. So, which shall it be?" He looked directly at Max.

Max gathered his thoughts and stood up. Since his was the final word, he was going to make an impression. He stood behind Solange and placed one hand on her shoulder. The room grew quiet in anticipation of his choice.

"Well, as Ditter put it, we have a few choices, really two, the mountains or the ocean. So, which to choose? On one hand, we have the younger crowd with the sprit of adventure, ready to tackle what I love, which is the ocean." He began to walk around the table and stopped between Klaus and Hermann. "On the other hand, we have the older generation—with the exception of young Hermann, who for some reason likes old people."

The crowd laughed. Hermann smiled and shrugged once more.

"But even the elders are in a conundrum as to where to ski." He now walked toward Ditter. "Now, I have been given many offers, some just plain wrong—yes, Ditter, I am talking about you."

More laughter.

"Others a bit more enticing."

This time Hermann spoke. "Now that is not fair, little sister."

The women chuckled.

"All in all, each offer was enticing, to say the least. But I digress. I think you are all thinking about this the wrong way. You must think outside the box!" Max was getting ready to close. "So, with much thought I have come to a conclusion." Max dragged it out a bit more. "You are all hunters, adventurers, and looking for excitement in one form or another and what seems like a difficult answer is actually the easiest!"

Each person at the table began to smile, thinking that he or she had won.

"Now, let me understand: What I choose is final, correct? You will all go where I say?"

Ditter responded, "Yes, your choice is final."

"Well, I choose…" He paused for effect. "Neither."

The crowd looked at each other, not quite understanding the answer, but Max quickly jumped in to save the day. "I choose adventure! I choose…" He let it hang in the air. "Costa Rica!"

"What?" a few called out.

"I asked all of you specific questions and I came to the conclusion that none of you had ever been there. So, you have the warm waters of Central America, you also have the jungles, which provide many adventures, from white-water rafting to volcanoes. You have the Latin spice, which I am sure you will all enjoy, and you have the hunting."

"Hunting what?" Ditter asked.

"Big game fish."

"Oh, I like that," Klaus said. "And I am sure my boy would like to meet the local fauna."

The women chuckled at the playboy in the family.

"Well, Father knows best." Hermann smiled a wide grin.

Ditter was still a bit disappointed, but his wife was ecstatic and he gave in. "Fine, but I just want to make it clear that I will be fishing the whole time I am there." He slammed his palm on the table. "Costa Rica it is!"

The applause filled the room and Max took a slight bow.

"Time for after-dinner drinks! Everyone to the library!" Ditter was first up, followed by the rest of the group. Olga and Max were the last to leave the dining hall.

"That was brave, Mr. DuMonde, but well played. It seems that you are a very creative thinker. Here, come with me. I am going to pour you a well-deserved drink."

She grabbed Max by the arm and led him into the library where talk of setting up the trip was the topic at hand.

Another hour of drinking and planning finished the night. The crowd diminished as the guests turned in. Max had said his goodbyes to the locals, who left to go back to their homes on the mountain. He shook hands with the younger crowd as they went upstairs. Max looked around the room from the plush chair he now occupied. It was empty except for the people sitting around the glass coffee table. He took a quick look at his watch and made up his mind. Max placed his empty brandy glass on an antique side table. He slapped his thighs and looked up at Ditter. "I want to thank you for an entertaining night." He stood up. "But I am afraid I have to fly out tomorrow, so I need my rest."

"I hope we will see more of you in the future, Max," Ditter said as he shook Max's hand. "Here is my contact information. I will be leaving tomorrow, as well. I need to be at the house for the construction inspectors. Klaus was kind enough to let me fly with them to Zurich on his way back to Austria. If you need anything, just call me."

Max took Ditter's card. On the back, in pen, was written what looked like his personal phone number and address in Zurich. "Thank you, Ditter. Your hospitality sure helps in my decision to return," Max said with a smile aimed toward Solange. "I wish I could join your family in Costa Rica."

"Well, at least you will know where we will be come Christmastime."

He turned to find Klaus standing next to him and shook his cold hand. "Goodnight and thank you again for your suggestion. It will be fun hunting those big game fish," Klaus said, showing his yellow teeth.

"Here, let me walk you to the door," Solange said as she sidestepped around Klaus.

They both walked into the foyer where Solange left Max alone as she went into the coat closet to retrieve his coat and visor.

Max was first to break the silence as he adjusted the visor on his head. "Will you see me off tomorrow?"

"Of course. My grandfather and I will take you to the airport."

"Don't forget to write down your information so I can look you up during my stay in Geneva," Max said as she opened the front door.

"Don't worry, I'll come find you now that I know where you will be staying," she said. The cold night air hit him as he stepped out the door. He turned to face her and paused, trying to figure out what to do next. Max then leaned in to give her a kiss on the cheek.

He was not surprised when Solange turned her face toward him, making a friendly goodnight kiss into much more. The tip of her tongue softly caressed his lips, looking for a way in. Max, who had never been one to hold back, parted his lips slightly, allowing their tongues to touch each other for a brief moment, and then it was over. Max just stood in awe as he saw Solange looking at him with bedroom eyes and a mischievous smirk.

"Goodnight, Max. I'll see you tomorrow."

"Goodnight," he said after the heavy wooden door closed in front of him.

He turned around and removed a silver cigarette case from his inside coat pocket. He put a small Belmont cigarette in his mouth, lit it, and took a deep drag, letting out the sweet smoke into the crisp, cold mountain air. Max looked up at the night sky and stared at the countless stars above. He flipped up his coat collar, walked onto the main road, turned left, and headed toward his hotel in the center of town.

Max's room was small and decorated in late 1980's décor. It had a queen-sized bed taking up most of the real estate, and two nightstands with reading lights hanging from the walls. The bathroom was like any other, except for the fact that the shower lacked a curtain. Max locked the door behind him as he walked into the warm room, undressed down to his underwear briefs, did his bathroom duties, hung his dress uniform back in its garment bag, and slipped into bed.

Max looked at his father's diaries stacked on the small desk against the opposite wall, then at his Omega Speedmaster moon watch. He gave in to the fact that he was too tired to read, so he turned off the room lights. A small sliver of light from outside penetrated through the window curtain, cutting a strip of yellow across Max's chest. He stared at the light, thinking about Solange. She was a beautiful woman. Her long body wrapped in the tight wool dress showed off her thin, muscular frame, but Max could only think about the kiss. He shuddered with anticipation. It had been some time since he had had that feeling about a woman. Unfortunately, those few weeks of passion so many years ago had been erased by his second accident in the service.

Max thought back to the day of the accident. That he had survived it was a miracle in itself. It happened during his Navy SEAL training—a high-low jump, just as it was named for: jump high, then open the chute low. That night the jump was to start at 30,000 feet. Everything was running like clockwork until his chute deployed.

He looked up like he'd been taught, and saw that his parachute had tangled. The ocean was rising. He released the primary chute and the secondary chute began to deploy. Max looked up; the second canopy was almost full. *Come on open, open, open.* He looked down. Water.

His thoughts then drifted to his time at the hospital. He could have made friends with a few of the nurses, but the drugs left him sexually inactive and depressed. His physical therapy and follow-up surgeries didn't make his stay any more pleasant. The last surgery was the most important one. His accident had left him with countless injuries, but the brain swelling was the most dramatic. He had spent many weeks without part of his skull, wearing a protective helmet to avoid any accidental injury that would have left him brain dead. Then the day arrived when his head would look normal once more. The Navy doctors who had worked on him presented him with the incredibly hard and protective titanium skull plate that was to become part of him for the rest of his life.

The plastic surgeon was a talented man and had managed to keep his head scar hidden from the casual observer, which made Max's life easier. At the end of his hospital stay, Max walked away with titanium plates covering both his leg bones, his right arm, shoulder, and his head, earning him his new nickname with his younger brothers: Wolverine.

After the hospital and therapy, Max was given a desk job. The SEAL teams were not an option anymore, but going back to flying was, if he could pass the airman's physical—which he accomplished, but with a caveat: fighter jets were now excluded. He would never again be able to fly the jets he loved so much. But as one door closed, another opened. The Navy, in all its wisdom and some dumb luck thrown in for good measure, was kind enough to give him the opportunity to fly other types of aircraft. Max was not about to become a cargo pilot, so he researched the test pilot program, which eventually led him to the Condor. He called in favors and found himself a few months later as head test pilot for the program. Max became proficient and brought new insight into its multi-role function. The Navy agreed and moved the Condor program to the next phase of testing on the carriers.

The plane did its job. He had proved that the system worked better than the drone helicopters and planes the armed forces were deploying. But that night, the night of the Condor's aircraft carrier test phase. The firefight. The pain in his chest. He could not breathe...the deck was coming up fast. *I have to land! I can't see! I can't breathe!*

"NO!" Max sat straight up in the bed, breathing hard. It took him a few seconds to realize where he was.

His hands went to his chest.

Good, no bandages.

He swung his legs over the edge of the bed and felt the cold rug fibers as his feet touched the wall-to-wall carpeting. He looked at his watch and realized that he had been asleep for less than two hours, got up, and went to relieve himself in the bathroom. He felt the wall until his fingers found the wooden doorframe. He closed his right eye, reached around for the light switch, and turned on the fluorescent light.

The toilet finished its cycle. Max stood in front of the mirror. His eyes now adjusted to the light, he turned on the faucet, filled the glass cup beside the sink, and drank the cool, silky water. After two cups, he put his head into the sink and splashed water on his face, cooling himself down.

Max took a deep breath as he looked at the scars on his body reflected in the mirror. He touched the recent ones under his ribcage, then ran his finger over the bumpy, 10-inch scar that cut across his waistline, and underneath it, the empty space where he'd once had an appendix. Christ, his body had taken a beating over the years. Maybe it was time to find a new way of life—one that did not put him in harm's way all the time. He smiled at his reflection in the mirror and said, "Yeah, but then you would be one bored son of a bitch."

He turned his head as he heard a soft knock on the door. He reached behind the bathroom door to put on the hotel's complimentary bathrobe. It was after tying it up that he noticed it was too small for him.

Max rubbed his head and looked through the peephole, and saw Solange fidgeting on the other side. He unlocked and opened the room's door.

"Are you all right, Max?"

"Solange. Um. Hi. I guess. Is there anything wrong? Are you okay?" Max struggled to shake off his sleepiness.

"I have been standing—I mean, contemplating knocking on your door. Then I heard you shout, so I did not know whether to knock. So I waited, then I saw your light turn on, so I knocked." She smiled. "So here I am. Are you all right?"

"Yeah, it was nothing," he said, giving his new reoccurring nightmare a casual wave off.

"You sure? Here..." Solange stepped through the half-open door. "Let me make sure that you are," she said, walking into the room and stopping in front of the bed. She turned around, taking in the small room, her eyes finishing their search on Max. "That robe looks too small for you."

"Listen, Solange." Max walked toward her.

She put her hand up. "Max, I'm not the type of girl that just lets herself into a man's room in the middle of the night."

Yeah, but here you are....

"Don't look at me like that."

Oh, shit, don't blow it now.

"Don't stand there and tell me that you don't feel what I feel. I mean, I am 29 years old, and I know that this connection we have doesn't come along every day."

Well, maybe when I was in my 20s it did...what was her name? Oh, yeah, Dai—

"Max!" Solange said in a stern voice.

Max was tired and unable to control his expression. "Sorry, Solange, it's just that I'm still wondering if I'm having a dream." *That should do it.*

Solange squinted.

Good. It worked. At least, I think.

She stepped closer to him. "If this is a dream you had better kiss me before you wake up."

Yep, it worked.

"And if it's not a dream, don't you think..." Max stopped talking as Solange's lips once again touched his. He felt his body shiver with excitement as their lips separated. They looked at each other for a second.

"Lieutenant Commander, what am I going to do with you?"

The bright sliver of the morning sun inched its way up Max's body until reaching his closed eyelids. Max turned his head but it was all the incentive he needed to wake up. He opened his right eye and raised his arm, blocking the rest of the light.

What time is it?

Max turned and focused on the red numbers coming from the alarm clock next to the bed. *Ten.*

"Ten!" He sat up and looked at the sun pouring through an opening in the curtain. He rubbed his eyes.

Damn, I haven't overslept in…. Wait a minute.

His head turned to look at the empty bed. A note lay on the soft down pillow. Max reached across and read it.

> *Max,*
> *I had a wonderful night last night. I'm sorry that I left in a hurry, but I had a planned breakfast with my mother. I will see you at 11 for your send-off.*
> *Solange*

Max got to his feet and stretched. He then fell forward, catching himself with his hands as they hit the floor, and did his 100 push-ups, followed by 100 sit-ups. He turned on the television, setting the channel to the BBC, picked up the menu lying next to the television, looked over his breakfast choices, and called room service.

Twenty minutes had passed when he heard a knock on the door. "*Servir de chambre.*"

Max opened the door, thanked the waitress, and signed the bill as she placed the tray on the small desk next to the television. He thanked her once more and closed the door.

Better call the airport.

He rang up the operator and got hold of the airport tower. After a brief conversation on the weather conditions he thanked them for the update and finished his breakfast. He gathered his personal items, put them beside the door, looked at his watch and figured he had enough time to call Pierre.

"Pierre? *Bonjour*, it's Max. How are you?"

"Max, *bonjour*, good to hear from you. How was the flight into Geneva?"

"I decided to stay the morning in Courchevel but I'm on my way out now before the storm comes in."

There was a pause. "Watch out for the storms in the mountains. They have a way of sneaking up on you."

"No worries, Pierre. Are you getting set to fly down to Madrid?"

"Yes, I will be heading out in a few days." Pierre paused. "I still have some adjustments to work out on the 'Giro, then I'm off."

"Well, have a safe flight, and I'll see you in Madrid, on or about the 26th."

"You have a safe flight, as well. *Au revoir.*"

Max heard Pierre hang up, and then did, as well. After getting dressed in his flight outfit, he took a last look around the small room. Satisfied, he picked up his luggage, opened the door, and headed down the hallway.

• • •

The day was crisp and clear, but off in the horizon Max could see that the weather was changing. The four of them stood on the tarmac, facing the Storch. Max shook Ditter's hand.

"Thank you again, Ditter, and I hope to see you soon."

Ditter looked at Solange. "Make sure you make his stay in Geneva a pleasant one." He looked at Max. "And if you find the time, come visit us in Zurich. I will be there until Friday, then I come back here. Hermann will be flying us back here, then it's back to Austria for him. Klaus? You coming back any time soon?"

"No, we will have to leave the skiing for another time. Steel production never stops." Klaus shook Max's hand. "The invitation is always open for the hunt."

"I'll do my best to make it out there one day." Max turned to see Hermann talking on his cell phone by a Pilatus turbo prop plane. Hermann waved at Max and Max waved back.

Ditter slapped Max hard on the back. "You better get on with it, before that storm comes in."

Max turned once more to Solange. "I'll give you a call."

Solange just smiled and put her arm around her grandfather's waist. "Have a safe flight," she said as they turned and walked away.

Max picked up his satchel and garment bag as he walked to the Storch, which was in the process of being fueled by Jean-Luc.

"*Bonjour*. How is she doing, Jean-Luc?"

The kid looked down from the wing. "*Très bien*, topping off the tank now. I will charge your credit card, if that is fine."

"*Merci*. You finish up there while I do my preflight."

Jean-Luc nodded and went back to pumping.

Max opened the hatch and stowed his bags in the rear compartment. He pulled out his fuel tester and began his walk-around to go through his routine preflight check. He walked in front of the plane and, starting at a distance, approached the Storch while taking an overall view of the plane. The tires looked good, and the plane was level, with no apparent sagging, even with the kid's weight on the wing. He checked the engine, making sure that all was ready for flight and the fluid levels were topped off. Right as he was about to close the engine hatch, he noticed something odd. Someone had wiped the oil off the serial number embedded into the engine block. The metal just looked cleaner than the rest of the engine. He looked up at Jean-Luc and asked him if he had been in the engine compartment.

"*Oui*. I topped off the engine oil, and the rest was in perfect shape."

"Thanks for doing that."

"Wait a few minutes before you check the fuel for water." Jean-Luc made sure the fuel cap was on tight and then he stepped off the Storch's strut. "It was nice to meet you, Max."

"Next time I'm in the area I'll take you up for a spin."

"Great! Try to make it back before spring though. That's when I leave for the city."

"*Au revoir,* Jean-Luc." Max shook Jean-Luc's hand and watched as he jogged toward the idling fuel truck. Once the fuel hose had been coiled back into the truck, he climbed in, waved out the window, and drove away.

Max finished his preflight, checking the fuel for water and finding a couple of drops. He buttoned up his WWI canvas coat, folded the map of his route onto his kneeboard, and climbed into the cockpit.

"Clear!" Max yelled out the window and started up the Argus engine. The propeller spun until the engine caught and started popping as each cylinder ignited, sending out a puff of smoke with each turn of the propeller. The Storch rocked as the propeller gained speed and settled down after Max adjusted the rpms to a comfortable idle.

Max watched as the engine warmed up. He called the tower and they gave him a clearance for his VFR flight to Geneva, followed by the take-off clearance. He pushed the throttle forward and eased off the brakes, steering the Storch to line it up with the runway's center line. Max checked that the runway and airspace were clear, and looked at his VistaNav GPS screen, making sure it was on and active. Satisfied, he pushed the throttle forward and the Storch began to roll. Right before the plane hit the downhill portion of the runway it lifted up and gained altitude, avoiding the updraft that had caught him by surprise the day before.

Max turned to a north-northwest heading, following his predetermined route on his map and scrolling across his color portable GPS screen. He adjusted his engine speed, and cruised along at 80 knots, heading toward Geneva, 60 miles away.

7

Sunday was a quiet day in Geneva. Max had returned from the neighboring town of Annemasse, where he had tied down the Storch at the local airport. He had spent the early part of the morning trying to find a way to put the Storch in one of the hangars, protecting it from the second winter storm that was due later on in the day. After a short search he had come across an old man in the airport's café who happened to own a maintenance shop in one of the smaller hangars, and agreed to put the Storch inside for some cash. Once the plane was secure and behind closed doors, Max took the tram back to Geneva.

He strolled down the Quai du Mont Blanc, one of the famous streets in Geneva running alongside the lake with a view of Mount Blanc on a clear day. It was off this street that Max found a small watch shop. One particular watch, hidden in the corner of the store's window, caught his attention, and it ended up around his left wrist after some bargaining.

Max walked across the street to an old wooden bench next to the lakeside. He sat and spent some time mesmerized by the view in front of him. The sun's absence made the day gloomy at best, but the graceful Jet d'Etau, a water fountain jet that reached over 400 feet in height, formed a beautiful spectacle as the light winds pushed on the falling water. In the distance, the menacing weather front kept Mount Blanc hidden from sight. Max sat back and relaxed as he thought about the night's activities.

The cold breeze strengthened as the time went by and eventually nature blew a sudden gale that sent a shiver throughout his body. Max stood up from the cold park bench and stomped his numbing feet, trying to get some warm blood to circulate. His stomach, in turn, told him it was time to go eat.

He took note of the hour, and admired his new watch. It was a typical automatic Brietling with its chronograph and round slide ruler, the old-fashioned way to calculate everything from rate of climb and descent, to local currency exchange. Max knew how to use it, but his iPhone had the same applications, and just made the job of calculating less time-consuming. But if the iPhone were to fail, his new watch would do the job.

The extra gadget that made the watch stand out from the others was an Electronic Locator Transmitter embedded within the casing. The hidden antenna, when extended from the watch casing, would send out an emergency beacon. This beacon would alert a local rescue military team. In turn, the emergency battery would then give the rescue team 48 hours to find a downed pilot. Max covered the watch with his coat sleeve and began to walk the five blocks to his hotel.

The Hotel d'Angleterre was also located on the Quai du Mont Blanc overlooking the beautiful lake. He was unable to get a room with a lake view due to his last-minute reservation, but a view didn't matter with the current weather conditions.

The wind had grown to a steady gale by the second block. Max turned his face away from it and caught sight of a small, red neon light flickering down a narrow alleyway. Intrigued by the Indian Cuisine sign, he turned away from the cold windy street and picked up his pace in anticipation of a warm and spicy curry dish.

The restaurant was small and squeezed in between a Laundromat and an apparel store. Max pushed in the old glass-paneled door, and a bell announced his presence.

A small brown man popped up from behind the counter and hurried toward Max. "Welcome, my friend! I am Hamsa," the owner said in broken French.

"Do you speak English?" Max asked, knowing that Hamsa was trying to sound French.

"Oh, this is a good omen!" he said, this time in his native Indian-British accent. "To think that on our opening day..." His hands went up into the air. "...you are our first customer!" The man bowed and led Max to the best seat in the house.

"Since I am your first customer, then let me give you the honor of choosing my meal for tonight."

Hamsa's face lit up. "You will not be disappointed, or the meal is on the house!" Hamsa claimed as he hurried to the back, disappearing through a thin doorway covered in hanging beads. A few seconds passed and Hamsa's head popped out through the beads. "Spicy or mild?"

"However you take it."

"Oh...very brave man," he laughed. "Very brave, indeed." His head disappeared back into the kitchen.

Max ate like a king for the next two hours. At the end of the meal he invited his hosts for a toast. Hamsa brought out his whole family and introduced them. His wife and her mother did the cooking, and his two sons did the heavy labor, lifting crates of food and washing dishes. His only daughter ran the cash register.

Max held up his glass and gave his toast. "May you and your family prosper so that one day you can look back and know that you gave the people in this city happiness and a newfound taste."

The family raised their glasses, toasted, and after many kisses from the grandmother, Max was led out the door.

The cold night air hit his sweaty face as he turned to speak to Hamsa. "I have been around the world, Hamsa, and to be honest, there are only a few restaurants that have left an impression on me. Yours has just been added to my list. I will pass the word around. Here is my card if you ever need me, and thank you again." He patted Hamsa on the back and stepped out onto the snow-covered sidewalk.

Max walked down the empty white street and waved back once more at Hamsa's family. He smiled and looked up at the snowflakes glimmering past the streetlight. During his feast the snowfall had intensified, and in the two hours that had passed a two-inch blanket of snow had fallen. Max turned his gloved hand up and caught a few falling snowflakes. He pivoted his hand, catching the streetlight's reflection on the flakes, and marveled at their beauty and intricate simplicity.

Then it hit him.

Something was off.

The surrounding energy shifted. Max kept his gaze straight and normal, but his eyes darted back and forth, taking in the surroundings, trying to note what was out of place. He concentrated on his senses. He could hear the faint sound of traffic in the distance, and closer, the sound of a warehouse fan turning as the slight breeze pushed on its blades. Closer still was the crunching of snow packing down under each step of his size-12 boots.

The adrenaline in his system began to pump throughout his body, increasing his heart rate and alertness. He listened to his steps until his senses picked out the anomaly. It was the sound of an extra step, and then another. Max stopped and the steps got louder and quicker.

Without his military training, Max would have been lying on the sidewalk bleeding from his scalp, but the training took hold just as the long wooden stick came around to make contact with his head. Max dropped and spun. His hands went up, grabbing hold of the attacking arm and pulling it down to the ground. The assailant fell forward and rolled in the snow, getting up quicker than Max had expected. Max lifted his body into a fighting stance as he looked over his target. The man was stocky and small, the worst kind of person to fight if one is much taller.

"Give me your wallet," the stocky man yelled in French.

"Come get it, shorty," Max said. He could tell from the man's posture that he was not intimidated, and began to worry that the guy had more than just a stick in his possession.

"Your wallet, now, or you're dead." The man took a quick look around and crunched his body into a smaller target.

Okay...he's bluffing. Max raised his hand, extending his middle finger. "International sign for fuck you, pal."

The man jumped forward, wielding his stick up for a strike, but Max was a split second quicker. He flew forward, thrusting up both hands and grabbing the arm with his left hand, but this time he did not let go. He spun his body away from the attack, using the attacker's forward motion, arcing his right arm out and in front of him, giving him enough gyroscopic momentum to end up back to back. A split second later, Max stepped out with his right leg, away from the attacker's back, who was still traveling forward. Max reached up with his free right hand and grabbed hold of the hand holding the stick. Now with both his hands holding on to the assailant's wrist and hand, Max twisted his torso away and down.

Max's body movement turned the attacker's wrist in one flowing move, which, in turn, rotated the arm at the shoulder, making the ligaments stretch, then snap. The force of the rotation was so great that the assailant's body lifted in the air and somersaulted to the ground while he screamed in agony. The scream subsided when the attacker's skull struck the snow-laced pavement, knocking him unconscious.

Max pinned the man down and scanned for the possibility of another attack, but saw none. He removed the attacker's facemask to reveal a mid-30s, acne-scarred hoodlum. The man was missing a few teeth and smelled of liquor. Max felt for a pulse. Satisfied that he had not killed the attacker, he stood up, looked around once more, and then calmed his breathing.

The body left a smooth track on the street as Max dragged it to the nearest dumpster. The man groaned as Max put him on top of some garbage bags, using the surrounding cardboard to cover him from the weather.

He stepped out into the street and walked toward the lake, then noticed something he had missed earlier: There was a slim sheet of snow covering a black Range Rover, as opposed to the two inches of powder on all the other cars surrounding it.

Max kept on his path, inconspicuously eyeing the black SUV ahead and to the right of him. Then the truck shifted.

Shit, there's someone in the car.

Max picked up his pace and went down the street to join up with some other pedestrians heading home. After a short, quick walk, he took a glance behind him. The street was empty of traffic. Max sighed as he walked up the front steps of his hotel.

He pushed the revolving door and was greeted by the warm air within the hotel lobby. Even though he was now warm and safe, his body shook from the adrenaline rush. He stepped into the elevator and looked at the front entrance of the hotel, waiting to see if he had been followed, but no one else came in as the elevator doors closed.

Max made sure his door was locked and secure once in his room. He took a warm shower, then picked up his phone and called his unit in San Diego, California, before crawling into the cold bed. He called Elena Vittoria, a longtime friend of the family, and mother to his best friend, Val Vittoria. They had a nice conversation. She told Max to stay out of trouble and gave him Val's new contact information in Germany.

The heavy snowfall continued outside of the Hotel d'Angleterre, as the city woke up to over a foot of powder draped on the empty streets. Max's sticky eyes scanned the dark room while he searched with his left hand for the television remote control, and after a few seconds the flat-screen television against the plain white wall lit up to the BBC channel. Max hit the mute button, got up from bed, and fell back down onto the carpeted floor for his morning exercise. He was about finished when there was a knock at the door. Max did two more sit-ups before letting in his continental breakfast. After signing and giving the room service lady her tip, he sat down and ate in silence, thinking of what he would find at the bank.

The hotel lobby seemed crowded for such a gloomy day as he maneuvered around a few morning zombies toward the concierge desk. Max stood behind an elderly British couple and stepped forward as they moved aside, waiting as the concierge made his call. Max leaned his arms on the cold marble stand and stared.

"*Oui, monsieur?*" Lukas the concierge asked, clearly annoyed by Max's stare.

"Good morning...Lukas," Max said after he read the nametag.

"*Bonjour*, may I help you, sir?"

"I just wanted to thank you for your recommendation of that fantastic Indian restaurant." Max turned to the couple next to him. "By far the best I have ever had."

The concierge looked at Max in confusion.

"Andhra, off Quai du Mont Blanc." He turned once more to the couple. "You have to go; it's only a few blocks from the hotel. I highly recommend it."

The concierge looked at the couple and asked, "Would you like me to make reservations at—?"

"Andhra," Max filled in.

"Yes, Andhra."

The couple nodded and Lukas looked through a small book until an Andhra business card dropped down onto his desk. He picked it up and looked suspiciously at Max.

"Make one for me, as well. Room 312. DuMonde, for two...tomorrow night. Eight-thirty if they can fit me in," Max said as he pointed at the card.

Lukas looked down once more and gave in as he started to dial the number. Max winked at the couple, spun on his heel, and gingerly stepped through the revolving brass door.

After a short walk in the cold morning air he entered a small café across the street from what had been his father's bank. Max ordered a latté, sat down, and waited until the bank opened. It didn't take him long to lose himself just watching the slow progress of a city's inhabitants waking up to a blizzard.

Enough time had passed as Max lifted his cup one last time, emptying the remaining drops, when he caught a glimpse of a familiar SUV. It looked like the black Range Rover from last night, just parked there nice and clean, unlike the surrounding vehicles on the street. He put his cup down and headed out of the café, leaving a small tip in his wake.

Max walked outside and toward the SUV. He stopped on the sidewalk as a bus crossed his path, pushing a V-shaped plow that piled the snow onto the curb of the street. He stepped down onto the frozen asphalt and crossed it, then walked up to the front window of the SUV, peered inside, and found nothing unusual within. Max shook his head and chuckled at his paranoia. He turned around and headed to the bank entrance.

A few sleepy security guards on hand making their morning rounds were the only souls in the building as he entered. The inside hall was a renaissance room flanked by white, fluted Corinthian columns reaching up to a painted, tin-plate mosaic ceiling. There was a small sign halfway down the wide marble hall explaining that the safe deposit vault lay above the curving flight of stairs.

Max climbed the stairs, taking in the splendor of the riches of such a bank. He studied the paintings on the walls depicting scenes of a bygone era. Max looked around once at the top and saw a chest-high wooden counter. A thick Bavarian woman dressed in a suit sat behind it, eyeing Max as he approached.

"*Bonjour*," said Max.

"*Monsieur, bonjour*; *Je suis est* Emily. *Comment puis-je vous aider?*" The plump woman asked how she could be of help.

Max pulled out the safe deposit key from around his neck and handed it to Emily. "My father has passed away, and left me his possessions," he said in

English, paused, and reached in for his father's death certificate, last will and testament, and lawyer's papers. "Here are the papers that his lawyer gave me to present to the bank."

The lady took the papers, looked them over, and motioned for Max to have a seat. "I will just be a moment while I go and get the manager." Emily switched to English, "You can hold on to the key," then waddled away.

Max walked over to a modern carpeted square in the middle of the hallway and sat down in one of the four sleek, black, Herman Miller leather chairs and waited. He felt small and insignificant in the imposing hall and was relieved when he saw a tall, thin, lanky man thanking Emily, who went back behind the counter.

"Monsieur DuMonde, my name is Marc Hieldel. My assistant has informed me of your request." He bowed, then lifted his hand and ran it through his oily, thinning gray hair. "You will have to fill out some forms. If you will come with me I will assist you as best I can."

Max stood and followed the thin man a few yards down the hallway and into his office.

After paperwork shuffling and a few phone calls, Max signed off on the safe deposit key, but not before having his handprint and retina scanned and stored in the bank's computer system.

The bank manager stood up, pulled down on his suit jacket, said, "If you will follow me, I will take you to the safe depository," and led Max into the hallway.

Max nodded and followed in tow. At the end of the hallway was a stainless steel door surrounded by a beautifully carved, marbled artistry frame. Next to the door was a small screen perched on its own marble fluted column.

"Please touch the screen." Max did and the screen lit up with a number pad much like the one on his iPhone. "Now enter your number code." Max entered his armed service serial number. The door responded with a satisfying *swoosh* to reveal an inner safe room with a round vault door built into the opposite wall. A security guard stood behind a stainless steel table. Embedded in the table was an LCD screen. As Max stepped in front of the table, the door he had just walked through closed.

"Please place your hand on the screen."

Max took note that the security man had his palm resting on the automatic gun next to his right hip. Max put his hand on the screen and watched as the screen scanned his hand, flickered, then turned green.

A flat metallic rectangle, perched on a pole, emerged from inside the table. It stopped its ascent in front of Max's face. He heard a clicking noise and a small hatch opened in the center of the rectangle.

"Place your right eye in front of the screen and hold still."

A lens inside the hole rotated and adjusted its focus; it clicked and flashed. A small green light at the top corner of the rectangle lit up, then turned off. A second later the small hatch closed, and the whole contraption lowered itself back into the desk.

Cool.

A second after the latch closed Max heard the inner mechanisms of the vault to his left rotate and click through their predetermined combination. He could see the arm-sized bolts retract from the surrounding steel frame. There was a small hissing sound and the massive door began to open. Max followed the manager and security guard through the new opening and into a room made up entirely of stainless steel. The metallic walls were embedded with safe deposit boxes of all types and sizes all around them.

"As you can see, only one safe owner is allowed at a time. No one can come in or leave as long as the main vault remains open. Your father has requested that you now be the sole proprietor of the box. This box has been given a permanent status in our bank, and you can leave it to whomever you wish. As you can tell, this is one of our larger deposit boxes." The door to the box looked to be around two feet square. "Your key, please." The manager put out his pale-white, bony hand for Max's key. He then inserted it, along with the guard's key, each into separate locks. A screen the size of a postage stamp lit up in the middle of the box. "Please place your thumb on the screen."

Once more Max did as he was told. Much like the outside screen, it too turned green, which allowed the manager and security guard to turn the keys. The one-inch-thick metallic door was pulled open and revealed a fitted metal case inside.

"You must repeat the same procedure when you are done," the manager said as Max watched the guard slide a four-foot box out of the wall.

The manager closed the door and turned the keys. He handed one back to Max and the other to the security guard, who was wrestling the box onto a rolling table cart.

"Your key will open the box. If you need anything, I will be in the vault's foyer." The manager handed Max his business card, shook his hand, and walked away.

Max stared at the four-foot-long box on the table of the private room within the vault. As soon as the door was closed and locked behind him, a single pinpoint LED light from above illuminated the box. He took a deep breath and rotated the key. The lid popped open. It was hinged in the center and Max lifted it until it lay flat on itself. A sealed white envelope lay within the steel box on top of what looked like a folded, black canvas duffel bag. He took the letter out and opened it.

> *Dear Max,*
> *This is the final phase of our journey. I won't keep you waiting too much longer. Of all my stories that you have read, here is the physical proof. Do what you will with what you find. I have provided you with a duffel if you wish to take some things with you, but know that this place will be the safest for them. Inside this envelope you will find a key to my flat in Geneva. Here is where I would spend my winters. The location is ideal for winter skiing. Most slopes are but a drive away. Well, I will leave you now to your inheritance.*
> *God speed, Son.*
> *Love, your father,*
> *Thomas*

Max took out the key within the envelope. Wrapped around the key was a paper with some numbers typed on it, and a small message saying "security code and address." He committed the address and code to memory and put the key and paper in his pocket. He put the letter back in the envelope, then laid the envelope down on the table and reached into the box to pull out the duffel. Under it was a wooden box. He lifted its lid to find a custom-fitted gun box containing a blued suppressed .22 caliber pistol.

Along with the pistol was a cleaning kit, four loaded clips, and a box of .22 low-muzzle-velocity bullets. He knew the weapon well; he had shot a similar pistol while going through his SEAL training. It was one of the many guns with which Max had become an expert marksman. He liked the .22, called the Amphibian, because one could shoot it under water.

He took it out of its fitted box and checked to see if it was loaded. It wasn't. Max held the gun out and aimed down the weapon's sights. He looked it over and found no inscription on it, but he knew it was the CIA Hi Standard, model H-D Military, the model the Amphibian .22 was based on. Satisfied, he put it back in its box, took the gun box out and shoved it in the black duffel bag. Next he saw an old leather briefcase lying on its side. Max sifted through some of its folders. He pulled out one; its contents were written in German.

Max chuckled at his father's close call in the Colombian jungle, and put the file back in the briefcase, but he couldn't get it to close. He looked in once more and found that a roll of blue paper lay flat on the bottom of the case, pushing up the thick folder. He took it out and unrolled it on the table, and saw that it was a set of blueprints of a structure of some kind. He managed to close the briefcase and placed it in the duffel, along with the blueprints.

Max peered in once more. Inside was what looked like a canvas rifle case and three separate plastic tubes, each around eight inches in diameter. He first pulled out the rifle case, then the three plastic tubes, and unzipped the case to find what looked like a vintage shotgun.

The deep gray steel was beautifully carved in intricate scrollwork, but it was different from any other shotgun he had seen; this one had three barrels, along with an exposed hammer for each. He unlocked the breach and the gun barrels folded down, exposing the chambers. Max was surprised to see the chambers were smaller than the typical 12-gauge shell. He looked back in the case and pulled out one of two plastic boxes, opened it and read the caliber. "Hmm…45-70. Oh man, it's a hunting rifle! Damn, that caliber could take down an elephant," he mumbled.

He closed the breach and put the stock up to his shoulder. Its barrels were short, around a foot and a half in length, definitely made for close quarter work. The shoulder stock was attached to the rifle via brass plates. Upon closer inspection, he figured out that the stock could be removed, making the rifle much more compact to carry. The shoulder stock was made from a deep-mahogany-stained wood with six holes running down its spine. The holes were there to hold six of the massive, three-inch-long bullets, which he inserted into place. The other box contained the same caliber shell, but instead of bullets they were filled with buckshot. He played with the rifle, taking aim and getting used to its weight and balance. Satisfied, he put it back in its case, then slid it into the duffel along with the ammunition. Next, he picked up one of the plastic tubes and twisted its end cap until it opened.

An oil painting lay unrolled in front of Max. At the bottom right of the painting was the artist's name.

Van Gogh. Holy shit!

In the next tube was a Matisse and lastly a Renoir.

"You have to be shitting me," he said, almost aghast.

Max could not believe it. His father had mentioned in the journal that he had taken some paintings, but hadn't mentioned who the artists were. By Max's calculations, what he had in front of him had to be worth more than a hundred million dollars. He looked around his private room to see if anyone was there. Max half-expected to be hit on the head and wake up in an alley empty-handed. He took a deep breath and slid each painting back into its plastic tube.

You guys stay here until I figure out what to do with you.

Max put the tubes back in the box, but the last tube hit something inside. He tipped the steel box over and a leather box slid into sight. The box was black, about a foot by a foot in measurement, and contained seven small drawers. He pulled on the leather strap of the top drawer, and just stared at what lay within.

There was a polite knock on the door. Max swiveled in his chair as he took out the gun box from the duffel, then removed the .22 from it, slapped a loaded magazine into it, and pulled back on the action. "Yes?" he said, pointing the loaded .22 at the center of the door.

"Is everything all right in there?" the manager asked.

"I need another five minutes, if you don't mind," Max said, annoyed at the interruption.

"Yes, sir."

Max listened as the manager walked away. He looked back down at the treasure his father had left him, pondering what to do next. He saw a small velvet pouch in the top drawer, put the gun down on the table and took a few specimens from the top drawer and placed them into the pouch. The top two of the drawers glowed green in Max's eyes as the LED light shone off the hundreds of cut emeralds. The other five drawers contained a few hundred brilliant, cut diamonds. He grabbed three of the dime-sized rocks and put them inside the pouch.

"I hate to do this, but the rest of you will have to wait."

He pushed closed all the drawers and put it, along with the paintings, back in the safe deposit box, and locked it. Max placed the velvet pouch in his pants pocket, and tried to figure out where to put the loaded .22. To his surprise, the inside chest pocket of the WWI coat was a perfect fit for it. He zipped up the duffel bag and touched the call button on the wall. Both the manager and security guard stood outside the room as Max opened the door.

The safe deposit box was locked into its wall space as Max and the manager stepped back into the foyer and watched the round vault door close and lock in place after Max had his retina scanned once more. Max walked up to the steel entrance and input his code on the flat screen inside the foyer. The steel door clicked a few times and slid open. The security guard stepped behind his desk, hand on his holstered weapon, and watched as Max followed the manager back out into the hallway.

Behind them the steel door swooshed closed with a resounding thump.

"I trust all is well?" the manager asked as he shook Max's empty hand and took a quick glance at the long duffel Max now carried.

"Yes, all is well," Max nodded. "Thank you for your help."

"Welcome to Swiss Security Bank, Mr. DuMonde. I hope you have a pleasant week." The manager turned and walked away and into his office, leaving Max to find his own way out of the bank.

Max walked the short distance to his hotel. The street was now busy and he felt uneasy knowing that in a span of a few minutes he had become a multimillionaire. The feeling was uncomfortable; he wasn't ready for it. He reached the hotel entrance and pushed himself in past a few more tourists, and stopped in his tracks when he saw Solange standing at the front desk. He walked up to her and tapped her on her shoulder.

"You're early," he said.

Solange jumped. "You scared me." She regained her composure. "I am so happy to see you!" Solange's smile went away as she noticed something off about Max. "Is there something wrong? You look...different." She tilted her head.

Oh nothing, it's just that my father made me a multimillionaire.

"Did your father leave you something good?" she asked, poking him and looking down at the duffel bag. "What's this?" Her finger hit the hard metal of the gun Max was concealing.

"Nothing. Here, come with me."

"What the hell is that?" she angrily whispered as Max led her toward the elevator.

"Let's go up to my room, and I will explain," Max said as he walked into the opened elevator. "Well, you coming or what?"

Solange pouted for a moment, gave in, and then stepped into the elevator.

Max dried himself after a cool shower while he looked at Solange's naked, sculpted body lying on his hotel bed. She was sound asleep, her flat stomach rising and falling with each breath. Max blushed at the thought of the last two hours.

They had ridden up the elevator in total silence, and neither spoke until they had reached the room. It was Solange who broke the silence. It took Max a few moments to explain what had transpired at the bank. He didn't elaborate, but mentioned that he had the gun because of the diamonds and emeralds he was carrying. Max showed her the stones, which seemed to satisfy Solange, but kept the rest of his inheritance to himself.

Max also mentioned his father's flat, and she in turn told him that she had reserved a room at an exclusive spa up in the mountains. Max was taken aback by her forwardness, but accepted the invitation.

Solange turned over and stretched out.

"Well, hello there, sleepyhead," said Max.

Solange grabbed the pillow and threw it at him. "Leave me alone, I'm exhausted."

"That is the best compliment I have ever heard," Max said as he put on his black turtleneck. "I'm going to head on out to check out my father's place. After that I'll rent a car and pick you up here, if you'd like. Then we can head out to your apartment and then up to the spa."

"Go ahead and check out," Solange said as she slid out of bed, dragging the bed sheet along with her into the bathroom. "I'll go on to my flat and you can pick me up there. I would recommend you rent an SUV, or anything with four-wheel-drive for our trip up."

Max watched as she passed him, dropped the bed sheet, and stepped into the shower.

Oh, now, that's tempting....

Max had a hard choice to make. He was half dressed, and could either attack, or recharge his batteries for tonight. "Screw it," he said as he took his clothes off.

"Five forty-six, Rue Jean-Charles Amat," the taxi driver said as he pulled up in front of a three-story concrete wall. The wall at first looked out of place, flanked as it was by the original brownstone buildings. But an old 10-foot-high wooden door built to the left of a stainless steel garage door gave it a sense of class and respect to the surrounding structures. It was very modern-looking, yet its drab, naked concrete walls let the façade blend well among the other structures.

Max stepped up to the door and noticed that it was carved with Arabic motifs throughout. He inserted the key and rotated it. The door clicked open and a beeping sound began to pulse from inside the building. Max pushed the heavy wooden door inward, put his bags next to the entrance, and rushed to dial in the corresponding numbers to turn off the alarm. It did. He saw a light switch next to the alarm panel and flicked it on.

Inside, the building depicted the exact simplicity of what was perceived from the street. The interior structure was almost nonexistent with 10-foot-high glass panels giving the illusion of a floating ceiling. In the center of the site lay an interior courtyard, white with the night's snow cover. A tall, blue pine tree 15 feet in diameter encompassed the rest of the courtyard, its branches drooping down from the weight of the snow. Farther back, he could see another glass room with wooden stairs rising up to a second floor.

Max closed the door behind him, walked forward, and stepped into a small living area. Two black, mid-century, modern, low horizontal couches facing each other occupied the center of the room. In between them was a low glass table. Jutting out from the wall to his left were four glass shelves displaying archeological artifacts illuminated from above. The opposite concrete wall was naked, adding to the contemporary design of the room. Walking farther down, Max turned his gaze right, where he caught a glimpse of the front of a car. He walked toward the glass door, opened it and stepped in.

The far wall from the entrance to the garage had numerous early 1920s racing posters. The opposite wall was covered in wall-to-wall tool cabinets. Four wheels piled on top of each other took up the far right corner next to the stainless steel garage door. Lastly was the glass wall to his left, through which one could look out into the interior courtyard. Taking up the rest of the garage was a beautiful silver car.

Max walked around the car. He ran his gloved fingers along its body, and took note that the wheels were winter-studded snow tires. He looked up to see that the four wheels in the corner were regular all-weather tires. Max knew the car at first sight. It was a 1980s revolutionary machine called the Audi UR-Quattro. The car was built for rally racing in Europe and gained fame as it took many first place trophies throughout the racing circuits. One of the main reasons the car succeeded was its new—for the day—all-wheel-drive system, which enabled the car to race at high speeds through rain, snow, gravel, and whatever else nature threw its way, in full control. The Quattro kept traction on hazardous surfaces while others slipped, crashed, or had to slow down on the trail.

Max looked at the car. He noticed that it seemed shorter than he had remembered. After a closer inspection of the interior, Max smiled and patted the hood of what he knew was one of a few public rally models that Audi had developed for homologation, for group B rallying. Just 500 of these street-legal cars had been made for the unique individuals who could afford them. The main difference from the normal production model was that the rally cars were race models adorned with the odd extras that made them street legal to drive. The regular production models were much longer, allowing for two more passengers in the rear seats. The production cars were heavier due to the use of steel body parts instead of fiberglass, like that of the rally cars. The engines had some major differences as well, in which the rally engine was balanced for racing and had much more horsepower.

He found the car keys hanging on a small hook up on the wall beside the glass door. He took the keys, put them in his pocket, and thanked his father yet again.

Max took his time walking through the glass house. The kitchen, a dining table, bar and another modern sofa accompanied by a Le Corbusier ottoman were in the back. Against the far back concrete wall was a six-by-10-foot splotched painting flanked on both sides by a bookshelf with an impressive collection of books. Max recognized a few of the famous writers, like Steven Coonts, Steven King, Mark Frost, Mathew Reilly; and his favorite,

J.K. Rowling, the *Harry Potter* novelist. Each one had been autographed by the author. Better still was the artist's signature on the painting. Jackson Pollock. Max stood in front of the painting for a good 10 minutes studying the genius's work, which was now his, and shook his head in disbelief.

Up the stairs a simple, low, modern Scandinavian bed, a closet and master bath took up the upstairs area. The main attraction to the master bedroom was the Picasso on the wall. Max took some time to study it, as well. He turned and looked into the courtyard and its magnificent blue pine. Across from the pine, and above the garage, was what seemed to be an enclosed, domed observatory. Max slid the glass wall open and stepped out onto the balcony. Looking down, he could tell that he was walking on the roof of the hall that connected the front of the house with the kitchen and dining room.

Max watched his step as he walked through the fresh powder toward the two-story-high, snow-covered domed structure. The entrance door was made of solid steel, which took a bit of pull to get it open. He entered into a wall-to-wall, dark-wood-paneled circular room with shelving every other panel. On the shelves lay more books and an assortment of old astrological globes, armillaries, and fantastic mechanized orreries—small, movable, mechanical depictions of the solar system.

The middle of the room contained a beautiful 55-gallon drum-sized brass telescope fitted onto a plush leather wing chair. The chair tilted back along the angle of the scope, giving its user a more comfortable position for long periods of viewing. Max walked up to the telescope and noticed a joystick, keyboard, and screen on the right armrest of the chair. He moved it forward and the whole contraption followed. Max ducked under the telescope, made himself comfortable in the plush chair, and gave the room a onceover.

He stepped out of the observatory and walked back into the bedroom to spend some time rummaging through his father's belongings. Max then went down to the kitchen, took a quick inventory of what he needed for a three-day stay, and headed to the garage.

With the alarm reset and the door locked behind him, Max stepped outside, holding the black duffel bag in his right hand, and walked around to the driver's side of the Audi. Once inside, he wrapped a bicycle cable around the base of the seat and secured the duffel, preventing any opportunist from walking away with the triple barreled rifle and .22 caliber pistol.

Max adjusted his body into the leather Recarro racing seat, and checked to see that the engine had warmed. He clicked the seat belt, then pushed in the clutch pedal, revved up the engine, placed the car in first gear, and released the clutch. The Audi's four tires spun on the slippery ground and the car moved sideways before the tires found their grip in the packed snow and quickly accelerated away.

Max had a wide grin on his face as he pulled into a supermarket's parking lot. He found a parking space near the front entrance, revved the engine once more, then turned the ignition to off.

"Man, what a ride!" he said as the Audi's engine went quiet. Max grabbed his wallet and his iPhone that displayed a map of his surroundings, and walked toward the supermarket's front entrance. Ten minutes passed before Max gingerly stepped out of the supermarket, holding two brown paper bags. He went around to the rear of the Audi, opened the trunk, and put the bag with the champagne bottles securely between his two suitcases, closed the trunk and walked around to the driver's side door and noticed it was unlocked.

Didn't I lock the door?

He shrugged it off and placed the other bag, which had all the fruits, bread, cheese, and meats, on the small rear seat next to the locked duffel bag. Max typed in Solange's address, waited a few moments for directions, then pulled out of the parking lot and turned left onto the street.

• • •

Solange's flat lay within the early 19th-century block halfway down and in front of the empty parking space that he pulled into. The front spoiler pushed away the small snowdrift that the city's snowplow had left behind and bounced over the mound, conquering its slippery incline as the permanent four-wheel-drive system pushed the car through.

"Nice car. Where did you get it?" Solange asked as she pushed open her building's front door with her foot and dragged a small suitcase through the opening.

"Well, looks like you're ready to go." Max smiled up at her from the bottom of the steps. "Oh, yes, the Audi." He turned back to look at the car. "My father left it to me." He noticed the ice on the steps as he walked up to help Solange with her bag.

"Interesting. It looks like the Audi rally cars from the '80s." She stepped off the last step and giggled as Max almost lost his footing.

Max tried to play it off and answered her question with a question. "Yes, it is. How did you know that?" He walked to the passenger's door and opened it for Solange. Once she was in, he closed her door.

Max walked around the car, opened the driver's door, and sat in the warm car seat.

Solange looked at him and said, "Just because I'm a girl doesn't mean I'm clueless as to cars. That and the fact that my grandfather is a rally racing fanatic, taking me to the races when I was small, helped a little."

"All right, since you're the rally race expert," he said, buckling his seatbelt, "be my copilot and show me the way."

Solange pointed straight. "That-a-way, sir!" she said in a poor American accent.

Max grinned, put the car in gear, and accelerated through the snow bank and down the street.

A few blocks behind them the driver of a black Range Rover followed the flashing green dot on the passenger's laptop screen. The dot left the main city grid and appeared on the Swiss highway system. A man with a full arm cast sat in the back seat, listening intently to the conversation taking place within the Audi, now a mile away.

Max and Solange enjoyed the pristine scenery as they turned off the highway and onto the twisting mountain road, which led up to the spa. "Can you translate written German to English?" he said as he shifted gears around a sharp turn.

"Yes. Why?"

"Well, my father left me a briefcase full of what looks to be old Nazi documentation of some kind." Max downshifted yet again, accelerating to pass a slow-moving truck. "I was wondering if you could take a quick look at it and translate some of it for me so I could get an idea of what we're looking at."

"Sure. Where are the papers?"

"Here." Max dug into his pants pocket. "Take this key and open the lock on the black bag behind you. There's an old leather briefcase inside it."

Solange reached back behind her seat, unlocked the bag, and pulled out the leather briefcase.

"Okay, open it up and tell me what you find."

"Smells old," Solange said as she pulled out a thick paper document and dropped it on her lap. "It looks like a collection of letters and files." She flipped through them. "They are in chronological order." She stopped at one particular page. Her finger ran across the page as she translated, "Device for extermination of units." As she read her curious look got more serious. "These are plans and some designs for some sort of extermination machine. Says here that they accidentally ran into the technology while experimenting with new sources of magnetic and radio frequencies. They learned they could put a unit within the machine and disintegrate it, with no residue." She then realized what she was looking at. "I...I think this machine was going to be used for exterminations in the concentration camps." She paused, taken aback by the realization.

Solange shook her head and continued, trying to understand what was written on the faded pages. "But they ran into a power problem. It seems that it would have taken too much electricity and money to make it 'economically viable' with the ever-increasing cost of the war." She flipped through a few more pages. "Some of these letters and notes are written by a Dr. Kammler, who looks to have led this project. He found another use for the device and asked the High Command for funds and manpower to build a functional machine. He was denied the request. Then the tone changes." She flipped a few more pages. "It looks like he managed to get approval through other means, and began to receive funds and manpower from the concentration camps. There is this letter from Himmler stating that funding was approved and an unlimited amount of labor would be provided. It is dated 1942."

Solange turned over the letter and found a much thicker file. "Phoenix Project. Top secret." She turned the page. "It's a chapter reference, chapters one through six. Chapter one, introduction. Two, main descriptions and electrical outputs. Three, test and analyses. Four, research. Five, application, and six, final conclusions and results." She turned the page and sighed.

"What is it?" Max asked.

"It's the stamp on the page." She paused. "It is an eagle perched on top of a swastika. Below it reads 'top secret, eyes only' along with a date."

"Okay, what is the date?"

"Nineteen forty-four."

Max took a quick look at the stamp, then at her. "Well, let's start with chapter one."

"Let me read it, then I will summarize it for you. I think that will make it easier for both of us," she said as she flipped over to the next page.

Max took the Audi to the limit on a few curves, almost losing control a couple times, testing how and which way would be the best to drive in snowy conditions. Max found that by accelerating into a turn, the all-wheel-drive would spin the wheels, drifting the car sideways, which would line up with the road at the apex of the turn, allowing him to accelerate in a straight line.

Every now and then Max would look toward Solange, who was concentrating on the pages in front of her. She turned the last page of the report and looked into the briefcase once more and retrieved a black envelope sealed by another wax Nazi seal. The seal was unbroken.

"Should I open it?"

Max looked at the thick black envelope with the red wax seal. "Might as well."

Solange opened the envelope. The seal cracked, then crumbled as she pulled back the fold and took out a thin black notebook. Inside it were countless handwritten mathematical calculations and what looked like underlined numerical answers with dates and times.

"What, already?" Max asked.

Solange turned to face Max. "This is a joke, right?"

"What is a joke?"

"What I'm reading."

"I told you, my father left it to me. I don't know what it is."

"Well, if it is real, and if everything on the pages I have read so far is true, then the Nazis accidentally invented a..." She paused as she found the correct page on her lap. "...a dark gate. Yes, that's what they called it."

Max laughed. "A dark gate? What does that mean?"

"Well, it's described as a hole in a three-dimensional space, creating another infinite fourth dimension. What is strange is this." She held up the black notebook. "It is filled with codes, dates, numbers, and calculations. The calculations are the same throughout the book, they just have different inputs, dates, and what looks like radio frequency numbers. What is crazy though are the dates. They are all over the place: some are in the 1970s, then the '90s, others are decades from now, and then there is this one, which is the only one written in red."

"Okay. So what does it say?"

She looked up at Max. "It reads November 23, 2010."

Max eased off the accelerator as he turned to Solange. "Tomorrow? What else is in there?"

Solange looked back into the case and pulled out a thin blue hardcover book, which she began to leaf through. "Looks like some sort of sign-in log book." She sat still as she read the signatures on the page staring back at her. Her eyes grew wide with shock as she analyzed one particular signature.

"What is it?"

Solange spoke softly. "The signature under Doctor Kammler's."

"Well, whose is it?"

She looked up, and stared out the windshield as millions of snowflakes fell all around them. "It's my grandfather's."

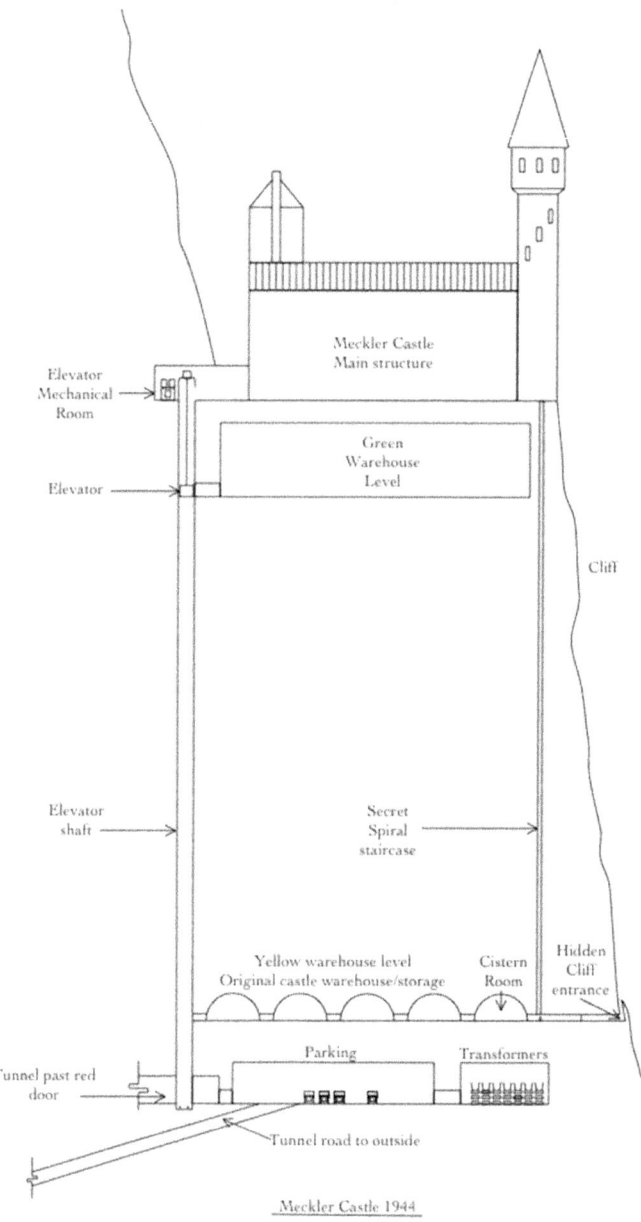

Meckler Castle 1944

8

Southeast Austria near the Swiss boarder, Winter, 1944

The wind speed coupled with the increasing snowfall made it difficult to concentrate on avoiding the 20-meter-tall pines flashing past the glass canopy of the Fi-156 Fieseler Storch observation-and-light-transport aircraft. The rudder swung left as the rest of the control surfaces flailed around, trying to keep the plane's wings level through the turn. At its controls, Lieutenant Ditter Von Ludger fought against the gusting winds as he banked hard once more, avoiding a majestic pine.

The SS general sitting in the back seat directed him to fly even lower, as the forward vision diminished. Ditter didn't like to be told how to fly, but the general was right. The night was fast approaching and the visibility quickly faded with every passing minute. By flying low he could keep an eye on the countless granite boulder tops peeking out through the snow-covered stream that followed the valley below. According to the general, this stream would eventually lead them to a runway.

"*Wir sind aus zehn kilometer,*" said his passenger.

"*Schließlich*, 10 kilometers left," Ditter whispered under his breath as he banked the Storch. It was dangerous for him to fly so low in an unknown area, but it was exhilarating at the same time.

He shivered as he adjusted his body on the seat. "*Verdamnt*, it is cold!" Ditter's body had yet to acclimate itself to the frigid Bavarian winters from his time serving in Africa and the Mediterranean. He had served with the Wüstennotstaffel rescue squadrons in the North African Theater and flown more than 100 wounded men, two at a time, throughout an intensive battle, before his injuries sustained in that encounter earned him the Knight's Cross. That accomplishment alone gave one of those wounded men, who was now his commander, the idea to reinstate him to another, and much safer, post.

Ditter had been sitting with a few Messerschmitt pilots earlier in the week when he saw the plane carrying his present passenger do a ground loop after its main gear had collapsed on landing. The SS passenger was physically shaken, but like most SS soldiers, he took it with a grunt and continued with his High Command orders.

He was at the wrong place at the wrong time when his commander volunteered him to fly the general the rest of the way. The flight itself wasn't the worry; it was the military non-disclosure papers he'd had to sign that concerned him most. The papers stated that he was to remain silent as to his destinations. He was not to solicit information to or from other officers, and he was to remain as the general's pilot until final release papers were signed from the High Command.

At worst, Ditter thought, he would have to put up with the Nazi general for a while; at best, he was not in the line of fire anymore. Either way, he was flying.

Ditter picked out the runway before the general called it out, but the increasing wind and low visibility would make landing a challenge. The Storch came down at a high rate of descent toward the snow-covered field. He began slipping the aircraft onto the short, snowy runway, knowing that the aircraft's small tail would make it difficult in the crosswind. It was the only fault the lieutenant found with his plane. Ditter flared out the plane at the last possible moment, and the skis attached to the landing gear sank into, then slid forward on the fresh, powdered snow, coming to a stop 25 meters from where the skids first touched the ground. Ditter took a moment to calm his nerves, relaxed his grip on the stick and looked around the makeshift runway.

The field he had landed on was the size of a typical football arena. To his left were a few tents, three troop transports, a bus, and what looked like a hangar. To his right were two fuel trucks, a Kubelwagen staff car, and another Storch tied down and covered in a camouflaged tarp.

A soldier on the ground directed them forward and to the right, between the two fuel trucks. Ditter pushed the throttle, giving just enough forward momentum to slide the plane into its designated tie-down area. The man in front of the plane crossed his wrist as the aircraft nestled itself neatly between the two trucks. Ditter pulled back on the throttle, which in turn stopped the plane's forward momentum, but kept the propeller lazily rotating at idle as he went over the shutdown checklist. He then pulled back on the red knob of the mixture control lever and starved the engine from the fuel supply. The engine complained as each cylinder went quiet and the two-meter-diameter, two-blade propeller gave one last turn before stopping in a vertical position. Ditter reached out, turned both magnetos to off, and then switched off the main battery supply.

"When can we depart?" the general asked as he removed his headset.

Ditter looked out through the generous glass canopy and sighed. The snowflakes began to fall at a greater rate as the cloud cover thickened. "Doesn't look good. We are lucky that we found this place when we did. Another 10 minutes and we would have spent the night camping."

"I didn't ask for a commentary, just an estimate of when we could head out," the general said with the usual arrogance of the Nazis who had crossed Ditter's path.

Asshole.

"Well, tomorrow if the weather lifts. If not, then we wait until it does."

"Fine. Grab your gear and come with me." It was an order, not a suggestion.

The mountain air was crisp and cold as the two of them crunched their way through the fresh snowfall to a waiting Kubelwagen staff car. Heavy with its new passengers, the rear wheels sank down and gripped the hard-packed snow as the car accelerated off the field and onto a winding gravel road that disappeared up into the mountain. Ditter looked back at his plane as they drove away, watching as the flight crew finished covering the Storch with a gray-and-white camouflage tarp.

Ditter was amazed at the thickness of the steel door they passed through. Beyond it lay a long, upslope concrete tunnel with a thick white line painted on both sides. The tunnel burrowed itself into the mountain as they passed the one-kilometer mark painted over the white lines. Ditter looked forward and saw no end to it. They sped up the tunnel, passing crews working in and out of secondary tunnels that ran parallel to the main one they now occupied. The first dozen tunnel doors were painted orange with a stenciled bomb painted on them, signifying that they were passing through the armory. New tunnels were being carved out of the granite rock two kilometers past the armory.

Ditter didn't see it at first until they had to stop and let a line of workers drag timber across the main tunnel. He noticed the workers were thin and almost non-human in appearance, and was shocked to realize this particular group was made up of children. He felt sick to his stomach when he saw an SS soldier shove a gun at one of the older ones, push her head forward, and laugh as they took turns shouting insults at them.

"Move faster, you worthless Jew!" said a towering blond soldier as he kicked a small child down. "Get up and move, I said!" His breath condensing in the cold tunnel made him look like an angry bull ready to attack.

The powerless child stood up and shuffled back into line.

Ditter was appalled. He had heard the rumors of Jewish labor camps, but he did not realize that children were being utilized as forced labor.

He knew better than to show any emotion as to what was occurring around him. Any hint would mean, in the eyes of the general sitting behind him, that he was disapproving of their leaders' orders. If this were to happen, he'd be digging tunnels alongside the prisoners.

The TEN KILOMETERS stencil passed by as the Kubelwagen pulled out of the concrete tunnel and up a small embankment, passed a guardrail, and parked in a designated parking space alongside a cargo truck and KDF wagon. Its engine hesitated to shut off as the driver removed the key from the ignition, and popped once more before it fell silent, allowing the tunnel's sounds to fill in the void. Ditter heard electrical transformers humming from a well-lit cavern to his right beyond the parking area. The sounds of impact hammers rumbled away into the tunnel they had just driven through.

Ditter stepped out of the car, grabbed his bag, and followed the general. *Jesus*....

He looked around at the massive room. He could clearly see the transformer station with its thick electrical wires strapped to the ceiling, running out of the cavern and radiating out like a spider's web. One of the wires provided power to fans the size of airplane propellers attached to steaming copper tubing mesh above his head. It was some sort of rudimentary heating system trying ineffectively to warm the air circulating through the tunnel system. To his left another massive, thick steel door stood ajar.

What is this place?

A lowly sergeant stood behind his metal desk and saluted at the sight of the general. He had the typical gray army uniform with a lime-green patch sewn above his upper left chest pocket.

"Heil Hitler!" the sergeant said as he stood stiff as a board, his right arm outstretched.

The general raised his right arm at the elbow. "Sergeant, this is my new pilot," he said in his deep, authoritative voice. He gave Ditter a quick look, took a moment, and seemed to have made up his mind. "See to it that he gets a blue pass, and a room for the night." He handed over his orders to the sergeant. The sergeant in turn handed him a multi-colored card on a lanyard, which he hung from his neck.

"Lieutenant," the general looked down at Ditter, "have me called when the weather clears." The general walked around the desk and through another steel doorframe. Beyond the frame lay another corridor and a red steel door flanked by two armed SS guards, who saluted. He waited as one of the guards opened the door marked RESTRICTED, RED PASS ONLY. Ditter got a glimpse beyond the door. The general purposely walked into a concrete semi-circular hall lined with gauges, tubing of different colors, and small control stations manned by people wearing white lab coats. The scene was abruptly cut off as the red door slid closed with a resounding thud.

Ditter looked down at the sergeant shuffling paper. "Excuse me, Sergeant, can you provide me with a car so I can run the corridor to the outside tomorrow morning?"

The sergeant spoke as he slid papers into a folder. "No need for that, Lieutenant. You'll be staying up in the castle. In one of the private suites." He looked up from his desk and gave Ditter a quick glance. "Consider yourself lucky that General Kammler cleared you. He usually puts his pilots down here in the tomb." The sergeant gave a small laugh. "Probably let you sleep up there due to the Knight's Cross." He briefly pointed to the black and silver cross pinned to the left chest pocket of Ditter's flight suit.

"What do you mean?" Ditter asked as he touched the cross.

"The general has great respect for men of combat, especially one who has earned the Knight's Cross." He sighed. "I have not been in combat, thus my position at this desk in the middle of this mountain."

"If you don't mind telling me..." Ditter looked around and at the two SS guards to see if they were listening. "Where are we? And what is this place?"

The sergeant's eyes narrowed. "That is classified information, Lieutenant, and if I were you, I'd not ask anybody else." The sergeant was all business again. "Sign here." Ditter pulled out his fountain pen and signed the thin blue book, taking up three lines with his elaborate signature below the general's signature. The sergeant gave him a nasty look. "Nice signature," he said sarcastically. "Here is your blue pass. Keep it with you at all times...if you do not wish to be shot." He paused and pointed to a truck-sized door opposite the red door. "Go to the top floor. Once there, you will be escorted to your room."

Ditter took the pass from the sergeant, thanked him, and walked past the desk and through the steel doorway. To his left were the two sentries guarding the red door. To the right of them was the elevator gate, but what caught his attention was the massive corridor he stood in. It stretched out into the distance for over a kilometer. He could see two Tiger tanks rumbling down the concrete tunnel, itself over 10 meters in height. He walked forward, looking on as the Tiger tanks turned and disappear from sight.

A third SS guard stepped out from the elevator and spoke, "Lieutenant, if you will come with me."

Ditter turned and followed the guard into the elevator.

• • •

The metal gate in front of him rattled as the elevator picked up speed. He grabbed hold of the windshield on a white-striped Kubelwagen occupying one-third of the space in the freight elevator. By its size, Ditter figured that even a truck could be lifted up to God knows where. He looked down; the floor was steel-plated with embedded rail tracks bisecting it.

As the elevator rose it passed a tunnel, its bare concrete walls painted with a horizontal yellow stripe. The SS guard to his right began to speak his rehearsed lines. "You are allowed in the white and blue zones in Meckler Castle." His accent was clearly Austrian. "The white zones are common areas, the blue zones are lower-ranking officer areas. You are not allowed in any other areas marked any other color. If you are found within a restricted area, you will be detained for questioning. The dining hall is a white zone. The officers' sitting hall, library, and upper sleeping quarters are blue level areas. You will take your meals between zero five hundred hours and zero seven hundred hours for breakfast, twelve hundred and fourteen hundred hours for lunch, and seventeen hundred to nineteen hundred hours for dinner. The officers' common area is open at all times." The guard looked him up and down, drawing a conclusion, and continued, "You are allowed outside in the hangar and runway until twenty one hundred hours. If you are found outside after that time you will be detained. You will have a telephone in your room, but you may not use the telephone for personal calls."

Runway?

The small, incandescent bulb dimly lit the elevator. Past the iron gate the rough-cut granite wall of the shaft flew on by as they rose up. The elevator operator slowed the lift down as they approached what looked like another level. A solid green door aligned with the elevator's gate as it stopped. The elevator operator slid the iron folding gate open and at the same time the green door split apart vertically, revealing an endless cavern cut into solid granite rock. Countless dim lights hung 20 meters above the floor, illuminating rows of crates stacked 10 meters high, which stretched away into the darkness.

A mechanic in a greasy jumpsuit, wearing a green-and-gray rectangular tag on his upper left chest, rushed in from the cavernous warehouse to retrieve the car inside the elevator. He jumped in and started the engine. The car popped at a lazy idle as the mechanic struggled to find first gear. After a few moments of crunching the transmission into gear, the car leaped forward, leaving a blue cloud of exhaust as it accelerated out of the elevator and into the maze of crates.

The elevator operator waved his hand, trying to dissipate the fumes as he reached up and pulled down on the upper half of the door. The lower half came up, meeting its twin in the middle. He then slid the elevator's gate closed, and shoved the control handle up. The elevator rattled once again as it climbed higher up the shaft. A few moments later they came to a shuddering stop. The SS guard slid open the metal gate, pushed aside a wide white door, and gestured to him. As soon as Ditter stepped out from the elevator, the gate shut behind him and the SS guard and his elevator were gone.

A corporal approached Ditter. "Sir, if you would come with me I will take you to your room."

Ditter nodded and follow in tow into Meckler Castle.

Ditter checked his aviator's watch: 10:30. All he wanted was to sleep, but he was kept awake by a constant, low humming noise that had begun a few minutes after dinner had been served. The monotone sound engulfed the castle, but all the officers around him seemed to ignore it.

After a hearty stew dinner, Ditter took it upon himself to go search out the secondary runway. The night had come quickly as the snowstorm engulfed the castle grounds. Once outside, the windswept virgin snow made it impossible to see farther than a few meters ahead. Ditter walked through the whiteout and startled an SS sentry making his rounds. The frozen soldier questioned him before pointing him in the right direction toward the far end of the castle.

Ditter would have felt more comfortable walking the small runway; that way, he would know what to expect if he were to return and land there at a later date. The runway lay parallel to the castle, and ran less than 100 meters south, where it ended at the cliff's edge. Ditter stood at the edge looking down into the abyss, its bottom obscured by the rising cloud cover below.

Satisfied, he turned back from the edge and walked north until he ran into what the sentry had told him would be the observatory tower. There was a corrugated, 10-meter-wide white metal door at its base, able to open wide enough to fit a plane through. It rattled as a strong gust blew against it. Ditter walked up to the man-sized door embedded within the larger structure and peeked through. Inside, a few mechanics pored over another Storch. Parked up against the far wall was the Kubelwagen that had ridden up the elevator with him earlier in the day. Next to it was another opening, its concrete sides painted green. Ditter assumed that the opening led to the cavernous warehouses he had caught glimpses of on his elevator ride.

Ditter pulled open the thin metal door and walked into the hangar. A gust of wind caught hold of the door and slammed it closed behind him, alerting the mechanics to his presence. The taller of the two mechanics looked over Ditter, who was still dressed in his flight suit and sporting the blue tag. He nodded, and asked him to grab a tool roll from the Kubelwagen against the far wall.

Ditter rummaged through the car and produced an oily canvas roll, heavy with tools, and walked to the Storch.

"*Danka*. Can you do me a favor and put these in the car?" The mechanic looked at his watch after handing Ditter two heavy parachutes. "It's 10 till. Better get going, Lieutenant, or you will get shot." Both mechanics laughed.

Ditter gave them a half-smile and walked away, parachutes in hand. He placed them in the car's back seat, took one more look around and hurried out the hangar and back to the castle to get some much-needed rest.

• • •

Ditter reached out and turned on the nightstand light. He got up from his bed and walked up to the dark-stained, wood-paneled wall and put his ear to it.

Where is that noise coming from? Better yet, when will it stop?

He moved along the cold wall, listening as the humming intensified the closer he got to the armoire. He stopped when he felt a cool, faint breeze escaping from one of the joints in the wall.

Looks like a hidden door.

Ditter spent the next few minutes working out the problem of how to open it, but it was a futile attempt, so he walked back toward his bed and fell face first into the mattress. The bed felt wonderful as he adjusted his body into the plush mattress. He rolled over and put the pillow over his head, trying to block out the humming, but to no avail. Defeated and tired from his trip, he gave in.

I am just going to have to live with it.

He reached over to the lamp jutting out from the elaborately carved wood wall, felt around for the switch, and pushed it.

The constant humming sound increased in decibels as a clicking and scraping sound resounded through the room. He took the pillow off his face, lifted his head, and looked at the armoire. The room, which was still lit from the weak bulb nestled within the metal arm lamp, got colder as stale air entered from a dark, ominous, rectangular hole where part of the wood-paneled wall once stood. It took him a few moments to register that the opening was a doorway. He looked to his left and discovered the wood knob now embedded within the decorative scrollwork carved in the wall. He ran his fingers over the switch and looked back at the ominous black hole a meter from the foot of his bed. Brushing aside the childhood fear that something might jump out of the hole, he got off the bed and walked to the opening. He peeked inside it, trying to adjust his eyes to the darkness within, and managed to make out the shapes of steps leading downward.

The tight, cold, musty passage looked to have not been used in years. Ditter decided to risk his little curiosity, and got redressed into his one-piece winter flight suit. He looked twice at the blue tag and decided to take it with him. He'd left his torch inside the Storch, but his American Zippo lighter was full of fuel, so that became his source of light as he stepped through the opening.

Ditter saw a lever to his left inside the passage. It was embedded into the cold concrete wall just past the opening. He pushed it up and the hidden wood panel slid closed next to him. Ditter took a moment to study the contraption. Satisfied that it would reopen if he pulled on it, he stepped deeper into the tunnel. The thin, claustrophobic hall turned 90 degrees right and then went on down, and turned once more into a gentle right-hand curve. Ditter managed the uneven steps and went down deeper into the structure, his lighter's weak flame only illuminating a meter of the passage in front of him at a time.

He navigated through the ever-thinning tunnel and squeezed his body through a narrow opening into a two-person-wide space. He moved his lighter around the space, illuminating the enclave, and noticed a semi-circular groove carved into the stone floor. A meter and a half above it and to the right was a rectangular metal door the size of a five-mark banknote. He reached up, unlocked the latch, and swung it open. Two rays of light shot through the small openings in the wall. Ditter looked through and stared into the library that was next to the sitting area, where earlier in the night he had leafed through a *National Geographic* magazine after dinner.

He deduced from his narrow and limited view that he was close to the gray-marbled fireplace opposite the entrance to the room. He looked around the best he could and held his breath, trying to listen for human sounds. The room seemed empty, so he closed the small opening. Two steps forward he found a lever within an indentation in the wall. He studied it, and guessed as to its function after noticing the odd spacing of the joints on the wall. He wrapped his gloved hand on the lever, and with some effort, pulled it out and away.

Clunk.

Click, click, click.

One of two Doric columns in the library that flanked the right side of the fireplace mantel swung inward, making a crunching sound as its metallic wheels rotated over some loose gravel in the groove of the floor. A moment later, Ditter emerged into the library. He looked around, and to his relief, the room was empty. One of the mantel's surface decorations had tilted out from its perch, revealing the mechanism to open the secret hatch from within the library. Ditter looked around the circular library. It was two stories tall, ending in a wagon-wheel rafter ceiling. A crystal chandelier hung from the center, hovering parallel to the upper balcony floor. The walls were lined with leather-bound books of all sizes; some old, others looked relatively new. There were eight leather high-back chairs facing each other and corralling a knee-high circular table in the center of the room. Ditter walked to one of the chairs in which someone had left an English version of a *Life* magazine. He picked it up, looked at it, then folded it into his chest map-pocket on the flight suit for some late-night reading. Ditter gave the room a quick last look and slipped back into the fireplace. Moments later, and back in the secret tunnel, the column ground back into place with a resounding thump, sealing Ditter back into the secret tunnel system.

The tunnel now split in two. To Ditter's left it led to another peephole, which gave an overall glance at the Great Room. Its high ceiling and dull granite walls absorbed what little light came from the clear glass sconces along both its sidewalls. The room was devoid of furniture, save for the crystal chandeliers that hung in the darkness of the rafters above the marbled floors, giving the castle an eerily abandoned feeling. To his right the tunnel led to two more peepholes and secret doors, one each for the dining hall and kitchen, where the tunnel system abruptly ended.

Disappointed at the stale outcome of his adventure, he went back up the tunnel, passed the hidden dining room and tripped over an uneven floor cobblestone, slamming into the opposite wall. As he pushed off the wall he felt it shift slightly.

What is this?

Ditter studied the wall in the dim light. It was different from the surrounding stone in that it was smooth. He crouched down and ran his hand on the floor over the raised stone, studied it for a moment, looked back at the smooth wall, and then pushed down on it with the palm of his hand. The cobblestone gave way and slid into the floor a few millimeters before springing back, but nothing happened. He then placed his boot on the stone and pushed down with greater force. The stone slid back into the floor and gave a resounding *click*. A half a second later the smooth wall slid into the rock to reveal yet another tunnel leading down into darkness.

The new tunnel's granite walls were rough and cut in a semi-circular arch, a few centimeters higher than him, and three times as wide as the previous passage. Ditter counted his strides as he headed down. It was built on a downslope and the farther he went, the colder it became.

Two hundred sixty steps later the weak flame from the Zippo illuminated evidence of a change ahead. He was at the end of the tunnel looking down at a circular flight of stairs cut into the granite. He noted the time and stepped down.

Five minutes later there was no end in sight. He looked back up, then made up his mind to keep on going. It took another 10 minutes before he stepped out off the claustrophobic spiral staircase and into another tunnel running left-to-right of his position. He took two deep breaths, relieved to be out of the stairway, and looked around. To his left he could see a wooden door, and to his right an ominous steel door. He chose the wooden door.

It was unlocked. Ditter unlatched it and pushed. A cold breeze blew past him and into the hall, replacing the stale air of the tunnel. He moved forward, and after a dozen steps, the tunnel opened onto a precarious ledge. The entrance to the tunnel from the outside was well hidden within a massive vertical crack on the cliff face. A thin path on his left disappeared into the thick cloud cover. From what he could see of the path, it was carved out of the rock face. Ditter put his back to the cliff wall and sidestepped down the path, where he came upon an old pulley mechanism. Taking in his surroundings and calculating his 15-minute descent, Ditter figured that he must be a few hundred meters below the castle's perch. The falling snow and cloud cover obscured everything else around him beyond the pulleys. Ditter, not wanting to risk slipping and falling to his death, decided to head back toward the entrance into the mountain.

He began to think about the pulley system and figured that it must have been a way to transport goods from below, although that spiral climb must have been hell on the castle's workforce carrying whatever was needed up top. He closed the wooden door behind him, passed the spiral staircase entrance on his right, and went to the steel door. Its rusty surface looked haunting in the semi-darkness. He put his ear to it, hearing the ever-present humming sound that now seemed to engulf the whole mountain. The door didn't have a handle, but next to it was a lever that jutted out from the rough-cut granite wall. He pushed it down and part of the steel door swung in.

Ditter was taken aback by the pungent smell of formaldehyde. He covered his nose with his wool scarf, turned off his lighter, and peeked through the opening. What lay in front of him looked much like the tunnels on the mountain roads back home, but this one was four car widths wider and stretched out roughly a football pitch in length. He scrunched down, squeezing himself through the one-meter-square opening, and stepped down onto a metal grate floor. The tunnel had the same lighting fixtures as the green warehouse. Below him the lights, and mirrored on both sides of him, dozens of evenly spaced square concrete cisterns, walked down toward the far end of the room. Ditter turned back to see that the opening he had squeezed through was part of a wall lined in steel panels. He looked around for some sort of mechanism to open the hatch if he were to close it, but found none, so he left it open and approached one of the cisterns.

It, along with the next dozen, was empty. Ditter walked up to the next one and froze as he made eye contact with a man submerged in a smoky liquid. It took him a few seconds to realize what he was looking at, and he was sickened by the number of human body parts floating around the severed head. He looked up and counted at least 40 more cisterns. Each looked to be filled with the foul-smelling liquid. A few seconds had passed after the gruesome discovery when the whine of dozens of electric motors spinning filled the space.

Ditter looked up at the ceiling; it was covered with manhole-sized openings. Inside them fans began turning. He felt the rush of fresh air coming from below him through the iron grate floor. It was an air-circulating system, keeping the room safe from excess fumes.

As the air-circulating system picked up speed he heard a metallic creak behind him.

"*Scheissen!*" Ditter grumbled as he sprinted toward the opening.

The pressure within the room was changing and was forcing closed the hatch he had used to gain access into it. Ditter could see the metal door slowly rotate on its hinges. He dove the last few meters, his hands outstretched, trying hard to reach the edge of the opening. But it was too late, and with a resounding thud, Ditter slid hard into the steel wall, locked out of his exit.

He desperately felt around the door for a latch or switch, trying to move the exposed rivets, but the ones he touched stayed in place. He stepped back from the wall, and looked it over once more.

"Idiot," he muttered.

The only way out beckoned from the other side of the room. Ditter turned, took a deep breath of the semi-clean air, and walked down the long corridor, catching glimpses of severed arms, legs, torsos, and the occasional half a face looking back at him. After the 20th cistern, he just focused on the door at the end of the corridor, trying hard to keep his eyes from wandering. He stood for a couple of tense seconds in front of a red door wide enough to drive a car through, before reaching out and turning the metal door handle. The door opened a few centimeters. Ditter took a peek at what lay on the other side.

It was yet another tunnel, taller and wider than the one he now occupied, but it looked familiar. The tunnel was well lit and its curved, bare concrete structure reached all the way down to the smooth concrete floor, which was lined with a rail track. It had a yellow stripe painted on its walls. Ditter figured it was most likely the first tunnel he had passed on the elevator ride up to the castle.

He stepped through and closed the red door to the cistern warehouse. Above the door the number 5 was stenciled in white paint. The tunnel ended to his right, so he turned left. His footsteps amplified, echoing off the walls as he walked through the tunnel. Every hundred strides he would come across a yellow steel door. The numbers stenciled above the doors in white paint receded in order. As Ditter approached each door, he would open it and peek inside. Warehouses 4, 3, and 2 were storage caverns piled to the ceiling in boxes and crates. The contents within the boxes were written on the sides. Warehouse 4 and 3 contained canned food; warehouse 2 had clothing, shoes, and the like.

Ditter stepped back out from warehouse 2 and looked down the tunnel. In the distance he could now see part of what looked like the elevator that had taken him up to the castle.

How the hell am I going to get back up without them taking me in for questioning?

Between him and the elevator was another warehouse carved out of the solid granite, the number 1 stenciled above the frame. If logic served right, it was the last storage cavern before the elevator. He was cautious since its door was open, and he could hear men hammering and dragging objects within. Ditter sidestepped inside and maneuvered around rows of trucks, Volkswagens, and BMW sidecar motorcycles arranged in single file. He took position behind a Schwimmwagen (an amphibious, Volkswagen-based four-wheel-drive car), and watched as a few men in overalls, sporting yellow-and-gray tags on their chests, unloaded crates from a forklift onto the floor.

A yell from afar caught his attention, followed by the sound of crates falling, which led to a sudden and deadly explosion. Everything happened at once—an alarm sounded, red lights began to strobe through the dense black smoke, and he heard yelling and the screams of an injured man. Ditter ran toward the fire and found five men battling it with metal fire extinguishers. One man dropped his empty extinguisher and ran past Ditter toward a fire hose next to the entrance. Ditter stepped behind him and helped unroll the hose. He stood by the valve and ordered the man to stretch the hose out toward the fire.

"Turn it on!" the man yelled as he grabbed hold of the spigot.

Ditter turned the valve to open, and the onrush of water made the hose rigid as it flowed through and out the nozzle.

Another man jumped in and helped control the nozzle, sending water out at a phenomenal rate. The two of them manhandled the hose as they started to move side to side, spraying the fire. Ditter walked forward to see how else he could help, just as an onslaught of armed SS soldiers came in from the main tunnel. A major leading the troops ran to Ditter and asked him what had happened.

Before Ditter could answer, he was looking down the barrel of the major's nine-millimeter side arm.

"Halt! You are not cleared for this area. What are you doing here?"

Ahhhh...how do I explain this?

"Sergeant, sequester this man!"

The storm troopers surrounded Ditter, MP 40 machine guns raised at the ready, when the concussion and heat from a secondary explosion engulfed them. They all scattered from the incoming flames. Ditter ran for the entrance and dived as a wall of fire chased after him.

"Don't shoot!" Ditter stepped out from behind the door.

The major put out flames on his uniform's sleeve, looked at Ditter, and raised his weapon. Ditter raised his arms in response. Then the major yelled at his men, "That's the saboteur, shoot him!"

Ditter was in shock as the first bullet grazed his shoulder. He quickly came to his senses and dove sideways away from the warehouse entrance and into the main tunnel. Another barrage of bullets followed, smacking into the far concrete wall behind where Ditter had stood. He rolled, and once on his feet, began to run away from certain death. As he rounded the curved tunnel, the elevator came into view.

Ditter saw the SS elevator guard whip up his MP 40 at the sight of the blue tag, but he was not quick enough. Ditter jumped forward and tackled the soldier, knocking him off his feet. They both fell. The SS soldier's head impacted the bumper of a Kubelwagen that was parked inside the elevator, breaking his neck in the process.

"*Scheissen!*" Ditter exhaled as he felt for a pulse and found none. He turned his head as rounds of bullets flew past him, ricocheting off the elevator's steel mesh walls. As quick as he could he shut the gate and reached out for the elevator lever and pushed it up, but not before another round of bullets came at him, bouncing around the elevator's inner metal structure. One of the bullets found its mark, finishing its path in Ditter's forearm.

Ditter winced and grabbed his forearm as the elevator shuddered and climbed up the shaft. He stood up and looked around, trying to figure out what to do next, when his eyes fell upon the Kubelwagen. On closer inspection, he noticed that it was the same car that had been in the hangar earlier in the night. This gave him an idea.

The first part of his plan failed as he stopped the elevator a bit late. The elevator was halfway between the opening of the green warehouse door. He slammed the control handle down and the elevator jolted to a stop as the power to it was shut down. Now he could hear commotion below as SS guards made their way up to him through the auxiliary elevator shaft ladder.

Ditter considered his options once more, and deterred from the original plan. He managed to force open the gate, jumped down onto the shaft edge, and pulled up the green warehouse door as a few more bullets ricocheted off the metal grate floor above his head. He climbed back up into the elevator, jumped in the car, and started the engine. Reaching up, he unhooked the soft top and pushed the hinged windshield forward, put the car in first gear, and floored the accelerator.

The metal windshield snapped right off as the Kubelwagen squeezed through the gap left between the elevator floor and the opening of the warehouse entrance, and fell six feet down. The front of the car took the brunt of the fall, crushing on impact. To Ditter's good fortune, he was still able to steer the car. He sped off into the maze of crates and toward a ramp at the far end of the green warehouse.

Ditter kept the accelerator floored, constantly looking back at the hunting party that was sure to come. He turned the car right, sliding it sideways on the smooth concrete floor, then shot up the ramped path where he flew the car through the truck-sized open warehouse door that led into the hangar. He stopped the car next to the Storch the mechanics had been working on a few hours before, jumped out, and ran to the main hangar control panel on the far wall and pressed the button that opened the hangar to the outside. The metal door squeaked, and inch-by-inch began to slide open. Ditter ran back across the hangar and jumped in the Storch, said a small prayer, closed his eyes, and hit the starter button. The propeller turned and the cylinders popped as the engine came to life. He laughed out loud as he moved the throttle forward. The plane shuddered, then began to roll toward the receding hangar door as he increased the throttle to take-off speed.

His grin faded as the front windscreen erupted under a hail of bullets that tore through the plane. Two of the bullets found Ditter. He winced in pain from his shoulder and thigh wounds as he felt the plane pick up forward speed, and went to push the throttle to full, but the whole throttle lever was missing.

He looked back into the hangar and knew he had one option left as he reached to open the hatch.

The plane gained speed and the tail rose as the sergeant commanding the barrage of bullets screamed to his men, "Destroy the plane!"

The bullets ripped through the cabin, wings, and fuel tanks. The heat from them ignited the fuel just as the plane left the ground.

The SS guards scattered as the fiery plane dove into the crowd of soldiers and exploded. Those few SS guards who were spared the misfortune of their comrades managed to catch a glimpse of a Kubelwagen crashing through the debris, wheels on fire, heading toward the edge of the runway. Two guards got to their knees and opened fire on the burning vehicle as it went over the edge of the runway into the dark abyss below.

Ditter knew they would be looking for his body once the weather cleared, so he folded up the parachute and threw it back into its pack. He couldn't help but laugh from the adrenaline rush he was feeling. He had no chance to escape in the Storch as it was being shot to pieces, so he had jumped out and run back toward the car, all under a hail of bullets. By some miracle he hadn't been hit in his mad dash. He dove and landed inside the car, strapping on one of the parachutes that he had dropped on the passenger's seat earlier in the night, all while driving through the hangar door and toward the flaming Storch as it crashed down into the SS guards. He knew it would be risky to jump from the cliff's edge, not knowing its exact height, but with the help of the car he figured he could manage to put enough distance between him and the rock wall, allowing the parachute to fully deploy...hopefully, before meeting the ground.

Ditter looked up into the thick cloud cover, listening for danger, but all he could hear was the wind blowing up and around him. He unzipped his winter flight suit and studied his wounds. The idea of surviving the following days seemed almost impossible. Ditter took out his utility knife and cut some of the parachute silk to dress his wounds. Once done, he zipped up, shouldered the parachute on his good shoulder, looked down at his compass, and began to limp south toward what he hoped would be the Swiss border.

9

Swiss Alps

———

Max awoke, shaking his head clear, trying to remember what had stirred him from his sleep. He sat up and checked out the room. His eyes adjusted as he stared out the balcony window from the comfort of the hotel room bed. He swung his legs over the side of the bed and sat in silence as he rubbed his hands on his face. It was 5:20 in the morning and he knew himself well enough to know that it would be futile to try to go back to sleep, so he slid off the bed, lay face down on the carpeted floor, and performed his morning exercises. Once finished he found his pants and boots, put them on, and walked to the balcony door, grabbing his aviator coat from the desk chair against the wall before stepping out into the cold. He pulled out his Zippo lighter and lit the small Belmont cigarette he had put in his mouth, took a long drag and looked back through the balcony at the silhouette of Solange's naked body inside their hotel room at the spa.

Outside, the floodlights cut through the dark, stormy dawn. Max wiped the inches of accumulated snow off the balcony railing and leaned back against the outside wall, staring at the millions of snowflakes falling from high above his perch. Individual ones glimmered as they crossed the beam of one of the hotel's lights and disappeared down the steep slope and over the cliff below his second-story balcony.

He thought about the briefcase and its contents. Was it just a theory... or had the Nazis actually built such a device? Had his father ever looked into it? What about Ditter's signature? It had him listed there as a pilot for the doctor. Either way, he knew that he had to present the case to his superiors. It was most likely a last-ditch attempt to try to turn the tide of the Second World War in one form or another, but the science behind it seemed something the United States might have an interest in, and he knew the right persons to give the information to: the Francis brothers—little mousy geniuses he'd met and befriended in Annapolis who now worked in Naval Intelligence.

Besides, they owed him one since it was Max and Val who'd finally found them the twin girls that took their virginity. Max gave a quick laugh at the thought of that night.

His first priority, though, was 20 feet away, and he figured that adding a few more days to something that had been hidden for over 60 years would not make a difference. He took one last drag of the small Venezuelan cigarette and flicked it out into the snow as he turned to step back inside.

"Leave it open. This room needs to let out some of the steam from the night's activities," Solange said while stretching her long body. She patted the bedside and Max began to walk toward the bed, but was interrupted by a soft knock at the door.

"What time did you order room service?" he asked.

"Six, then we have massages at seven." She covered her naked body with the thin bed sheet and put a pillow over her face.

"Well, good thing they're early, 'cause I am starving," Max said through his yawn while walking to the door. He reached out, unlocked it, turned the handle, and pulled.

Max froze as the cold steel from a suppressed MP5 submachine gun pushed up against his temple.

"Don't move and stay quiet," commanded in English a whispering, thickly accented German voice. "Hands where I can see them."

Max raised his hands as his heart rate picked up. A rush of adrenaline shot through his body.

"Good, now back up."

Max knew that he was not facing an amateur by the way the man moved and the equipment he carried. Of special interest was the submachine gun pointed at his head. He knew the weapon well. It was the SEAL's weapon of choice for silent, close-quarter combat. He had used it many times and knew its deadly power. The fact that it was the suppressor model, one that could shoot a full clip of bullets at a target in silence, didn't make the situation any more comforting.

The black-hooded man spoke in German to someone behind him, still staring down his sights at Max. "Clear."

The room filled with three clones of the first man, each pointing his own deadly weapon at Max.

Crap, now there are four.

"Don't make any sudden moves, Solange," Max said, and for breaking the silence was hit hard by the muzzle of the MP5. Max staggered back and caught himself on the edge of the bed. He could feel the warm blood trickling down the side of his head as he moved closer to Solange. His calf then rubbed against the butt of his father's .22, which he had stuffed between the mattresses earlier that night.

"What the hell is this?" Solange shouted as she removed the pillow from her face.

One of the black-clad soldiers pointed his MP5 at Solange and motioned for her to be silent. She did as she was told.

Two of the soldiers parted and let a fifth man come in.

It was Solange who spoke first.

"Father?"

Klaus Wehr looked coldly at Solange wrapped up in the bed sheet.

"Wehr, what is this?" Max asked with authority.

"We are here to reclaim property that was stolen from us."

"Come again?" Max asked.

"You have items in your possession that do not belong to you." Wehr paused and looked around as if deciding whether to continue. "Lieutenant Commander, your plane, the Fi-156 Storch, belonged to Doctor Hans Kammler, attaché to Germany's High Command and servant of the SS. Along with that, you also have paperwork that is of great importance to us."

"If I might ask, who are *us?*" Max asked.

"I am General Klaus Wehr of the German SS Phoenix command," he said proudly.

Max looked toward the closet. *Phoenix Command?*

"Now, the papers please."

"I have no clue what you're talking about," Max said, looking up at Wehr.

"Do you honestly take us for fools? I have been looking for that specific type of aircraft for a long time. So, when our people notified us of one we had never seen before flying south of Paris, I had them keep an eye on the Storch. Once you landed and tied down in Courchevel, we flew in to take a closer look. By Chance Ditter invited you to dinner—ha, strange how the world works. So, after dinner and as you slept in your room that night, I had my men search out the serial numbers of your plane. To my delight, they matched the plane that was stolen from Doctor Kammler so many years ago in Colombia." He smirked with pleasure as he continued the story. "In 1966, when my team and I arrived at the doctor's estate, we found him dead in his study. Worse, we found that the contents in his safe were missing. All was lost, I thought, until we searched the property and discovered that the doctor's plane was also missing. We looked for years, but none of the aircraft we found matched the doctor's, and we had almost given up hope until you re-opened that door. I knew then that there might be a chance."

Shit, I am running out of time. Keep him talking. "A chance at what?"

"A chance for our race to rule once more. You see, I was never told the specifics about what the papers held. I was told to be patient, and that all would come to fruition. It took 20 years for that to happen. Finally, it was my time to serve, but that moment was taken away from me, by your father, I suppose. But now we have found our plane, and all we needed was proof that you had the papers, as well. That is when your curiosity, and my daughter, helped in the search."

Max turned to look at Solange.

"No, she's not part of this, but the fact remains that she did translate the information to you, and the transmitter in your car picked up that conversation, leading us here." Wehr spread his arms out. "Now, if you will, the papers please."

Max looked toward the closet once again. Wehr immediately walked to it, opened its door, and removed the briefcase containing the Nazi files. He took a moment to review what was inside, and produced the thin black notebook. He flipped through it and stopped when he found what he was looking for. Wehr pulled out his own notebook and compared the numbers on the pages. He let out a sigh and turned to his men.

"Our calculations were wrong, but now we have what we came for and there is little time to prepare. Hermann and Wolf, stay here with me; the rest clear the path to the helicopters."

One of the two commandos closest to the door reached out and inched it open. He exited to the right as the second followed closing the door behind him.

Good, two down, three to go. Hermann's by the door, Wolf's next to the balcony. Think... what now?

Wehr picked up Solange's clothes and threw them at her. "Get dressed. You are coming with us."

"No."

Wehr motioned to Wolf, who shot a silent burst at Solange's pillow. Solange froze in fear as the feathers from the pillow danced in the still air.

"Solange, go with them," Max said. "I'll find you."

Solange dressed in front of all of them. Wehr reached out, grabbed her, and forcibly began to lead her out of the room behind Hermann.

"What do we do with the American?" Wolf asked.

Wehr turned to look at Max. "He knows too much. Take him with us, then we'll throw him out of the helicopter."

"N—!" Solange started before Wehr clamped his hand over her mouth.

Crap, not good. I need a distraction. Adrenaline poured into Max's system; his heart rate increased exponentially. He had to do something—anything— or he was a dead man.

Knock, knock.

Everybody turned to the door except for Max, who took the small window of opportunity and made his move. He reached down, grabbed the .22 from under the mattress, and leapt at Wolf, managing to get off two shots...one missing Wolf, the other penetrating his lower jaw.

Wolf was dead before Max tackled him through the open balcony. They both tumbled over the railing, falling 15 feet down onto the steep snow-covered slope. Max and the body began to slide toward the cliff's edge. The sound of bullets thudded all around him and sent snow up and over him. Max flipped and grabbed Wolf's body, placing it between him and the raining bullets.

The bullets traveled alongside Max and found their mark, burying themselves in Wolf's limbs and bulletproof jacket. Max relaxed for a second when the shooting stopped, but tensed immediately as he and Wolf's lifeless body flew off the cliff's edge.

• • •

"Just leave it outside. I'll get it in a moment," Wehr told the waiter through the door.

He listened as the waiter walked away, and then looked at Hermann.

"He's dead. If the bullets didn't kill him, the 100-meter fall did," Hermann said as he took off his mask. "What do we do about the other loose end?"

"Get eyes on him for now. He's the only other person who knows. If he does anything, take him out."

"Understood." Hermann began to speak into his throat mike. He looked up at his father. "Done."

"Good. Let's go," Wehr said, still holding his hand over Solange's mouth.

Solange gave Hermann a cold stare of hatred as Wehr led her out the room and to the emergency exit door to their right.

Max came to atop Wolf's body on a small outcropping jutting from the side of the cliff's granite wall. Beside him was the thick trunk of the tree that had stopped his fall into the abyss below. He had gone over the edge, but seconds into free-fall had been caught by the tip of a pine tree. The tree bent with the force of both him and the body, then threw them back against the cliff face, where they'd slid down and become wedged between the tree and rock face.

Max looked up as he heard two helicopters fly overhead, and watched the strobe lights disappear into the heavy snowfall. He looked down at his right hand, which still held the .22, and put it back inside his coat. Wolf's twisted body lay at his feet. Max knelt down in the small space and began to inspect the body. He took note that the MP5 was missing, but an automatic gun was still in its thigh holster. He removed the thin gun and inspected it. It was a Glock 36, with the exception that the one he now held had a longer clip that held more bullets, and it was suppressed. He made sure it was loaded and put it, along with its extra clips, in one of his coat pockets. Next he removed Wolf's bulletproof vest. The vest had a multitude of pockets. Max checked each one and found six magazine clips for the missing MP5, a radio, a gun-cleaning kit, two energy bars, a flashlight and a small, flat, plastic bottle of water.

Max removed his aviator coat and shook as the cold wind blew against his bare skin. He took the fleece-lined jacket off the body and slipped it on. Next he slid into the bulletproof vest, and finally covered it all up with his coat.

Max put on the leather gloves that he kept in the aviator jacket's chest pocket and tied up his leather boots for the climb ahead. He stuck the flashlight in his mouth, pointed it at the granite wall, and swung his arms in a circular motion, trying to circulate warm blood into his numbing fingers while looking up at the cracks and imperfections on the wall and calculating the easiest route up the face. He took hold of Wolf's body and pried it up and out of the wedge. He slid it over the outcropping and watched as the falling body disappeared into the dense mist below.

Max stuck his hand into a crevasse and made a fist, which wedged his hand in place, and pulled himself up. He did the same with the other hand

and alternated as he began to scale the side of the cliff. After a few slippery minutes of climbing he was kneeling on the edge, flashlight off, looking up at the hotel and to his balcony. The balcony door to his room was shut and the lights within were off.

He hunched down and walked around the building's perimeter to the front of the hotel to enter through the lobby, which was empty save for the night shift desk clerk, who was asleep at the front desk. Max tried to shake him awake. The clerk slipped off his chair and fell hard to the ground. On closer inspection, Max saw that the man had a hole above his right eye where a small caliber bullet had entered.

A scream came from Max's left. Down the hall he saw one of the hotel maids staring at him in horror.

"No, it's not...." Max tried to explain, but the maid ran off. "Aw, crap," he said as he stared at his image in the wall mirror of him holding the Glock in his right hand.

I have to get out of here!

He spun and ran out the front of the hotel to his car.

The snow crunched under the weight of his boots when a whistling sound passed next to his ear. He immediately knew what it was and crouched down as he picked up his speed, looking for the origin of the bullet, and saw a man shooting at him 20 meters away from the side of a black Range Rover. Max took aim with his newly acquired Glock and responded with a silent burst. The shooter dove away from his SUV and over a snow bank.

Max jumped a small mound and found himself face to face with the man from the night in the alley. The man reached for the gun at his side, but Max swung his gun forward and point blank shot him in the chest before he could draw his weapon. The man flew back from the force of the .45 caliber bullet and tumbled back into the snow.

Max looked at the Audi. The driver's side door was open and mist exited through the tailpipe. He closed the trunk, ran around to the front and jumped in, slammed the car into first gear and skidded away, picking up speed as he fishtailed out of the parking area and onto the main road.

"Thanks for warming it up for me!" Max yelled as he passed the squirming man on the ground. The Audi plowed through a snow bank, sending a spray of fresh powder up into the air. He kept close to the mountainside as he left the parking area, being careful on the sharp turn as the car drifted onto the snow-covered mountain road. Max took a quick glance at the rearview mirror and caught a glimpse of the bouncing headlights of the black Range Rover flying around the bend behind him.

"Don't these guys ever quit?" Max heard three smacks on the side of the Audi, and leaned down into the passenger's seat. "You have got to be fucking kidding me!" he screamed as he regained control of the Audi and accelerated out of the turn. "You want me? Come and get me!" Max downshifted and the four wheels spun as they searched for a grip on the slick road.

The new Range Rover was no match for the old Audi, but its driver was persistent, and Max found it hard to outpace the SUV as he concentrated on not slipping off the road and keeping his speed up. The car drifted at every turn as he slid down the alpine road toward the sharpest outside turn he remembered on the way up. It was there where he would set his trap.

Max took the turn to make his snow tracks look like the others behind him, but this time he turned off the headlights and let the car spin away from him until it faced the opposite direction. The car slid over to the side and Max reached back for the duffel bag. He had only seconds as he took the keys from his pocket and fumbled them into the lock. The door flew open as he hurried out and ran over to a small pine tree near the apex of the turn.

The Range Rover came fast around a far turn and picked up speed on the straightaway. Just as the driver of the SUV began his turn, Max stepped out from behind the tree, and took aim with the loaded and cocked vintage triple rifle.

BOOM!

The shoulder stock dug into him as the 45-70 bullet exploded out the top barrel and flew at the left front tire. The tire exploded as Max took aim, moved his index finger to the second trigger, and squeezed. This time the rear wheel disintegrated. The SUV lost traction, sliding uncontrollably until it disappeared over the edge, taking the guardrail with it. The muffled sounds of the Range Rover tumbling over diminished the farther it fell down the cliff side.

Max stood on the edge of the road, finger on the third trigger, aiming the triple rifle down into the ravine, and waited in the silence of the storm. Satisfied he was safe, he walked back to the Audi. The Audi then spun 180 degrees, and Max headed down the mountain road, back toward Geneva.

Max sat in the warmth of the Audi's cabin, looking over the deactivated Russian-made tracker that he'd found under the driver's seat. He turned it around a few times in his hand, then looked out through the windshield at the deserted street that ran past his father's flat. Walking into the house could be a trap, but not one soul had walked along the street since he had arrived 45 minutes ago. He would have to make it a short stay.

It had been four hours since the incident at the spa, giving him enough time to go over everything that had happened. Max was sure that the authorities would have the information from his credit card charges in the hotel. Also, Interpol would find out which guests were missing once the poor maid—the one who saw him standing over the dead body of the front desk clerk—gave her description of the armed man. Put two and two together, and match that description to his passport photo in the system, show it to the eyewitness, and they would have their main suspect.

Max was sure that he wouldn't be implicated in the murder of the desk clerk because the bullet in the clerk's head was not from his gun or the Glock he now possessed, and with time, the ballistic experts would know that; but Max did not have the weeks it would take for an investigation to clear him. He figured he had less than 24 hours to get the girl, and if time allowed, stop whatever the Nazis were up to.

Nazis. I can't believe I'm even thinking it.

He'd started to pull a plan together, but he was missing a piece of the puzzle: Ditter.

Max had pulled over at one of the many gas stations along the way back to the city and used a pay phone to reach Val, knowing he was less than two hours away, but could not be contacted. Pierre, however, had changed his flight plan and was on his way to Geneva. Hopefully, Val would have received his message and maybe he could convince the military to help him out, but for now it was all up in the air.

Max debated making the next call, but his gut told him to trust Ditter. He looked at his iPhone, making sure it was off and the sim card removed so it couldn't be tracked.

Max scanned the snow-covered street once more and turned off the engine. He stepped out and casually walked down the sidewalk until reaching the front door of his father's place. The snow was undisturbed, which was a good sign. He unlocked and pushed in the heavy front door, stepped through, leaving it slightly open for a quick getaway.

Something did not feel right. He took the Glock out and held it ready for action as he scanned the now silent alarm panel.

The alarm's off. FUCK!

The glass shelves next to him exploded, along with the sofa to his left, forcing Max to run away from the front door. He sprinted as fast as he could from the foyer and the flying shards of glass, furniture, and plaster, and headed straight through the glass hallway, shooting back at the unseen attacker in the courtyard. The glass around him fragmented behind every stride he took, as the bullets traveling through the broken glass ended their path in the red brick wall to his left. Max was at top speed, fleeing the raining death as he reached the end of the hall, where he propelled himself up and over the stainless steel bar.

The smacking of suppressed nine-millimeter bullets riddled the bar, but did not penetrate its thick stainless steel skin. Max readied himself for the right moment as liquor and glass from the shattered bottles rained over him. Then the whispered shooting stopped.

Max took the opening, jumped over the bar, and ran through the broken glass wall toward the pine tree in the middle of the courtyard. He found his target in the final steps of reloading his MP5, and shot him in the head. In one fluid motion he dropped the empty Glock, grabbed the MP5 from the still-standing dead man's hands, and chambered in a round. Using the tree as cover, he scanned the kitchen and second floor for more targets.

The tree began to splinter as another barrage of bullets hit around Max's head. Max let the new assailant finish his tree-trimming exercise, then peeked out the other side and saw his target's exposed right foot. He took careful aim and shot the foot. The man behind the steel column in the garage screamed and rushed Max.

Max, who did not expect the man to rush him, ran backward, shooting the sides of the tree, discouraging his target from going around it, while still keeping the tree between him and his target. Once back inside the house, Max leapt behind the low sofa and fired a final burst at his target's face.

One of the bullets hit its mark and the back of the man's head burst. Breathing heavily, Max scanned the lower floor once more. He turned to go up the back stairs and stopped frozen in his tracks.

A tall man in a gray pinstriped suit was pointing a small gun at his head from behind the kitchen counter.

Fuck.

"You're empty. Gun down, now," the man said calmly.

Max obeyed. If he were to go for the .22 in his jacket pocket he'd be dead. Once again he needed a distraction.

"On your knees, hands where I can see them," the tall man said, then pulled out his cell phone and spoke. "He killed my two men, but I have him. Do you want me to bring him in?"

The man smiled and Max knew the answer.

He was going to die.

Max waited for the opportunity to go for his gun and die fighting, but the time never came.

The man flipped closed his phone and pulled the trigger.

A bullet left the barrel, traveled its short distance, and hit its target.

Max stared in disbelief. He was still on his knees, hand in his pocket holding his .22 as the headless body of the once tall man collapsed to the floor.

The assassin had pulled the trigger just as another bullet had smashed into the side of his head, sending the dead body sideways and the bullet off its intended target.

Max turned to look for the starting trajectory of the mystery bullet. He focused on another man standing next to the pine tree, holding one of the dead assailants' guns.

"Hey, Max," the man said as he walked toward him.

"Hey, Val." Max let out the breath he had been holding. "Good timing."

Val let out a short laugh as he helped his friend up and took note of the .22 in Max's hand. "At first I thought you were on your knees, pleading for him not to kill you. But now that I see the .22 in your hand, well, I knew you could have never been such a pussy." Val smiled wide and sat down on the couch, giving the destroyed interior a good look. "Nice place you got here." Val waved his hands around. "Excluding all the bodies, broken glass, and bullet holes, of course." He then looked up at his best friend. "So, what's the story this time?"

Max picked out the radial engine sound before the 'Giro was in sight. The winged aircraft with its four rotating rotor blades came down to their position in the middle of a snow-covered pasture east of Geneva. The 'Giro made a constant swish-whooping sound as it flared and stopped five feet from where it had landed. Its radial engine throttled up, creating its own miniature blizzard of snow across the field as it taxied over to Max and Val.

They both leaned against the car, watching the 'Giro's engine shut down and its rotors come to a stop. A hatch on the left side opened, and Pierre unfolded his tall, thin body out onto the wing. He waved at Max and jumped down to the snow-covered ground.

"Val, this is my friend, Pierre."

They shook hands and nodded. Pierre looked at Max. "Max, what is going on? You don't look to be in any sort of trouble."

"Max has left tons of trouble in his wake," Val laughed. "It's just not caught up to us... yet."

"That's why we are meeting here. I must ask you a great favor and you can decline if you wish," Max said.

Pierre seemed uncertain. "*Mon ami*, I feel like I have known you since you were a young child." He kicked some snow around with his boot, then looked up. "What is it you need of me?"

"I need you and the 'Giro; we need to fly to Zurich and pick up a man there. Then we are off to here." Max unrolled an old blueprint on the hood of the Audi.

"Meckler Castle. Never heard of it," Pierre said as he studied the drawings. "Where is it?"

"We don't know, but I may know a man who could help us find it: Major Ditter Von Ludger."

"Who?"

"A man I met in Courchevel. How are you doing on fuel?"

"I have enough to get us to Zurich, but we will have to get fuel there."

"Good. I will explain the situation on the way." Max turned to Val. "You know what to do. I will contact you with the coordinates. If you can't convince them, so be it. Either case, we will pick you up before we head out."

"Are you sure you can trust this Ditter character?"

"My gut tells me yes. But I need to be careful; so far two family members are not as nice as I thought they were. Either way, I'll get the information."

"Don't worry. I got your back, pal, like always." Val smiled, saluted Max, and got into the Audi.

Max watched as Val accelerated away from them, and then turned to Pierre. "Would you mind giving me a lesson on how to fly this thing?"

"After you," Pierre said as he slapped Max on his shoulder.

The teakettle whistled and spit water vapor into the kitchen as Ditter rushed in and took it off the stove. He poured the tea into a blue coffee mug and leaned up against the kitchen island counter. *"Wir werden es zwischen elf und eins sein ... mit meinem Glück zeigen sie sich eine Minute vor einem."* he complained to the hot mug in his hands about the contractors inspection time frame.

Ditter took a sip of the hot tea and reveled in the silence. He was home alone and the complete lack of voices was music to his ears. No bickering about the maids or the weather or whatever else the women in the house could think of. Pure, unadulterated silence. His moment was short-lived when the house phone rang.

"Hallo?"

"It's Max. I am close by. Can I come over?"

"Close by? I thought you were in Geneva," Ditter answered in English.

"Change of plans. I'll tell you all about it in five minutes."

The phone line was cut off. Ditter looked at the phone, wondering what Max was doing in Zurich. He shrugged, hung up, and took a cookie from a jar on his way back to his office.

He stood at the window behind his desk, looking out into the forest.

• • •

A man lying in a prone position on top of a waterproof blanket about 50 yards inside the forest watched through his sniper scope as Ditter drank from his mug. From this distance the shot would be an easy one. He adjusted his earpiece as a voice crackled through.

"Yes, sir, target received a call from an American called Max." He listened to the instructions coming through his ear piece. "Yes, sir. I will take them both out when they are together. Understood."

Now things got a bit more complicated. He called in his second, who sat next to the driver in a car a block from the house. "We have a go on target plus one. Switch to secondary plan."

Max stepped off the light-rail trolley at Zurich Klusplatz, walked a few yards down the street, and took a right off Witikonerstrasse, blending into the crowd as he walked north to Hegibachstrasse. He turned east to Hitzigweg. At the end of the street and to the right stood Ditter's home. The street was quiet and the white winter snowfall had started to turn gray from the dirt kicked up by the occasional passing car. As he rounded the street he looked around, analyzing the parked cars in sight. Up ahead was a forest of trees stripped bare from the cold winter, the odd green pine dotting the bleak forest with a hint of color peeking through the white snow that still clung to its branches.

It was too quiet for his liking.

Ditter's house was perched on the top of a hill. Its back yard was the forest, and in front lay a view of downtown Zurich. The house was a two-story with what looked like good attic space. It was designed in the typical Bavarian mountain style with whitewashed walls and blue trim. The garage sat 100 feet from the front of the home and dug into the hill the house was built on.

Max looked around as he stepped up the stairs leading away from the street, and once at the front door, rang the bell. After a few moments Ditter unlocked the door.

"Ditter, we need to talk...somewhere away from the windows." He pushed himself in and slammed the door behind him.

"What are you talking about?" Ditter asked as he watched Max peek into the kitchen.

"There are two people a block away, sitting in a car and watching the house. Odds are there could be more." Max walked by Ditter.

"Max, hold on." Ditter grabbed him by the arm. "I don't understand? What do you mean by watching my house?"

"Ditter, I am going to ask you once, and trust me, I will know if you're lying when you answer."

"Ask me what? What is going on?"

"Are you involved with a place called Meckler Castle?"

Ditter froze in place. "I have not heard that name in many, many years. How do you know about it?"

"Never mind that. Where is it?" Max grabbed both Ditter's arms and squeezed.

"Max, let go of me. Now!"

Max looked into Ditter's eyes and loosened his grip. "Where?" he asked once more.

"It is in Austria close to the Swiss border, but I really don't know since I flew there from the north in a snow storm and escaped to the south on foot."

Max looked past Ditter as he put the sentence he had just heard into perspective. He looked back at Ditter and let go of his grip. "What do you mean, escaped?"

Ditter smiled. "I'll tell you my story if you tell me yours."

"Ditter...they took Solange and tried to have me killed."

"Solange? Killed? They? What do you mean?"

"I'll tell you that on the ride to the airfield."

"No, tell me now!" Ditter insisted.

"Klaus and Hermann Wehr took her to Meckler Castle. Something is happening tonight and they tried to have me killed. We need to go. You need to take me there."

Ditter paused for a moment, then he turned. "I.... Here, come with me."

Max's reaction was quick as the door to the study opened and a red dot appeared on Ditter's forehead. He dove, tackling Ditter just as the office window shattered and a bullet hit the wall behind them. A split second later dozens of bullets began to pepper the room as Max dragged Ditter back into the hallway.

The front door burst open. Max pulled out his Glock and began firing at the front door, holding back the assassin.

Ditter took hold of Max and yelled at him, "Follow me!"

Max slipped on the area rug as he scrambled to get up. The hall then erupted as thousands of wood splinters flew in all directions as the assassin at the door let loose his MP5. Max dove through the kitchen door. He slid across the tile floor, stopping against the center kitchen island. The assassin burst into the room, submachine gun blazing, just as Max grabbed hold of the teakettle and threw its boiling hot water at him.

The assassin lifted his arm to block the water, which gave Max a small window of opportunity. He kicked up his left foot and knocked the MP5 from his hands. The assassin quickly reached in for his sidearm, but Max slapped it away.

It was now a hand-to-hand fight. Max threw a one-two punch combination that was blocked and returned with a swift kick to Max's belly. Max turned just in time to reduce the impact of the blow, but left his left side open to attack, which the assassin took advantage of by striking Max hard in his rib cage. Max stumbled back and caught himself on the kitchen counter, where there was a set of kitchen knives. He reached out for the wood block and was hit once more in the kidney.

Max fell to the floor and was about to get pummeled when out of nowhere a frying pan flew across the kitchen, hitting the assassin in the head, but not before he managed to grab one of the knives on the counter. Max got up and looked at his attacker as he lost his balance. Clearly, Ditter's efforts made the odds better for Max, who launched himself at the knife just as the assassin lunged forward. Max was cut, but not before he grabbed hold of the hand wielding the knife and twisted it into the assassin's belly.

Luckily for the assassin, his bulletproof vest stopped the knife. Max, feeling the resistance of the vest, spun and wrapped his arm around the assassin's neck, twisted his head, and cleanly snapped the spinal cord. The body flopped to the floor. Ditter grabbed Max when he heard the office door being kicked open, and pulled him into a side closet that led down some stairs.

"Move!" Ditter yelled and Max obeyed, running after him down a thin tunnel just as a flash-bang grenade went off at the stairs behind them. The loud bang echoed through the tunnel and came close to rupturing Max's eardrums. Max stammered and reached a metal door that Ditter held open as he screamed at Max, whose ears were ringing, to hurry. He ran through and Ditter shut the door and locked it.

They were now inside the garage. To Max's left was a 1960s Jaguar E type and to his right a Mercedes G wagon. Ditter went for the SUV. "I drive!" he said as Max went around and threw himself into the passenger's seat just as two bullets cut through the steel door and hit the back of the Jag.

Ditter started the Mercedes wagon, and its V8 engine came roaring to life. He popped the clutch and burst through the closed garage door. The garage door split in two as the wagon leapt out into the slick street. They slid sideways, but Ditter knew what he was doing and controlled the skid as they flew past the sidewalk. Thirty seconds later a Volkswagen Passat spun 180 degrees, bounced off Ditter's neighbor's wall, and accelerated away to give chase.

"Well, I guess this makes you one of the good guys," Max said as he wrapped his scarf around his cut hand.

"We have company," Ditter said as he took a quick glance in the rearview mirror.

"We need to get somewhere busy. Head to the center of town."

"No. I have a better plan."

"I'm all ears!"

"Help me with the cross streets."

Suddenly, the rear glass exploded as a bullet hit the top left-hand corner of the trunk door.

"Clear!" Max yelled as they came to a cross street, letting Ditter know that there was no cross traffic. Ditter spun the steering wheel and made another quick left-hand turn onto Aurorastrasse.

Any other day the long winding road would have been a pleasure to enjoy sitting on the passenger's side, but today was not that type of day as the wagon slid sideways, passing a police car. Max made eye contact with the police officer in the cruiser. He was in mid-sip of his Starbucks coffee when the wagon flew past in front of him. The officer floored it and missed crashing into the Passat as he entered the road, fishtailing as it, too, joined the chase.

"Police are in it now. Can we lose them?"

"Not if they call in the helicopter." Ditter shifted his body securely into his seat. "Here we go! Hold on!"

The street did a slow turn to the left, abutting a golf course, and Ditter took the path less followed as he plowed through the golf cart path and onto the golf course. White powder snow flew in all directions as the wagon bounced onto the fairway. Ditter turned his head from side to side, as if looking for something familiar. "Ha!" he exclaimed and corrected his path, heading in the direction of a mound.

The wagon flew onto the mound and caught some air before settling back down on the soft snow. The Passat followed the same path, but the police officer was off target. He took the left side and plunged into a sand trap hidden by the snow.

The wagon passed 60 miles per hour as it cut its path through the golf course. Up ahead was another road. Ditter accelerated as he took out a metal pedestrian pole and jumped onto the road, then aimed left, breaking through a chain strung across a side road and entering one of the many forest trails. The Passat followed, not giving up an inch.

"I know these woods like the back of my hand," Ditter said as he swung the steering wheel left and right, coming so close to the trees that he managed to rip off the side mirrors. The Passat was not doing as well as the four-by-four Mercedes, and Ditter managed to build up a considerable lead.

"We need to get to Dubendorf Airfield," Max said.

"Let's lose them first."

Max looked back and watched as the Passat slipped and slid through the woods. They came into an open area the size of a baseball diamond and Ditter gunned it. The Passat also made it there, but the wagon was long gone. The car stopped, then spun on its wheels and headed back the way they had come.

"Looks like we lost them."

"You sure? I don't want to give up this lead."

"Yes. How do we get to the airport?"

Ditter turned the wheel onto another trail and eased up on the accelerator. After a few minutes they left the forest and jumped on a local road, then pulled onto Untere Greerenstrasse. Both of them kept a keen eye on all the cars around them. The assassins were still out there. The road wound through a beautiful section of forest and opened up into another small town.

"Go to that field." Max pointed to an open field north of a small town. "Where are we?"

"The town up ahead is Düendorf. What is the plan?" Ditter asked as the wagon bounced off the road and onto a field.

"Park it under the trees. I have someone at the airport who can get us out of here." Max flipped open the prepaid cell phone he'd bought in Geneva and dialed a number. He looked at the compass on the dashboard "We're southwest of Düendorf, parked in the forest tree line. Silver SUV Mercedes Benz G wagon. Pick us up; I don't want to risk showing up at the airfield. Bring her down quick; we need to leave fast." Max flipped closed the phone and looked at Ditter, who was staring out into the field.

"What is going on, Max?" Ditter asked, clearly shaken.

Max told him everything that had happened before he arrived at Ditter's house. Shocked, Ditter turned off the SUV and they both stepped out.

"I have known the Wehrs for a very long time. Christ, the man even married my former daughter-in-law."

"No one ever knows what happens behind closed doors, Ditter."

"But to hide something like this. To keep it secret for so long..."

"Yes, but you managed to keep the knowledge of the castle a secret, as well."

"I will not argue that point."

"What happened there?" Max asked as the cell phone rang. He flipped it open. "Good...I see you, just keep that heading."

Ditter looked up at the sky as he heard the sound of a radial engine.

Two thousand feet above them, Pierre looked through a pair of binoculars at the SUV in the middle of the field, and then scanned the area once more for any other cars or people.

Max kept the phone to his ear as he watched the 'Giro.

"I see you...looks clear. How is the ground?" asked Pierre.

Max went out into the field and walked around. "Six inch—sorry, 10 centimeters soft, then the ground is frozen."

"Coming down."

Pierre throttled down and banked the 'Giro to the left, putting it into a high velocity, spiraling descent. Ditter watched in amazement as the strange aircraft from above corkscrewed its way down toward him.

The 'Giro leveled out at 200 feet, then did a quick fly-by and swung its tail around. Pierre then expertly coaxed the aircraft down onto the soft snow a few car lengths from the Mercedes. Max and Ditter both jumped out from the tree cover and jogged to it. Once at the 'Giro's side, Max opened the hatch and they both climbed in.

Ditter smiled at Max. "What a beautiful machine!"

Max nodded and adjusted the Bose headphones around his ears as he sat in the copilot's seat. He buckled himself in as Pierre began to throttle up.

Pierre reached up and put his hand on the rotor clutch activator, and waited for the rotor to spin up. The rotor spun past 150 revolutions per minute and he disconnected the clutch, released the brakes, and the 'Giro hopped forward a few feet. Max felt the pressure on the seat as Pierre pulled back on the yoke and performed a short, high-angle-of-attack take-off.

Max reached back and touched the noise cancellation button on Ditter's headset. "Better?" Max spoke through the headphone's microphone.

"Yes, thank you."

"Ditter, this is Pierre Bouvier. Pierre, meet Ditter Von Ludger." He looked right, then left. "Keep a lookout for the police helicopters."

Pierre looked around, searching the horizon and kept the 'Giro low. "I don't see any helicopters; looks like we are clear. I will keep this bearing for another 10 minutes, then we head to the meeting point."

"Sounds good to me." Max looked back at Ditter. "We have no clue as to the location of this castle. Which way do we go?"

"How well do you know the Alps, Pierre?" Ditter asked.

"I used to fly rescue helicopter missions in them about 20 years ago."

The 'Giro bucked as it flew through some unstable air.

"Good. Then you know how to fly down close to them." Ditter looked down at the map Max had given him, and with his finger traced an imaginary line. "Head east toward the border of Liechtenstein and Switzerland. We follow the river south to Sargans where it turns southeast until the town of Karlihof. From there we fly east to Schiers. After that, it's a guessing game."

"You don't know its location?" Pierre asked.

"I really couldn't tell you. I escaped from the castle in 1944, and it took me three days of hiking before I saw the village of Schiers from atop a peak, and by that time I was half dead. I would have never made it if I hadn't stumbled into a high alpine summer cattle shed. So between the wandering and the time gone by, it may take us a while to find the castle."

Pierre and Max looked at each other, then back at Ditter.

"What happened? How did you escape?" Max asked.

Ditter looked out the window and smiled at how lucky he had been so many years ago, and began to tell his story.

The small town of Schiers was located in a valley surrounded by mountains. Ditter looked through his binoculars. "You have to head up that valley." He pointed with his bony finger as he spoke through his microphone.

Pierre nodded and aimed the nose of the 'Giro northeast up the valley, increasing altitude as the ground came up under them.

"Great! Just got a text message from the brothers," Val said from the back seat.

Ditter looked at the new member of the group surrounded by bags of climbing equipment and clothes.

"Which one?" asked Max.

"Xavier. Christ, his freakin' code is a pain in my ass. Okay...if I am decoding this right, it seems like someone, as in you, poked the hornet's nest."

Val and Max had discussed involving the military in this situation. They knew the only way to approach the military would be through their old friends the Francis brothers, who now worked in Naval Intelligence—Jack in San Diego, Xavier in Washington. The brothers had a cryptic way to send information over the Internet. So, they took it upon themselves to teach Val and Max the code many years ago.

"By the way, Max, you owe me big for all this climbing shit. I maxed out my credit card. Fuck, shit is expensive when the U.S. government doesn't give it to you."

"Never mind that. What's it say?" Max asked about the message.

"It took them a while to respond, but it seems that your man is on a list. Lucky for us they have a few interested parties that are willing to stick their necks out for a promotion. I relayed that once we find the castle I will transmit the GPS coordinates to them. Then we'll know what type of support we'll get."

"You must have told them a hell of a story."

"Yeah, that and the fact that the bodies of three professional assassins were found in your father's place helped a little. They wanted your ass at the embassy to answer questions, but I told them you were 'missing.' That put a stop to that...for the time being, anyway, but eventually you are gonna have a hell of a week answering questions. Fuck…in reality we are ALL going to have a hell of a week! Thanks for all this, Max…" Val said sarcastically as the 'Giro bounced through some more unstable air.

It was hard flying for Pierre as the 'Giro battled the high winds whipping around the mountain peaks. After an hour of weaving in and out of valleys, Ditter spotted what he was looking for.

"There! It looks like a plain at the base of that cliff…" He paused, searching for any evidence of a man-made structure through the ever-present cloud cover, but couldn't find one. "It has to be here…somewhere," Ditter said in desperation.

The world was white and gray all around the 'Giro. Only back in the town, miles away, was there any sign of life.

"Wait…a…minute…" Val whispered as he pushed his binoculars against the Plexiglas window. "Damn, that's good camouflage, looks like the castle's walls and roof are made from the same material as the mountain, so it blends right into the granite cliff." He pointed at the mountain. "The straight lines gave it away. Ditter, look at the top of the peak, then scan down inside that narrow valley, and what do you know…we have ourselves a castle!"

"I see it!" Ditter said, excited. "There it is! Meckler Castle."

"Going to be a bitch getting in there without being seen," Val said as he looked over the castle through his binoculars.

Max flew the 'Giro as Pierre studied the structure.

"There is the Storch!" Pierre said. "Oh, yes, I can make that landing; there is more than enough space. Here, let me have the controls."

Pierre handed over his binoculars to Max, and took control of the 'Giro's yoke. Max looked over the castle, trying hard to make mental notes of everything he saw. He studied the small runway. A few people were dragging his Storch into a hangar. He then scanned down the cliff face, looking for the small rectangular cliff entrance Ditter had mentioned.

"Well, at least we won't have to climb that far." It was Val again who spotted the cliff entrance. "I'd be worried about the sentries, though. They have a whole bunch. I count 50 so far."

"Pierre, keep it straight and level. Let's fly off their field of view before we turn. They might have radar, so use the mountain to shield our signature as we turn back to that patch of dead grass we saw earlier. We will have to do some quick climbing so we are not caught up there in the dark." He looked back at Ditter. "Are you up for it, Ditter?"

Ditter nodded as he stared at the castle through the frosted glass, lost in thought.

10

The red light had never switched on during his shift, but today was different. Not only was it on, but the center of the five-foot-wide curved computer screen lit up, showing a text message:

OMEGA ALERT

Corporal Martinez freaked out.

It was real!

He switched on his cell phone and punched in his code. He scrolled past two app screens until he found the app he was looking for. Sudoku. Martinez started a new game and pressed the numbers on the screen. The screen flickered, then turned black, showing him two phone numbers and a phrase under it. He was standing when he made the call to an office 30 stories above him.

The secretary answering the phone spoke into her headset. "General West's office."

"Good morning, ma'am. This is Corporal Martinez. I have a level-one message for the general."

"Authorization code?"

"Four two seven."

The secretary typed in the code. The computer screen icon spun for a second, then gave the "clear" code.

"Patching you through."

"General West here," answered a sharp, stern voice.

"Sir, your travel agent called. All is set for your trip," Martinez said.

There was a small pause on the phone line. "I will be down in two minutes."

Martinez ended the call and dialed the second number.

"This is Martinez. Code Omega."

Martinez placed the phone back in his pocket and sat down. "Shit, this must be big," he said as he went through the log-in protocols.

Exactly two minutes later, General West was standing alone at Martinez's terminal typing his passcode into the curved clear glass screen. In front of him hummed the gigantic super-computer, which ran over 250,000 processors grouped in 72 racks/cabinets connected by a high-speed optical network taking up a room the size of three basketball courts. The keyboard minimized from under his fingers and slid, in icon form, to the left side of the touch-sensitive screen. A new message appeared in the center, followed by a soothing woman's voice.

"I need retinal scan and voice recognition, General West," said the computer.

West stepped to the right and leaned forward, placing his right eye in front of a dime-sized, oval red screen. "This is General West, security code angels, west, two, six, nine, romeo, bravo. Confirm voice and retinal scan," he said to the machine.

The screen flashed, the general leaned back, and the computer spoke once again.

"Thank you for the proper identification, General. Message as follows."

The computer screen flashed once more, revealing another text message. The general took his time reading the coded message and its translation. He reached up and with his fingers slid the message over to the right, revealing another file beneath. After a few minutes of rearranging pictures and transcripts on the 60-inch touch screen, he stepped back and took it all in.

"Interesting," he whispered. He went over his options. The general had read about this particular experiment when he'd been briefed in the NSA special warfare office. He had heard of about a dozen such secrets, one more troubling and revealing than the next. This one in particular was of great interest in that the only proof of its existence was the paperwork on the project; the actual machine had been destroyed. The U.S. Army engineers and scientists had tried to reverse-engineer the destroyed machine, but had been unable to. That machine, or what was left of it, was now permanently housed in a secret location in the Nevada desert. The small archive of files told of the true nature of its purpose, and how it was powered. It also contained a brief note of the construction of another, but its location was unknown. What was now important, to him, was to get his hands on the technology. What the machine did was interesting, but unproven. There was no evidence that it worked. So what was of interest to him was what made it work, specifically the electric boosting technology. His goal now was to hand it over to Omega before the U.S. government got wind of what was going on.

West had to calculate the risks. To activate the procedure code and get nothing of importance would be disappointing to Omega.

Omega was the name he'd picked for the group with no name. It was the word used for the activation code, so why not name them the same? Three percent of all patents and loot recovered, that was his price for treason...but man, what a beautiful price.

His choice to become a member had been a simple one. Omega knew he played dirty and they had a file thick enough to prove it. Not only did that tasty morsel motivate him to join, but also the fact that he was to be killed if he declined had sealed the deal. West had heard stories about all the people who had declined Omega's invitation: Lincoln, the Kennedy brothers, even Reagan, who had survived the first assassination attempt and was given a second chance, which he'd accepted. Even his childhood hero, but because of his patriotism, General Patton, had been assassinated after his meeting. As far as West could tell, anyone could spin stories, but the death of another Omega man close to him made him presume otherwise. He never had contact with them directly, but the acts Omega pulled, using him as a middleman, were impressive ones. They were true masters of deception, intelligence, and knew how to put on a show. They had their hands in everything and infiltrated everyone, in one form or another.

He had to be smart and think ahead of the game. With the information he now had in hand, the most feasible action for him would be to send in a covert team, eliminate all involved, keep it quiet, and bring the technology back to the States. The general could already see the money rolling in. He would just have to be very careful with his plans, but that was why they had chosen him.

The general tapped on the screen and dragged the information folder onto the flash drive icon. After a moment he removed the fingernail-sized flash drive. West tapped another command on the screen and the computer spoke.

"Thank you, General West," said the soothing voice of the computer. "Please scan to close file zero, one, two, six, six, nine."

West leaned forward once more. The computer closed the file, and the screen settled back to its original scanning configuration.

He spun on his heels and walked to the sealed, bulletproof glass door at the far end of the narrow room and placed his palm on the tilted green screen. The screen flickered as it read the general's prints, and the door slid open. Martinez gave the general a quick look, and saluted him as he passed by and entered the secure elevator.

"Thank you, Colonel. See to it that I have the full report on my desk within the hour. Have the C-130 fueled up and ready to go when the weather turns. I want them ready and able to take on the winter storm. We need to test them to their limits. Notify German command of our exercises. That will be all." West excused his team and waited until his conference room was empty. He finally looked up from the inch-thick stack of papers and leaned back into his leather high-back chair. He took a deep breath as he went over his plan for the hundredth time and reached up to his military ribbons, where he pulled out the hidden flash drive that contained all the information on the Omega alert.

West twirled the flash drive in his fingers. The key lay in the team that had found the information. They were en route to a destination and once he had the coordinates from them, he could pull the trigger on the plan. Lucky for him, the Omega software had given him a head start. Only his people knew about what was going on, but eventually others would find out. The key was to control how the information dam would burst. The computer had calculated a 93-percent chance that the machine was located somewhere in the Alps. That information alone had given him enough to start the ball rolling earlier in the day.

The cover story was perfect. A mock mountain exercise in the middle of a storm. It was all coming together.

The BlackBerry alarm vibrated on the desk. It was time. West stood up and walked out of his office. "I will be out for 10 minutes. Hold all my calls."

West's secretary replied with a nod.

The general exited the waiting room, walked past two Marine sentries, turned left, and trod the long Pentagon hallway outside of his office for five minutes before he got to the unmarked door to a secure boardroom on his floor. He put his thumb on the scanner and waited. The door clicked open, West walked in, and faced another locked door. He closed the first door behind him and took one step forward.

"Voice confirmation please."

West spoke his name and serial number. The lights turned off in the hall and the door in front of him slid open. The room was the size of six cubicles and painted white. A round, white table took up most of the space and was surrounded by four mid-century modern chairs, two of which were occupied by men he had never seen before. It was amazing to him that he was holding the meeting in the very same building, and more than ever he respected Omega's power.

"West, sit down. Do you have information?"

"Yes. Gentleman, we have an Omega alert. It's file 17, the Phoenix Project."

The thin man in the Navy uniform typed it into his computer and waited two seconds for the information to upload. "Good, very good," he said as he read the information off his computer screen. "This is your call. How do you want to play it?"

"Once we receive the coordinates as to where the machine is, I will authorize an information and first-strike team to hold and secure the venue."

An Air Force colonel to the right of the Naval officer typed away on his aluminum Mac Book Pro. "Where is this information coming from?" he asked.

"From a SEAL team commander not affiliated with us. He will be given help so we can maintain eyes on the objective before our collection team arrives. I have a dedicated situation room up and ready with its clone room receiving and recording. Once done, we will have full personnel termination orders."

"Good. I will set up the European strike team to proceed, and await the 'Go' code. It will be your show from here on. The strike team will have their orders come from you. We will have no further contact until the mission is accomplished. Your authentication codes will arrive within the hour."

West placed his flash drive in the center of the table. "All the information is here."

The thin Naval officer grabbed the flash drive and inserted it into his own aluminum Mac Book Pro, and began to type away. The other colonel looked up from his screen. "Thank you, and good luck, General."

West stood up, spun around, and waited for the door to open. He stepped through and the door slid closed behind him. Outside the room and back in the small hallway he put his thumb to the screen until the door clicked open. He stepped through and into the public hallway. West remained still for a moment and let out the breath he had been holding. He gathered his composure as he walked back to his office, all the while mentally analyzing the mission ahead.

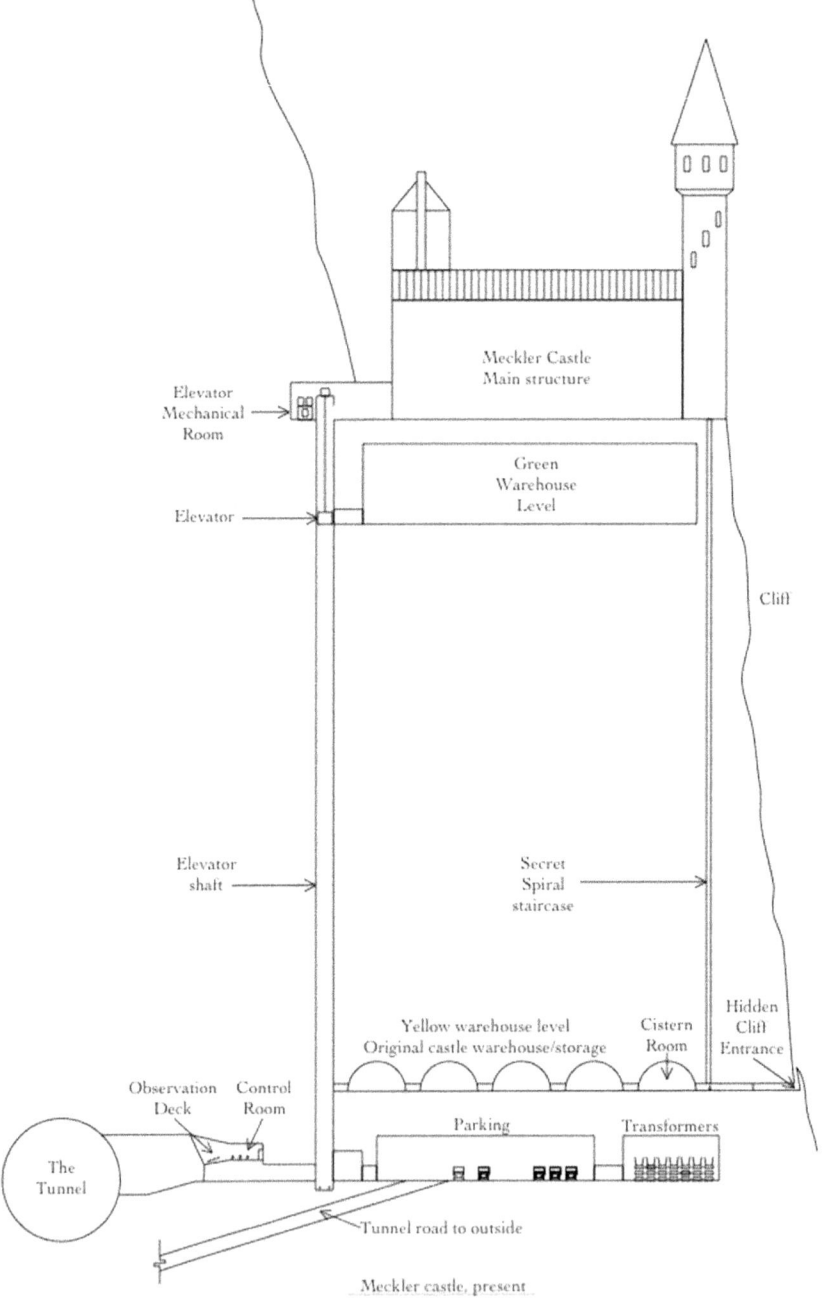

Meckler Castle, present

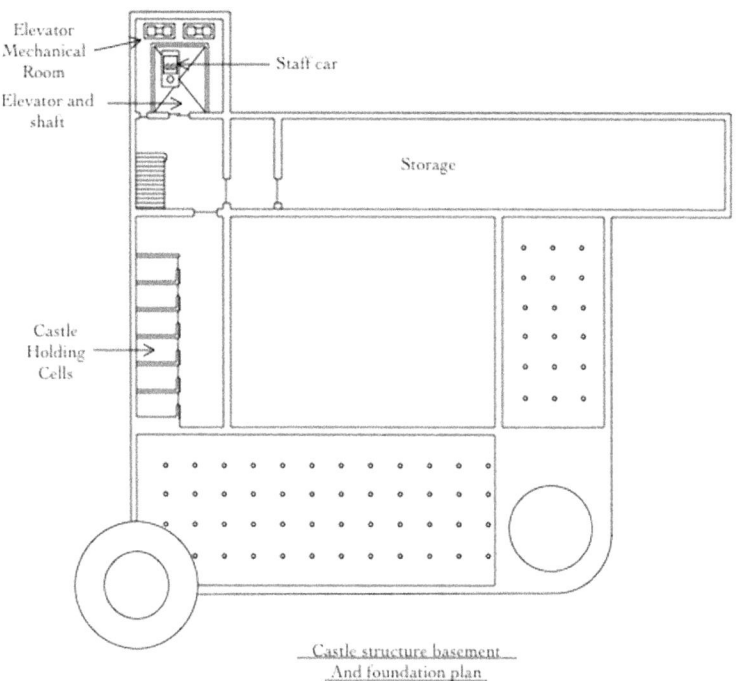

Castle structure basement
And foundation plan

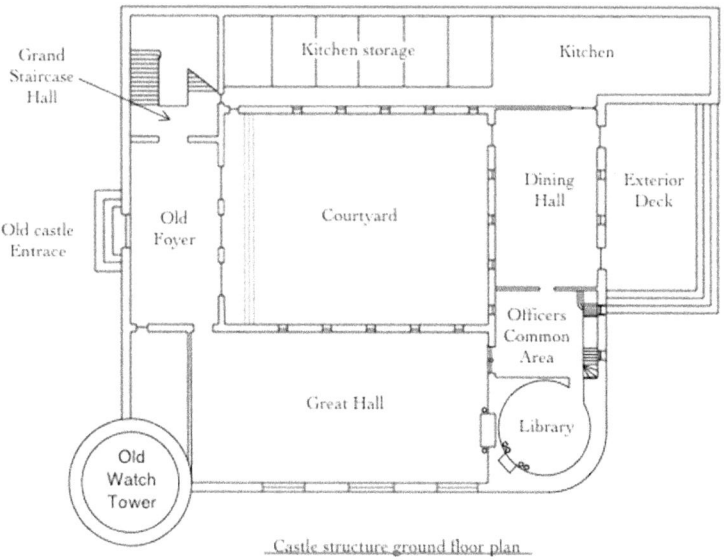

Castle structure ground floor plan

217

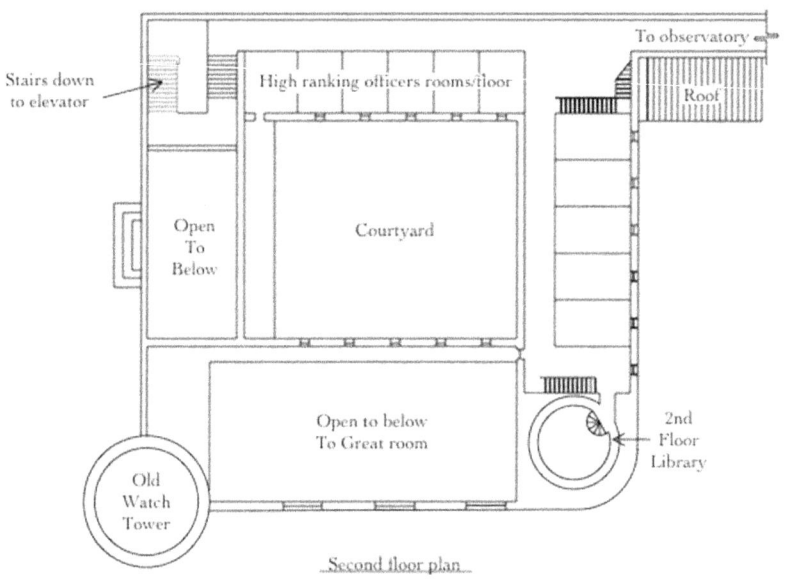

Stairs down
to elevator

High ranking officers rooms/floor

To observatory

Roof

Open
To
Below

Courtyard

Open to below
To Great room

2nd
Floor
Library

Old
Watch
Tower

Second floor plan

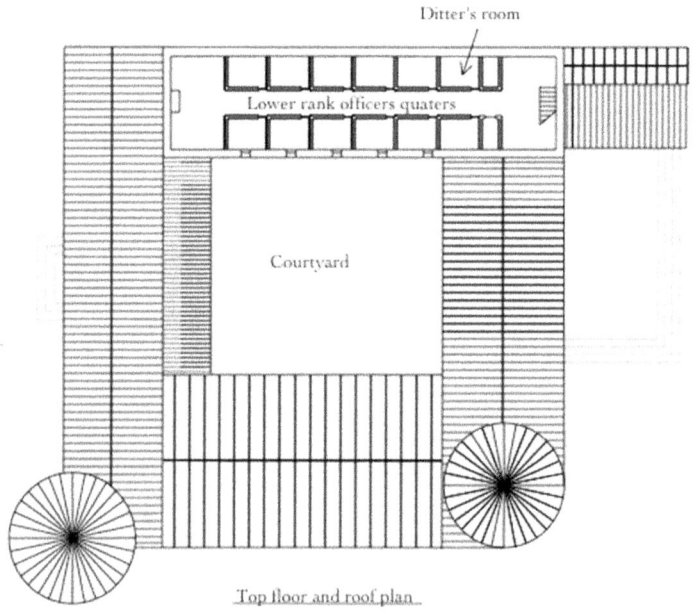

Ditter's room

Lower rank officers quaters

Courtyard

Top floor and roof plan

218

11

Alps, on the border of Austria and Switzerland

The carved-out path in the granite wall that snaked its way up the cliff side would have made the climb easy were it not for the build-up of snow and ice. And, as if to add excitement to the climb, the sun had begun to set, which made it a real challenge to all three climbers.

Max kept an eye on the descending cloud cover above them. At first it was a blessing, keeping them shielded from view, but in the past hour it had grown thicker, now threatening to engulf them before they could reach the opening on the cliff face.

Max stepped forward as the cloud cover cut off his view of Ditter, who was leading the group up toward the rock face entrance to the castle.

"Ditter?" Max called as he pulled on the stretched climbing rope in front of him.

Ditter poked his hooded face out from behind a rock outcropping, and a small cloud of condensed air exited his mouth as he said, "This way, Max." Ditter pointed up to the thin crevasse that ran up the cliff side. "The path goes vertical now. Here's where the climbing gets hard."

Max studied the small crevasse and put his back to one side of the cold granite wall. With his feet he began to push up against the opposite wall. It was slow going at first, but once Max felt at ease with his grip he shimmied up.

The dense cloud cover had engulfed Max by the time he reached the small, flat step jutting out of the crevasse he was in. Above him was an old wooden pulley. Max peeked over, but could not see more than a few feet forward, so he pulled himself up from the hole and carefully walked the icy path. After a few steps he found the opening in the side of the inner wall. He took out a finger-sized waterproof pelican LED flashlight from his pocket and pointed its beam into the dark hole. All Max could see was a rough-cut, thin granite cave curving away from him.

Max stepped into the cave, holding the Glock 36 at the ready. After a few moments his eyes picked out what he was looking for—a wood door. The door was closed and the hall leading up to it lay empty, both good signs. He backed up and, once out on the ledge, began looking for a suitable place to set up the climbing equipment. He began to hammer the arrow pitons into the granite wall. Even though there was the existing pulley, Max was not going to take any chances using it and set up his own pulleys. Once secure, he attached the locking carabineers to the protruding pitons, followed by the pulleys, and threaded the 50-foot climbing rope through it. He then ran the rope around a second pulley, which hung a foot above and to the side of the edge, and let the rope drop down the crevasse.

Ditter caught the rope, tied it to his waist climbing harness, then pulled twice, signaling to Max that he was ready to climb. Max found a good foothold and began to pull. The pulleys made easy work of hauling Ditter up the crevasse. Once up, Ditter stood behind Max and helped him pull Val up. Val made quick work as he grabbed the edge and pushed himself over. Once they were all up on the ledge, Max turned and retrieved the equipment that Val had tied up to the end of the climbing rope.

Ditter watched from the thin edge as Max and Val put on bulletproof vests and checked the guns and ammunition. Max carried the .22 in his aviator coat along with the suppressed Glock, the vintage triple barrel rifle, and he wore the bulletproof vest that he had taken off one of the assassins. Val stood on the other side, the most heavily armed of the bunch, with the two assassins' MP5s, one in his hand, the other strapped to his back. He now wore Wolf's tactical bulletproof vest, which was loaded with ammunition for the MP5s.

Ditter felt odd wearing the bulletproof vest and holding the suppressed Glock in his hands, but was glad to have a weapon. "Okay, we leave the ropes ready. Odds are that we are going to have to move fast. Val, you lead."

Ditter stood back and watched as Val performed a slow scan of the tunnel ahead. Val would look the walls up and down, then the floor, and step forward. It took him some time to reach the wood door. Once there, he ran a small rectangular black device around the frame.

"Its not wired," he said, pulling the door out a half an inch. Then he placed what looked like a dentist's mirror through the small opening and reflected the light around the inside of the door's frame. "Looks good inside."

He pulled the door open and stepped through. Max and Ditter followed. Val saw the spiral steps opening on the right and stopped. He raised his hand and they all gathered in a small circle.

"Looks like no one has been through here since I walked these halls," Ditter said.

Val nodded, recalling Ditter's story. "I concur, but still...look out for any sort of wiring, just in case. Okay, this is where we kiss and say goodbye."

"I think we should stick together. We saw how many sentries there were up top. We don't know what we are stepping into," Ditter said.

"Ditter, you and Max have a job, and that is to get Solange. It's my job to find out if there's something more sinister going on."

"I understand, but I would feel more comfortable with the two of you."

"Yeah, me too, especially with this lazy, no-good soldier covering your back."

Ditter jerked his head and looked at Max.

"Ditter, don't worry; we both know what we're doing. Now let's go get our girl." Max tapped on his ear. "I don't think we will get much use out of these radio transmitters inside these tunnels, but we should be okay once we're in the castle. In any case, we keep to the plan—radio silence until we have the girl. I'll click the transmitter three times. Now, Val, if you see something worth talking about, take note and we will see what we do once we are back here. Any questions?"

Val and Ditter shook their heads. Max fist-bumped Val, and stepped up the spiral staircase.

• • •

Max stared aimlessly at the stairs circling up above him. It had been 15 minutes since they had started the climb, and he was getting frustrated and a bit claustrophobic. He had just begun to wonder when the stairs would end when the ceiling began to flatten out. Curiosity struck as he studied the odd shape above his head, trying to figure out what it was. He took one more step up where there was none, and stumbled forward, catching himself in a small hole in the wall.

They had reached the top.

Thank God.

Max looked into the shoebox hole he had used as a handhold. A metal ring swung lazily within. He looked up at the ceiling, then back down at the ring.

"Huh."

"What is it?" Ditter asked, breathless from the climb.

Max aimed his light beam up at the ceiling and found what he was looking for. "Well, good, if we use it. Bad, if they do." He pointed at a boulder as wide as the stairway walls, dangling above their heads.

"*Scheissen.* Did not see that..." Ditter said, taking a long, deep breath, "when I was last here."

"Easy to miss when you're on your way down, looking down at the stairs, not up at the ceiling."

"You have a point." Ditter looked past Max and down the tunnel. "The tunnel slopes up until we hit a granite door. Once past that we are in the castle." He pointed up the dark tunnel.

Max hunched over to avoid the tunnel's low ceiling and walked forward until he came up to a cross tunnel. He stepped in and accidentally pressed down on the raised cobblestone on the floor. A heavy granite door behind him slid closed, separating him from Ditter. Max reached out to stop it, but pulled his hand out at the last second as the door thumped shut. He looked down and found the switch, and pushed down on the cobblestone once more. The door clicked, then slid open. "Cool...I take it this is the granite door you mentioned," Max said as Ditter stepped through. "Good to know it can only be opened from the inside."

"I did not think it would have remained open all these years. At least now we know I was the last one in these tunnels." Ditter pointed to the left. "That way is the kitchen, and to the right is the Great Hall, library, and the room I came in through."

"Well, let's be a couple of Peeping Toms, then." Max winked at Ditter.

The kitchen was bustling with energy. Max saw 10 men working the area, preparing meals. He gave Ditter his place, and Ditter listened. After a few minutes, he smiled and closed the peephole.

"She will be taking dinner in her guarded room, but no mention where she is in the castle. It seems that she broke one of the guards' noses, and they were all arguing about who was to take the food to her."

"Well, she's here, which is good and bad, but it's a start. Let's go see what's happening elsewhere," Max said as he aimed his flashlight up the thin corridor.

The SS major's clicking heels resonated through the castle library. Ditter could see through the peephole that the room had changed décor since his last visit. The major addressed the officer sitting behind the desk, his back to Ditter.

"General, Phoenix Project is ahead of schedule. The last three evolutions have achieved a 100-percent retrieval rate. We have now almost three battalions—close to 1,500 men—going through medical and orientation. They will be fully armed and ready within the hour. The Phoenix evolution is now on schedule with another five transports within the next week. We have run the last two EMS Hive tests at 100-percent power. The new magnetic rails are holding power with minimal acceptable drain. All systems are go and ready for countdown and activation."

"What have we heard from the Zurich team?"

"After the targets escaped into the forest, the team backtracked and split up. The Mercedes wagon was spotted in the woods and the neighbors reported seeing two men boarding a helicopter. The helicopter headed west and was not seen again." The major handed the general a report.

"Continue," the general said as he scanned the report.

"The aircraft spotted earlier has not returned, and the radar scans show the skies clear of aircraft out to 50 miles, except for the occasional crossing of commercial passenger flights above 30,000 feet." The major took a short breath. "Activity is now Condition Two. All security teams are at their posts and ready for orders. The biologics teams are set up and ready for extraction. 'All clear' will be given once the cargo is secure. Time for activation will be—" He took a quick glance at his wristwatch. "—in 82 minutes, sir."

The general thought for a moment. "Alert all teams to Condition One."

"Yes, sir."

"Inform the doctor that we will be down in...30 minutes. Have Fraulein Ludger at the control room's observation deck by the time I get there. That is all, Major."

The tall, blond-haired man in the black SS uniform clicked his heels together and shot out his right arm in a perfect Nazi salute, and exited the room. The general turned in his chair and took a minute to relax in the glow of the crackling fireplace.

Three shelves up running along the wooden column abutted to the wall, Ditter stared in shock at Wehr, who was dressed in an SS general's uniform. He closed the peephole and turned on his flashlight. "Max, we have less than 30 minutes to find Solange."

"Why?"

"They are taking her down to the observation deck. Whatever that means."

"Observation deck?" Max asked, but Ditter left it at that as he hurried up the tunnel. Ditter found the peephole to the room, looked through, and hit the switch on the wall. The door opened in toward him, revealing a wall of cardboard boxes. It took them some time as they both worked together to gain access.

Max passed Ditter and headed to the room's door. He slowly opened it and took a quick look into the hallway. The hall was dark. To his left he could see stairs and the glow of light coming from below. "Okay, Ditter. You stay here until I get back," he whispered.

"No, I'm going with you. I know this castle better than you."

"Don't worry, I'm just going to scout the hallways to make sure all is clear. I'll be back in a few minutes."

Ditter grabbed Max by his arm. "Don't be a hero. If you are not back in five, I'm coming after you."

"It's a deal." He winked, admiring Ditter's tenacity.

He arrived at the top of a stairway after a short walk. Muffled voices wafted up. The conversation stopped and was replaced by a techno beat.

Television.

Max headed down the stairs. He poked his head out into the hallway at the last step, and took a quick, two-second scan of what lay ahead.

Small flat-screen TV. Keyboard. iMac on top of an elaborate wooden desk. Long hallway, stairs at the end. Twenty-five meters. Chair pulled out, ashtray with unlit pipe on the tabletop. Smell of vanilla tobacco in the air. Nobody in sight.

He stepped around the corner and quietly walked a few yards past three dark-stained wooden doors, and ended up at the desk. He walked around, scanned it, and found a pad with names and measurements.

A toilet flushed behind one of the three doors. Max looked up from the desk, his brain working out an escape, when one of the doors began to open. Max instinctively jumped over the desk and ran full speed to the door, hitting it hard. As the door went back on its hinges, it slammed into the face of a portly man. The man, in turn, hit the back of his head against the bathroom sink, knocking him unconscious.

Max peeked around the door to find an old man dressed in a black uniform lying unconscious on the white marble floor. He reached down and pulled the cloth measuring tape off his neck. Max took one more look at his surroundings and smiled as he formulated a plan.

Ditter began to look around the room and in the boxes. He found black SS visors and caps wrapped in clear plastic. He looked at his watch once more, grunted, and moved toward the door. As he reached for the knob, the door swung open.

In the door frame stood an SS major.

Ditter raised his gun, but it was too late. The major dove forward and caught Ditter's armed hand.

"Ditter, relax!"

Ditter struggled, but stopped when he recognized the major's voice.

"What?" Ditter looked up from the uniform and realized Max was staring back at him. "What the hell are you doing in that uniform? I almost shot you."

Max looked at the gun in Ditter's hands. "Yeah, I guess that was stupid of me. Won't happen again. Anyway, I think we just found our way in." Max held up a SS colonel's uniform, and looked past Ditter to the visor on top of a box. He walked to it, took off the plastic covering and put it on his head. "Hey, it fits!"

Ditter took the hat off Max's head, went to another box and put a new hat back on Max. "They would have noticed that a major was not wearing the correct officer's visor." Ditter held up the first visor. "Look, no silver piping."

"Good thing you're here," Max smiled, and looked him over. "Now let's get you fitted."

• • •

Ditter, now dressed in a colonel's uniform, told Max that he would do all the talking if they came across anyone. As they walked down the hall, Ditter assured Max that they had properly dressed for the occasion. "You will be fine...just don't talk."

"Don't worry about me. Even though I can't speak the language, I can at least understand some of what they're saying."

"The good thing is that in the SS, the lower ranks never spoke in the presence of a commanding officer, unless they were addressed, ordered to, or had a message to relay."

They took a turn and headed into a wider hallway.

Up ahead, two lieutenants were talking. Ditter proceeded to reprimand Max for not having his paperwork ready for the up-and-coming fictitious meeting. The lieutenants, not wanting any part of the rage, lowered their gaze and tried to look busy as the colonel and his assistant walked by.

Max looked once more at his watch. They had less than five minutes to find Solange. Ditter pushed out a painted wood door and stepped into the grand stairway hall. A beautiful marble staircase ran the circumference of the three-story-tall room.

Ditter looked down from their perch to the bottom of the stairs, stopped, and turned to face Max. "See the two guards down below?" Ditter followed Max's eyes as they darted to the guards against the far wall, flanking a white door two stories down. "That is the elevator shaft. If we wait here she is bound to show up, but what do we do then?"

"We go with her." A full minute passed and next to the bottom of the staircase a door opened and Solange exited. "Ditter, here she comes."

Ditter tensed and looked back to see Solange being escorted by two armed SS sergeants. "Follow my lead," he said as he stepped down past the foyer entrance and down to the basement level.

"Are you sure about these red tags, Ditter?" Max asked, referring to the red tags found in the locked drawer of the tailor's desk.

"Yes, I'm sure...at least, that was the way they worked over 60 years ago. Now be quiet." Ditter straightened up, stepped onto the basement floor and headed to the elevator shaft.

"Sergeant."

Solange and the two sergeants turned to see who was addressing them. Solange gasped as she realized it was her grandfather in the black SS uniform.

Both sergeants saluted simultaneously, causing a saluting chain reaction to the two corporals guarding the elevator gate.

Ditter raised his right arm from the elbow. He turned to meet eyes with his granddaughter and spoke. "Fraulein Ludger, your father has asked me to accompany you down to the observation deck and explain what we are about to see." Ditter stepped aside just enough to let Solange see Max. Max had a blank stare, mostly due to the fact he had no idea what Ditter was saying.

"Pardon me, Colonel, but we must stay with Fraulein Ludger at all times."

"I did not order you to leave, did I, Sergeant?" Ditter acted as pompous as he could.

The sergeant thought for a moment and gave in. "I apologize, Herr Colonel."

Ditter just stared at the sergeant, trying to make the man uncomfortable. Satisfied that he had been intimidating enough, he turned to Solange. "The general has told me that you have not been a cooperative guest." Ditter laughed and turned to the sergeant with the bandaged nose, who in turn gave a slightly humiliated smile. "I hope that you will not be breaking my nose, as well."

A metallic shudder resonated behind the white, six-foot-wide door. One of the corporals turned and pulled it open. Behind it was an ornate iron gate. Ditter watched as the elevator stopped, aligning its steel floor with the castle's dark wood floor. "Ah, here is the elevator. Sergeant, if you will?" Ditter faced Max as the corporal slid open the gate and the sergeants' escorted Solange into the elevator. "Major, I know you are a busy man, and I have work to do before the countdown, but could you spare me a few minutes on our way down, before I let you go about your business?"

Max, still lost as to what was being discussed, just clicked his heels and did a slight bow in response. Ditter gave a slight nod to Max to follow him and they both stepped into the elevator. Max walked past Solange and the two sergeants, putting himself behind the group.

"Fraulein, did you know that the first time I rode this elevator I was a lowly lieutenant trying to earn my way up the promotion ladder? Who knew that so many decades later our great plan would still be in the works."

Ditter looked back at Max to make sure he was in position. Max pointed his chin to the grand stairway. Ditter looked over as the elevator operator closed the iron gates.

General Wehr was beginning to go down the stairs from the grand foyer when the sound of the metal gate closing caught his attention. He turned around, and saw, past the elevator gate, Solange, her guards, and an officer.

Max was the first one to catch the look on Wehr's face as he recognized Ditter in the colonel's uniform. The elevator operator had just turned the lever when the general took out his gun as he shouted, "Alarm!" He pointed at the elevator and got off a shot. The bullets ricocheted off the iron gate. "Stop that elevator! Intruders!"

The soldiers guarding the elevator shaft turned and joined Wehr as they shot a burst at the passing elevator roof as it dropped out of sight.

Max was already fighting a close-combat, hand-to-hand battle inside the moving elevator with the big sergeant. Being the first to see Wehr's reaction, Max had drawn his .22 and shot the closest sergeant in the head. The other sergeant's reflexes were quicker than Max had anticipated, and Max's bullet missed its intended target.

The sergeant knocked the .22 out of Max's hand and began delivering a multitude of punches that Max managed to block. Max, in return, hit the sergeant straight on the broken nose. He felt the nose flatten as the punch shattered the cartilage within, spraying blood on Max's hand and uniform. The sergeant grabbed his face in pain and Max took the opportunity to land three blows to his abdomen.

Ditter and Solange were busy, as well, both fighting the armed elevator operator. Ditter repeatedly hammered the butt of his gun into the operator's face as Solange kicked him wherever she could.

Max's blows didn't do much, since they hit the sergeant's bulletproof vest. The sergeant, furious now, lunged at Max, picked him up off his feet, and carried him to the far elevator wall. Max spread his arms out and swung them back in, slapping both of the sergeant's ears, rupturing his eardrums.

The sergeant let go and stumbled back. He reached over his back and grabbed his MP5. Max did the same, looking for the Glock, but his opponent was quicker on the draw.

The sergeant took aim, and his head exploded, spraying blood, bone, and brain matter onto the sidewall of the elevator.

Max turned to see Ditter's suppressed gun barrel smoking from the bullet that had just left it. Ditter looked at Max and asked if he was all right.

"Yeah. Solange, you okay?"

"I thought you were dead, Max," she said, accompanied by a small sob.

"Not yet, honey, not yet." Max put his hand on Ditter's raised gun, pushing it down. "You had to do it, Ditter."

"Yes, I did," Ditter whispered, taking one more second to contemplate what had happened, then he ran over to the elevator control handle. "It's a long run to the hangar. Are you ready?" he asked Solange as the elevator stopped.

Max pressed the communications button on the transmitter in his pocket three times. The elevator stopped in front of a green door. "What's behind the green door?" he asked Ditter.

"It's the green warehouse I told you about. We will have to run to the hangar if we don't find a car." Ditter slid the gate open.

Max picked up his .22. "I'm ready!"

Ditter pulled down on the bottom half of the green door. It slid down, and at the same time the top half slid up, revealing the extensive warehouse, and 20 fully armed SS soldiers pointing their weapons at them.

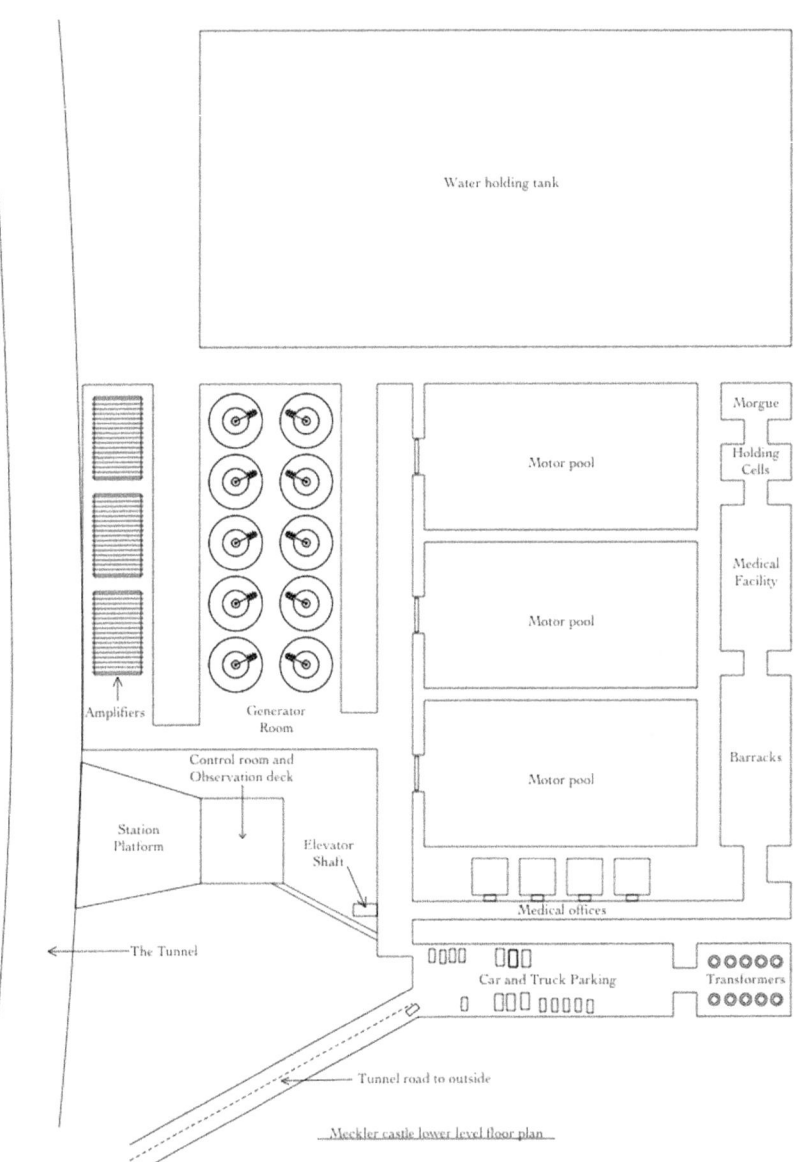

Water holding tank

Morgue

Holding Cells

Motor pool

Medical Facility

Motor pool

Amplifiers

Generator Room

Barracks

Control room and Observation deck

Motor pool

Station Platform

Elevator Shaft

Medical offices

The Tunnel

Car and Truck Parking

Transformers

Tunnel road to outside

Meckler castle lower level floor plan

12

Meckler Castle control room, November 23, 2010

Max's left eyebrow bled a continuous stream as he was thrown on and then cuffed to a heavy metal chair. His vision was blurred from losing consciousness, but he was aware that he was not the only one in the room as countless voices echoed from somewhere behind him.

A cold splash of water hit Max in the face.

"Thanks, that felt good." He managed a crooked grin at Hermann Wehr, who was holding a metal bucket. Wehr's fist flew, hitting Max, and sending one of his lower teeth flying out of his mouth. Max spat a glob of bloody saliva onto the black SS suit he still wore. "Good to see you, too, Hermann." He blinked hard, trying to focus and get a reading on his situation.

Hermann lifted his hand once more, but was stopped by his father's raspy voice.

"That's enough, Hermann. You can do what you want with him when we are done, but for now I want him to see what he failed to stop."

"All I wanted was the girl. I don't much care for your goose-stepping bullshit." Max spat out another mouthful of blood and saliva as he spoke.

General Wehr shook his head. "You have no idea what you have come across."

Max looked to his left and saw that Ditter and Solange were in similar chairs, handcuffed and gagged. It was then that he began to take in the surrounding space. He was seated in a theater-style room, with three rows of seats in front of him. To his right and back were a series of control stations. To his left, past Ditter, was a wall lined with what looked like servers. The room was white all over; even the iMacs were white. In front of him was a dark, wall-to-wall glass viewing window that reflected the rest of the room behind him, showing a crowd of men and women dressed in white doctor-type coats. It reminded Max of a NASA control room. The area also felt like that of a clean room, but it wasn't. His blood on the floor made that clear. Max looked up once more when he heard Wehr speak.

"Ditter, Ditter...." Klaus looked down at him, shaking his head. "I guess you are wondering how all this could be. How could a man who had escaped this place find himself here once more? Well, the answer is in the castle's logbooks. And you, Herr Von Ludger, caused some serious problems back in your day. Did you know that you are the only person to have ever known about this place outside of the Order? That is right, you were never indoctrinated. We had such high hopes, but then you had to go and sabotage your future." Klaus was starting to enjoy himself. "So, when I came across the notes on your escape I figured that the lowly lieutenant on the pages had met his death when he flew off the cliff in a car. A car!" Klaus laughed and shook his head. "You are one crazy old man! So it was to my surprise when I ran into you so many years after the war. I was a young man making my way in the world, trying to climb up that political ladder at that heads-of-state dinner. Remember? You told me your name and I did not think twice about it until you mentioned that you had flown in the war. So I did a bit of background checking on you, and what do you know? I had found the only man to successfully infiltrate the castle, cause damage to the infrastructure, take out a squad of SS guards, and escape." Klaus clapped his hands in a sarcastic cheer to Ditter.

"Since it had been so many years after the war and you had stayed quiet about the incident, I decided to sit back and watch you from afar. And then I met your widowed daughter-in-law, Olga." He smirked at the odds of him falling for her. "Love!"

Ditter stared him down.

"Oh, you don't think a man like me could love? Well, I can, and still do. Question is, will she stay alongside her man when all this is revealed?" He looked at his reflection in the glass wall. "Turn on the floodlights!"

The control room's lights dimmed and an immense room came to life in front of Max, just past the glass enclosure. A camera crew stepped into view, pointing a digital camcorder and spotlight at Wehr.

"What am I looking at, Wehr?" Max asked as he coughed, spraying a fine mist of bloody saliva onto the seat in front of him.

"You are looking at the beginning. You will see the New World Order reborn from this room. We will have control of world industries through the use of fear. We will conquer anyone who opposes us. We will rightfully take back that which was taken from us so long ago. We will once again become the master race."

"Wehr, I think you have been spending too much time playing soldi—"

The punch came out of nowhere. Max almost lost consciousness. Hermann picked up the bucket and poured the remaining ice-cold water over Max's head.

"Thank you, Hermann. Lieutenant Commander, you are trying my patience, but since my son will be killing you soon, I will allow your slander. Now if you don't mind, I will continue."

This time, Max kept his mouth shut.

This can't be. It's not possible. This guy is fucking nuts.

Max stared into Wehr's eyes. He took another long look at his surroundings, and then it hit him: *The crazy fucker is going to do it. After over 60 years he is actually doing it.* He looked at Wehr and tried to listen to what the man was saying through the ever-increasing humming noise.

"I digress. The sniper's bullet killed the general and left that scared 12-year-old this scar that fateful day in Berlin." Wehr reached up and caressed the scar hidden from view by the years of anger etched on his face. "But not before I was told about this." Wehr reached out with his hands, gesturing all around him. "He told me about what would happen and how I could bring back our dream of the one true race. Unfortunately, he was unable to tell me everything, but he said enough to lead us here. This will be the most important event the world has ever seen. Your life and mine are about to change. In a few moments it will all come to light and the final pieces to the puzzle will be in my hands to continue that which was lost. We will make the world bow to us. Soon we will have all we need. Soon we will be feared and respected once more." Wehr's crazed eyes grew wide. He took a deep breath and regained his composure. "I was the only one left with the secret." He looked back down at Max. "I was the only one left standing when the bombs fell. It was a miracle."

"Sir, countdown in one minute," said one of the technicians behind a control center.

"Can you believe it?" Wehr once again became excited at the thoughts racing through his head. His son looked at him in awe. "They left it all to a 12-year-old boy. It was I who was destined. It was I who would bring it all back!" Wehr pulled down on his uniform jacket and turned to face the empty room beyond the thick glass wall.

"Technology has been kind and allowed us to upgrade the systems since they were last tested. I couldn't risk 60-year-old equipment malfunctioning at this critical moment." Klaus laughed at his own joke. "We had all the codes except one—the most important one. All we needed next was the correct frequency, and time of activation, which you so kindly provided for us." He held up the thin black notebook that he had taken from Max back at the spa. "What are the odds? Incredible! Using the other codes we have tested and tweaked the computers so that today we would have a perfect evolution. The first couple were..." He searched the room for the correct word. "...messy. But eventually my team of scientists got it right and now we have a steady stream coming through!"

Klaus flipped through the notebook, then looked up as a female said, "Sir, it's time. Thirty seconds and counting." Klaus looked out into the staging area beyond the thick glass and regained his composure.

The film crew directed the camera to frame Wehr within the shot.

Behind them the control room increased in activity. "Rockets one through 16 are green. The Bell's accelerating past 600 knots, and climbing," said one voice in German.

"Ring's counter-rotation stable. Electrical current on and active. Electromagnets running full capacity. Systems reaching one gigawatt," someone with a South African English accent said in the background. "Center ring passing 12,000 rpms and climbing, all systems are armed and ready."

"Now, watch, and see as the New World Order returns!"

All the remaining nonessential personnel stopped what they were doing and looked up.

Max felt a strange vibration as his chair began to shake. The room lights flickered, then turned off. The sound grew louder and louder. His chair began shaking uncontrollably.

The left side of the tunnel grew brighter with every passing second. A red strobe light came on as a female voice counted down. All around them hard drives began to whirl and keyboards clicked as the rehearsed, machine-like dance occurred behind him.

"Six..."

"Initiating radar frequency," said another voice in French.

"Five...four..."

"Gate stabilization at 100 percent!" the South African voice shouted over the ear-piercing humming.

Inside the staging area, beyond the safety of the control room, water sprinklers came on, sending a constant spray inside the tunnel.

The sound became unbearable. Max's insides began to vibrate with every passing sound wave.

"Three..."

"Servers have control!"

His eyes squinted as he saw the staging area glow white-hot. Wehr, to his right, began laughing uncontrollably.

"Two...one..."

The darkness was now light, and in front of him stood the closed sliding door, its glass cracked outward from where the bullet had lodged a split second ago. His mind was still and all was quiet.

"You all right?" asked a voice next to him.

"Yeah...it's quiet. What was that light?"

"I don't know."

His hand went up and touched the bullet—it was hot. *Strange*, he thought. His eyes began to focus past the bullet wedged in the plate glass and on the winter wonderland past it.

"It's beautiful outside today."

He saw the white snow falling on the shapes behind the cracked plate glass. Where was he? What was it he was doing? He looked down at the machine gun and cocked his head as if trying to remember what had just happened. He looked past the cracked window again.

People...white statues of people....

"Sir?"

"Yes?"

"Oh, my God. Dean!" Collins grabbed Dean and dragged him past the second door. "Get down...NOW!"

Max could not believe it. A moment ago there was nothing, then the next there was the biggest subway train he had ever seen. The train glimmered white as if it had just come in from a blizzard. The spray of water had turned to snow.

Max looked the train up and down and figured that most of it was hidden out of sight.

"She is beautiful, isn't she, Hermann? Beautiful!"

All around them cheers erupted.

Max saw as the father and son team hugged each other passionately. He could have almost sworn he saw Wehr cry.

Max looked at the scene that unfolded in front of him. The train's outer skin was now starting to condense as vapor began to rise away from it. A yellow strobe light was drowned out as the hundreds of spotlights began to illuminate the staging area, which had suddenly turned into some sort of subway station. Behind him the scientists were back at work describing what they read on the screens.

"Phoenix evolution is at a 100-percent retrieval rate. Open decompression gate one, five percent."

"Electromagnetic plates reversal on and active. The Bell has come to a complete stop. Temperatures stable. Ring speed decreasing at a stable rate," said another voice.

"Prepare maintenance team for next evolution 64 hours 32 minutes on my mark. In three, two, one, mark."

"Oxygen levels increasing. Two minutes to level one for chamber door opening."

Max looked over the train and concentrated his gaze on the far left subway car. There was something off about the metal. He squinted. Right near the middle of the subway car, above the window line, was a hole big enough to fit a man. He pondered the problem, when suddenly the whole car expanded outward and burst into thousands of pieces.

It took less than a second for the concussion to hit the observation room glass wall, imploding it. Both Wehrs were sucked in through the new opening, followed by the camera crew, guards, and a couple of the scientists screaming past him. Max was saved the short ride into the subway station, as he was held firm to his chair by handcuffs.

The alarms went off all over the room's terminals. People started screaming at each other as steel plates slid across the destroyed window, effectively sealing the control room from the vacuum within the station.

"Open all the vents! We need to resupply the tunnel with air!"

Max looked around, trying to get his bearings. Loose sheets of paper danced in midair to the beat of the red strobe lights and wailing alarms. Then he felt something odd—a tingling in his numb hands as if the handcuffs had been loosened. He brought up his arms and the handcuffs were gone.

What the...?

He looked down at his wrists, then up at Solange and Ditter, and kneeling next to them was a man in a lab coat. Max climbed over the rows of seats and violently swung his limp right fist at the scientist's head, trying to knock him out, but the strike was blocked.

"Jesus, Max, you look like shit." Val smiled as he held on to his friend's wrist.

Max relaxed his guard and dropped his fighting stance. "Great timing, as always. How the hell did you get in here?"

"Man, can we talk about that when we get the fuck out of Dodge?" Val said as he un-cuffed Ditter. "Let's go." He pushed Ditter and Solange forward toward the server wall to their left.

"By the way, nice job on the train," Max said as he crunched down next to the seats, trying hard not to be seen by the scientists scrambling around the control room.

"If it were any other day I'd take credit for it. But today, that wasn't my work." Val handed Max his .22. "I got it off one of your guards before they went flying through the window. Almost got sucked out myself. Lucky for you my foot got stuck under one of the seats!" Val reached the server and stepped around it.

Max took the gun and checked that it was loaded. "Thanks. You're always one step ahead of the game."

They followed Val from the observation room and into a small hole in the wall beside one of the countless servers. Max was last in line as he stepped through and shut the hatch, leaving the chaos of the control room behind him.

Max looked at his new surroundings. The inside of the tunnel was lined with tubes and wires of all thicknesses and colors. They extended away in both directions from where he stood. Max bent down under one of the pipes as he rushed forward.

"Let's *go*," Ditter said.

Max hurried, trying hard to see the obstructions on the floor and avoiding the overhead pipes that were dimly illuminated by the unevenly spaced incandescent light bulbs. After some time he stepped into a cross tunnel to find Ditter and Solange hugging each other. Once Solange saw Max, she let go of her grandfather and ran to him, kissing him hard on his cut lip. Max winced at the pain, but kissed her back.

"Thank God we escaped."

"Well, we're not out of this yet. Val, what do we have here?" Max asked as he looked at their surroundings.

"First, introduce me to the lady, then we talk business." Val smiled at Solange.

"Solange, this is my best friend, Val."

Solange went over and gave Val a big kiss and a hug.

Val blushed.

"That was for saving us," Solange turned her attention to Max. "How do we get out of here?"

"Well, that depends." Max turned to Val. "How's the situation looking?"

"Pardon my French, but the situation is all fucked up. First, no offense, Ditter, but you should have warned me about all the body parts in the cistern warehouse. That room was fucked up. Then after I spent a few minutes puking out my dinner, I noticed that I was passing out from a lack of O_2."

Ditter looked at Val. "Sorry, I did not figure that after 60 years they would have still been doing experiments."

"Seems that they got it right this time, though," muttered Max.

"Yeah, whatever. Anyway, I had to hold my breath and hope that the door on the opposite side was unlocked, and luckily for all of us it was. Well, it led into this tunnel with a yellow stripe and it too was empty, but I did find a couple of storerooms with boxes and shit, and that's when I found these service tunnels. Man, this place is fuckin' immense. Ditter, let me tell you that you have yet to see what we are standing in. I actually ran across an electrical processing plant as big as the Hoover Dam. The tunnels went farther on, but I was pressed for time. Then I heard the strange humming sound. So, like a cat, I went to go check it out."

Max rechecked the MP5. "That's when you found us?"

"And then some."

Max jumped, as did the others, when they heard the loud rapping of machine gun fire. The cross tunnel they were in began to spark as the nine-millimeter bullets ricocheted off the walls and tubes around them. Val grabbed Ditter and Solange from the line of fire and pulled them to safety.

"Val, is that the way out?" Max asked as he fired his MP5 down the tunnel.

"Yeah, we just follow the yellow tube next to you; that will take us to the cistern room level. Come on, I'll cover you." This time Val shot his MP5, keeping the attackers at bay.

"No, you guys go. I'll draw them toward me and hold them back for a while."

"Max, no!" Solange screamed over the sound of the firing machine guns.

"Don't worry about me! I'll be with you in no time!"

Max winked as he saw Val toss his vest at him.

"You need it more than I do. Good luck! First one at the bar buys the drinks, and don't worry, I'll take care of your girl!" Val let out another round of bullets down the tunnel, then grabbed Solange and pulled her away.

The sound of gunfire diminished the farther away they got. Solange was angry about having left Max, but the big guy behind her would not listen. "Damn it! How could you leave him, Val? He is your best friend!"

"Honey. First...keep your voice down; and second, my friend back there is now in his element."

"What do you mean?"

"Max is the best man I've ever met at the art of one-man war. I'd worry for the other guys if I were you."

Val took point once he thought that they were ahead of any danger. He slowed his pace down at the cross tunnels, which in turn helped give Solange and Ditter time to catch their breath.

"Not much farther n—"

Solange stood in shock as two wires shot out from a dark cross tunnel and into Val's chest. He started shaking uncontrollably. Ditter ran toward Val, pushed Solange aside, and knocked the wires away from Val's chest with his outstretched arms.

Val fell to his knees, dropping his weapon in the process. He was conscious, but weak when three men clad in dark uniforms ran forward and knocked Ditter and Solange down with a strike from their weapons.

Val tried to raise his hand as the third man came toward him, but he couldn't. The man stood above him, smiled, and spoke in a South African English accent. "I'm going to have me some fun torturing this *Kaffir*."

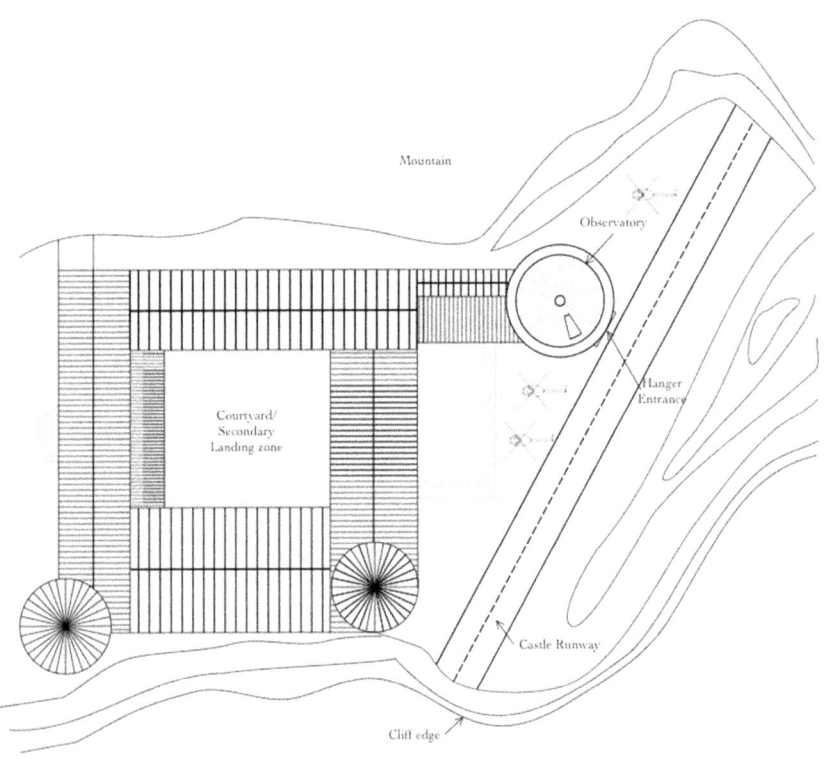

Mountain

Observatory

Hanger
Entrance

Courtyard/
Secondary
Landing zone

Castle Runway

Cliff edge

Meckler castle roof and site plan

246

13

Meckler Castle Battle

Corporal Ramirez, a member of Val's SEAL team, lay hidden below a white tarp outside and across from the castle's runway, overlooking the helicopters and the sentries guarding them. The SEAL team had arrived at the site via a very difficult high-altitude parachute jump that landed the team close to the peak of the mountain. From there they'd scaled down the cliff face and taken cover on the far side of the runway.

"I have two tangos smoking cigarettes 10 meters from the helicopter to the south, and two more by the hangar door," he said into his neck mike and waited for a reply. Ramirez shifted under the white camouflaged tarp, 50 meters northwest of the castle runway.

"Roger," Monk replied, the team's highest-ranking member and the direct link to headquarters.

Ramirez watched as the men by the helicopter began to jerk around like rag dolls, their arms flailing about.

"We have a situation." Ramirez aimed his sniper rifle sight away from the fallen bodies and toward the two guards next to the hangar, who began to perform the same dance, but this time he could see the blood. "Monk, something is really fucked up here; all four of my targets are down." Then he saw them. Eight men landed in front of the hangar door, followed by their gray-and-white parachutes. The men unhooked their parachutes as soon as they touched the ground and split into two-by-two formations. Ramirez called out their movements over the radio. "Are we expecting company?"

"I don't know what's going on. Intelligence says that we're the only strike team. Can you identify the weapons?"

"Hold on." Ramirez took out his 25 magnification binoculars and began to study the soldiers. "Monk, I count eight weapons, all urban assault rifles of some kind, two with scopes. They all look to be wearing biologic suits."

"Roger. Keep a tally of their movements. I need to contact headquarters." He switched frequencies. "Nest. Eagle." Monk paused, waiting for a reply.

"Go, Eagle."

"Hostiles. Eight. Took out sentries and securing landing zone."

"Eagle, copy. Relaying."

An Army second lieutenant from behind a 27-inch computer screen in a 20-by-20-foot situation room a few stories below the Pentagon ground floor, turned his head and spoke to General West. "Sir?"

"Orders still stand. Observe and report," said General West.

West paced in front of the five flat-screen televisions on the wall as the second lieutenant gave the orders to Monk. The center screen showed a live satellite view of the castle from above. Within this view five green dots fluctuated in intensity, depicting the exact positions of the Eagle team members who'd parachuted in from 35,000 feet, and taken positions around the perimeter of the runway next to the castle.

The far left screen showed the infrared view of the center screen. West could see how Omega's covert team had split into pairs. Three pair hit the helicopters, the remaining pair worked on the hangar door.

West looked down at his watch, and headed to his computer terminal at the back of the room. He sat down, punched in his code, and the screen split into four. Unbeknownst to the rest of the room, every action that was sent, taken, or seen was duplicated in another smaller situation room somewhere else inside the Pentagon; Omega's control room.

West had connections to both rooms, and through his computer terminal was giving duplicate orders. So far everything was going as planned. West typed in a few more codes and the exact position of the Navy SEAL team was sent out to Omega's mercenaries now entering the castle. The instructions were specific: Eliminate all personnel after recovery mission was complete.

Best-case scenario for West was to take the whole castle and make the events of the night disappear in the Pentagon archives. This would make Omega happy. Worst case was to hit a massive defensive force and have to retrieve as much information as possible before sending in the Army Rangers. The key to his secondary plan was to have his people out before the Rangers stepped in.

The current plan was still in effect. The rest of Omega's covert team would land after the satellite, which West had access to, failed. From there, radio communications would be taken over by the Omega covert team, who now had all the Go codes. The SEALs would remain in place as observers until the covert team had accomplished the mission. Finally, either the covert team would take over the premises, then terminate the SEAL team, and/or if they ran into heavy resistance, would gather all the intelligence possible, destroy all the evidence (which included setting off an Electro Magnetic Pulse bomb which would destroy anything electric), then evacuate via helicopters, leaving the Rangers to pick up the mess.

West knew that failure to occupy and hold the castle was not in his favor. Omega would not look too kindly upon that, and would most likely terminate his own involvement with them via heart attack, car accident, or countless other ways to kill him without suspicion.

Omega had picked him for his forward thinking, though. That was what he was best at, always thinking 10 steps ahead of the rest. West stared at the blip on the far left screen on the wall depicting the flight path of all the aircraft in the air. Of particular interest to him was the Ranger's C-130 on its way to the castle. This was his wild card, and if all hell broke loose he would bring them in.

It was all a waiting game now. The Omega mercenaries had strict orders for radio silence. Since Bluetooth communication had a limited 40-foot signal strength it was the preferred method of communication between them. This minimized any accidental discovery of their transmissions from an outside source. His real-time intelligence was the SEAL team members watching the castle from afar, and by luck, the transmissions they had with the personnel inside. West clicked on the lower screen to bring up the files of Val Vittoria and Max DuMonde.

He studied them once more, trying to see if he could pick out anything else from the two-dimensional descriptions on the computer screen in front of him. Val was a grunt by every sense of the word. He, like DuMonde, had started his Navy life at the Naval Academy, graduated, and headed to flight school. From there they'd split to fly different aircraft. Vittoria chose helicopters, which led him to the Osprey Program, and DuMonde jets, finishing up with the F-18 Super Hornet.

They'd done tours in Iraq, Afghanistan, and Pakistan before they'd unexpectedly joined the SEAL training program, and finished the training with high marks. DuMonde never entered the active teams because he was injured in a skydiving training accident; Vittoria had saved his life.

Both worked well together, and they had the ability to think through problems in high-stress situations. West thought about his contingency plan; the one that only he had knowledge of. So far it would be a 98-percent chance that he didn't need to implement the Ranger strike force...so far.

He calculated the C-130's estimated time of arrival over the castle and sent a coded message giving Omega's team a new mission statement: to either take over the castle, or recover all the information and evacuate within two hours.

West leaned back in the leather chair, which creaked and stretched under his heavy, muscular body. He put his hands behind his neck and stretched as he looked over the screens on the wall. The game was on.

The concussion of the explosion threw Dean and Collins 15 feet from the secondary door in the subway train. Collins was the first to get up and survey the damage. The door he had dragged his friend through had closed seconds before Dean's satchel charge had gone off. It had absorbed the deadly impact of the explosion, but sustained irreparable damage.

"Damn, I owe you another one!" Dean said as he stood up.

"That you do, sir." Collins tried to look through the intact but shattered glass. He pressed his hand to a small crack in the door seal and noticed that the pressure was equal on both sides. "Sir, I think there's air back in the tunnel; we can't go this way, so let's double back to Bill. God knows we need the firepower when we run into the SS again."

"On the way out remind me to pick up the charge we left behind. I think we're going to need it."

"Will do." Collins passed Dean, taking point as they stepped through the subway train toward the rear exit.

Dean looked in amazement at his surroundings. His boots crunched the new, powdery snow beneath him. "That wasn't there before..." he said as they sneaked past a gigantic metal door that took up the full height of the tunnel. Inside, they could see soldiers and crew moving a crane toward the opening. "Keep going. Too many of them."

They were now in search of the small room where they'd last seen Bill.

We should have seen it by now.... No, wait...there it is. Train must have moved while we were in it.

Dean was first to climb up the curved wall and once at the door, he looked through the window. The room seemed different. There was a small, upright, flat rectangle on the desk against the wall that had not been there before. Worse, Bill was nowhere to be seen.

"I think we passed the room. Bill's not in this one and it just looks... different." Dean looked above the door at the flashing green light, grabbed the door handle, and pulled. The door slid smoothly into the wall. They both stepped in, and turned their heads when they heard a rumbling coming from within the tunnel.

Dean and Collins both poked their heads out the door opening and watched in disbelief. "What the fuck is that?" Collins asked.

"They're rotating in different directions." Dean whispered to his friend, who was staring awestruck at the sight heading toward them.

The machine was huge, bigger and stranger than anything he had ever seen. It took up the full diameter of the tunnel.

"Christ, must be close to 10 stories high!" Collins said.

The strange part about it was its shape. The whole structure was smooth and aerodynamic, composed of seven rings, each smaller than the previous, turning in opposite directions from each other. The final and smallest ring contained hundreds of antennas radiating from its inner circumference. At the base of each antenna were cylindrical bowls, like dinner-plate-sized dimples on a golf ball.

Both men leaned back as the ringed structure passed by the door. Its metallic outer surface covered the opening.

Dean began to count. When he got to 20 the back end of the machine slid past. He stuck his head out the opening once more and took a long look at the machine as it retreated away.

"That thing must be at least 20 meters long."

"What do you want to do?"

"I doubt this explosive charge will do much. We'll just leave it to the Army boys to figure out. Let's find Bill and Vic, 'cause we're going to need to create as much confusion in this place as possible until the armored division gets here." Dean looked at his watch. "Which should be any time soon."

"What do you make of this?" Collins pointed at the flat, thin rectangular object on the desk.

"Don't know."

"That's a strange typewriter." Collins looked at the letters on the thin board, and then turned to see Dean open another smaller, sliding door opposite from the door they had entered.

"Never mind that," Dean said.

Collins took one last look at the flat object and followed Dean into the tunnel beyond the door.

Dean had taken point within the small maintenance tunnel. They both maneuvered themselves around a jigsaw puzzle of pipes of all sizes and colors and stopped when they stepped into a spherical connecting cross tunnel. The tunnel radiated out into five paths.

"Collins. Take the left tunnel, follow the gray pipes, and I'll keep to the red pipes. Walk it for five minutes, then come on back. If I'm not back in 10, come after me and I'll do the same with you."

"See you in 10."

Dean turned and headed down his tunnel, listening to the surrounding sounds. He looked at his watch after some time. *Five minutes.*

Machine gun fire erupted farther down the tunnel. He was surprised at the rate of fire; it was almost twice as fast as the MP-40 German submachine gun. He reached up and unscrewed the light bulb above his head. Then he crouched down next to a concrete outcrop, checked that the clip in his grease gun was secure, and cocked his Schofield. There was a loud explosion, followed by a lone figure in the distance running toward him.

Dean kept his barrel down, being careful not to accidentally shoot Collins, who was also running around in the tunnels. The man down the narrow tunnel took cover inside a small slit in the wall 10 meters in front of him. Shortly after, more figures, clad in black, ran past the slit and toward Dean's position. The lead figure stopped and crouched, raising a fist up into the air. He then raised one finger and pointed twice to Dean's position. Another man stepped forward and threw a round ball at him.

Oh, shit!

Dean had nowhere to go, and the only protection was the small concrete outcropping. He watched as the grenade flew toward him, hit the edge of the outcropping, then bounced away as it fell onto the floor and rolled into a small drainage hole.

Of all the dumb luck.

The explosion was muffled, but sent concrete flying in all directions. Dean took a close look at himself to find that he was still intact, then aimed his grease gun through the dust cloud and sent out a burst of copper toward the enemy. In response, a hail of bullets began to pepper his cover at an extreme rate.

All of a sudden the firing just stopped.

Dean peeked down the tunnel through the thick dust, unable to see more than two feet in front of him. Then a shadow came out of the cloud, shooting once. The bullet ricocheted off the concrete pillar next to his head just as Dean swung out of his perch, but it was too late. The SS uniformed man knocked the machine gun out of his hands.

Dean jabbed his right hand up, knocking the gun from the SS man's hand and sending it flying at the opposite wall. He took the split-second opening and threw an uppercut at the enemy's jaw, but missed as the soldier ducked and weaved, in turn landing a hard kick in Dean's stomach. Dean flew back, momentarily blacking out as the back of his head bounced off the hard concrete wall. Dean regained sight as he saw a fist coming straight at his nose, but it never made contact.

The fist remained in midair inches from Dean's face. His focus turned from the bloody knuckles to the man's face, which had cocked to the side in question. He took advantage of the unforeseen distraction and kicked the SS soldier in the groin, knocking the breath out of him. Dean quick-drew his 1875 Schofield, but the soldier swung both hands up in a cross pattern, made hard contact with Dean's hand before he got a bead, and sent the Schofield flying away.

Now unarmed, Dean reached up to the K-bar knife on his chest and pulled down and out, and lunged forward. The soldier spun out to his left, grabbing his hand in the process. Now they were both back to back, but only for a split second. The soldier stepped out and turned Dean's arm back toward his shoulder. Dean, in an effort to shake himself loose, leaped up into the air, using the pipes on the curved wall to gain footing, and pushed himself off the wall, somersaulted backward, and landed hard on his side. The soldier, still holding Dean's wrist, twisted it, causing great pain, and forced Dean to turn onto his stomach and to simultaneously drop the knife.

Dean knew he had lost the fight and accepted defeat, but then he heard the familiar puff of a suppressed M3-A1. The soldier flew off his feet and onto his back as the .45 caliber copper bullet hit him straight in the chest. Dean lifted his head and saw Collins holding the smoking barrel of the grease gun.

"Never seen anybody fight like that before. I had to wait until he kicked your ass before I had a clean shot."

"He didn't kick my ass, I let him win," Dean said as Collins helped him up off the ground.

"No... I did kick your ass," Max mumbled.

Collins and Dean both jumped back as they saw the soldier squirm on the floor.

"You mind not pointing that cannon at me?" Max asked, taking a deep breath as he grabbed his chest. "You're late."

"Excuse me? Who are you?" Dean asked.

Collins kept his grease gun pointed at Max.

"What? Aren't you guys with Val's team?"

"No. Who the fuck is Val?" Dean had picked up his Schofield and now pointed it at Max.

What is up with the uniforms? "Wait a minute, that's an M3-A1," Max said as he looked over the grease gun. "And what the hell are you doing with that old Schofield?"

"Well, he knows his weapons. Are you American?"

"What kind of question is that? Of course I am, and so are you. What the fuck is going on?"

"You tell us! You're the one with the SS uniform."

"Oh, this thing—" He was about to answer but was cut off.

"You a spy?"

"What?"

"Who won the World Series in '39?"

"Nineteen thirty-nine? How the fuck should I know?"

"That's good enough for me." Collins moved the suppressed barrel closer to Max's head.

"No, wait." Dean held his hand up. "You a U.S. soldier?"

"Yes, I'm a lieutenant commander, U.S. Navy."

"What's the Navy doing here?"

"Well, aren't you guys Navy, as well?"

"No, Marines."

"Jarheads?"

Dean smirked at the insult. "Son, what's your name, rank, and serial number?"

"Lieutenant Commander Max DuMonde, U.S. Navy." He rattled off his serial number.

"DuMonde?"

Collins and Dean looked at each other.

"Yes. Now who are you?" Max asked as he heard a noise coming down the tunnel. "Scratch that. Now that we are clear that we are fighting on the same side, can we get out of here before they send more fucking Nazis after us?"

Dean looked down the tunnel and back at the swollen face of the Navy officer. "Get up."

Max stood up and rubbed his chest. "Man, that .45 really packs a punch." Max pulled out the ceramic plate inside the bulletproof tactical vest and held it up.

"What are you wearing?"

"A vest," Max said to Dean as if it were a stupid question.

"Got to get me one of those," Collins said as he let his guard down.

Max turned around and walked away.

"Where you going?" Dean called after Max.

"Need guns and ammo, and a new plate." Max bent down and picked up the .22, which had lodged itself between a yellow-and-gray pipe.

"Freeze! Drop the gun now!" Dean aimed the cocked Schofield at Max's back. "No guns for you until I can verify who you are."

Max aimed his .22 away from Dean and Collins and shot one of the squirming bodies on the floor. "If I wanted you dead, I would have killed you by now," Max said as he removed the now empty clip from the .22 and replaced it with a fresh one. He pulled back on the action, reloaded the weapon, then slid it in between the uniform belt and his pants. "Now, Wild Bill, may I grab these guns? God knows we are going to need them to get out of this hell hole."

"Wild Bill...now that was funny!" Collins laughed.

"Don't do that again. I almost shot you." Dean pointed the Schofield away from Max.

"Shoot me, don't shoot me...either way we need each other to get the hell out of here, Marine."

"Fine, but keep an eye on him, Collins." Dean turned to look at Max. "And I'm a major."

Max nodded. "How you guys doing on ammo? Oh, and that reminds me, who the fuck assigned you those old grease guns?"

"Old? These are the best we have for special operations."

Max was confused. "This is going to sound kind of weird, but how did you guys end up here?"

"We parachuted in."

Max handed Dean an MP5.

Dean looked the gun over. "What type of weapon is this?"

Max looked at Dean, then at Collins, then at their uniforms.

Oh...my...God.

Max could not hide his shocked expression. "You've never seen that type of submachine gun before, have you?" It was more a statement than a question.

"No, why? Should I have? Why are you looking at me like that?"

"Let's find a safer place, then I'll explain it to you." He looked at Collins. "What's your name?"

"Collins, Master Sergeant Collins. *Sir*," he said, drawing out the "sir."

"Sergeant, you and the major here should don those vests."

"Why, Commander?"

"It'll be stupid if you don't and take one in the chest...now that you've traveled so far," Max mumbled the end of the sentence.

Dean and Collins agreed. They remove their packs and began to clumsily put the vests on. Max stepped in and helped them tighten the vests.

"It has to be tight. What you got in them packs?"

"Ammo, grenades, rations, first aid kit."

Max thought it over. "Leave everything but the ammo, grenades, and one first aid kit. We need to be light, and if things go as planned, we should have some help on the way."

"Well, the First Armored Division should be right around the bend."

Max tried to ignore the comment, still in a state of disbelief. He looked past them. "Collins, where did you come from just now?"

"Down that tunnel," he said and pointed with the barrel of his M3-A1. "I ran into some medical offices before I turned back."

"Yeah, I know the place. We should be able to get to the warehouse levels from there."

"How do you know the area?"

"That's where Hermann...the general's son, used me for a punching bag. They then dragged me past some barracks, a hospital, the holding cells and ended at the morgue. I thought I was a dead man. But it seems that Wehr's ego saved me."

"I was wondering what had happened to your face," Dean said as he uncocked the Schofield, spun it once, and slid it back in the cross-draw holster.

Max checked out the fancy gun work and was a bit impressed. "Are you done playing with that toy?" he jabbed. Dean squinted at him. Max smiled. "Okay, then let's head out."

Collins stepped over and around the maze of pipes and after a couple hundred paces stopped in his tracks. He raised his fist and pointed to his ear. Max and Dean both heard it, as well—the painful screams of a man being tortured.

They moved until they could see the reverse side of the office's ceiling tiles hanging from the concrete above them.

It was then that the man doing the screaming told off his torturer. "Go fuck yourself, you Aryan fuck!"

The humming sound of electricity was soon followed by the man's scream.

"Val…" Max whispered. "I have to get to him," he said to Dean.

Dean nodded and Max withdrew his .22 as he crawled in the direction of the electric humming. Max stopped and looked down through the crack in one of the ceiling tiles.

Val was strapped naked to a metal chair. Electrodes and wires had been stuck to his skin all around his groin area. Two men in black uniforms laughed as one of them shut off the electricity and spoke with a heavy English South African tone. "Where is your *Kaffir* lover friend?"

Val spit on his face. The humming increased once again and Val grunted through the pain and slumped once the electricity stopped. "Johan, would you like to give blacky here a tr—"

Johan was confused when his partner did not finish the sentence. The man stood there in mid-thought and then fell forward. Johan rushed to his side and was met with the same fate; a .22 copper bullet to the top of his head.

Max moved one of the square plaster ceiling tiles and dropped down onto the white tile floor of the medical room, careful not to slip on the blood. He motioned to Val to scream and opened the door. A guard stood outside in an empty hall facing away from him. Max aimed and shot the guard in the head. He caught the falling body and dragged it into the room, shut the door, and watched as Collins dropped down from the ceiling.

Max went up to Val, who smirked at him. "Take it easy when you pull out those electrodes, *sailor*."

"I'm glad to see that you still have your sense of humor."

"Yeah, so who are these guys?"

"Commander Val Vittoria meet Master Sergeant Collins and Major..."

"Dean DuMonde," Dean said, finishing Max's sentence.

Max froze at the sound of the name.

Collins had cut the duct tape around one of Val's arms and began to cut the tape off the other arm when he saw Max step back and lean against the far wall.

"What is it, Commander?" Dean asked.

"Your name is DuMonde?" Val said. "You guys have the same oddball last name. What are the odds of that? Remove that camouflage paint from your face and you kinda look alike, as well." Val slowly got up from the metal chair.

"Yeah." Max shook his head, trying to get a grip of what was unfolding. "Major, I have a question. Now, just bear with me. Is your wife's name Olive?"

"How the hell did you know that?" Dean asked, clearly surprised. "Have we ever met?" He thought about it. "No. Only other Max DuMonde I know is my brother," he said quietly.

"No, we have never met. Hold on, let me get my bearings. Val, if you are here, where are Solange and Ditter?"

"Last time I saw them, they were in a holding cell."

"By the morgue?"

"Yes."

"Collins, help Val look around for some painkillers and bandages to patch us up."

Collins started going through the drawers in the room as Val got dressed.

Max then turned to Dean. "Major, could you step over here for a moment?"

As Dean walked over to him at the other side of the long medical room, Max wondered how he was going to tell him the truth about his situation.

"What is it, Commander?"

"Max, Major. You can call me Max."

"Okay, Max. What is it?"

"Bear with me. What day is it, Major?"

"April 30th."

"And what year is it?" Max had to make sure this was really happening.

"What?"

"Just answer the question. What year is it?"

"Nineteen forty-five, of course. Why?"

How do I tell them? Max took a deep breath, "Sir, you and I have stumbled on one of the greatest inventions ever made. This place, everything that was built around us, was built for one purpose."

"What purpose is that?"

"To see that the Third Reich's master plan would never fail."

"But it has failed. The Russians are inside Berlin; the Nazi forces are all but gone. There is nothing they can do to win, let alone turn the outcome of this war."

"Yes. That is what we were all meant to *believe*. Until you and I found this." Max spread out his arms.

"You mean that thing in the tunnel? What can that thing do to change the war?"

"It is not changing the war, it's just moving it someplace else."

"Someplace else? What are you talking about? Where?"

Max looked into his grandfather's eyes. "The 21st century."

14

They stepped through the service tunnels and moved past the hospital ward below them, which was filling up with patients.

"Where did all these Nazis come from?" Val asked as he stepped over a light blue pipe.

"Look to be victims from our little show back at the subway station," Collins whispered as he tailed Val.

"That was you? Nice job!" said Val.

"Thank you...I guess," responded Collins.

They arrived above the morgue after navigating through the maze of tunnels. Max crawled down onto his stomach and lifted one of the plaster ceiling tiles, and peeked into the dark room. He put it back in place and turned to his team. "Apart from the dead bodies, it's empty. Val, what's farther down the tunnel?"

"We make a left up ahead and that leads us to the power station water supply, but the tunnels loop back around and split. One side, the one with all the red pipes, goes to the power station and the observation room where I found you. The yellow pipes lead us back to the warehouses. And those gray pipes take you to the motor pool. It could be an alternate escape route or we could get sandwiched. Either way we are looking at around 10 minutes to get to the yellow warehouse."

Max thought about it for a moment. "Okay, then we grab Solange and Ditter and head out the way we came and follow the yellow brick road. At least we know where it ends up."

"Hold on there, Max. Who are Solange and Ditter?" Dean asked.

"She's his girlfriend," Val snickered.

"What? We are risking capture for a girl? I think our main priority is to stop whatever the hell is going on here."

Max looked toward Dean. "Frankly, Major, we don't have enough manpower to do much damage. So my plan is to get the girl and her grandfather, leave this dungeon, and then call in the troops. If that's all right with you."

There was a few seconds of silence. "Lieutenant Commander, right now I don't quite grasp or know what's going on, but since it looks like you have your mind set, and splitting our firepower would be suicide, I will go with your plan. But if we do have the opportunity to do some damage, I'm going to take it," Dean said forcefully.

Val pushed himself past Max. "If you guys are done, we have work to do." He removed one of the tiles and jumped down into the morgue.

Max lay on the cold concrete floor and looked through the small slit under the door, catching a glimpse of three pairs of shoes. Two were standing next to a steel door and the other looked to be at a desk.

Max pushed himself up and turned to Val. "I've got a plan."

• • •

It was the guard closest to the morgue's door who first heard the sound.

"What are you doing, Corporal?" the sergeant behind one of the two metal desks called out.

"Heard a noise, going to check it out."

"Private, go with him. And remember that we are on high alert."

The corporal and private walked the 20 steps to the morgue's entrance, and heard the sound again.

"Shit! It's moaning. One of our guys is still alive!"

They ran to the door and opened it to find a naked dead body flying toward them.

"Jesus!" was the last word the private uttered as .45 caliber bullets entered him and the corporal. The sergeant at the desk had managed to escape the deadly wall of copper as he opened and fell through the thick metal door with only two bullets lodged in his body.

Max ran to the doorway the sergeant had escaped through, opened it, and was greeted by a crowd of SS soldiers running toward the cellblock, intent on killing him.

Max shut and locked the door. "We've got company!" he yelled as a barrage of bullets began to dent the metal.

Val was working on the cell lock when Max stepped next to him and whispered in his ear, "Take your time, why don't you?"

"Go fuck yourself."

Click.

The door opened and Solange was the first to run out and hug Val.

"This is neither the time, nor the place to make your boyfriend jealous," Val smiled at Solange.

"If we are all done with this moment, I would like to leave," Dean said to Val.

"See, Max, I told you jarhead officers have a sense of humor."

Another barrage of bullets riddled the door. This time it was Collins who spoke. "One thing I have learned in my time is that these Nazis are not as dumb as you think. So it's a matter of time before they figure it out and blow up that nice little door behind us."

Max stepped next to Solange and placed a gentle hand on her arm. "You all right?" he asked.

"Yes. You don't look so good."

"I'll be fine. Come on, let's get you out of here." He pointed to the morgue's open door as another barrage of bullets slammed into the door behind them. "Change of plans. We go the long way. Val, you have point."

Max was the last one up into the ceiling. A loud explosion tore through the holding block, sending the door flying off its hinges across the hall, embedding itself into the concrete wall.

Max put the roof tile back in its place and hurried down the tunnel right behind Dean. After a short sprint, Max grabbed Dean by his shoulder. Dean turned and looked at Max, who held his finger up to his lips. "They're in the tunnels."

Dean nodded when he heard the sounds echoing throughout the tunnel. "What do you want to do about it?"

Max looked through a small glass window embedded in the wall. "Do you still have those explosive charges?"

"Yeah, why?"

"Wanna do some damage?" He grinned at Dean.

Dean was beginning to like this guy. "Sure, what do you have in mind?"

"Quick, set the timer to 10 minutes and put it—" Max looked around for a spot. "Here. Yeah, that should do the trick."

"What are you talking about?"

"You and our Nazi friends down the tunnel will find out in 10 minutes. Check your watch and let's go. Trust me, you do not want to be anywhere in this area when that charge goes off." Max slapped Dean's back as he ran past him.

"Crazy Navy swab," Dean muttered as he set the charge, then ran to catch up.

Max passed each member of the group and told them that they had to pick up the pace. Val, who was now leading the group, kept his concentration on the tunnel ahead as Max explained his little diversion.

"Man, you should have asked me first. What happens if we run into trouble?" Val then raised his MP5 and emptied it at the dark tunnel ahead. "Cover!" he yelled back. "This is what I was talking about!"

Instinctively, Max took cover as a barrage of bullets ricocheted off the concrete column he had hidden behind. He waited a moment and began to shoot into the dark void. Val reloaded and looked back, making sure the rest of the group had taken cover.

"Great! What now, genius?" Val yelled at Max as a volley of deadly hot copper was exchanged.

"Reloading!" Max yelled.

Val took up position and shot in burst mode at the unseen enemy as Max reloaded.

Max looked back when he heard the distinctive sound of the grease gun going off.

"We are taking fire!" Collins yelled as he reloaded and Dean shot into the dark tunnel.

Fuck! Sandwiched.

"They are making us use all our ammunition!" Max said.

"You think?" Val yelled sarcastically. "Reloading!"

Max took up position and began to shoot in the dark as Val reloaded.

"Shit! Grenade!" Dean yelled from behind.

Max turned to see Dean jump forward, grab a long stick grenade, and throw it back into the dark tunnel. The grenade flew through the air and hit another grenade coming the opposite way. Dean's grenade exploded and ignited the second grenade, causing part of the tunnel to give way.

The concussion from the two grenades going off simultaneously shook everyone within the tunnel. Max could barely hear Dean yelling at him from the after-effect of the explosion, but he knew what he was saying. Max grabbed Val, who was busy putting holes in the tunnel walls, and motioned him to look back.

"Got it!" Val said, "Go! Go! Go! I'll cover!" he yelled as he saw Max grab Solange and Ditter and disappear into a dark hole. Val stepped back until he was back to back with Collins, both shooting in opposite directions. Then he saw Dean pull out two satchel charges and throw one in each direction before dropping through the hole. Collins then grabbed Val, and pulled him off his feet and down into the dark hole in the floor of the tunnel.

Val fell eight feet onto wooden crates below and rolled several times before he was dragged, again by Collins, with the extra pull from Dean, down the pile of boxes and behind what looked like a truck. They managed to take cover behind it as both satchel charges went off, disintegrating everything in the tunnel above their heads. The German halftrack truck they now took cover behind took the brunt of the explosion, along with the wooden crates around it, which were now on fire, giving the giant chamber an eerie glow.

"That was fun!" Val said to Collins as he stood up and looked at the hundreds of trucks, cars, and equipment surrounding them.

Collins slapped Val on his back. "You're all right in my book!"

"Thanks, man. And thank you for pulling me out."

"Kiss already!" Max said as he surveyed their new location. It was another warehouse carved out of the mountain, much like the green warehouse, except this one had a painted gray horizontal line adorning its walls and was filled to capacity with vehicles of all types, all neatly lined up in rows that stretched out toward a door embedded into the far wall, two football fields away.

"Val, how far were we from the elevator shaft when we hit that ambush?"

"Still had a ways to go. A few hundred meters, I'd guess."

"Six minutes, Commander," Dean said.

Max looked at his watch, then back at Dean. He jumped up onto a WWII Tiger tank and scanned the area. "Collins, you know how to drive this thing?"

"Sure, if it runs."

"Well, lucky for us the Nazis have been fueling up. Look at the gas truck over there. Spread out and find a tank that has been filled up. And hurry!"

The group fanned out, and 20 seconds later Max heard the engine of a Tiger tank come to life. They all arrived at Collins's new toy.

"Hop in," he said as his head stuck out a small hatch.

It was a tight fit in the cabin.

Max noticed that Dean was not among them. "Where's the major, Collins?"

"Right on top of you. Here, grab these. I figured we could use them," Dean answered from above the open commander's tank hatch.

Max reached up and grabbed a heavy tank shell. He brought it down, looked around in the cabin, and found the ammunition storage.

"How many did you get?"

"Just two, and this ammunition belt for the machine gun. It's all I could carry."

"That will have to do, then. Collins, floor it!"

The Tiger tank jumped forward and began to crawl over motorcycles and Volkswagens, its steel tracks crushing them under its tonnage of weight until it reached the center of the chamber, which was clear of obstructions all the way to the entrance into the warehouse at the far end. Collins accelerated at full throttle with a clear view of the exit. It took them all of one minute to get to the warehouse door. Once there, Dean and Max got out to inspect it.

"There, hit the switch," Max said, pointing at a metal box with three buttons: top was green, middle yellow, and bottom red.

Dean pressed the green button on the electric box and a grinding sound emanated from the steel door as it began to open.

"Max, this is cutting it too close," Dean said.

Max looked at Dean. "Shall we?" He waved Dean ahead of him. Dean led first with the grease gun as he peeked into the tunnel behind the opening door.

In front, the tunnel wall extended to his right and left. It was lit and Dean could see that to the right, the tunnel ended, but to the left it kept going to another cross tunnel a few hundred yards away. Unfortunately, that was also the same direction from which a couple hundred uniformed SS soldiers were running toward them.

Dean stepped back into the warehouse and looked at Max. "Well, I thought I'd make it out of this war, but now I'm not so sure."

Max saw the flood of angry Nazis headed his way. "You might be right." He winked at Dean and looked at his watch, then at the door, and made up his mind. "Get in the tank, Dean. We are going for a ride! Val! Make sure that machine gun and that cannon are loaded. Ditter, Solange, when I say 'fire,' you guys cover your ears and hold on."

Max studied the door and figured that it had opened enough for the tank to pass through when Ditter asked the question on everyone's minds. "Max, what was it that was going to happen in six minutes?"

The tank shook slightly as a deep and distant explosion vibrated through the complex. Max looked down at Ditter. "That! Let's get out of here! Punch it, Collins!"

Hermann Wehr led the charge to the warehouse where the alarm system had detected one of the motor pool doors opening. A troop carrier rumbled past him, carrying a few dozen men ready and willing to fight to the death.

He looked past the speeding truck and was caught off guard as the mouth of the warehouse spit out a Tiger tank. The tank slid sideways and slammed into the opposite wall, collapsing part of the tunnel's ceiling on top of it. Hermann stopped in his tracks and watched as the tank skidded on the slick concrete floor, and accelerated straight for them.

The main gun from the tank erupted in a ball of fire as its deadly shell spit out from the barrel and found the troop carrier's engine bay, exploding, and turning it into a twisted metal inferno, disintegrating its passengers.

"Spread out!" Hermann shouted as the tank's front machine gun turret fired into the main crowd of soldiers, killing over 20 of his men. Hermann dove aside to avoid the deadly arc of fire from the tank, and waited until it passed.

He got up from his prone position and surveyed the carnage until he found what he was looking for. He picked up the weapon and pointed the rocket-propelled grenade at the weak end of the Tiger tank: its rear engine bay.

"Now it's my turn!" Hermann yelled as he turned on the laser sight, aimed the weapon, and grinned.

Just as Hermann was about to squeeze the trigger he felt a rumbling at his feet. He took a second to look around and saw his men dropping their weapons and running in the same direction as the tank.

Hermann felt the cool breeze hit the back of his neck, and turned his head. Directly behind him, a 20-foot wall of water embedded with tumbling cars, trucks, and motorcycles rolled toward him. He turned back around, took aim, and fired just as the wall of water engulfed him.

• • •

"Faster, Collins! We're about to take a bath!"

"What is he talking about, Val?" Solange asked.

"Well, your boyfriend had the smart idea to blow the water-holding tank that provided power to the electric generators." The machine gun erupted another burst at the crowd outside of the tank. "Unfortunately, he did not know what I knew, and in the future I would tell him to ask for permission before he gets any harebrained ideas."

"Know what?" Ditter asked as he crunched down when a barrage of bullets ricocheted off their steel protective cocoon.

"Oh...nothing big." He shrugged his shoulders. "Just that the water-holding tank is a little bigger than he thought, which is why I did not even think about it."

"How big a tank are we talking about?" Max asked.

"Size of a small lake, maybe a little more."

"How was I supposed to know that? You said that it was a river of some kind!" Max said as he looked through the tank's periscope in front of him. "Ditter, tell Collins where to go!"

Ditter looked out through another periscope and told Collins to keep it straight as Val kept up his rant. "Yeah, a river that fed the underground lake. Man, it was all over the televisions in the observation room!"

"Sorry, didn't notice since I was busy looking at the time machi—"

They were all thrown forward as Hermann's rocket smacked and exploded at the rear end of the engine bay. The tank began to sputter and slow down. Steam from the radiator began to seep inside the cabin.

"We're hit!" Collins called from the driver's seat.

"Gee, what gave it away?" Val asked as he looked at Max with a dumb expression on his face.

They were all thrown back again as the wall of water lifted and pushed the tank through the tunnel. They could hear and feel it inside tank as vehicles kept bouncing off the thick steel skin of the Tiger tank.

"Now this is what I call a water ride!" Val yelled as water began to seep in through any opening in the tank.

Their tank spurted one last time and shut off.

Ditter looked out through his thick glass periscope. "We need to make a right turn into the elevator shaft."

Crap, what do we do now? Max looked around the small cabin and saw there was one shell left. *That's it!* "Dean, we need to turn the main gun left. Val, load the gun!" Max pointed left with his outstretched arm as he looked out his periscope.

"I got it!" Dean yelled as he grabbed a handle and furiously turned it counterclockwise. Behind him, Max handed Val the remaining shell.

"More, turn it more!"

Val opened the breach and water began to rush into the cabin while he wrestled the shell into the barrel. "Fuck! Almost there," he grunted as he pushed his whole body into it and forced the breach closed. "Got it!"

Shit! Too late.

"Val! Fire...now!"

Boom!

The concussion of the exploding powder pushed the shell, along with a ton of water, out the barrel and in turn the pressure of so much mass moved the tank sideways just as they passed the elevator shaft. Luckily, the right tank track caught the edge of the concrete shaft floor and slipped down into the shaft. The tank teetered for a few moments before it took a slow reverse dive into the elevator shaft and sank down until it settled flat on the bottom, 30 feet below the rising water's surface.

Water began filling inside the tank compartment at a phenomenal rate. As the weak light bulb inside flickered off, Max knew that they had only seconds to get out. He turned on his flashlight. "Everybody ready to go!"

They all nodded and shook uncontrollably in the freezing water as it filled the lower part of the compartment. "Okay, we have to wait until the interior floods before I can open the hatch, so everyone make sure you're free from getting you're clothes snagged. I don't want to get this far and lose one of you to drowning." Max's lower lip trembled as the water soaked his wool uniform.

The water was up to his waist and climbing.

"Dean, you go first and make sure it's clear up top, then Ditter, Solange, Collins, Val, then me. Val and I can hold our breath for a couple of minutes so we'll bring up anyone who might get stuck."

The water was now up to their necks.

"When you're out, head for the elevator's auxiliary ladder on one of the side walls," Ditter chattered.

"You heard the man! It should only take a few seconds to get out. Deep breath. Now!"

They all took a deep breath and held it as the water filled up the remaining air pocket in the tank. Max shone his flashlight up at the hatch as Dean waited for the pressure to equalize so he could open it.

Dean was the first one out. He broke the surface and was relieved to find the shaft empty. One by one, they all emerged from the dark water and swam to the rung ladder attached to the wall. Dean helped Ditter and Solange grab the ladder with their shaking hands as the water leveled off inside the shaft.

Val was the last one up onto the yellow warehouse floor. "Follow me!" he said as he ran toward the warehouse door marked with the number 2. Once inside, he retrieved an ax from the wall, and began to chop on one of the countless wooden boxes piled up to the ceiling. He reached in and pulled out some gray wool blankets. "Dry yourselves." Val searched again for the right name on the boxes. He found what he was looking for and chopped away once more. This time he pulled out some gray mechanic's coveralls, and gave them to Solange and Ditter. "Layer them on." He reached in again and produced more for the rest of the team.

"Good, let's head to the cistern room. From there, Pierre is an hour's walk once we are at the base of the cliff," Max said.

"What about Val's team?" Ditter asked.

"We will contact them to get the hell out of here, if they are up there to begin with."

They headed out to the end of the long tunnel to the door of the cistern warehouse. As they were about to open it, a distant voice called out to them.

"Don't move! You are trapped."

Ah, fuck.

Max turned around and saw over 20 men 30 yards away pointing their MP40s at them.

"Disarm!"

Max put his MP5 down. The others followed reluctantly.

"The general wants you all dead," the officer said, pointing his small caliber weapon at Max.

Max focused his eyes past the gun to a small round object that rolled up to where the Nazi was standing.

Oh, shit.

"Grenade!" one of the soldiers yelled right before it went off.

Body parts were thrown in every direction. Luckily for Max and his team, they were far enough away to not get hit by the grenade's shrapnel. The Nazi soldiers that were left alive turned and tried to return fire as hundreds of bullets tore them apart.

Max opened the door to the cistern warehouse as Dean, Collins, and Val picked up their weapons. "Get up! Run to the end of the room!" Val yelled as he grabbed Ditter with one hand and Solange with the other.

"Wait, aren't they your guys?" Collins asked, confused with what was happening around him.

"Not with those guns! We use MP5s and M4s!" Max explained as he grabbed Collins, right before a wall of bullets tore apart the open door. "Shit! Run as fast as you can!" Max shouted.

Dean and Max threw two grenades each through the door opening before they took off at a full sprint down the chamber. Halfway through, Max began to feel lightheaded from the lack of oxygen in the room. Max ducked when Val, who had reached the opening in the wall to the secret passage, let out a volley of bullets. Just as Max got to the opening he saw the "Oh, shit" look in Val's eyes.

Max turned around in time to see one of the men at the opposite end of the warehouse shoulder a tube and fire a rocket.

"Everyone down!" Max screamed as he dove through the opening and into the secret hallway. Right behind, and slightly above, a electronically-guided rocket-propelled grenade threaded itself into the opening in the steel wall and through the hallway, screaming past the group as they lay flat on the floor, and finishing its trajectory at the ancient wooden door. The rocket tip explosive ignited, disintegrating the door and collapsing the tunnel exit.

Max was amazed that they were all still alive and kicked shut the iron door.

"Up the stairs! Go! Go! Go!"

They got up and followed Ditter up the curved stairway. Max was last in line. Another rocket blew the iron door off its hinges and flew directly toward him. Max instinctively ducked as the door bounced off the side rock face, narrowly missing him.

"Holy fuck! It doesn't get any closer than that!" Val yelled as he picked up his friend. "Come on, man. We got to book if we are going to stay ahead of the game."

"Who the hell was that?" Max asked Val as he stepped up the spiral staircase.

"Don't know, but I'd venture to guess that we either got some mercs on our ass, or the Swiss are mighty pissed off we didn't tell them we were having a small war in their back yard."

"But how would they know?"

"Who the fuck cares? I just hope our boys are upstairs roasting marshmallows for us."

"Yeah, we could use their help right about now, 'cause I am really getting tired of all this shooting shit!"

They caught up with Ditter and Solange, who were having a hard time running up the steps.

"What do you have left in your packs, Dean?" Max asked as he also struggled for breath.

"Five grenades and about 200 rounds each. Why?"

"Just checking our status."

"And?"

"Unless Val's boys are waiting for us, we're screwed."

"Why?"

"We're up on a mountaintop where the only means of escape are a World War II plane and an even older 'Giro, which, if they don't have cover fire, will be shot down before they leave the ground."

"Mountaintop? But—" Dean stopped, trying to rationalize, shook his head, and focused on the situation at hand. "So, what do you propose?"

"I don't know. I guess we'll figure it out when the time comes."

"What? Didn't you have a contingency plan before you went in?" Collins shouted from above.

"Yeah, but I didn't expect to run into the Third Reich."

"Well, that could throw a damper on things," said Dean.

"You're telling me," Val whispered.

The ascent up the stairs was slowing to a crawl. Ditter was having a hard time and they all took turns helping him. At first he refused, but after a few minutes more he gave in. Max trailed behind, making sure they were safe from the mercs, when he noticed an odd but familiar smell emanating from below. He stopped and looked down the stairs when the smell finally hit his memory bank.

You've got to be kidding me.

Max had to make sure and he stuck his hand out. The air below had indeed increased in temperature. "Guys, I know you're tired, but I think it's time we pick it up."

"What is it, Max?" Dean asked.

"You sure you want to know?"

"Yes."

"Flamethrower."

The burning fuel smell and heat from the flamethrower below gave them all a newfound strength. Dean and Val now had all the remaining grenades and, at intervals, would roll one down the stairs.

"How much farther?" Solange asked from above.

"Almost there. Val, take Ditter for me, and give me your load."

Max handed over Ditter and received Val's weapon and ammunition in return.

"That's it?"

"Yep, we are running out of BBs."

"Dean, give me the grenades and take point with Collins. I'll cover the rear."

Max shouldered Val's MP5 and reloaded his own with the last full clip. As he ran up the stairs, he carefully reloaded any spare bullets into one clip.

Seventy-five rounds. Not good.

Max was placing the remaining clip in his vest pocket when flames came shooting from below. At that same moment, Max dropped one of his grenades and yelled up, "Go! Go! Go!"

The walls shook from the grenade's detonation, followed shortly by another far-off concussion. Max climbed as fast as he could through the falling dust as the walls shook yet again. He picked up his pace and began to take the stairs three at a time, trying hard to get enough distance between himself and the fiery death from below.

"We're at the top!" Dean yell down.

Thank God!

The whole tunnel lit up like a Christmas tree as hundreds of bullets ricocheted off the walls. Two found their mark, embedding themselves into Max's vest and left arm. He yelled as the hot copper fragments penetrated his flesh. In return, he sent his last grenade and 39 copper slugs down the stairwell. He turned and jumped the last five steps, landing hard on the flat rock floor as a wall of fire engulfed his lower body. Max began to roll as the gasoline jelly burnt through the layered jumpsuit legs. He took off the vest, and tore off the burning material, while at the same time Dean and Collins emptied their machine guns down the stairs to keep the enemy at bay. Max reached up from the ground and pulled the iron ring embedded into the wall, which activated the boulder booby trap.

The ring gave way.

But nothing else happened.

Oh, come on!

Max pushed himself off the ground and started to run down the tunnel behind Dean and Collins. He turned his head to look behind him, and caught a glimpse of a man in a thick black bodysuit wearing what looked like a motorcycle helmet. The man turned, bracing himself from Dean's .45 caliber bullets, and aimed the nozzle of the flamethrower down the tunnel.

It was too late.

The man squeezed the trigger just as another blast went off in the castle above them close to where they stood. The explosion created a concussion wave, which reverberated through the walls, in turn rattling the century-old gear mechanism that spun and released the pin holding the three-ton boulder. Max stood there in awe as the boulder fell straight down and flattened the man holding the flamethrower. It hovered for a moment before it began its deadly fall down the spiral staircase.

Val ran to Max, stopped, and began to laugh as his friend stood half naked in charred long underwear. Lucky for Max his father's leather boots had taken the brunt of the fire and heat.

"You are the luckiest fucker I know!" Val said as he picked up the vest and handed it back to Max.

Max put the vest over his exposed skin and looked at the flattened body. "Val, was that a G-8 that guy was wearing?"

"Looked like it."

"Why the hell would they be wearing biological suits?"

"Well, it's not just a biological suit anymore, it's now made of synthetic spider silk, and dragon-skin bulletproof technologies, making it the lightest bulletproof full body suit ever made."

"Really? I would have guessed they were years from that."

"Technology has advanced, but to be honest, I thought they were in the prototype stage. Which leads me to believe that those guys must be spooks."

"Yes, but why would they attack us?"

"The spooks don't care who they kill as long as the job gets done. But to your point, you would think they would give us a break." Val slapped Max's back as they both jogged up the tunnel toward the others.

The floor shook again as another distant explosion went off.

"Looks like your boys are having themselves some fun," Dean said as he walked toward them.

"Sure does." Val gave Max a look.

"Well, we will find out soon enough, but first let's get some clothes on me."

15

"Rodent, this is Eagle, do you copy? Rodent, this is Eagle, do you copy?" Frustrated, Monk pressed his throat mike and said, "Nest, no contact yet."

A voice sounded in his earpiece. "Eagle, orders still stand. Observe and report," First Lieutenant Carpenter said.

• • •

General West stood quietly behind Carpenter, monitoring the radio chatter. He took a quick look at the center screen in the situation room and noted the time. His covert team was already in the castle carrying out their own separate orders to recover all the information possible, secure the site, and eliminate all within. West studied the far left screen showing the radar image of the area. An Air Force C-130, carrying two Ranger units, was headed to the drop-off point 20 minutes away. His timing had to be right if he was going to use the Rangers. He couldn't risk the Army units running into his team if things began to go south.

If his insertion team ran into trouble it would become an intelligence-gathering mission. Once done, they had standing orders to destroy all evidence and disappear before the Rangers dropped in. The Rangers would then take over and clean up any loose ends. Reports would be lost. Soldiers would keep their silence. West would then have to make sure he would control the investigation team.

On the other hand, if all went as planned—as he suspected it would—he would not deviate the Ranger squadron. They would run their preplanned military exercise. The Omega team had the best weapons and protection, which increased their success rate twofold. Like the Rangers, Omega would secure the site. Then they would send him to secretly oversee the project.

• • •

Back up in the high Alps, Monk looked at the Motorola's radio screen. "Come on, Commander..." he urged.

"Eag...is...ent...co..."

Monk smiled as the voice of his commanding officer crackled through the airwaves. "Nest. I think we have contact." He went back to the Motorola.

"Rodent, this is Eagle. You're breaking up."

"Is this better?" Val's voice came clearly over the small communications device.

"Yes, Rodent. Copy you, five-by-five."

"Five-by-five. Lay it out for me, Eagle," Val said, asking Monk to describe the situation from his perspective.

"SNAFU, sir. Ordered by headquarters to remain at post and observe. Suggest you evac through hangar. Will have cover. We have unfriendlies in compound, eight paratroopers about 20 minutes ago, followed by about 30 more, 10 minutes ago. Paratroopers are unknown; we believe to be mercs. We have ourselves a serious firefight within the castle. Sir. Again, you will have cover once at hangar, but before there you are on your own."

"Where is the main concentration?"

"They are all inside now. Two-thirds went in through the castle, the other third through hangar. I have two eagle eyes ready for cover, plus four heavy assault. Waiting for your orders."

"Roger. We will come up through the hangar. Will contact as soon as in area. Stand by to cover. Do you have retreat plan effective?"

"Sir, we are all jumpers if necessary, but will stay for incoming if possible."

"Roger. Rodent out."

"Good hunting, sir. Eagle out."

• • •

Val switched frequencies. "Pierre?"

"Oui?"

"Wheels up!"

"D'accord."

Val turned to face Max from the window ledge to see that he was dressed in his aviator's getup and shook his head. "By the way, Baron, have I told you that you look ridiculous in that getup?"

"Save it, Val. I think he looks dashing." Val was surprised to hear Solange's voice. Both she and Ditter had been very quiet since the stairwell incident.

"So, you two okay?"

"We will be, once we get out of here."

"Don't worry, miss, I think we should be safe by now," Collins said.

"Yes and no," Val said, then jumped down from the windowsill and brushed the snow off his pants.

"I hate it when he speaks like a Chinese prophet," Max said as he tied the belt of his aviator coat.

"By the way, you take care of that arm?" Val asked.

"Yeah, the bullet fragment was in the surface tissue. No big deal. Collins pulled it out."

"Aren't you the brave one," Val snickered.

"If you don't mind, Val, how do we get out of here?" a frustrated Dean asked.

Val looked down to the ground 50 feet below, and analyzed the situation. "You're not gonna like it."

"Swell. What now?"

"Ditter, can you get us to the hangar from the warehouse you told us about?"

"Yes, the ramp up to the hangar is at the far end."

"Okay, we can't go out this window...no ropes, and the castle is a battle zone. Only option is that we have to take the long way to the green warehouse."

"What do you mean?" asked Solange.

"He means we have to run all the way back down only to go back up again through the elevator shaft," said Max.

"Is there any other way to the green warehouse?" Solange interjected.

"Yes...what the lady said. And what do we do when we run into the bad guys? What? We'll just throw these empty guns at them when they start shooting at us?" Collins said sarcastically.

Max looked at Ditter. "Ditter, is that our only choice?" he asked.

"That is the only way to the green warehouse, up the elevator shaft."

"Okay, that settles it. We take the Ditter way out," said Val.

"What way?" asked Dean.

"We find a mode of transport in the green warehouse, preferably a tank like before, and drive up and out into the hangar."

"Well, as I recall, there are no tanks in the green warehouse, and I didn't see any cars when they captured us," Ditter said.

"We will just have to cross that bridge when we get to it," Max said.

"Yes, but what do we do if we run into trouble?" asked Collins once more.

Max walked back toward the entrance of the room's secret passage. "What do we have left firepower-wise?"

"I have my .45 and Dean the Schofield, and one clip each for the grease guns. Oh, and the De Lisle rifles. They have the .45 clips and are interchangeable. What about you guys?" asked Collins.

Val checked his MP5. He had one clip left. "Well, I guess we have to make them count!" he said.

Max picked up the triple rifle he had hidden behind a box and loaded the breach. Dean curiously looked on and was about to ask a question when Max spoke. "I have this..." he said as he snapped the elephant rifle closed. "Take out the clips and leave the rifles. Ready?"

Collins and Dean removed the clips from the rifles and placed them in their pockets.

"Dean, Collins, you are behind me." Max looked at the exhausted group, "Okay. Let's do this!" he said as he stepped back into the secret passage.

• • •

The sounds of rapid gunfire grew louder the closer they came to the library's secret entrance. Max heard muffled yelling coming from the peephole. He stopped and motioned for everyone to be quiet.

"What are you doing?" asked Dean. "We don't have time for this..." he whispered into Max's ear.

"Give me a sec, will ya?" Max said as he opened the peephole hatch. He saw two soldiers sporting red-cross armbands salute and head out the room's door. He could see Wehr as he adjusted a wooden crate on his desk, then proceeded to attack it with a pry bar. He dug into its sides until the top gave way, revealing what was inside.

Wehr reached in and pulled out a glass cube. Inside the cube was a perfect black sphere. He put it next to the Tiffany lamp to get a better look in the dim light. As the orb got closer to the lamp, the light bulb started to become brighter, as if more power was being sent into it. Wehr curiously put the orb closer to the bulb and squinted his eyes as the light grew in intensity, until the bulb burst. He looked at the orb suspiciously, then carefully put it in an aluminum briefcase next to the crate.

Another explosion shook the room, and Wehr looked up at the chandelier's crystals as they collided into each other. He reached into the crate once more and pulled out three long, golden metallic tubes, put two of them in the briefcase, and studied the third in his hand.

Wehr smiled at this newfound artifact and reached back into the crate, pulling out a folder. He looked from the folder to the object, as if reading instructions. Wehr twisted the object in his hand and with a soft click pulled out a scroll and unrolled it onto the table. He looked at the scroll and ran his index finger down it, studying the folder at the same time. A knock came from the door, followed by another distant explosion.

"Ditter, come here, see if you can hear anything," Max whispered as he stepped away from the wall.

"Do we really have time for this?" Dean asked again through clenched teeth.

"Just a few more seconds."

Ditter squeezed through to the peephole and looked into the library. Inside he saw Wehr close an aluminum briefcase and toggle a latch hidden below the tabletop in between two decorative carvings on the side paneling of the desk. The latch rotated, activating a secondary latch that protruded out the right side of the desk. Wehr went to it, reached out, and opened a hidden compartment. He stuffed the briefcase within, shut the hatch, reset the desk's mechanisms, and looked up as he heard the knock on the door once more. "Enter!"

• • •

"What do you mean the elevator is down?" Wehr grunted at the lieutenant.

"Sir, five men took over the elevator and booby-trapped it. We have regained control of the elevator's mechanical room, but if we move the elevator it will be destroyed," he said as someone moaned from the corner. The lieutenant couldn't take his eyes off the man lying on the couch.

"Pay attention! What is our status?"

The young man's eyes reverted back to Wehr. "Sir, they have us out-gunned. We are losing many men. The loss of the elevator and the recent flood have broken our troop numbers in half. We have won over the basement storage room and castle armory and are bringing over all the ammunition here, sir."

"What about my pilots?"

"They were all lost in the initial attack, sir."

"And my son?"

"We lost contact with him when the flood hit."

"Anything else, Lieutenant?"

"Yes, sir." The young soldier chose his words carefully and continued. "We were in the middle of transporting the canisters when they took the elevator. They now have control of them...sir."

Wehr slammed his fists down onto the desk, making the objects on it jump. He looked down, his eyes darting back and forth, examining every object on the table as if looking for a solution. He looked up. "Helicopters?"

"The helicopters that were outside the hangar look to have been damaged in the attack. The one in the hangar was under repair so we have to assume it is also down. The Storch was operational before the attack, but we have no further updates as to its condition."

"Do we have contact with the last remaining helicopter in the valley?"

"No, sir. We lost control of the communications room. But we might be able to contact them via the helicopter's radio in the hangar."

Wehr stared at the swinging chandelier. "We need to get to the hangar." He turned to look at the body on the couch. "We are going to need men."

"Yes, sir!" The lieutenant saluted, spun around, and hurried out.

As he opened the door, an officer wearing a brown leather jacket stacked a crate of ammunition against the wall outside. Wehr locked eyes on the major and called out to him. "Major, turn around."

The major did as he was told and Wehr's eyes lit up. "Come closer! Are you a pilot in the Luftwaffe?" It was a rhetorical question. Wehr knew that he was upon seeing the Luftwaffe pilot's badge on the man's jacket.

"Yes, sir," the pilot said as he looked curiously at the man lying on the couch in the far corner of the room.

"What is your name? And what type of aircraft do you fly?" Wehr knew now that his best chance to get out alive was using the major to pilot the Storch.

"My name is Major Otto Von Ludger, sir, and I am currently head test pilot for the Kolibri program," Otto said as he took a longer look toward the couch.

• • •

Behind the library wall Ditter stumbled back in shock at what he had just witnessed. He looked around aimlessly at all the faces in the passage, his mouth open, trying to speak. His hands shook as he reached into his inside chest pocket and pulled out his wallet.

"What is it? Are you all right? What did you hear?" Max asked.

"He is alive...alive after all these years...he is alive." Ditter pulled out an old, faded picture from the wallet, looked at it, then looked through the peephole once more.

"Who is alive? Ditter, who are you talking about?" Max asked as he grabbed Ditter's arms.

"It's...it's Otto."

"Ditter, what's going on?"

Ditter looked into Max's eyes, then Solange's. "Otto Von Ludger, my brother."

• • •

Ludger. "Kolibri program?" Wehr asked, now looking at the major with newfound interest.

"Yes, sir. Vertical lift aircraft program, sir. Helicopters."

Wehr smiled and stepped out from behind his desk. "We need to move... now. Major, I will be in need of your services. Please remain in the room while I find the medics." Wehr left the library, closing the door behind him.

Otto took in the hundreds of books lining the walls of the circular, two-story room. Then he heard a groan to his left and he focused once more on the tufted red leather couch. Lying on it was a man covered by a gray blanket. The man moved and the blanket slipped to the floor. His arms flailed as he tried to grab it. Otto approached him to see if he could help. The man then turned his head and lazily stared back at Otto. *"Wo bin ich?"* he mumbled before passing out. Otto leaned in closer, not sure he was looking at what he thought he was looking at.

An eerie silence engulfed him as all the gunfire and explosions in the background faded away. Otto stood silently looking down, his mind swirling with everything that had happened up to this moment, and suddenly it all made sense. He now knew why he was there.

Otto stood there, looking at the man lying unconscious on the leather couch, and didn't noticed as the column of the fireplace mantel moved aside. Max, Ditter, and Dean came out. Dean crouched on one knee, pointing his grease gun at the library's door.

"Otto."

Otto turned, surprised to hear such a familiar voice, and saw an old man. He was about to reach for his gun when he caught a glimpse of the old man's partner, who swung around and pointed the submachine gun at him and shook his head. The man then sidestepped over to the thick wooden door, locked it, and took one of the chairs in the room, propping it against the door.

"Ditter, hurry it up. We don't have much time," Max said.

"American?"

"Yes, American! Now, Ditter!"

"Otto, don't you recognize me?"

Otto turned his head to see the third man with what looked like a triple barrel shotgun walk to the opposite corner, pointing his weapon at the couch, as the other American soldier watched over him and the door.

"You do look familiar. Where are you from?"

"It is going to be hard to believe, but I'm your brother."

Otto paused for a moment. "You're a fool! A crazy old fool! My brother died in the winter of '44."

"No, I didn't. I escaped to Switzerland."

"Old man, how could you be my brother when I am older than him, or you, even in your crazy world—"

"We ripped our picture before we left our town, remember? Look here, I have it." Ditter reached out with the ripped picture in hand.

Otto in turn pulled his out and they placed them side by side. The old man's picture was old and faded, but Otto could still recognize himself. The rips matched perfectly. He looked up. "Brother? What happened to your face? Your hands? Were you in an accident? Did you get burnt?"

"How do I explain…. Remember reading H.G. Wells' *The Time Machine?*"

"What?" He shook his head. "What did you just say?"

The door rattled as someone tried to enter.

"Come on...let's move!" Dean growled back.

"There isn't much time."

Otto just blankly stared at his brother, as if lost in a dream.

"Otto, we must go—now!"

Somebody shoved hard on the door, but the lock held.

Otto nodded and touched his brother's arm. "Is it really you, Ditter?"

"Yes, it is. Now come with me and I'll explain."

"Max, let's go. What the hell?" said Dean. Max was carrying a man on his shoulder. "We can't take anyone else with us." Dean spun away from Max and took careful aim at the door when it was hit harder, splintering the wood around the lock. The chair kept it from opening. "Put that body down!"

"Trust me, this guy will come in handy."

Ditter stared at Max and the body draped across his shoulders.

"What the fuck are you talking about?" Dean grunted.

"The Germans won't shoot us as long as we have him," Max said.

Max passed the desk and paused as he saw a folder and a notebook next to the wooden crate. He thought about it for a quick second, then grabbed both items off the table and put them into his coat's chest pocket as he rushed to the fireplace. First through the mantel opening was Ditter, then Otto. Max swung the body's feet around to Dean and they both carried it through the hole. Once in, Dean hit the lever up, closing the secret entrance to the fireplace. The column started to move, but not before Wehr burst into the library and watched as the mantel's column slid into place.

Wehr jumped forward and desperately clawed at the fireplace mantel as it locked shut. He then turned around and yelled at the group of SS men behind him. "I need explosives! Now!"

Dean heard the order through the thick granite wall as he helped Max carry the body away from the library and through the passage. "Max, who the hell is this?" he asked, trying to see the face in the dark tunnel.

"You sure you want to know, Major?"

"Yes, Max, who?"

"Adolf Hitler."

16

Max told Val to take point as he and Dean took some time to rig the tunnel's sliding stone door shut. This gave them temporary relief from Wehr, who was sure to come after them one way or another. But it didn't solve the problem of the mercenaries running wild within the complex. Eventually, they would run into them.

Both Max and Dean started down the spiral staircase lugging Hitler between them. They stepped carefully around the flattened, disfigured bodies of the men they had fought earlier. Max, who started to struggle with Hitler's unconscious body, held back the urge to vomit as he passed the last member of the mercenary group, who was now stuck flat to the wall.

Max looked over the squashed body and noticed that his weapon was missing.

Dean saw that, as well. "Looks like they are all missing their weapons."

"Yeah, Val probably picked them up on the way down." Max stepped down a couple of more flights to find Ditter and Otto talking. "What's the hold up?" He laid Hitler down on the stairs.

"It looks like Val found something," Ditter said.

Max walked past Otto, who gave him a worried look.

"Ditter, tell your brother that I would be feeling the same way if I were in his shoes."

Ditter translated and Otto responded, "He says that there is no way you could."

"Right. And according to Max here I'm standing in the 21st century," Dean said from behind. Max in turn laughed at the fact that his supposedly dead grandfather was next to him.

"Dean..." Max took a moment to see if it was the right time to tell him he was his grandson, thought better of it, and changed the subject. "Check the stats on you-know-who."

Dean bent down on one knee and looked Hitler over.

"He's out. Doped. Probably morphine."

"Let's keep him that way; we don't want him to run off on us." He looked at Ditter. "Ditter, keep an eye on him while we go down to see what's up."

Ditter nodded, looked down, and the realization of who he was looking at left him speechless as Max and Dean proceeded farther down the stairs.

A few steps down Max ran into Solange. "You're doing better, I see," Max said.

Solange smiled at him and gave him a kiss on the lips. "That's for just in case."

"Don't ever think that way." He gave her his crooked smirk and walked on down where he found Collins looking over one of the mercenary weapons, admiring their complexity.

"Don't shoot yourself in the foot," Dean said.

Collins held up his finger to his lips. "Looks like Val found a hole into the green warehouse. He's checking it out," he whispered.

"Really?" Max went down, making sure that his flashlight was off, and bumped into Val.

"Seems like our grenade loosened the stone, and the boulder did the rest," Val whispered. "What do you think?"

Max looked past the two-foot-wide hole and into the green warehouse. "We got lucky...thank God..."

"Yeah, but with our luck..."

"Yeah, I don't like it either, but we had to come through here anyway."

"You know what they say…never look a gift horse in the mouth."

Max looked at the sniper rifle strapped to Val's back. "Yeah, yeah. What else did you scavenge back there?"

"Apart from this .50 cal, an HK416 that Collins has taken a liking to. Oh, yeah…and these little guys."

Max looked at the little brown, baseball-sized grenades that had caused so much havoc earlier in the night.

"Good, those will come in handy."

"Here, you take the sniper rifle; you were always a better shot. I'll go first," said Val.

"Have fun."

Val began to climb down the hole in the side of the stairwell wall. The hole was a few yards above the ground from the warehouse floor, so a fall wouldn't hurt. Once down, he hid behind some boxes, watching the warehouse as Max began his descent.

BUZZZZZZZ!

Max slipped when five out of about 30 bullets penetrated his vest and one his thigh. Unluckily for the shooters, Val had seen the barrel flash and launched two grenades at the spot. The grenades blew up consecutively.

"Max! Take them out!" Val turned when there was no return fire and saw his friend lying still on the floor. "Oh, no you don't!" Val reached down, felt for a pulse, and found one. "Collins, get down here and bring the medic kit."

Collins was immediately by Max's side and motioned Val to cover. The buzzing sound of the mercenaries' Gatling guns went off in the distance. "He's just knocked out by the fall," Collins said as he checked the thigh.

"Let's go, soldiers. On me," Val said as Dean came down the hole. He took the sniper rifle and headed toward the area where the grenades had detonated, and found two bodies. The suits had survived the explosion but the helmets were destroyed.

"I'm going up on those boxes. Collins, you and Dean try to bring them out into the open," Val said as he climbed up. He lay down and took aim into the semi-lit warehouse.

Val watched through the 10-magnification scope as Dean and Collins snaked around the hundreds of crates. Another volley of bullets buzzed and Val took aim at the muzzle flash before squeezing the trigger.

The .50 caliber rifle kicked back hard into Val's shoulder. The rifle spit out its projectile toward its intended target, another wooden crate. The bullet entered the crate, passed through an engine block within it, and exited the other side, severing the mercenary's helmeted head and sending it up into the air.

The other two mercenaries stood in shock as they watched the body of their sergeant squirt a stream of blood out from the neck stump. A split second later one of the two remaining mercenaries went flying sideways. The new G-8 suit was no match for the force of a .50 caliber bullet.

The last man began to run, but was lifted off the ground as the bullets from Collins's newly acquired HK416 assault rifle ripped through the glass of the helmet, killing him instantly.

Dean and Collins approached the bodies with caution. They bypassed the headless one and nudged the others, looking for any signs of life. There were none.

"Look at that machine gun...its like a Gatling gun," said Collins as Dean looked over the three-barrel machine gun. It was belt fed and had a steel rail that connected it to a metal, rectangular backpack, which housed the ammunition.

"That could come in handy..." said Dean.

"Sure could. Want to take it?"

"Not now. Priority is to get back to the team."

"Okay." Collins looked around one more time. "Clear!" Collins yelled out to Val.

Val scanned the area. Satisfied they were now alone, he responded back. As a precaution, Val kept an eye on Dean and Collins while they made their way toward the elevator shaft.

• • •

"You okay, buddy?" Val asked as he walked up to Max.

"Yeah, bullet went through my thigh. Ditter stopped the bleeding, glued me up, and gave me this nice adrenaline shot."

An explosion occurred within the tunnel and Val looked up at the hole. Below it he noted the body wrapped in the gray blanket now nestled up against the warehouse wall. "Yeah, that adrenaline is a miracle-maker. Who's that?"

"Insurance," Max said.

"Well, we leave him."

"No. He's our wild card. As long as we have him, the Nazis won't shoot at us."

"You sure about that?"

"Oh, yes, I'm sure."

"All right. You take the body." Val pointed at Otto.

Ditter translated and Otto picked Hitler up from the ground.

"We might have an issue," Dean said as he ran over to them.

"What is it?" Max asked.

"It looks like some sort of a detonation device, but I've never seen one like it."

"What's it attached to?"

"Explosive plastic, but that's not the problem."

"Well, what is?"

"The canisters that the explosives are attached to. I don't know what's in them, but it can't be good."

"How long?"

"Seven minutes. But we found a truck. Collins is working on hot-wiring it."

"Crap. Let's go then." Max fell in step, limping behind Dean. He looked back to make sure everybody was together.

"I need some help here! I have no clue what's going on under this hood!" Collins yelled.

"Val, go help Collins before he does something stupid with the computer system in the truck. Ditter, take Otto and Solange with you. See if you can help out."

Val dashed toward Collins, followed closely by Ditter, Solange, and Otto, who now carried Hitler over his shoulder.

Max and Dean stopped a distance from the elevator shaft, where they studied the timer from afar. Max walked over to a few jumbled crates to the left of the elevator, removed his trench coat, and placed it, along with his triple rifle and the .22, on top of one of the crates. He looked back at Dean. "Give me your Schofield."

"Why?"

"These things can be sensitive to magnetic disturbances." Max took the Schofield and put it on top of his coat.

They both walked up to the shaft and lay down on the floor to look under the elevator, since its floor was raised slightly above the warehouse level. "Emergency brakes have been tampered with, but there's no explosives from what I can see," Dean said.

Max stood and aimed his flashlight up at the hoisting cables. "Looks like the cables have been rigged. Here, help me push this crate."

They pushed one of the taller wooden crates next to the elevator and Max climbed up. He pointed his flashlight at the inch-thick cables and ran the light down until he came across the explosives charge.

Crap, accelerometer switch. "Looks like a motion sensor attached to a timer. It's active, so the question is: How long do we have if we step in to disarm it?" Max pressed the talk button on the Motorola two-way radio. "How we doing on the truck, Val? We need to get out of here ASAP."

"It's a fucking hybrid. I sent Ditter and Solange to see if they can find the keys on one of the bodies. What's our time frame?"

"Five minutes."

"If I can't get this thing to run in the next minute we are going to have a problem."

• • •

"What do you want to do?" Max's voice crackled through the two-way radio speaker.

"First, stop talking to me so I can concentrate." Val paused as he removed the plastic engine cover. "Hold on, looks promising. Give me another 30 seconds." Val looked at the countless wires and found what he was looking for. "One more sec. Okay, I think I...I got it!" The truck's diesel engine started to hum as Val slammed the hood down. "Let's g—"

"Don't move, Val," Collins said from behind the driver's seat.

Val saw that Collins was staring somewhere behind him. He turned around and slipped his sniper rifle off his shoulder, dropping it to the floor.

"Nobody move and stay quiet," Wehr said. He held a .32 caliber gun against Solange's temple. Behind him, four SS soldiers aimed their weapons— two at Ditter and Otto, the other two at Val and Collins. The remaining men in the group carefully put Hitler down on the ground. "Out of the truck now!" spat Wehr to Collins.

"You just said nobody move," Val said with a smirk.

Wehr aimed his gun at Val, then fired.

Val's body spun as the bullet penetrated his left shoulder. Solange let out a scream that was stopped by the hot barrel of Wehr's gun pushing up against her jaw.

Val got up, pressing his right hand onto his bleeding left shoulder.

Wehr aimed his gun at Val once more. "I said, quiet."

• • •

The SS soldiers that managed to get the jump on Max and Dean kept their distance as they escorted them to the side of the truck.

"General, they have wired the canisters with some sort of explosive device set to go off in three minutes."

Wehr thought it out, then looked at Max. "I was going to kill you, but I think I'll let you live an extra few minutes and let the Sarin gas do its thing."

Max looked back at the canisters, then at Solange.

"Don't worry, Commander, she'll live, as will Ditter. Trust me, the last thing I need is my wife mad at me." Wehr laughed at his own sick joke, and waved his small army into the truck. He pointed his gun at Otto. "You're flying us out, so get in. Corporal, how is the Fuhrer doing?"

"Sir, he is still unconscious, but vitals are stable."

"Good. Gentleman, step back, if you will." Wehr climbed into the truck, paused, then turned back to face Max. "You know what? I have changed my mind. You are too much trouble. I think I'll kill you now." Wehr took aim, squeezed the trigger and shot Max in the head.

Solange screamed in horror. Max's head snapped back as the bullet hit his forehead slightly above his left eyebrow. His body went limp and collapsed to the floor.

The truck accelerated away and Val rushed to the side of his best friend's body. "No! No! No!" Val grunted through his teeth as he held up Max's limp head. Collins and Dean stood in shock, then moved back a few paces.

"Val. We have to go."

Val was quiet as he looked down at his friend's face.

"Val..." Dean urged him sympathetically.

"I know...I know." Val closed his eyes to the pain that began to swell up within him. He squeezed his friend's hand one last time.

And it squeezed back.

Max's body convulsed. He gasped for air as his arms reached out. A primal scream echoed through the warehouse as he reached up to his friend. Max's arms flailed, looking for a hold. Val reached out and grabbed his friend, who was growling in anger, trying to get up.

"Relax! Relax! You have been shot. Relax, Max..." Val lowered his voice.

Both Dean and Collins looked at each other in disbelief. Val stared in shock, too.

"Buddy, can you hear me? Say something," Val pleaded with him.

"Ahhh, my...my head!" His left hand went up to the gash on his forehead. "Shit. Pain killers. Get me more pain killers...now!" Max staggered up with Val's help, only to fall back down.

"What the fuck, Max! You're alive! How the fuck?" Collins asked, almost aghast at seeing a dead man living.

Max looked up. His eyes rolled as the world spun uncontrollably, and he threw up all over himself and Val. During Max's convulsions Dean caught a glimpse of metal inside the bleeding scar, which ran across the left side of Max's forehead.

Val could not believe it and held Max's head upright, popping more painkillers into his friend's mouth. "Here, take a sip. Dean, help me out."

Dean rushed to Max's side.

Max tried to focus but everything was blurry. "How long was I out?"

"Only a few seconds, buddy," said Val.

Dean watched as blood trickled between Max's fingers.

Max let out a painful laugh. "Thank God I asked the doctors to make the titanium plate thicker than normal." He smirked at his forward thinking. The small caliber bullet was no match for the thick titanium plate that covered most of the left side of his head. "Ah, man, it hurts…." He grabbed his throbbing head once more.

"Fuck! All this is just fucking insane! First he takes a .45 in the chest, then one in the arm and leg and now in the fucking head, and he's still ticking? Jesus Christ! What's next, Superman?" Collins shouted as he stepped by them and watched the truck reach the far ramp. It turned and headed up into the hangar. "And now that I think about it, what the *fuck* did he mean by 'the Fuhrer'?"

Collins turned around to see Dean and Val help Max up. They turned and walked back to the boxes next to the elevator shaft.

Collins ran toward Dean, who holstered his Schofield and grabbed Max's .22 and rifle from under the trench coat. Dean looked over the triple barrel rifle, then at Max, and it suddenly hit him. He gasped for a brief moment, placed the revelation aside in his mind, and threw the rifle at Collins, who caught it in midair.

"Glad they didn't see these!" said Collins as he held up the rifle, "So, what now?" asked Collins.

"Val has an idea. Go with Max; he will explain. We don't have much time." Dean handed over Max and the .22 to Collins, turned, and disappeared into the maze of boxes.

Collins slipped the .22 in Max's belt and draped Max's coat over him. Val in turn ran past them toward the elevator shaft.

"Where is he going?" Collins asked Max.

Max clumsily put on his coat and looked back at Val. "Don't worry, he'll be right behind us. Now, let's get back to the stairs." He pointed in the general direction of where they had entered the warehouse. "We need to move fast."

Collins put Max's arm around his shoulder for support. "What is Val going to do?"

Max smiled and pressed the makeshift bandage on his bleeding forehead. "Hopefully, buy us a couple of seconds."

Val heard the sound of boots running across the cold concrete floor and turned, catching a glimpse of Dean lumbering back toward the hole in the wall, hauling two helmets, two Gatling guns, and an HK416. He waited until Dean had climbed up through the hole. The timer on the canisters read 58 seconds and counting. He then took a deep breath and stepped onto the elevator floor—all the while looking up at the hoisting cable.

Beep.

He stepped out of the elevator and climbed up the wooden crate to get a better look at the explosives detonator.

Let's see how much time we have....

The detonator counted down.

Eight.

Seven.

Oh shit! Change of plans!

Val jumped down off the wooden crate and fell flat on the floor. He scrambled up and staggered sideways, trying hard to keep his balance.

"Four!" Val yelled out loud as he turned the corner away from the elevator.

"Three!"

The pain in Val's shoulder intensified with every stride.

"Two!" He could now see the hole in the wall.

"One!" Val reached the entrance and began to climb into it just as two gloved hands grabbed him, pulling him up as the explosives went off.

The explosion ripped through two of the four hoisting cables. The blast reverberated down and into the canisters, loosening one that tipped over onto its side and rolled toward the elevator's opening. The elevator shifted and bounced as one of the two remaining cables snapped. The last cable stretched, and one by one each individual steel band began to snap. In one tense moment, the remaining strands ruptured in unison, sending the elevator plummeting down and into the 30 feet of water at the bottom of the shaft. On its way down, the roof edge of the elevator sliced down onto the loose canister's valve, ripping it off and releasing the Sarin gas into the atmosphere. The canister flew into the warehouse and rolled uncontrollably until it embedded itself into one of the countless wooden crates, which stopped its trajectory.

At the same time, but below water, the elevator came to rest on top of the Tiger tank. The secondary timer counted down to zero, and the plastic explosives ignited, sending a huge fireball of debris and Sarin gas into the surrounding water and up the elevator shaft.

Time was of the essence as Val put on the G-8 suit that Max had brought down to him. He had heard the elevator screech and fall, splashing down into the water below, but he also heard the distinctive hissing sound of a high-pressure canister releasing its contents as it bounced off the boxes in the warehouse.

"I figured you wouldn't make it up the stairs quick enough, so I brought down one of the suits for you," Max said through his helmet as he helped Val suit up. "We're lucky these suits are multi-layered; the interior cooling suit held most of the bodies together." Max held up Val's helmet. Inside were the remains of blood and bile that the previous owner had spat out when the boulder crushed him.

"I managed to clean it up a bit, but I'm afraid it's not going to smell too good—shit!" Max said as rats started to run up the stairwell.

"Shut up and zip me up!" Val said as he put on his helmet.

Max carefully sealed Val's suit and helped him secure the helmet as they clumsily stepped up the stairs. One of the rats by Val's feet began to convulse, urinating and defecating all over itself and Val's sealed boots. The rat then vomited blood and stopped moving.

"That was disgusting. Here, let me check your re-breather...good, you're green. We keep going up. I don't want to expose these suits in case one of us has a leak. Once at the top we head to the hangar through the kitchen's trap door."

"Ship Five, do you read? Over."

"Loud and clear. We have been trying to communicate with base for the past half hour, over."

"This is General Wehr. We have been compromised. We need immediate evacuation now."

"Roger that. Where is the extraction point?"

"Hangar door. If the landing zone is hot, head to officers' landing pad."

"Extraction at hangar entrance. Secondary extraction point at officers' landing pad. Engine running, will be there in five."

"Copy, five minutes ETA. Out."

Wehr dropped the headset on the helicopter's seat, glad that the radio inside the helicopter still functioned. He turned around and looked at his small army of dedicated men. He was proud of them, but he knew their ordeal was far from over.

"Sir, the Storch is ready."

"No need; we have a helicopter on the way. Men, I can only take four of you, the rest will be suppressing any incoming fire upon pick-up. If the landing zone gets too hot, you are to clear a path for us to the officers' landing pad. Is that understood?"

"Yes, sir!" they responded.

"Lieutenant!"

"Kaufmann. Sir!"

"Kaufmann, you are squad leader. It is your duty to make sure the Fuhrer gets to the helicopter. I will need the two medics and the best shot of the group."

"That would be Sergeant Nidder, sir."

A tall blond man stepped forward, carrying the .50 caliber rifle he had liberated from Val. "Sir, I am honored and will protect our Fuhrer to the death."

"Is the runway clear?" Wehr asked one of the soldiers as they stepped back into the hangar through a small side door.

"Yes, sir."

"Good. Kaufmann, open the hangar doors and form a perimeter." He spoke to the medics. "Get the Fuhrer onto the stretcher."

Wehr then turned his attention to the three people kneeling down next to the Storch. He took his time walking over as the sounds of rotating gears echoed off the walls as they began to pull open the hangar door.

"Well, it seems that you have all reached the end of this interesting journey and I am happy to say that you have a choice."

"*Du Hurensohn*. You are a disgrace to the German people and you will be held accountable for your actions," Ditter spat at Wehr.

"Accountable? Yes, I will be viewed as the savior of our people. Because of me, the New World Order will live on for 1,000 years. Right now, as we speak, thousands upon thousands of true followers are gathering at points around the globe, all with one goal in mind: to reach the New Germany. From here, we will launch a new front. We now have all the pieces and can execute our plan—the plan that will put Germany back as a true world power." He took a deep breath as the cold mountain air entered the hangar. "Now, for your choices. You can die right here, right now, or you can join us."

"Go to hell," Ditter spat.

"Fine. Private, shoot them all."

Wehr looked on as Solange began to cry.

Ditter turned to his granddaughter. "Don't worry, *Meine liebe*. We will be together again, soon."

The sergeant behind him cocked his gun. Ditter managed a small smile. The sergeant aimed the gun at the back of Ditter's head and pulled the trigger.

Blood squirted over Solange's face and hair as she watched her grandfather stare blankly at her as his body collapsed to the floor. She closed her eyes at the sight.

The sergeant sidestepped behind Solange, aimed once again, and squeezed the trigger. This time it was Otto who was sprayed with blood and brain matter. More gunfire broke out around him. Everyone fanned out, leaving him alone with the bodies of Solange and Ditter. But something was not right. He looked back to see that the executioner was lying flat on the concrete floor. He tried to comprehend what was happening, and it hit him. He crawled over to Solange and picked her up, leaving Ditter's body behind as he ran toward the Storch.

Solange opened her eyes to see that she was being carried. She fought herself loose and tried to run away, but was caught again.

"Solange! Stay down!" Otto screamed.

"*Grandpere!*" she screamed as Otto dragged her away.

"We have to get to the plane! I promised Ditter I would get you out of here if he couldn't!"

Solange turned and looked at Otto, seeing that he, too, was crying.

"But why? Why him?"

All around them bullets bounced off the rough granite walls of the hangar. The two medics carrying Hitler took cover behind one of the destroyed helicopters outside.

"Solange, we have to go. It is what he would have wanted."

More gunfire went off around them as Otto opened the hatch and helped Solange in, then jumped into the pilot's seat.

Solange looked at her grandfather's body one last time as the engine started. Otto did not wait for the engine to warm up and pushed the throttle full forward.

"They are taking the plane!" Wehr screamed as he tried to shoot at the Storch, but was held down by the incoming fire.

• • •

Monk spoke quickly into his mike as he took aim from the side of the mountain slope. "Keep them pinned down until the plane is out off danger. Crap! He is going the wrong way! Smitty, Philips, see who is flying that plane!"

• • •

Otto maneuvered the plane to the left and accelerated. Moments later he cut the power when a mountain of snow filled his windshield. He applied the brakes and full right rudder. The Storch skidded sideways as the wings swung around. The left wingtip scratched the frozen mountain face, but he managed a full turn.

Otto took a deep breath, readying himself, and froze when he saw two men clad in white camouflaged outfits pointing their equally white rifles at him.

• • •

"Take cover! Here comes the helicopter!" Sergeant Nidder yelled when he saw the helicopter do a sharp bank toward the castle.

Wehr reached up into the now bullet-ridden helicopter in the hangar, and grabbed the headset. He squeezed the trigger that controlled the radio transmission and screamed into the small microphone. "Abort! Abort! Taking heavy fire! Head to the secondary landing zone!"

Wehr's rescue helicopter reacted to the call and pulled up and away from the hangar's entrance.

"Kaufmann! Clear a path! We must get to the second landing zone."

"*Jawohl!*"

The rate of fire coming from the mountainside across from the hangar was intense. Kaufmann expertly ordered half his men to suppress the fire, and the other half of his team to start to clear a path toward the secondary inner courtyard landing zone.

As the point team and Wehr's small group cleared around the bend, the fire suppression team began to regroup, losing three of the five-man team as they turned the corner away from the line of fire.

Kaufmann's group, now reduced to seven men, maneuvered themselves into the castle's dining room, all the while surrounding Wehr and the Fuhrer as they cleared the room.

BUZZZZZZZ!

A sudden hail of bullets took out two of the point men as they reach the stone archway leading to the common room. Kaufmann lobbed two grenades toward the suit-clad intruders, and was cut in half as he tried to head back for cover.

Outside, the helicopter was beginning its descent. The remaining suppression team split in half. Two desperately covered the rear as the suited men advanced from the common room. The other three formed a perimeter around the landing helicopter.

The helicopter hovered a foot off the ground, blowing the accumulated snow up and around. The intense pressure created by the rotor blades formed a blizzard-like atmosphere in the courtyard, which hid the helicopter from sight. Wehr took the opportunity and blindly headed in the general direction of the helicopter, followed closely by Nidder.

The two medics carrying the stretcher followed Nidder through the man-made blizzard, when another volley, this time from the opposite direction, cut down the three perimeter soldiers, along with one of the medics. Wehr and Nidder both dove into the cabin of the helicopter.

The remaining medic struggled with his burden until another burst of fire killed him and the helicopter's pilot. The copilot pulled up on the collective, lifting the helicopter from the inner courtyard.

Wehr clutched the Fuhrer's hand as Nidder, from inside the passenger's compartment, tried to hold off the assault on the helicopter. Another volley of bullets shattered the Plexiglas dome around the copilot. Wehr tightened his grip as the helicopter rose, but the dead weight of the body was too much of a burden as it lifted off the stretcher. Hitler slipped from his grasp and fell on top of the bodies below as the helicopter climbed up and out of the courtyard.

Wehr desperately looked down from the helicopter's cabin and saw a group of four suit-clad men fanning out into the courtyard from under the courtyard balcony, surrounding the Fuhrer. They picked him up and fought their way out of the courtyard in the direction of the hangar through the dining hall. He then saw more suit-clad men exiting through the common room courtyard door, giving chase, and firing their weapons at the smaller group before he lost sight. He stared in disbelief as the thought ran through his head...*DuMonde?*

17

Two suit-clad men lay directly in Max's path. Their Gatling guns began spinning, but Max was quicker on the draw and let loose two 45-70 bullets, one for each man. The bullets hit their targets just as the Gatling guns began to fire. The force from Max's bullets picked both men up off their feet, killing them instantly.

"Clear!" yelled Max and he ran forward into the dining hall.

"Jesus H. Christ on a popsicle stick!" Val yelled as he shot back at the advancing mercenary force. "I need more firepower!"

Max turned around and shot his triple rifle. The 45-70 bullet hit its target, knocking the first man back onto his advancing team. The mercenaries then took cover, not wanting to feel the wrath of Max's weapon. Max spun back around and reloaded as Dean took up position next to Val, and both fired their Gatling guns as they ran backwards. Once inside the dining hall, Max turned right and shot twice at the secondary force coming in from the common room. The mercenaries again took cover, giving Max and his team enough time to exit out onto the exterior deck. Collins clumsily followed Max as he labored with the weight of the body on his shoulders. Val and Dean worked their way across the deck, keeping the mercenaries, who were now in the dining room, at bay. They finally arrived at the steps leading down to the runway and had covered enough distance that each could take turns firing their Gatling guns.

Max was close to the hangar, running along the outside wall of the castle, when he removed his helmet and unzipped his biological suit. He took out the Motorola two-way radio and spoke into it. "Eagle, this is Rodent."

"Copy, Rodent. What is your location? Over."

"We are heading to the hangar. We are a group of five. Be advised we have biological suits on."

"Copy that. We are holding a strange plane at the end of the runway. There is a woman and man inside."

"Have your men tell them to head south and land at the first town they see."

"Roger."

Max was approaching the circular wall of the observatory when he saw the Storch fly up and away.

"Eagle, we need some major backup. We have unfriendlies advancing on our tail. Transport on its way. Beware, Sarin gas has been released in the facility. Recommend calling HAZMAT. We are coming around the wall to hangar now!"

"Roger, understood. I have you in my sights. You are clear. We have your back. Out."

Max switched the channel on the Motorola and spoke as he turned the corner. "Pierre! Do you copy?"

"*Oui.*"

"Land that fucker now! We need to get out of here and fast!"

"Roger, coming down now."

Max helped Collins with Hitler and they both dragged the man down the runway. They all instinctively ducked as the whizzing of bullets flew above their heads.

"Keep going! Those are our guys shooting."

Max looked up at the dark, cloud-covered sky while the long-distance firefight took place. He didn't like their situation, and knew that they were all sitting ducks in the middle of the runway. The only way out was Pierre.

Come on, Pierre, where are you?

The firefight intensified as the mercenaries gained ground. Then, as if from nowhere, the 'Giro fell out through the clouds, landing hard five yards ahead of them. They all got up and followed Max as he avoided the spinning rotors, approaching the 'Giro from the left side.

Max held the hatch open. Val jumped in first, grabbed Hitler, and threw him back against the plush leather seat.

"Val, break out the window! We're going to need all the fire suppression possible!" Max said as Collins, then Dean, jumped into the 'Giro.

"Go! Go! Go!" Max yelled as he shut the hatch.

A few rounds hit the front right window. Pierre instinctively ducked as he pushed the lever, releasing the rotor blades from the engine control shaft. They were spinning above maximum rpms when the 'Giro lurched forward from the propeller's pull. The 'Giro picked up speed and lifted off the ground only 10 yards from where it had touched down. The undercarriage extended and Pierre banked sharply away from the hangar entrance as he gained altitude.

As the 'Giro banked, Val and Dean fired their Gatling guns into the crowd of mercenaries, silencing them enough for a safe escape.

"Eagle, what is the status on reinforcements?" Max yelled into his Motorola before they were out of range of the SEAL team.

"Rodent, a full platoon of HAZMAT and first-strike biologics team is on the way." Monk paused as he shot another round at the suit-clad mercenaries. "I'm afraid we can't hold them off much longer, over."

"You've done all you can, gentlemen, time to get out of Dodge," Max said.

"Copy. Out."

• • •

"You heard the man! Let's jump!" Monk shouted as he shot another burst at the incoming mercenaries.

Monk covered for his team as each jumped off the cliff into the abyss. He cocked the grenade launcher under his rifle and fired it. By the time the smoke had cleared, Monk was gone.

Max put his Motorola receiver down and turned to see Pierre wearing night vision goggles strapped to his head. They were out of danger. Better yet, he knew that the SEAL team, which had saved their lives, had jumped off the cliff and were landing softly on the flat plateau 1,000 feet below the castle's perch. He uncocked his rifle hammers and laid the weapon down between the front seats.

Max was also relieved to know that Solange flew off to safety in his Storch. He took a deep breath, looked back and made eye contact with his 32-year-old grandfather. Dean nodded his head. Val had taken Hitler's seat and put him on the floor. Collins just stared out the left window. Max thought of what Dean must be thinking. He thought about how it would affect both Dean and Collins to find out how much the world had really changed.

Max looked on as Collins squinted into the night and jerked forward until his forehead touched the cold frosted glass.

The world seemed to slow down as Collins turned his head toward Max, and yelled, "DIVE!"

Sergeant Nidder held the crosshairs of his scope on the 'Giro pilot's head and squeezed the trigger. The .50 caliber bullet trajectory was dead on, but just as the bullet entered the side window, the 'Giro dipped down into a dive, saving Pierre as the bullet nicked the top of his headset.

"Did you get him?" Wehr screamed.

"No, sir, the aircraft dove at the last second!" Nidder yelled over the rushing wind inside the helicopter cabin.

"Forget the pilot, take out the engine!" Wehr said. He turned when he heard an alarm go off inside the helicopter. "What the hell is that?" he screamed at the pilot.

"Sir, we are very low on fuel. The tank must have been hit in the recovery attempt!"

"What are you telling me?"

"We only have a few minutes' remaining fuel."

"Nidder. Shoot that fucking engine apart!"

Nidder opened fire on the 'Giro.

• • •

Max yelled, "They are shooting at the engine! Collins, get them off our tail!"

Collins stuck the HK416 out the window and started shooting back. It became a midair battle. Wehr had even joined in, shooting his gun at the fleeing 'Giro.

"I'm out!" yelled Collins.

This time it was Val who took aim at the pursuing helicopter. The hail of bullets from Val's Gatling gun peppered Wehr's helicopter as it took evasive maneuvers.

Nidder reloaded the 10-shot .50 caliber semi-automatic rifle and shot back. One of his bullets found its target, and ripped through the top cylinder of the radial engine.

The engine began to sputter, then caught fire. Oil began to flow out onto the windshield. "We lost the engine!" Pierre screamed over the sound of the Gatling gunfire.

· · ·

The helicopter pilot tried to maintain altitude and speed as the fuel began to run out. "General, we are starting to lose power."

Wehr could hear the turbine engine fluctuating as its fuel supply dwindled, and was taken aback as he was suddenly hit by Nidder's spraying arterial blood when one of the bullets tore through his throat. He watched as the man slumped and fell out of the helicopter into the darkness below.

"Sir, now we are losing oil pressure!" the helicopter pilot screamed.

"No! I didn't come this far to lose again! I can't let the world get hold of him!" Wehr reached down and opened a green case. "He must not be captured!" He produced a Russian, rocket-propelled launcher. "If the Order can't have him, nobody can!"

Wehr put the rocket launcher on his shoulder, aimed the laser sight at the 'Giro, and squeezed the trigger. A three-foot flame exited out of the rear of the long tube. The wire-guided rocket led by Wehr's mad eyes tracked toward the 'Giro. Wehr realized he was going to miss and pressed a second trigger. The rocket flashed hot white, detonating in front of the 'Giro, destroying what was left of the radial engine.

· · ·

"Ahhh!" Pierre screamed. "I can't see! I can't see!"

Max took the night vision goggles from Pierre and yelled at him over the rushing wind in the cabin. "I have control! You'll be fine in a minute or so!"

"Max, he's got to be reloading by now! Do something!" The Gatling gun went silent. "I am out!" Dean gave his Gatling gun to Collins. "We are below the helicopter. I can't shoot through our rotors!" screamed Collins over the howling wind.

Max looked at the airspeed as he put on the night vision goggles and saw that they were over the 'Giro's maximum allowable speed. He had to slow down—but if he did, they were as good as dead. If he sped up, he would rip the rotors from the hub.

Max looked over his shoulder and faintly saw Wehr loading his weapon. This was it. He had to do something. Then it hit him—the pictures he had seen in his father's hangar, next to the drafting table, on the wall. "Hold on!" he screamed as he pulled back hard on the yoke. "Collins, shoot through the ceiling when I tell you to!"

"But that will shear off the rotors!"

"It's our only chance!" Max groaned as he began to feel the increasing gravitational force on his body.

Wehr was bracing himself in the helicopter, trying to get a good angle shot at the 'Giro when he lost sight of it as it crossed in front of the helicopter. It then pulled up and went vertical, flipping over as Wehr's helicopter passed under.

The 'Giro was now upside down and directly over Wehr.

"Now! Shoot!" Max yelled at Collins.

Collins's Gatling gun spit fire through the canopy glass. Inside the 'Giro was mayhem as the fire from the Gatling gun strobed crazily and hot, empty shells bounced all around the interior of the cabin. The bullets exiting the barrels ripped through the rotors, shearing them. They continued their deadly path, tearing through the helicopter below, killing the pilot and wounding Wehr on the shoulder and leg.

Wehr collapsed onto his knees in pain and dropped the rocket launcher, which in turn rolled out the cabin door. He looked forward to find half of the pilot's face gone. Beyond that he saw a mountain peak through the cracked window of the doomed helicopter.

Wehr held on to the pilot's seat, watching as the mountain filled the windshield, and screamed the last two seconds of his life.

Max was too busy trying to maintain control to have had the pleasure of watching Wehr crash into the mountain. Luckily for all of them, he knew that the model PA-19 Cabin 'Giro was a surface-controlled 'Giro, which mimicked the exact aerodynamic control of a regular plane. Unfortunately, its wings were smaller, because most of the lift came from the rotor blades.

Max pulled harder on the yoke, trying to maintain a reasonable cruise speed to allow for the 'Giro to fly the farthest distance at their current altitude. But it was a futile attempt as the increasing air pressure began to tear at the delicate fabric-covered fuselage. A loud snap shook the cabin as both wheels were ripped off by the force of the wind, giving the 'Giro less wind resistance, thus increasing its speed. The rush of wind entering the cabin intensified with every second.

"Max, you have to slow her down! You're going to rip the wings off!" Pierre yelled as he rubbed his eyes, trying to focus on the airspeed indicator. He noticed that the needle was pegged.

Max desperately searched and found what could be their salvation. "I want everybody to make sure they are buckled up! I see what looks like a snow-covered pasture ahead! I'm going to try to land on the downslope!" he yelled over the howling, hurricane-force winds entering the cabin.

"Ahhh, crap, here we go again," Val moaned.

"He knows what he's doing, right?" Dean asked as the pasture got closer.

"If anyone can get us down, it's Max, but just in case, it was nice knowing you." Val flashed his bright white teeth.

The 'Giro zoomed over some tall pines. Max kept the nose pointed down. The flat, snow-covered pasture filled the windshield as he tried his hardest to gauge their altitude through the night vision goggles.

Crap, I can't see it! When do I flare? Keep your cool, keep your cool. Oh, oh...OH!

Max pulled hard on the yoke and the nose came up. The 'Giro's belly hit the snow hard and bounced.

"Hold on!" Max screamed as he pushed the yoke forward once more, then back, overcorrecting the bounce.

The air pressure flowing over the elevators was so great that it ripped them clean off. The 'Giro slammed back down, uncontrolled, onto the soft, powdery snow, digging itself a trench.

The snow broke the front windshield and it started pouring into the cabin. The 'Giro's wings ripped off, and the fuselage started to slide on its side until it hit a snow bank, flew up sideways into the air, and began to roll uncontrollably, over and over. Anything not tied down in the cabin flew out. The side door and windows were now gone.

The 'Giro stopped rolling when it hit another snow bank, but kept its momentum across the open pasture until it reached the forest's edge. The trees came up much too fast and the 'Giro crashed hard into one of them. The force of the collision collapsed what was left of the engine and its mount, and finally brought the destroyed 'Giro and its passengers within to a complete stop.

The beeping sound was driving him crazy. He reached over to shut off the alarm, but it didn't turn off. He picked up the alarm clock and banged it against the counter, but it kept on beeping. He grabbed the alarm with both hands and smashed it against the night table, breaking it into a thousand pieces, yet it kept on beeping.

Then he heard a voice.

Who's there? What's going on? Shut off the beeping!

His breathing stopped. He was choking.

Help me!

He opened his mouth, but he couldn't speak. Then it all went black. He couldn't see.

What the fuck is going on? Somebody help me! He screamed, but no one could hear him.

The pain started to creep in. His chest was killing him. His face felt numb, as if it was floating.

"Max. Max. Can you here me? Open your eyes. You're safe now."

Max shook his head. The breathing came back, but it took effort. The darkness was now gray, but getting brighter. He opened his eyes, but everything was blurry. He shut them again, bringing his hands to his face. His face felt strange...bumpy, swollen. It hurt as he rubbed his eyes.

"Son, don't do that. You're going to rip your stitches off."

Son? I don't have a father. He is dead. He left me his plane. Wait a minute... Solange, Val, my grandfather. What? Oh my God! Where am I?

"Max, open your eyes. I have lowered the lights."

He knew that voice.

Max opened his eyes again. It was now dim and he could see a figure dressed in a khaki uniform.

The face... it looks familiar. The eyes.

The face began to come into focus, but he still did not clearly recognize it. It took him a few more seconds.

"Granddad?" Max whispered in a raspy voice.

Dean approached the side of Max's hospital bed. "Yes, Max, it's me. Don't worry, you're safe now," he said as he held tightly to Max's hand.

18

"It is with great honor that the President of the United States awards to you the Navy Cross for uncommon valor against overwhelming enemy forces..."

Max looked curiously around the small British Naval hospital conference room, which had all its furniture shoved against the walls. He was able to stand now, and was gradually healing from the injuries he had suffered three weeks ago in the Swiss Alps. His gunshot wounds were now small scars; his face, which had swollen beyond recognition, was now just purple and red under his eyes. His broken nose was still taped and would require one more surgery before it would look normal again. Worst of all was the fractured leg that the doctors said would have needed to be amputated if it had not had the titanium plates surrounding the bones that held it together.

"...and then willingly sacrificed himself for his unit when he..."

Max leaned on the antique climbing pick ax cane that his grandfather had bought for him in Paris earlier in the week. He looked at Val, who stood beside him receiving the award the admiral had just pinned on his own chest a minute ago. Val looked good. At the end of the day, they all looked good, except him. The fact that Max had had the yoke in front of him, and his face continuously slammed into it as the 'Giro flipped and rolled, made him the worst-looking of the bunch.

"It is with great honor that I have been chosen to hand deliver these awards."

The admiral had finished pinning Val and stepped back from the group. He was addressing them all. Max didn't care, though. He just wanted out of the hospital. He wanted to go see Solange and comfort her, but he knew he couldn't.

Ditter.... When Max heard, he'd cried. Even though he had known him just a few days, they had become friends. Solange took it the hardest. She'd lost her grandfather, but gained a granduncle, who happened to be a few years older than her. She was confused. In fact, everyone was confused. She didn't know whether to be happy for Otto and Eva—they themselves were having a difficult time coming to grips with the reality of the situation—or sad for her *grandmere*. She even asked for Max to stay away for a while. Max knew the reality. Whatever connection they had had been erased that fateful night three weeks ago.

Max did have one thing to look forward to—his grandfather. Dean had spent every day he could next to Max's bedside. It was proving hard for Dean to adjust to the 21st century. The thing he complained about most was the way the world moved so fast. Max figured that he would be having a hard time because all that he knew, and everyone he loved, were now gone. But he had Max, and they were going to make the best of it. As soon as Max was released he was heading back to the United States with him.

Collins reacted much the same way Dean had, but funny enough, at the end of the day, they both thought it right to stay with the Marines. The U.S. government, on the other hand, was harder to convince, but after two weeks the interrogators went away. In their place a Pentagon Army general named West stepped in and cleared them all. The general took good care of all of them. They all got what they wanted in return for their silence. The fact that West had approved for Dean and Collins to collect over 60 years of pay was also a nice bonus.

The admiral was wrapping up his speech when General West, who was standing silently in the corner, locked eyes with Max. Max didn't much like the man, even less so when the general had picked his grandfather to be second-in-command of the Phoenix Project research and development team, in conjunction with the Swiss and Austrian governments. The general was to be the head of the project, overseeing every aspect. Dean had convinced Max that, since he was now a full-blown colonel, things would be fine.

The general gave Max one last penetrating stare, then spoke to his adjutant. "Lieutenant, get the car ready," West said as he looked at the four men in front of him. He thought about how close he had come to failure and eventual death, but his quick thinking had kept Omega happy at the end.

The mercenary team he'd sent in had failed part of their mission, but had gathered all the intelligence necessary to give West the ammunition he needed to survive. He had brilliantly cleaned up the mess, leaving no trace of the team's existence. The Sarin gas had been his saving grace. Because of the leak, he'd had no use for the Army Rangers. A HAZMAT team had been sent to the site. The fact that it took them hours to arrive gave him all the time in the world to complete the mission.

They did manage to download critical information from the computer banks before setting off the electromagnetic pulse bomb that erased all files and data pertaining to the machine. He knew that eventually the joint taskforce would reverse-engineer a way into the inner workings of the machine, but he had given Omega a head start. The electrical booster technology alone was enough to guarantee a payday. His actions—or inactions, to be precise— would give Omega enough of a head start to make the proper arrangements at the patent offices to lock in the potential money-making devices that would one day allow the human race abilities beyond imagination.

West was desperate not to lose his life. He began pulling all his favors to get the head position of the project, and once that was done, Omega had backed off. They now knew that he controlled the project from every angle, and Omega could use that for the benefit of slowing the government research even more, if needed.

West was now satisfied, but he knew that he would have to keep an eye out for Commander Vittoria and newly promoted Commander Max DuMonde. Maybe he could use them on his team. He would have to keep that option open. In any case, if anything were to happen and he needed their help, he could always use his ultimate bargaining chip—Max DuMonde's grandfather.

Max stood proudly at attention and saluted the admiral before they exited the room. A few minutes later Max, Val, Dean, and Collins stood outside in a small adjacent room, shaking hands and talking about their assignments. Val looked at Max and finally asked him the question on everyone's mind.

"What are you going to do now that you're retired?" Val paused. "Shit man, I still can't believe it," he finished. Val was the first person Max told and was still in disbelief as to his decision.

"Well, not fully retired. I am still in the reserves. Besides, this body can't take any more punishment."

"Really, Max...what the hell are you going to do in the civilian world?" Val persisted.

"Who knows? Maybe I'll take on an instructors job at the SEALs just for kicks...if I get too bored. I did promise Pierre I'd help him recover the 'Giro from the mountain valley this summer."

"He's still pissed, huh?"

"Not so much now, but yes."

"Um, maybe you'll find you-know-who's body out there."

"Yeah, maybe. Anyway..." Max turned to Dean, changing the conversation. "So, you will be in charge at Meckler Castle?"

"Well, I have to keep busy." Dean smiled, knowing that everyone he knew and loved was now dead. Taking the job was an easy choice; it kept him busy and away from the realities of the outside world.

"I'll give you a call before I arrive with Pierre; that way you can give me a tour of the castle in peace and quiet."

"No worries, son. Take it easy and recoup. I'll see you in two weeks." He paused and looked down at his leather briefcase. "But before I leave, I have something for you." He put the briefcase on a chair and opened it, took out a scratched-up wood box, and handed it over to Max. "Took me a few days to find a box for it, but it is of the same decade."

Max lifted the worn-out wooden box. Nestled neatly in its own velvet compartment was Dean's 1875 Schofield revolver. Max looked up in surprise.

"This revolver was given to me by my father, James, your great-grandfather. It belonged to Jake DuMonde, his brother. It has been passed down through generations, and has become a sort of good luck charm in the family. It originally came with the triple rifle you carried, which was lost in the crash. So please try to find it and bring them back together. Anyway, like my father did for me, I now pass it on to you."

"I don't know what to say."

"Just take care of it and keep it close. You never know when you are going to need some luck." Dean stuck his hand out and shook Max's hand. "Val, Collins, I'll see you two around." Dean turned and left.

The three of them stared at the gun. It was Collins who spoke first. "That gun has had a very interesting life. For one, it saved my ass in Italy. I'll tell you about it some time. Right now I need to catch the train north. Seems that I have quite a few of my kin running around. Then I need to take some time to figure out this world. Once I get bored with learning, I'm off to San Diego. Going to give the SEALs a run."

"Watch out for Waxal at SEAL training," Max said.

"Will do, Commander."

"Yeah, watch your fucking mouth, as well. When you graduate give me a call. You will always have a spot on my team," Val said.

"Aye-aye, Commander," Collins said with a crisp salute.

They all shook hands. Max and Val watched Collins walk away.

They stood in silence, each reflecting on the past few weeks.

"Well, let's go. You owe me a beer," Max said, breaking the silence.

"I owe you a beer? I don't fucking think so!"

They walked down the hall and got louder the closer they got to the exit.

"Do I have to remind you how many times I saved your life?"

"Oh, you have to be kidding me. Do you honestly want to go there?"

The automatic doors opened to reveal a gloomy English day. Max put his arm around Val's shoulder and leaned on him as his friend helped him down the steps.

The wet, brown mop danced its way back and forth on the cheap linoleum floor. All around, the sounds of the desperate and ill echoed through the halls. It was late in the day and the new shift was about to come through. The custodian looked at his watch as the lock on the outside security gate buzzed open for the fresh meat of the new semester.

They were all new students from the sound of their fancy, hard shoes tap dancing on the floor as they made their rounds. He knew that eventually all the new students would trade their expensive designer shoes for the more practical and comfortable sneakers that the veteran staff wore.

He studied them carefully. One of them would have to do, but which one? It was all a waiting game now. He would study their routine. He would watch their mannerisms. One would show his or her weakness, and then he would act...but for now he had to wait.

It had to be timed perfectly. It had to look and feel normal for it to happen without suspicion. The plan was perfect; all he needed was the last element, and it was somewhere among the crowd of new students.

"The workload will be very tiring for you new students, but you will learn to adapt. This is Ward C. We take special precautions to make sure every individual is taken care of to the best of our abilities," Dr. Winecot, head of the psychiatric department, said flatly. "There are many rules and regulations. I expect them to be followed to the letter."

The group shuffled forward.

Dr. Winecot continued. "We have the best record in the European Union and have not had an incident here within the last five years. Although prior to that, a first-year student was brutally raped and dismembered."

Winecot looked around as if to find the right door.

"Now that I have your attention, we will look into the more dangerous patients on this floor. Most are a danger to others, some to themselves. For example, patient 34257."

Winecot walked up to the clipboard-sized window and peered in.

"Patient 34257 is a very peculiar case of delusional disorder. The patient can be very violent, so we keep him sedated most of the time. We have all tried to reach him, but he is too far gone. That said, we consider him a challenge for any of you students."

"What is his delusion?" asked a small brunette as she approached the door.

"He was brought to us two months ago after being found wandering in the Alps. We think that he lived in a mountain cabin. Nobody in the area in which he was found knew him. He is in his late 50s, and is suffering from the beginning stages of Huntington's disease. He has been medicated to alleviate the tremors and mental instabilities. The biggest hurdle that we are facing is his persona delusion. The man claims he is Adolf Hitler. Although he does bear some sort of resemblance, he can't seem to get around the fact that if he were indeed Adolf Hitler, he would be over 120 years old."

A few of the students laughed.

"Doctor, how do we get permission to evaluate and study patient 34257?"

"And you are?"

"Miss Monserrat," she said as she stood up on her tiptoes to peer through the window.

Inside the room was a man curled up on a plastic mattress. He had short-cropped hair and a week-old beard.

"Miss Monserrat, you can contact me tomorrow after rounds. I will make the necessary arrangements if you are up to the challenge of handling Adolf, along with your other patient load. Let's move on, shall we? Custodian...? Yes, you. You are new here, aren't you?"

"Yes."

"Well, this is the time I do my rounds and I would greatly appreciate it if you could wipe the floors after I am finished."

"That can be arranged, Doctor."

"Thank you. And what is your name?"

"Hermann. Hermann Wehr."

About the Author

Robert Blanchard was born 1969 in Geneva, Switzerland. As a small boy he lived in Italy, Puerto Rico and Venezuela, before moving to the United States. He graduated with a B.A. from Regis University and went on to receive his Masters at the University of Colorado. He lives in Miami, Florida.

For more about Robert Blanchard and the sequel you can visit his site at
www.Phoenixproject-thenovel.com

www.ingramcontent.com/pod-product-compliance
Lightning Source LLC
Chambersburg PA
CBHW060512180626
46817CB00002B/349